SHAUN HUTSON

Death Day

Published by Caffeine Nights Publishing 2016

Copyright © Shaun Hutson 2016
First published in Great Britain in 1987 by
Star Books, A Division of W. H. Alien & Co plc
Published in 1990 by Sphere Books Ltd
Reprinted 1990
Published by Warner Books 1992
Reprinted 1993 Copyright © Shaun Hutson, 1986

Published in Great Britain by
Caffeine Nights Publishing
4 Eton Close
Walderslade
Chatham
Kent
ME5 9AT

www.caffeinenights.com

British Library Cataloguing in Publication Data.
A CIP catalogue record for this book is available from the British Library
ISBN: 978-1-910720-18-9

Cover design by
Mark (Wills) Williams

Everything else by
Default, Luck and Accident

Also by Shaun Hutson:

ASSASSIN
BODY COUNT
BREEDING GROUND
CAPTIVES
COMPULSION
DEADHEAD
DYING WORDS
EPITAPH
EREBUS
EXIT WOUNDS
HEATHEN
HELL TO PAY
HYBRID
KNIFE EDGE
LAST RITES
LUCY'S CHILD
MONOLITH
NECESSARY EVIL
NEMESIS
PURITY
RELICS
RENEGADES
SHADOWS
SLUGS
SPAWN
STOLEN ANGELS
THE SKULL
TWISTED SOULS
UNMARKED GRAVES
VICTIMS
WARHOL'S PROPHECY
WHITE GHOST

Hammer Novelizations
TWINS OF EVIL
X THE UNKNOWN
THE REVENGE OF FRANKENSTEIN

DEATH DAY

His body moved slightly and she saw his hands slowly pull the covers down. June found herself staring at the back of his head, then he rolled over and looked right at her.

She would have screamed had he not fastened one powerful hand around her throat. He pulled her close and she felt and smelled his fetid breath on her face.

His eyes were gone.

No whites, no pupils. Nothing. Just two blood red orbs which swelled like crimson blisters from the dark skin which surrounded them. Saliva ran in a crystal river from both corners of his mouth, his red lips flecked with spittle. The nostrils flared as he tightened his grip on her throat...

Death Day

SHAUN HUTSON

AUTHOR'S NOTE

Originally written in 1981, DEATH DAY was first published in the United States under the pseudonym of Robert Neville.

The reason I chose the name Robert Neville was after the character in I AM LEGEND which had been a major influence on the novel itself. Well, not the Richard Matheson book itself but one of its adaptations, THE OMEGA MAN (1971) with Charlton Heston. I had always loved that film and had always wanted to write a novel similar to it. Had the appalling Will Smith version been around when I was young I would probably have given up horror and started writing comedy!

If I'm honest I can't remember exactly where the initial idea came from. All I can remember is that I'd just had a novel called THE SKULL published by a company called Hamlyn Paperbacks (they did lots of horror back in the early 80's) and wrote DEATH DAY to offer them as my next book but they turned it down, so I decided to look for an agent who eventually got it published in America by a company called Leisure Books in 1982. It wasn't published in this country until 1987 and there were a couple of small scenes added near the beginning as I remember, including a torture scene.

The artwork used on the cover was very similar to the American artwork and emphasised the amulet that features in the book and triggers the horrific happenings. Those of you who've already read it will know what I mean but I won't spoil it for anyone just discovering the book.

DEATH DAY is still one of the most "traditional" horror books I've ever done. It owes a lot to the Hammer films that influenced me so much when I was growing up and it owes a huge debt to THE OMEGA MAN, I openly admit that. Some of the plot elements would be re-used in EREBUS because at the time (1982) I didn't think that DEATH DAY would ever be published in this country. I hope I didn't plagiarise myself but I'm sure my readers would have told me by now! The whole idea of a town gradually being taken over by a force of evil with just a handful of people left to combat it fascinated me then and still does to an extent but it's such a staple (almost cliché) of the horror genre that I tend to steer clear of it these days but back then I just wanted to do it and see how far I could push the idea. I don't think I've ever said this before but there was also a planned sequel that never came off which is a pity because DEATH DAY was very successful and I think the material for a sequel was there.

That just brings me briefly to the whole subject of sequels and leaving novels open ended. Most of my early stuff, in fact most of my books throughout the last 30 years, have been open ended and people have invariably asked if that was to allow for a sequel and nine times out of ten the answer was no. I think SLUGS was the only book that I consciously planned to do a sequel even before it was published. The others have finished with open endings just to show that events are ongoing, that what you've read about is continuing. I know it seems obvious but I just wanted to clear that up. For instance, RENEGADES was always intended to be a standalone novel, I had no idea there'd be 3 sequels! If the opportunity is there and the book does well, then that's a different matter but usually each novel is written to be a one-off. To be honest, I never really know until I get to the end!

Maybe there'll be a DEATH DAY 2, only time will tell.

Shaun Hutson 2016

This book is dedicated, as always, to my wonderful daughter, Kelly.

Acknowledgements

I would like to thank the following people for their help or encouragement. Meg Davis. Darren Laws and Holly Andrews at Caffeine Nights. Rod Smallwood and Phantom Music. Steve, Bruce, Dave, Nicko, Janick and Adrian. Thanks to my Mum too, for different reasons. Cineworld Milton Keynes, especially Mark, Mel, Adam, Phillip, Dani, Alun, Hannah, James, Phil and Rae. Thanks also to the Broadway Cinema in Letchworth.

My thanks to all my readers as ever.

'Hell hath no limits,
nor is circumscribed in one self place;
for
where we are is Hell,
And
where Hell is must we ever be...'

- Christopher Marlowe

PROLOGUE

The woman was thrown to the floor of the tiny cell, her face ground into the reeking straw which covered the stone. She made few sounds, even as a heavy boot was driven into her ribs. She felt bone splinter and the air was torn from her. Powerful hands dragged her to her feet, pinning her against the cold wall. Her head was wrenched up by her long hair until she was face to face with the tallest of the three men.

His face was shrouded by deep shadows, some caused by the gloom inside the cell, but most by the wide brim of his hat. He stood in silence, watching her through heavily lidded eyes. She met his stare, the merest trace of a smile on her lips.

The two men on either side of her suddenly released their grip on her wrists and began tearing her clothes from her. Her full breasts swung into view, already marked with numerous scratches and red welts. She did little to resist as they tore the last clothing from her and then slammed her, naked, back against the wall.

The tall man reached into his pocket and pulled something out. It looked like a piece of wood, as thick as a man's finger but it bore a needle like point of steel. He touched the point to a place close by her right nipple and pushed.

Now she broke her silence and screamed as the steel punctured her flesh. Blood welled up and dripped from her wound.

He repeated the procedure until her chest was reduced to a bleeding ruin. He reached lower, pushing it into her belly.

Pain lanced through her and she felt as if she would pass out but rough hands tugged at her hair and face, slapping hard until she found her vision clearing.

The tall man stepped back, pocketing the pointed implement.

'Speak,' he said, quietly. 'Where is your master?'

The woman met his gaze but did not answer.

She felt one of her arms being forced up her back, the strain on the joint becoming intolerable.

'Where is your master?' the tall man repeated.

Her shoulder felt as though it were burning as yet more pressure was exerted on her twisted limb.

She opened her mouth in silent agony.

There was a loud crack as the arm broke, unable to withstand any more such pressure. The bone snapped above the elbow, the power exerted on it so great that the shoulder was dislocated too.

The woman screamed loudly.

'You think he would hesitate to speak your name where he in your position now?' the man asked her.

Her head sagged forward for a moment and the tall man nodded towards his companions who immediately took a firmer hold on the woman's arms and began dragging her from the cell. Along a narrow dripping corridor they took her until they reached a larger room. There they secured her to the stone wall with shackles and one of them hurled some water at her. It revived her, the clear liquid dripping from her body, mingling with the blood which had congealed there.

She saw the tall man reach for the branding iron, its tip white hot as he pulled it from the brazier. A flicker of fear passed behind her eyes as he approached her with it, the glowing end mere inches from her face.

'What is the secret of the circlet?' he asked.

She gritted her teeth and shook her head.

The iron came closer until she could feel the heat then, in a moment of mind numbing agony; she felt it touch her cheek. Her scream rose mightily within the room as the burning metal seared her flesh, a great raw welt rising beneath the brand. The acrid stench of her burnt skin filled her nostrils and she passed out.

More water was flung at her, hands slapped hard at her - cheeks until she regained consciousness.

The tall man remained before her, the branding iron still burning hot.

She closed her eyes, tears spilling down her cheeks.

'Why prolong the pain?' the tall man asked her. 'Speak now. Is it true that the circlet only afflicts those who are first to touch it?' He moved the glowing iron closer. 'Only those who are first to touch the amulet are tainted. Is that true?'

She didn't answer.

He snarled and pressed the red hot rod to her breast.

It took much longer to revive the woman this time but when she did eventually come round she felt heat between her spread legs. The iron had been re-heated and now, the probing brand, white hot, hovered precious inches from that most sensitive area.

'Is it true about the amulet?' the tall man asked her, the rod like some burning, agonizingly hot penis. It quivered between her legs.

'Yes,' she shrieked. 'The first to touch the amulet is tainted but none thereafter until my Master has held it again.'

The tall man smiled and turned away from her. He replaced the branding iron in the coals and turned back to face the woman. She felt sick, the pain which racked her body gripping her like a fist. The other two men unshackled her and dragged her from the room, back along the corridor but this time up into the daylight.

There were hundreds of people standing outside the building. They shouted things at her as she was thrown to the ground amongst them. Some spat at her. But the babble died down as the tall man emerged into the light.

'Let all know that in this, the year of Our Lord 1596,' he began. 'This woman has confessed to the sins of which she was accused. She knows the secret of the amulet and he who holds it.'

He pointed an accusing finger at her.

'There is but one punishment for this blasphemy.'

It took but a moment for them to find a rope and secure a stout knot. Two of them looped it round her neck and dragged her to the nearest tree, where they took hold of the end and tugged her up into the air. She kicked and struggled for what seemed like an eternity, spittle and blood dribbling over her cracked lips but, eventually, her movements ceased and only the wind stirred her motionless form.

'We have dealt with the disciple,' said the tall man. 'Let us destroy the Master.'

There was a roar of approval from the crowd, many brandishing pitchforks and clubs above their heads.

'Let us rid ourselves of this pestilence forever,' the tall man said. 'We know where its source lies, let us erase it from God's earth.'

He set off, followed by the maddened crowd. They knew their destination and there was a firm determination about them.

However, many shuddered as, overhead, dark clouds began to gather and the first soundless fork of lightning rent the air.

'Be not afraid, God is with us,' the tall man called.

The storm clouds gathered in huge black masses. Like dark warnings.

PART

ONE

One

There was a dampness in the morning air which promised rain.

The sky was heavy with clouds, great, grey, washed out billows which scudded across the heavens, pushed by the strong breeze. The same breeze which stirred the naked branches of trees. They stood defiantly against the wind, shaking skeletal fingers at an invisible defiler which rocked and battered their flimsy forms. Birds huddled in the branches, feathers stirred and ruffled by the strengthening gusts.

Rain-soaked piles of leaves lay in tightly packed masses about the tree bases.

Seasonal transition had nature in limbo. The time when winter has passed but the earth has not yet erupted into that frenzy of greenery which is spring. That time was still to come.

There had been more rain during the night. Enough to darken the concrete paths of Medworth. The town had its fair share of rain, standing, as it did, in the rolling hills of Derby-shire. The nearest town of any size lay twenty miles away to the west, but the people of Medworth were content with their own patch of miniature metropolis. The town was small; a population which struggled to reach nine thousand, but there was plenty of work within the town itself. It was built around a large shopping centre. The shops themselves employed more than a third of the total labour force, many of the rest being accounted for by the town's small industrial estate built a mile or so out. It consisted of a small iron foundry and brewery as well as a number of smaller factories.

The few farms which were scattered on the hills nearby were concerned mainly with arable crops, the odd scatterings of livestock kept for the benefit of the individual farmers rather than for any serious commercial purposes.

To call Medworth a thriving community would have been an overstatement, but it ticked along comfortably, satisfied with its own seclusion.

There was little entertainment to be found. The old cinema had closed down two years earlier and now remained nothing more than an eyesore in the centre of town. A large building, almost imposing in its obsolescence, it stood at the top of the main street, now just a darkened shell.

Its presence represented a reminder of the past, of a time when life was lived at a slower pace. Progress had come slowly and almost resentfully to Medworth.

By eight o'clock that morning there were people in the streets, and, an hour later, another working day had begun.

Two

Tom Lambert brought the Capri to a halt and switched off the engine. He looked out of the side window and read the sign which spanned the iron gates.

'Two Meadows.'

In ordinary circumstances he would have smiled. The name of the cemetery always amused him. After all, it was built on a hillside two miles outside of town. Not a meadow in sight.

Lambert sighed and ran a hand through his short brown hair, catching sight of his own pale face in the rear view mirror as he did so. He readjusted it, as though not wanting to see his reflection. The wind rustled quietly around the car, somehow far away. It seemed to him as though, here inside, he was insulated against all sound and sensations.

He wished it was an insulation against his own emotions.

As he climbed out of the car, Lambert realized just how cold the wind was. He shook himself and pulled up the collar of his leather jacket before reaching onto the back seat to retrieve a bunch of carnations. He sniffed them. No scent.

Greenhouse variety. He locked the door and pocketed the keys.

His feet clattered noisily on the pebble driveway of the cemetery. He wondered why they had never bothered to pave the path. It wound right through the cemetery before disappearing out of another gate a mile and a half further on. That was one of the things which always amazed Lambert. The sheer size of the place. There seemed enough plot acreage to bury half the population of Britain, never mind the occupants of Medworth.

He continued up the path, passing the first rows of gravestones. The plots were in various states of disrepair according to their age or the consciences of those who had buried someone there. Few of the older graves bore flowers. An urn might sport a few withered blooms but most were bare.

To Lambert's right, along a broken path, stood the church. Its great steel-braced oak doors were closed. The bell tower, topped by the twisted black spire, dominated the bleak skyline and as he looked up, he could see the battered weather vane twisting in the wind.

Almost thankfully, he reached the footpath which led off from the main drive. The noise of the crackling pebbles was beginning to grate on his nerves and as he walked along the muddy path between the rows of gravestones he was pleased by the silence. It was broken only by the mournful sighing of the wind in the nearby trees. They stood like sentries, watching him pick his way through the maze of stone memories, and if they could have spoken they would have known this young man. Lambert had been coming here at the same time for the last two weeks and he wondered how much longer he would continue to do so. Perhaps his entire life would be spent edging his way between marked and unmarked graves, looking for one in particular. The same one he came to every morning at nine o'clock.

Beneath the shade of a huge oak tree, he found it.

Amidst the brown and grey of the cemetery, the plot stood out with an almost unnatural blaze of radiance. Flowers of every kind were laid across it, some still wrapped with the cellophane in which they'd been brought. He bent and picked off two fallen leaves which had found their way from the low tree branch onto the grave. Lambert lowered his head. He didn't need to read the inscription for he had it burned into his mind. It was there constantly, gnawing away at him like some kind of parasite.

'Michael Lambert-Died January 5th 1984'

He had been twenty.

Lambert thought that most of his emotion was spent but, as he bent to lay the bunch of carnations on the grave, a single tear slipped from his eye corner and rolled down his cheek. He straightened up, wiping it away. He stared down at the grave. His brother's grave. He gritted his teeth until his jaws ached. He wanted to shout, to scream at the top of his voice. Why? Why did it have to be Mike?

He spun round in a paroxysm of helpless rage, driving one fist as hard as he could into the solid bark of the oak. Pain shot up his arm but he ignored it, his back now turned to the grave as if he could feel his brother's eyes staring out reproachfully it him. Images flashed into his mind.

The car. The screaming of brakes. The explosion.

Oh Jesus Christ, he wanted to scream again.

Lambert felt the tears running more swiftly down his cheeks now as the thoughts returned with a clarity which sickened him. Living with the memory was bad enough, if only it weren't so vivid...

They had gone out that night, ten of them including Mike and himself. What was it blokes liked to call it, the last fling? Stag night, booze up, piss party, call it what you like. It had been the night before Mike was due to get married. A right little cracker he was landing too. Sally. He couldn't remember her last name, but he realized what a lucky man Mike was. Lambert himself was to have been the best man. He was going to drive Mike home that night, he was going to be the one who kept his eye on his baby brother. (There was three years between them, Mike was twenty, Lambert had just turned twenty-three.) He was the one who was going to stay sober, let Mike get boozed up, let him enjoy his last night.

Now, as he remembered how prophetic that statement turned out to be, Lambert hated himself even more.

They had carried on drinking late into the night but it had been Mike who had remained sober, Lambert himself who had got pissed. So pissed he asked Mike to drive them home. So pissed he had not closed his car door properly (the thing that probably saved his own life). So pissed he'd forgotten Mike had only passed his driving test a few weeks earlier and had no experience at night driving.

And now he remembered, how the car went out of control as it hit the patch of black ice. How the car swerved and he was thrown clear while Mike struggled with the wheel, trying to avoid the lamp post.

Drunk and in pain, Lambert had seen the car smash into the lamp post. Seen Mike catapulted through the windscreen, heard his scream of agony as the jagged glass shredded his face and upper body. Then Lambert had crawled across to his brother's body and sat with him, ignoring the blood which had splashed for fifteen feet across the pavement, ignoring the pieces of glass embedded in Mike's face and neck, the final spoutings of his blood jetting darkly into the night.

When the ambulance arrived, Lambert had been sitting on the pavement holding his dead brother's hand. At that precise moment of course he didn't know that Mike was dead. He only realized that when the two ambulancemen lifted the shattered body. There was a dull thud and the head dropped to the ground, the neck severed by the savage cuts.

At that point, Lambert had collapsed.

And now, he found the courage to look back at his brother's grave. He wiped the tears away, suddenly becoming aware of just how cold the wind was getting. He shivered, cold in spirit as well as body.

'Shit,' he said aloud, shaking his head. He inhaled, held the breath then let it out very slowly.

The family had been very understanding about it. God, how fucking ironic, how bloody magnanimous of them, he thought. Never mind about your brother, it wasn't your fault. He felt suddenly angry. So, maybe it wasn't his fault, but, he told himself, what good were consolations when you had to live with the thought for the rest of your life?

He'd woken screaming for nights afterwards.

Debbie understood, she always understood. He thanked God he had her. They'd been married two years but already he wondered what the hell he'd have done without her. If he hadn't had her with him during the last couple of weeks he'd have gone up the wall. Everyone had been very understanding but it had done nothing to ease the guilt. He wondered what would.

There had been nothing about it in the news- papers. Lambert knew Charles Burton, the man who ran The Medworth Chronicle. The two men disliked one another but Lambert had managed to persuade him not to mention his name in the local rag. It wouldn't have done his reputation much good either.

He'd been surprised that he hadn't heard more from Divisional HQ in Nottingham. Lambert, as head of Medworth's small police force, could do without the kind of publicity which the crash might have brought. He was surprised he hadn't been asked to resign or some such drastic measure, but, as Debbie had said to him at the time, he hadn't killed his own brother. He had only been involved in the accident which had taken his life.

Lambert was the only one who felt like a murderer.

He lingered a moment longer, then, almost reluctantly, he turned and made his way back along the path between the graves until he reached the gravel drive.

It was after nine but he was in no hurry. He'd been told to take a month off. Get his thoughts back into one piece. The men under him were all capable. Capable enough at least to run things until he returned.

He walked, head bowed, collar turned up against the wind. Lost in his own thoughts, he almost bumped into the tall man coming through the cemetery gates.

The man was carrying a pick over his shoulder and there was a younger man behind wearing a pair of bright orange overalls.

Lambert sidestepped the pair who continued up the gravel drive, their mud-caked boots making it sound as if they were walking on cornflakes. Lambert saw their council van parked across the road outside the vicarage. There was movement in the bay window of the building and Lambert saw Father Ridley standing inside. He waved cheerfully to the young man who raised a hand in weary acknowledgement. He fumbled in his pocket for his keys and unlocked the car door. He slid behind the wheel, started the engine and swung the car round, pointing it down the hill in the direction of the town. Lambert flicked on the radio but, after a moment or two found that he didn't feel like listening to music. He switched the set off.

He drove the rest of the way in silence.

Three

'It'll take until next Christmas to clear this lot,' said Ray Mackenzie, dropping his pick dejectedly.

He was looking at a patch of ground about half the size of a football pitch, surrounded on three sides by densely planted trees. Some had even encroached into the heavily overgrown area itself. The grass and weeds were waist high in places and, as Mackenzie stepped forward, he snagged his arm on a particularly tall gorse bush. He muttered something to himself and kicked at it.

The area was beyond the main part of the cemetery, two hundred yards or more from the central driveway along which they had just come. Situated in a slight hollow, it was effectively masked from the rest of the area. Only the fact that the top halves of the trees poked up above the rim of the crest testified to its existence. The grass was neatly cut only up to the very edge of the crest then it sloped down into the area where the two men stood. Nature run riot.

'Fancy letting it get in this state in the first place,' complained the younger of the two men.

Steve Pike had quite fancied the idea of working for the council at first. Weeding the flower beds in the town gardens, cutting the grass in the park? It had seemed like a good idea. As he surveyed the expanse of twisted gorse, bracken, heather and waist high grass he began to have second thoughts.

Father Ridley had called the council offices and asked if they could send some men to clear a patch of ground for him.

'Well,' said Mackenzie. 'Standing here looking at it isn't going to make it go away.'

With that he drove his pick into the ground, turning a large clod. He grimaced as he saw the size of the worm which clung to it. He broke the clod with his pick and continued digging. Steve stood watching him.

'Come on,' snapped Mackenzie. 'Get the sickle and cut some of that stuff down ' He pointed to a dense growth of ragweed which was fully two feet high. Steve went to the canvas bag they had brought with them and pulled out the sickle, then he set to work, hacking away at the recalcitrant plants. Mackenzie swapped his pick for a shovel and was soon turning the earth. But it was quite a battle.

Steve too found that the roots of the bramble and gorse bushes went deeper than he thought. Great thick tendrils of root clung to the earth like bony fingers.

They worked on. Yet despite the fury of their exertions, both men began to notice something odd. Both were soaked in sweat but both could feel their bodies trembling from the cold. A cold the like of which neither had experienced before. A deep, penetrating cold which was almost oppressive. Mackenzie stopped digging and looked up.

Another thirty minutes and the men decided that it was time they stopped for a while. Steve looked around. They had done quite well considering the size of the problem. At least a quarter of the overgrown area had been cleared, the earth now dark beneath their feet. Mackenzie looked at his watch. The second hand was frozen. It had stopped, the hands pointing to 9:30. He shook it and grunted.

'What's up?' asked Steve, taking the fag he was offered.

'My bloody watch has stopped,' Mackenzie told him.

Steve rolled up his sleeve, his forehead creasing. He tapped the face of his own timepiece.

'So has mine,' he exclaimed, extending his arm so that Mackenzie could see. The twin hands were immobile.

Stuck at 9:30.

Lambert parked the Capri in the small driveway beside the house and got out. The next door cat scampered across the front lawn as he walked up the path to the back door and he hissed at it.

The startled animal spun round and fled off through a hole in the fence. Lambert smiled thinly to himself.

He found his back door key and let himself in. It was after nine-thirty so he knew that Debbie would be gone. She always left well before nine, sometimes before he even drove for the cemetery. The kitchen smelt of pine and new wood, and Lambert inhaled deeply. He crossed to the kitchen table and sat down, noting that two letters were propped up against the tea pot. He smiled again. Although the letters were addressed to Mr and Mrs T. Lambert, Debbie had left them for him to open. She always did. He considered the envelopes for a moment then dropped them back onto the table and crossed to the sink to fill the kettle. He stood for a moment, looking out of the back window, thinking how badly the grass needed cutting. The gardens on either side were in a worse state and that, at least, comforted him somewhat.

Their house was roomy, semi-detached, with three bedrooms, a dining room, kitchen, and spacious living room. The third bedroom was to be used as a nursery when, and if, the need ever arose. Lambert looked down into the aluminium bottom of the sink and saw his own distorted image staring back at him. At the present time, there was no talk of children. Both he and Debbie had promising careers: he was one of the youngest Inspectors in the Midlands force and Debbie was chief librarian at the large Victorian looking building in the centre of Medworth. Lambert shook his head. An Inspector in charge of a force of less than twelve. That was police logic for you.

The shrill whistling of the kettle interrupted his thoughts. He made the tea, poured himself a cup and carried it into the living room where the daily paper was waiting on the arm of his chair. Debbie again. God how he loved that girl. He suddenly began to feel warmer, the incidents of the morning gradually subsiding. Diminishing but never fading.

He flicked through the paper, hardly seeing the words, then he folded it up and stuck it in the paper rack. Lambert gazed across at the bay window.

It was the inactivity more than anything which wore him down. The same routine every day, stuck in the house trying to find jobs that he'd already done two days before. The doctor had told him to rest for a month after the accident, but the time was dragging into an eternity. He glanced down at the phone on the table beside his chair and rubbed his chin contemplatively. Should he ring the station? Just to find out if they needed him for anything?

He grunted and turned away, warming his hands around the mug of steaming tea. He eyed the phone again but, instead, went and retrieved the letters from the kitchen. He tore the first of them open, knowing from the 'Private' stamp on the top left hand corner that it was a bill of some sort. Electricity. He muttered something to himself and re-folded it then tore open the second.

It was from his mother. He read it briefly, not really seeing the words on the blue tinted pages. Everything was all right, his father was fine. Hope he was feeling better. Etc., etc., etc. Tactfully no mention of Mike. He pushed the letter to one side and finished his tea. The same old crap every time. Debbie usually replied to them. Lambert picked up the letter once more and read the line which never failed to annoy him.

'Your father is fine.'

He threw it down. Father. Fucking stepfather. His own father had been dead for ten years. Lambert had watched him die, day by day. A little at a time. He remembered coming home from school every dinner time when he was twelve and finding his father sitting at the table, the bottle of whisky gripped in his palsied hand. Lambert hated him for his drinking, he hated him for what it had made him. But most of all, he hated his mother because she was the reason his father had begun drinking in the first place.

Her and her fancy man. Mr Ted bloody Grover. 'Your father.' His new father, his fucking stepfather.

He tore the letter up savagely, hurling the pieces away from him in rage, his breath coming in short gasps.

Cirrhosis of the liver had caused his real father's death. Or precipitated it anyway. Lambert remembered finding him that day. His head thrown back, his eyes open. The yellow blobs of vomit still on his lips, the empty bottle gripped in his rigid fingers. Choked on his own puke.

Why was it, Lambert thought, that the painful memories always stayed more vivid than the pleasant ones? To him at any rate.

He reached for the file and dialled Medworth police station. The phone rang a couple of times, then was picked up.

'Medworth Police Station,' the voice said.

Lambert smiled, recognizing the voice as sergeant Vic Hayes.

'Morning, Vic,' he said.

'How you keeping, sir?'

'Not bad. What's doing?'

There was a pause at the other end as Hayes tried to think of something he could tell his superior. His tone sounded almost apologetic, 'Nothing really. Mrs Short lost her purse in the Bingo hall, she thinks it was nicked. Two kids took a bike from outside old man Sudbury's shop and I've got bloody flu, that's all I can tell you.'

The sentence was finished off with an almighty sneeze.

Lambert nodded, 'So there's nothing worth me coming in for?'

'No, sir. Anyway, aren't you supposed to be resting? I heard that the doctor gave you a month off.'

'How the hell do you know that?' asked Lambert, good naturedly'.

'I bumped into your wife the other day,' Hayes explained. There was silence for a moment, then the sergeant said, 'By the way, sir, we were all very sorry about what happened.'

Lambert cut him short, 'Thanks.' He moved hurriedly on. 'Look, Vic, if anything does turn up, let me know, will you? Sitting at home here is driving me up the bloody wall.'

'Will do, sir.'

They said their goodbyes and Lambert hung up, plunged once more into the silence of the room. He clapped his hands together as if trying to shake himself free of the lethargy which gripped him. He got up, tired of the silence, and crossed to the record player. He selected the loudest recording that they had in their collection and dropped it onto the turntable.

Someone thundered out 'Long Live Rock & Roll' and Lambert went back into the kitchen to make himself some breakfast.

Already, the emotions were slipping to the back of his mind, waiting to be stirred perhaps the next day, but, for now, he began to feel brighter.

'Long Live Rock & Roll' blasted on.

Debbie Lambert looked at her watch and noted with delight that it was nearly one o'clock. She took off her glasses and massaged the bridge of her nose between thumb and forefinger. There was a nagging ache behind her eyes and she closed them for a moment. The ledgers lay before her as if defying her to carry on work. This was the only part of her job she hated. Cataloguing. She was thankful it only happened once a year. Every book in the library, all 35,624 of them, had to be listed by author, publisher and serial number. She'd been working at it now for more than a week and hadn't even got half way. She resolved to take some of it home with her that night.

Mondays were usually quiet, but today there were agitated babblings from the direction of the children's section. A party of twenty kids from the local infants' school had been brought in with the idea of introducing them to the delights of a library. Debbie could see two of the little darlings giggling uncontrollably as they pawed through a book on early erotic art. She barely suppressed a grin herself, especially when the kids looked up and saw her watching them. They both turned the colour of a pillar box and hurriedly replaced the book.

'Don't you just love kids?' said Susan Howard, struggling past with an armful of books.

Debbie raised one eyebrow questioningly and Susan laughed. Nice girl, thought Debbie, about twenty, a year or so younger than herself. They got on well together. All the staff in the building did. There were just four of them: herself, Susan, Mrs Grady and Miss Baxter (who took care of the research section, or reference library as everyone else liked to call it). Debbie had wondered whether Miss Baxter would resent being under a woman more than thirty years younger than herself, but there had been no animosity shown. The previous head librarian had died three years before and few people suspected that the job would go to someone as young as Debbie, but her aptitude for the job was undeniable. She had, since she took over, tried to change the image of the building some-what. She disliked the staid, Victorian picture of libraries which most people had. Of old spinsters in long skirts and horn-rimmed glasses hobbling about the corridors, and endless leather-bound dusty volumes which no one ever read. Since she had taken over, more youngsters had joined. Attracted no doubt by the presence of Susan, and, she hoped, herself. More men were members now than ever before.

She dropped her glasses into her handbag and stood up, shaking her legs to restore the circulation. She'd been sitting in more or less the same position for nearly four hours, bent over the ledgers and her shoulders and legs felt as if someone had been kicking her. She exhaled deeply and swept a hand through her shoulder length blonde hair.

'Sue,' she called quietly, 'I'm just popping out for lunch.'

The other girl nodded and struggled on with her armful of books.

Debbie walked out, the noise of her high heels clicking conspicuously on the polished wooden floor. As she reached the exit door she eyed her reflection in the glass and smiled. She had a good figure, slim hipped, the small curve of her bottom accentuated by the tight jeans which she wore. The thick jumper which covered her upper body concealed her pert breasts and made her look shapeless, but she dressed for comfort, not show.

As she stepped out into the street, an arm enfolded her waist and she spun round anxiously.

It was Lambert.

Debbie smiled broadly and kissed him.

'I thought you were at home,' she said happily.

He shrugged, 'I ran out of things to do. You were the last resort.' He smiled as she punched him on the arm.

'Cheeky sod,' she giggled. 'I was just going for lunch.'

'I know.'

'My God, you're not a policeman for nothing, are you?' she said sarcastically, trying not to smile.

He slapped her hard across the backside. 'Come on, Miss Librarian, let me buy you some lunch.'

The nearest cafe was busy but they found a seat near the window and Debbie sat down while Lambert fetched the lunch, picking food out from beneath the plastic fronted cabinets. He returned with a laden tray and began unloading it onto the table.

As they ate, she told him about her morning's work and about the kids. He smiled a lot. A little too much perhaps. She reached across the table to clutch his hand.

'You all right?' she asked.

He nodded, 'I walked down here to meet you,' he told her, 'I needed the air.'

She smiled, then trying to sound brighter, 'Were those letters anything important this morning?'

He told her about the bill. 'The other one was from my mother.'

'What did she have to say? Or do you want me to read it when I get home?'

'I torethe fucking thing up,' snapped Lambert.

Two women on the table next to them looked round, and the policeman met their stare. They returned quickly to their tea, and gossip.

'What did it say?' asked Debbie, squeezing his hand tighter.

He shrugged and took a sip of his tea before answering, 'The same old shit. Same as always. I don't know why the hell she can't just leave me alone. I never asked her to start writing in the first place.' He slammed his cup down with a little bit too much force, making a loud crack.

The two women looked round again and this time Lambert thought about saying something. But he returned his gaze to Debbie. Her eyes were wide, searching his own, trying to find something that lay beneath his visible feelings.

There was a long silence between them. The only sound was that of many voices talking at once, each lost in their own world, making sense alone but, combined, becoming a noisy babble of nonsense. People around them chatted about the weather, their families, their jobs. The everyday monotony of life.

'I phoned the station,' said Lambert, at last.

'Why?' asked Debbie.

'I wondered if there was anything I could do, or if they needed me.'

Debbie looked at him reproachfully, 'Tom, the doctor told you to rest. You're not supposed to be at work. Sod the bloody station. They can run things without you.'

'I can't sit at home all day doing nothing,' he protested, 'it's driving me crazy.'

'Well, going back to the station isn't going to help either.'

'At least it might give me something else to think about. That's what I need, something to take my mind off what's been happening. You don't understand what it's like, Debbie,' he gripped her hand. 'I relive that bloody accident, that night, every time I visit Mike's grave. Even when I'm not there, it's still with me, you don't forget something like that easily.'

'No one expects you to. Just stop blaming yourself.' She didn't know whether to be angry with him, or feel pity.

'Shit,' he said it through clenched teeth, his head bowed.

She watched him for long seconds, a feeling of total helplessness slowly enveloping her. Finally he looked up and swallowed hard, 'I'm sorry,' he whispered.

'Don't be,' she told him.

He shook his head, moisture brimming in his eyes. He exhaled deeply, 'I asked Hayes to get in touch with me if they need me anytime.'

She opened her mouth to speak but he raised his hand, 'It's the only way, Debbie. I'll go off my head otherwise.'

They finished eating. He looked across the table at her and smiled. She glanced up at the clock on the wall of the cafe and saw that it was approaching two o'clock.

'I've got to be getting back,' she said, reluctantly.

'I'll walk you,' he said, standing up.

The town was busier as they walked back to the library. People were looking in shop windows and talking on street corners. A number spoke to the young couple as they walked, as both were well known within the town.

When they reached the steps of the building, Lambert put his arms around his wife's waist and kissed her.

'What will you do this afternoon?' she asked.

'Never mind me,' he said, smiling. 'You get back to your cataloguing.'

He turned to leave but she caught his arm and pulled him to her, her lips seeking his. He felt her moist tongue flick over the hard edges of his teeth before plunging further into the warm wetness of his mouth. He responded almost ferociously, pressing her close to him, anxious to feel her body against his own. Finally she pulled back. He ran an index finger across her soft cheek and smiled.

'See you later,' he said.

As he turned, she called after him and he stopped, listening.

'Tom,' she said, 'I love you.'

He smiled, 'I know.' And he walked off.

Four

Steve Pike poured himself another cup of tomato soup from the thermos and watched the steam rising from the thick red liquid. He took a sip, wincing at the plastic taste, but he persevered, taking a draw on his fag to deaden the flavour.

'Want some?' he asked, pushing the cup towards Mackenzie.

The other man shook his head, and after stuffing the remains of a sandwich into his mouth, pulled a small metal flask from the pocket of his parka.

He took a hefty swing and smacked his lips, 'Stuff your soup,' he said, 'I'll stick to this.'

From where he sat, ignoring the dampness which was seeping through the seat of his trousers, Mackenzie could see the church clock. Its metal hands were at three-twenty. He glanced down at his own watch once more. Despite winding, it still wasn't working. Bloody Russian crap. Next time he'd get a Timex.

Squatting on the dark earth, Steve looked around. They were well across the clearing, almost halfway. The high grass and weeds had been cut down behind them; tomorrow they would cut down the remaining vegetation and, after that, dig it all into the soil.

'We'll go as far as that tree stump today,' said Mackenzie, pointing to a gnarled knob of wood which jutted out of the climbing grass like a beacon. It stood about two feet high but was nearly that width across the neatly cut base.

Someone, many years ago, had chopped it down and, what was more, they had done it with amazing precision. The severed trunk was as smooth as Formica on its darkened diameter. It reminded Steve of a table, as if it had grown in that shape for some purpose.

'That's going to take some shifting,' said Mackenzie, taking another pull from his hip flask, 'I bet the bloody roots go down for yards.'

Steve looked around the clearing: the darkened area of earth strewn with chopped down grass, and that which lay beyond, rampant with clotted outcrops of weed. Not a wild flower in sight.

'I wonder why they wanted it cleared?' he said.

'Well,' said Mackenzie, 'it is a bloody eyesore.

Christ, I shouldn't think it's been seen to since the fucking cemetery was opened.'

Steve wasn't satisfied. 'But it's out of sight of the rest of the place, you can't even see it from the driveway.'

Mackenzie turned on him irritably, 'What the bloody hell does it matter why they want it cleared? Perhaps they're expecting lots of people to peg out and they want somewhere to put them. How the bleeding hell should I know why they want it cleared?'

'All right, keep your shirt on. I was just curious.'

Mackenzie grunted. 'Why bother about it? As long as we get paid for doing it I couldn't give a bugger what they want it for.' He drained the last drops of brandy from his flask. He shook the flask and dropped it back into his pocket.

'I'll tell you what,' he said. 'It's getting colder. I reckon we'll have a frost tonight.'

'It is bloody cold,' said Steve, softly, almost to himself.

He threw what was left of his soup onto the ground and pushed his thermos into his lunchbox.

Grumbling, they returned to cutting down the sea of weeds and grass. Mackenzie straightened up sporadically and massaged the small of his back, groaning with the ache that had settled there. He drove his spade down hard and felt it connect with something solid. He pawed away the earth and saw a root as thick as his arm. And the tree stump was more than three feet away. He groaned inwardly. Shifting it was going to be harder than he'd anticipated. He lifted the spade above his head and brought it crashing down on the root, severing it with a powerful blow.

'Steve.'

The youngster turned.

'There's a couple of hatchets in the work bag. Go and get them. We'll chop the bloody thing free.'

Steve nodded and headed off to fetch the tools.

Then he heard Mackenzie call again. 'And bring the crow bars too.'

He returned a moment later with the tools to find Mackenzie leaning on the tree stump. He took an axe from Steve and set to work, hacking through the thick roots until the sweat began to soak into his coat. But neither of them removed their jackets because it was getting so cold. Mackenzie could feel the biting iciness catching in his throat and he half expected to see his laboured breath frosting before him in the freezing air. Steve too, slashed away at the tentacles of root, watching as sap oozed, blood-like, into the earth.

It took them nearly half an hour to free the stump.

Panting, Mackenzie picked up the crow bar and motioned for Steve to do the same. They slid the clawed prongs under two sides of the stump and, at a given signal, pressed down on the iron levers as hard as they could. Their faces turned bright red with the effort and veins stood out angrily on both men's foreheads.

'Hold it a minute,' gasped Mackenzie.

Steve was fit to drop. He had never known exertion like this in his life and, if he had his way, he'd never have it again. They tried again but the stump remained stuck fast as if driven into the soil with some gigantic steam hammer. It was like trying to pull a masonry nail from a wall with your fingers.

'Couldn't we both try it from the same side at once?' offered Steve, not really caring now whether they moved the bloody thing or not. He didn't know why they just couldn't have gone round it.

Side by side, they prized the crow bars deep beneath the stump, Mackenzie eventually shouting in angry frustration.

'Fuck the bloody thing.' He threw his bar to the ground and stood, hands on hips, staring at the recalcitrant stump which seemed to grin back at him as much to say, you might as well forget it.

'Does it matter that much?' Steve asked timidly.

Mackenzie exploded, 'Of course it matters, you stupid little bastard. How the hell are they supposed to turn it into a fucking burial plot with that stuck in the middle?'

He retrieved his bar.

'Come on,' he snarled and they set to work again. To Mackenzie, it had become a matter of pride; he intended moving that stump if he had to stay there all night and do it.

There was a slight creak and it lifted an inch. They pressed down harder and it lifted a little more.

'It's moving,' shouted Mackenzie, triumphantly.

Inch by agonizing inch, the tree stump rose, bringing with it more thick roots which hung like hardened veins from its dirt encrusted base.

It lifted a foot. Then eighteen inches, a great sucking sound filling the air as it began to come free.

Then they noticed the smell. A fetid, choking stench which smelt like excrement and made them gag. Steve felt his muscles contract, the hot bile clawing its way up from his stomach.

'Keep pushing,' shouted Mackenzie, tearing the lump of wood from its earthy home until the many-rooted base was at a ninety degree angle to the ground. Both men put their shoulders to it, preparing to push it over.

It was then that they looked down into the hole.

Mackenzie opened his mouth to scream but no sound would escape. The cry caught in his throat and rasped away. His eyes, riveted to the sight below him, bulged madly, the blood vessels in the whites threatening to burst. Steve made no attempt to stop himself and vomited violently, not quite daring to believe what he saw.

Lying in the hole, its body coated in thick slime, was a slug the size of small dog. Its body was a sickly greyish white colour, covered from head to tail with thick slime. As the horrified men stood transfixed, its twin antennae slowly grew towards them, lengthening like car aerials, until they had reached their full height. The bulbous eyes waved gently at the end of the antenna and the abomination slithered forward.

With a scream of sheer horrified revulsion, Mackenzie snatched up the crowbar and struck the creature. It made a hideous gurgling noise, the antenna retracting swiftly. Mackenzie struck again but, seeing that the blows were having little effect, he grabbed the axe, lying discarded by the tree stump and brought it down with terrifying force on the monstrous thing.

His blow split it in half and, a shower of virulent pus-like blood spouted into the air, some of it spattering him. Screaming like a maniac he brought the axe down again, this time splitting the thing lengthways. A reeking porridge of blackened entrails spilled onto the ground, the stench nearly making Mackenzie faint. Sobbing now, he brought the axe down once more, this time slicing off one of the antenna. He sank to his knees, the slimy mixture of yellow blood and dark viscera covering him. He gripped the axe and screamed.

Steve Pike lay unconscious behind him.

It was a full hour before Mackenzie was able to think clearly, or even to look at what remained of the thing in the hole. God alone knew how long it had been there, what it had fed on... And only now did he see that it had been lying on something. A box of some sort.

Steve had come to about twenty minutes ago, seen the creature's body and thrown up again. Mackenzie didn't blame him. Now both of them sat looking down into the hole left by the torn up tree stump, wondering what was in the box on which the slug had been lying.

'It looks like a coffin,' said Steve, quietly. Mackenzie nodded and leapt forward, tentatively touching the wooden lid. It was soft to the touch, like mildew. He poked it with the crow bar and a lump fell off. Both men stepped back.

'What if there's another one of those things in there?' said Steve, apprehensively.

Mackenzie ignored him and stepped down into the hole. Christ, it was deep, a good three feet deep, the rim of it level with his waist.

The sky above was growing dark and he had to squint to read what was on the lid.

'It's a name or something,' he said.

Steve swallowed hard and looked around him. The wind had sprung up and the trees were rustling nervously. 'For Christ's sake hurry, Mack,' he said. Night was drawing in fast, clouds gathering like premonitory warnings above the cemetery. Birds, returning to their nests, were black arrowheads against the purple sky.

Mackenzie bent and looked closer. There was a name plate but the name had been scratched out making it unreadable. Only the date was visible, caked over with the mud of four hundred years.

1596.

'Christ, it's old,' said Mackenzie.

He slid his crow bar under one corner of the lid and wrenched it open.

Both men found themselves looking in at a skeleton.

'Jesus,' groaned Steve, noticing that the empty eye sockets had been stuffed with rag. The blackened skeleton lay in what remained of a shroud, now little more than rotted wisps of linen. The mouth was open, drawn wide in a way that made it look as though it were screaming.

But the most striking thing was the medallion. It hung around the neck of the skeleton, almost dazzling in its brilliance. As if the rigours of time had been unable to make an impression on it.

'Fucking hell,' gasped Steve, 'it must be worth a fortune.'

The medallion consisted of a single flat circle of gold suspended on a thick chain. There was an inscription in the middle, and more jumbled lettering around the rim of the circlet but, as Mackenzie leant forward, he could see that it was no language he recognized. He hazarded a guess at Latin and would have been pleased to know that his theory was right.

'Shouldn't we tell the vicar about this?' Steve wanted to know.

Mackenzie shot him a warning glance, 'You're joking. After what we've been through getting this, I want a souvenir.' Reaching down, he ripped the medallion from around the neck of the corpse. Smiling, he studied it lying in the palm of his hand.

'A fortune,' he said quietly. It was then that he noticed the slight sensation of warmth in his palm. At first he dismissed it as imagination, or the sweat of his exertions. But the neat grew stronger, the skin on the palm of his hand began to sizzle and, as he watched, the medallion began to glow.

He dropped it with a startled grunt. It stared back at him from the damp earth.

'The bloody thing burned me,' he said, looking up at Steve.

The younger man frowned and looked down at the medallion. He reached forward and prodded it with his fingers.

'Seems alright to me,' he said, picking it up.

Mackenzie snatched it from him, holding it for a moment or two. Nothing happened. Perhaps it had been his imagination. He looked down at the palm of his hand. There was a scorch mark the size of a milk bottle top on the flesh of his hand.

He dropped the medallion into his pocket and picked up his spade.

'Let's fill it in,' he said.

'I still think we should tell the vicar,' Steve persisted, shovelling earth.

'Shut up and keep digging.'

They buried the coffin and its skeletal occupant and the slug then set off back to the cemetery proper. Mackenzie was quiet, staring ahead of him as he walked, and Steve had to hurry to keep up with him.

'What are you going to do with the medallion?' the youngster asked.

'Mind your own fucking business,' rasped Mackenzie.

Steve swallowed hard, disturbed by the tone of the older man's voice. What he had just seen had caused him enough trouble, he didn't want to end his first working day with a fight.

When they reached the van, parked outside the cemetery, they dumped their tools in the back and Mackenzie threw the ignition keys to Steve.

'You drive,' he ordered, 'I've got a blinding headache.'

Steve didn't argue. He got in, started the van and drove off towards Medworth. Mackenzie sat silently beside him, head bowed, his breathing low and guttural.

The youngster put his foot down. He would be pleased to get home.

Five

Debbie Lambert turned the big master key in the door of the library and smiled at the three women behind her.

'Another day, another dollar,' she grinned.

The women said their goodnights on the steps of the library then went their separate ways into the chill night. Although it was only six-fifteen, frost was already beginning to speckle the roads and pavements. It would be black ice by ten that night.

Debbie shivered and walked around the side of the building to the car park. She was struggling under the weight of a large plastic carrier bag she held. It was jammed full of ledgers. Reluctantly she had, as expected, been forced to take some work home with her.

After dumping the carrier on the passenger seat she slid behind the wheel and started the engine of the Mini. It spluttered a little then burst into life and she guided the car out into the street in the direction of home.

The journey didn't take her long. Their house stood on a small private estate about ten minutes from the centre of town, in a street with only six houses on each side of the road. As she turned into the street she could see lights blazing from the living room windows of their house. She parked her Mini behind Lambert's Capri and walked around to the back door.

The smell of cooking met her as she entered the kitchen, and she sniffed appreciatively. Lambert, dressed in a plastic apron with a bra and knickers drawn on it, was standing by the cooker stirring the contents of a large saucepan.

Debbie took one look at him and began laughing.

'I bet this never happens to Robert Carrier,' he said, grinning.

She crossed the kitchen and kissed him, peering into the saucepan.

'What is it?' she asked.

'What is it?' he mimicked her. 'It's stew, woman, what does it look like?'

She nipped the end of his nose and retreated into the living room. There, she dumped her carrier bag full of ledgers on the coffee table and called to Lambert that she was going to change her clothes. He shouted something about slaving over a hot stove and she laughed as she bounded up the stairs.

His mood had changed, she thought with relief. But that had been the problem since the accident. His temper and character seemed to fluctuate wildly. One minute he was happy, the next he was plunged back into the abyss of self-reproach and guilt. Debbie removed her clothes and left them in an untidy heap on the end of the bed. She fumbled in the drawer for a t-shirt, stood before the mirror, unhooked her bra and threw it to one side before pulling on the t-shirt.

Her nipples strained darkly against the white material. She slid into a pair of faded jeans, patched so many times she'd lost count, and padded, barefoot, downstairs.

Lambert was ladling out the stew when she walked into the dining room.

They ate slowly, at a leisurely pace, chatting about this and that, feeling the tensions of the day slowly drain away.

He poured her another glass of wine and sat down again, gazing across the table at her as she drank.

'I'm going back to work at the end of the week,' he said quietly.

She paused, her glass midway to her lips and asked why.

'Because I can't sit around like this any longer.'

'You know what the doctor said.'

'Oh, sod the doctor. He doesn't know what it's like. Sitting here every day and night thinking about that bloody accident. I need to go back. I need something to occupy my mind.'

'You said yourself that there was nothing doing.'

'I know,' he took a sip of his wine, 'but at least I wouldn't be shut up here in the house all the time.'

'Just give it a little longer, Tom,' she asked.

'It's been a fortnight now,' he said, his voice growing to a volume which he didn't intend. He looked down at the patterned table cloth and then across to her again. 'I don't think I'll ever be able to face it, so I might as well just keep running.' He drained his glass and poured himself another.

'And what happens when you can't run anymore?' she wanted to know.

He had no answer.

Ray Mackenzie stood on the pavement outside his house as the van drove away and rubbed his eyes. Christ, the bloody headache was getting worse and now his eyes were starting to throb. He felt if he hadn't slept for a week. He looked up into the dark sky and inhaled deeply. As he walked, the medallion bumped against his thigh, secure in his trouser pocket.

There was a small tricycle lying outside the back door and he bumped his shin against it as he rounded the corner. Snarling, he lashed out at it, sending the tiny object hurtling across the yard.

Inside, June Mackenzie sighed. It looked like one of those nights. She had been expecting him for the last hour and a half. He'd probably been down the pub for a couple of pints. Well, she'd give him a piece of her mind when he came in. Half past seven. What sort of time did he call this? It was the same every day, wondering if he'd be home straight from work or down the bloody pub with his mates. She had put up with it for the ten years they had been married but she sometimes wondered how much more she could stand. If not for Michelle, now nearly five, she would have left him long ago. At thirty-four, she felt that life was somehow passing her by. Even if he'd offer to take her out once in a while that would be something. But no, same routine every night. He came home, stinking of booze. Had his dinner, went back down the pub until nine then flopped in front of the TV for the rest of the evening. Christ, what a way to live a life. His idea of a great night out was sitting and watching a darts match down the local. He'd asked her to come with him occasionally but there was no one to look after Michelle and, besides, she didn't fancy sitting with a bunch of boozy men all night, cracking jokes about their wives' frigidity.

June shook her head. There must be more to life than this?

She had thought about trying to get a flat for herself and Michelle but the waiting list was four years long and, with the child just starting school she didn't want to move too far away. Besides, her own measly wage could never support them. She worked part time as a cleaner in a car showroom but there had been talk of cut-backs and she was beginning to wonder how much longer they would keep her on. Ray didn't earn a lot. Just enough to pay the rent and the H.P. They had everything on H.P. If he ever lost his job and the payments couldn't be met, half the house would be repossessed. She shuddered at the thought.

The back door flew open and Mackenzie staggered in.

'Who left that fucking thing outside the door?' he shouted, rubbing his bruised shin.

'Do you have to shout?' she demanded, 'do you want the whole street to hear you?'

He walked off into the living room, grunting at Michelle who was playing on the rug in front of the gas fire.

'Your dinner is ready,' called June, 'and has been for the last hour.'

He ignored her and stormed upstairs, his heavy boots crashing heavily across the landing.

She knew that he must have gone into their bedroom. She shook her head angrily.

'What's the matter with Daddy?' asked Michelle.

Mackenzie moved about the bedroom without turning on the lights. His headache had grown steadily worse and he found that bright light aggravated it. Despite the blackness in the room, broken only by the dull glow of the street lamp outside, he moved with assurance. Sitting on one corner of the bed, he pulled the medallion from his pocket and studied it. He guessed by its weight that it must be solid, a good pound and a half. He tried to guess at the value but the persistent buzzing pain which throbbed behind his eyes and in his temples made rational thought impossible. He sighed, disturbed at the intensity of the pain. It felt as if someone were driving red hot nails into his scalp. He stood up, shakily and crossed to a drawer where he pulled out his wife's jewel box. It was wooden, the top carved ornately, making it look more valuable than it actually was. He flipped it open, emptying its meagre contents onto the floor. Then, carefully, he laid the medallion inside. It seemed to wink mockingly at him and, for a moment, a wave of icy air enveloped him. He shut the box lid and it passed. He hid the small box beneath his pillow and walked out of the bedroom.

When he entered the kitchen, his dinner was on the table. It had dried up long ago, the chips looking like mummified fingers.

'I don't want any dinner,' he growled, raising one hand to shield his eyes from the bright glow of the kitchen's fluorescents.

'Look,' said June, 'it's not my fault it's like that. If you'd come home at the right time.'

He cut her short. 'No fucking dinner.' He screamed the words, grabbing the plate and flinging it at the far wall where it shattered, splattering food in all directions. He turned on her, spittle sticking in white blobs to his lips. June was suddenly afraid.

She took a step backward, watching him as he glanced up at the light. He hissed and covered his eyes as if the white glow were causing him pain.

He rushed to the switch and slapped it off, plunging the room into darkness.

'Ray,' said June, her tone softening, wondering just what was happening, 'what's the matter?'

'Light,' he grunted, 'can't stand the light.' He turned and stalked into the living room, recoiling madly from the shaded hundred and fifty watt that illuminated the room.

'Turn it off,' he screamed and dashed for the switch.

The room was now lit only by the glow of the television screen and Mackenzie growled something as he stood looking at it. Michelle got to her feet and ran to her mother, suddenly frightened by her father's behaviour. He put both hands to his head and moaned, slumping into one corner of the room, head down.

June crossed to the phone and began dialling, 'I'm going to get a doctor,' she said.

Mackenzie leapt to his feet and was across the room in a second, his hand closing around his wife's wrist in a grip which threatened to snap the bone. She gasped and tried to pull away. The phone dropped uselessly from her hand and swung by its cord. His voice almost a whisper, now surprisingly calm, Mackenzie said, 'No doctor.'

She looked down at the hand which gripped her arm and tried to pull away. Mackenzie smiled, his eyes blazing in the reflected glare of the TV. He released his grip and pushed June away. She bumped into a chair and nearly fell.

'What the hell is wrong with you?' she said, becoming angry, 'had too much to drink?'

He snarled and stepped towards her, bringing his arm back then striking forward with the back of his hand. The blow lifted June off her feet and sent her crashing into the metal guard of the gas fire. She rolled forward, blood weeping from her split lip. Still stunned from the force of the blow, she peered up at him. Mackenzie stood, legs astride, glaring down at her, his eyes narrowed to protect himself from the light of the TV.

'You bastard,' she said softly. 'You mad bastard.'

Michelle began to cry. She had been standing in the doorway between kitchen and living room and had seen it all. Now she watched as her father turned and stormed out of the room, his feet slamming up the stairs. She heard the sound of a door being smashed shut. Then she ran to her mother who had managed to drag herself up onto her knees. She caught the little girl and hugged her to her chest, feeling her own blood dripping slowly down her chin.

This time he'd gone too far.

June looked up at the clock on the mantelpiece. It said ten thirty-five.

She had put Michelle to bed two hours before and had sat, alone, staring blankly at the television. There had been no sound from Ray. She had gone up there once and tried to open the door but found that he had locked it from the inside. She licked a tongue across the swollen cleft in her lip. The bastard must have fallen asleep. She had called his name but there had been no answer. Not a sound from inside the bedroom. She had then gone to the child's bedroom at the far end of the landing and peeked in. Michelle had been asleep, a ragged old Snoopy clutched between her tiny hands.

Then June had returned to the living room. She had sat there all this time. Wondering what to do. If Ray wouldn't open the door, she'd just have to sleep on the sofa. She gritted her teeth. God, would she give it to him in the morning!

She waited ten more minutes, until the hands of the clock had crawled onto ten forty five, then she moved quickly through the house, locking doors and windows, pulling plugs and prepared to go upstairs. She double checked the back door. Burglars had always been one of her biggest fears. Though, God knew, they had nothing worth taking. Nevertheless, she pulled the bolts tight, peering out of the small window into the darkness beyond. The street lights still glowed like trapped fireflies and one or two lamps burned in front rooms but apart from that, the street was quiet.

She closed the hall door behind her and walked wearily up the stairs. As she reached the landing, she cautiously opened the door to Michelle's room. The child was still sleeping. June smiled and pulled it shut. Then she padded along to her own bedroom. There was no sound from inside and she put her hand on the knob, expecting to find it twist impotently in her grip.

Instead, the door opened.

She half smiled. The sod must have come to his senses. June went in, closing the door quickly behind her. Mackenzie was lying in bed, his head covered by the blankets, facing away from her. She undressed quickly and slid into bed beside him. He grunted as she did so, a deep guttural sound which made her sit up. His body moved slightly and she saw his hand slowly pull the covers down. June found herself staring at the back of his head.

'Ray,' she whispered, touching his shoulder.

He didn't move.

'Ray.' She shook him harder and this time he rolled over and looked straight at her.

She would have screamed had he not fastened one powerful hand around her throat. He pulled her close and she felt and smelt his fetid breath on her face.

His eyes were gone.

No whites, no pupils. Nothing. Just two blood red orbs which swelled like crimson blisters from the dark skin which surrounded them. Saliva ran in a crystal river from both corners of his mouth, his red lips flecked with spittle. The nostrils flared as he tightened his grip on her throat and she made a gurgling noise and tried to pull his hand away.

He was on his knees now, above her, bringing more pressure down on her, as if he wanted to force her through the very bed itself. She struck out at him, her long fingernails raking his skin and tearing three bloody furrows but he kept up the pressure, that insane grin still smeared across his face. The rictus which showed his yellowed teeth, dripped mucous. June saw white stars dancing before her eyes and she knew she was blacking out. Then, suddenly, and with a force far beyond that of a normal man, he lifted her in that one hand and threw her across the room.

She slammed into the wall, cracking her head. June slumped down, clinging desperately to consciousness. She had one thought. One rational thought in a world gone mad. She must get to Michelle.

But the creature with the burning red eyes, the creature which had been her husband, rose slowly from the bed and walked purposefully towards her.

She staggered to her feet, wondering if she could make it to the bedroom door. If only she could get past, lock him in....

Dazed, she bolted for safety but Mackenzie caught her arm and, with terrifying force, hurled her backwards. She slammed into the dressing table, her head snapping forward to smash into the mirror which splintered. Shards of glass sprayed out into the room, one of them falling at Mackenzie's feet. He bent and picked it up. Razor sharp, it was the length of a milk bottle. He could see his own vile reflection in it as he advanced on her.

June began sobbing, blood pouring down her face from a cut on her forehead. She tried to scream but it came out as a strangled cough. She raised a hand to ward him off but he brought the shard of mirror sweeping down and it carved off her thumb.

'Ray,' she croaked and he was upon her.

The bedroom door opened slowly and Michelle stood there. The noises from her parents' room had woken her. Now she stood quietly, watching as her mother died, bleeding from a dozen savage wounds. The child didn't move, her eyes riveted to the slaughtered body.

There was a movement beside her and she looked up, not quite realizing that the thing with the burning red eyes which stood above her, clutching a length of blood splattered mirror, had once been her father.

Six

Debbie yawned and took off her glasses. She shook her head and sighed deeply. The ledgers stared back up at her, defiantly. Her eyes were beginning to grow tired and she could feel the pain gradually gnawing its way from her shoulder to her neck and up the back of her head. She leant back in her chair and stretched, letting out a moan. The room, lit only by the light of the table lamp, seemed to crowd in on her and she promised herself that she would finish in half an hour. She'd been at it solid for three hours.

'Enough.'

Lambert slapped his hand down on the ledger spread out in front of her and she jumped.

'Christ,' she said, 'you frightened me.'

'Wrap your gums round that,' he said, handing her a steaming mug of coffee.

He stood behind her and rested his hands on her shoulders, massaging gently. She purred contentedly.

'Call it a night, Debbie,' he insisted, his fingers working more strongly. She flexed her shoulders, enjoying his expert touch.

'What have you been doing?' she asked him, closing her eyes.

'Watching TV, reading. Nothing much.'

She took a sip of her coffee, squirming as one of his hands slipped down and touched her breast. She reached up and held it, pressing his hand to her bosom. He responded by squeezing it, feeling the nipple grow hard beneath his palm. He ran his free hand through her blonde hair, tracing one finger across her cheek until he reached her mouth. She parted her lips slightly and licked at the end of the probing digit. He pulled it away and allowed his hand to find its way to her other breast. Both hands now clamped firmly on the pert mounds, he gently rubbed them, becoming aroused himself by Debbie's tiny moans of pleasure.

She put down her coffee and swung round on the swivel chair to face him. He smiled down at her, watching as she pulled off her t-shirt, revealing her firm breasts, the hardened nipples now pink buds.

She reached forward and fumbled with his belt, pulling it free and undoing the top button of his jeans, slowly easing the zipper down. She pulled him closer to her, excited by the sight of his erection. She bent low and kissed him and he groaned from the sensations in that most sensitive area. Her lips fastened around his swollen organ and she drew him still closer, bringing her hands round to grip his buttocks. He held her head, not wanting her to stop the motion of her mouth and tongue but also wanting to enjoy her more fully. Gently, he pulled away and knelt before her, helping her to slip out of her own jeans and knickers.

She raised one foot which he caught and kissed taking each toe into his mouth in turn before allowing his tongue to flick its way up the inside of her leg towards her own pulsing desire.

She edged forward on the chair, giving him better access and, as his tongue parted her nest of light hair, she gasped. He plunged deeper, allowing his probing tongue to taste her flowing juices and she pressed hard against his face until he put his hands beneath her and lifted her to the floor, impaling her on his erection.

Slowly at first, but then with increasing urgency, Debbie moved back and forth until her gasps became cries, mingled with his own muffled gasps of pleasure as they reached a peak together and he buried his head between her breasts.

As the sensations subsided, they lay beside one another, aware only of the warm glow from the other's body and the plaintive howling of the wind outside.

Debbie leant over him and kissed his chest before looking into his face. He smiled up at her and stroked her cheek with one hand.

'Maybe cataloguing isn't so bad after all,' she said and they both laughed, holding one another tightly. They lay there on the floor, naked, for a little while then Debbie said:

'I wonder what it's like to go through life without someone to love. Without someone who loves you?' She twisted the hairs on his chest into little spirals with her index finger.

Lambert shrugged, 'I've never thought about it.'

She smiled, 'What was it Shakespeare said, "It's better to have loved and lost, than never to have loved at all."'

'Something like that,' said Lambert, trying to suppress a smile.

'What's so funny?' Debbie wanted to know.

'You're very philosophical.'

'Am I getting boring?' She looked into his eyes.

He tutted and sighed, 'I might have to give that some thought.'

She pinched him.

'Ouch,' he said, sitting up, 'you bitch.'

She giggled.

'Assaulting a police officer is a very serious offence,' said Lambert in an officious voice. 'You have been warned.'

'And what if I do it again?' she asked, teasingly.

'I shall have to consider my verdict carefully.'

Debbie kissed him on the cheek, 'how about an early night?'

He agreed.

Lambert sat up, sweat coating his body. He stared wildly around the room, his breath coming in gasps. Glancing down at the alarm clock he noticed that it was four a.m. The luminous arms of the clock glowed like gangrenous glow worms in the darkness. Beside him, Debbie stirred, murmured something in her sleep, and was silent again.

As carefully as he could, Lambert swung himself out of bed and padded to the bathroom. He turned on the cold tap, filled the basin with water and splashed his face. As he looked up, a haggard face stared back at him from the bathroom mirror. The dark lines under his eyes looked as if someone had drawn them with charcoal. He peered down into the clear water and splashed more onto his face.

When he was sure he had calmed down, he let the clear liquid out of the basin and padded back to the bedroom, pausing on the way to look out into the night. He could see nothing. Not a light anywhere, just the watery moon slowly being smothered by banks of thick cloud. He shivered, realizing that he was still naked, and hurried back into bed.

He closed his eyes and waited for sleep, but it wouldn't come. No peaceful oblivion, just that same stubborn image. The one which had woken him in the first place.

The car careening towards the lamp post, smashing into it. His brother hurtling through the windscreen, while he sat in the road watching.

Morning was a long time coming.

Seven

Maureen Bayliss piled the last of the breakfast dishes in the sink and looked at her watch. She sighed. Time to get the kids off to school. The washing up could wait until she got back.

'Mum. Mum, I can't find my boots,' shouted little Ronnie Bayliss from the living room.

Maureen hurried to the door and pressed a finger to her lips. 'Don't shout,' she rebuked. 'Your Dad's trying to get some sleep.'

She looked up at the ceiling as if fearing that her husband, Jack, had been woken by their son's frenzied howlings. Jack worked nights at Medworths Foundry, and if he was disturbed while trying to sleep, he'd be like a bear with a sore back for the rest of the day. That she could do without. She told Ronnie that his football boots were in the kitchen and he pushed past her to find them, eventually stuffing them into the red vinyl bag along with his other games equipment.

'Is Carol ready?' asked Maureen, glancing once more at her watch. 'We're going to be late.'

A moment later, the hall door opened and Carol Bayliss emerged. She was a year younger than Ronnie, about six, and Maureen was pleased that they went to the same school so that the boy could keep his eye on her. Carol was a quiet child, withdrawn. Exactly the opposite of Ronnie. Just the type of child whom other kids seem to find a source of amusement. She herself had been to the school twice to report instances of Carol being bullied by older girls and she didn't intend letting it happen again.

Now she helped the child into her navy blazer and straightened her pig-tails, kissing her lightly on the top of the head.

Maureen peered out of the living room window and saw that the sun was shining, but she put on her leather coat just in case. There were dark cloud gathering to the east and she didn't fancy getting caught in a shower on the way back from the school. She struggled with the buttons, horrified to see that she was indeed putting on weight as Jack had told her. She breathed in and managed to button it, hardly daring to exhale for fear of the buttons flying across the room.

'Everybody ready?' she said, and the kids scurried out of the front door before her.

She followed, closing the door as quietly as possible so as not to wake Jack, and headed up the garden path. As she turned the corner, she couldn't help but notice that the curtains of the Mackenzie house were still drawn. It was unusual for June to be so haphazard, thought Maureen. She was usually a stickler for detail. They had lived next door to one another for the last ten years and had become close friends, both of them having their children about the same time. Now they walked, with the kids, to school every morning, did their shopping together and generally went about their business as one.

Ronnie opened the gate which led down the path to the front door of the Mackenzie house and, as Maureen followed him, she saw that upstairs curtains were drawn as well. They've probably slept in, she thought to herself and reached for the brass knocker, smiling to herself, imagining June's panic when she realized what had happened.

Maureen struck hard, stepping back in surprise as the door swung open. Ronnie was about to dash in when she grabbed him.

'Let's go and wake them up,' he said, leering mischievously.

Maureen suddenly felt uneasy. Why should the front door be open when all the curtains were drawn? Perhaps Ray had gone out early that morning and forgotten to close it behind him. Perhaps they hadn't locked it the night before, there had been a strong wind after all.

Perhaps....

Perhaps what?

Maureen took a step back, pulling Ronnie with her. He looked up at her, 'What is it, Mum?'

'Come on,' she said, 'trying not to convey the note of anxiety in her voice. No, why lie to yourself Maureen Bayliss, she thought, for some unknown reason you are scared. There's something wrong here.

She locked the gate behind them and told the kids to stand still while she went and fetched Jack. She fumbled in her purse for the front door key, went in and rushed upstairs. She pushed open the bedroom door, waking Jack immediately. He rolled onto his back, his eyes bleary.

'God, what is it, love?' he said, trying not to sound irritable.

'It's next door,' she told him. 'The curtains are all drawn and there's no answer when I knock.'

'They probably just overslept.'

He tried to roll over again but she pulled him back, 'Jack, for Christ sake, the front door is open.'

'So what?' He was losing control of his temper.

'There might be something wrong,' she persisted.

He snorted, 'Like what?'

'You never know, you read of all sorts of things happening these days, they might all be dead. Burglars or something.'

He waved her away, 'You're going to have to stop reading The News of the World. Things like that don't happen around here, love. This is Medworth, not bloody New York.'

'Then I'm going to phone the police,' she told him, heading for the landing.

He swung himself out of bed and caught her at the bedroom door. She could see that he was angry. 'All right, I'll go and look.' He pulled on his dressing gown and stormed off down the stairs.

'You're not going like that?' she asked.

He turned as he reached the front door, 'Why not? They're going to think I'm off my bloody head when I walk in there and they're all tucked up in bed anyway. I might as well look the part.' Muttering to himself, he headed out into the street.

Ronnie and Carol saw him coming and started to laugh.

'You can shut up too,' he said and headed down the path towards the Mackenzie house.

Maureen ran after him and he paused at the door, still open. 'You'd better wait here,' he said, sarcastically. 'I mean, if they have all been butchered, the killer might still be around.' He shook his head and banged on the open door.

'Ray,' he shouted.

The house greeted him with silence.

Mrs Baldwin from across the road passed by, giving Jack Bayliss a funny look. She turned her nose up and walked on. He bowed mockingly and the old lady hurried past. Ronnie and Carol laughed again.

Jack took a step inside and shouted once more. There was no answer, no sound of movement. Nothing. The hall door to his left was closed, the staircase straight ahead of him. The curtains at the top of the landing were drawn, plunging the house into a kind of murky twilight. He walked into the hall and pushed open the door. Christ, it was dark in there. He swallowed hard, squinting into the gloom, and called again.

Silence.

He took a step into the room, casting a furtive glance around. Jack could feel the tension building within him as he padded towards the closed kitchen door and, he almost hit the roof when he felt a hand on his shoulder.

Scarcely stifling a yell he turned to find Maureen standing there.

'Did you have to do that?' he panted, his heart thudding against his ribs.

'I told you there was something wrong," she persisted.

He peered into the kitchen and found nothing, discovering his scepticism rapidly draining away.

His tone, when he spoke again, had lost its flippancy.

'I'm going to look upstairs,' he told her. 'You wait in the hall.'

As he ascended the stairs he looked around.

Nothing had been disturbed; whatever had happened it hadn't been a visitation by burglars.

He reached the landing and looked around. There were four doors facing him, set in a kind of L shape. He leant over the banister and saw Maureen looking up at him. Angry with himself for allowing the atmosphere to affect him, he opened the door nearest to him and looked in.

A child's room, he realized from the scattering of toys on the floor and the flowered bedspread. No sign of anyone. He closed that door and moved to the second. It was an airing cupboard. He tutted and was about to open the third door when something caught his eye.

It was lying outside the door of the fourth room, which was, itself, slightly ajar. He crossed cautiously to the discarded object and picked it up. It was a toy, a stuffed animal. Of course, Carol had one. It was Snoopy.

He dropped it when he noticed the blood which covered its floppy head.

His eyes suddenly darted round the darkened landing, flitting from door to door. Fear and anger vied for control of his emotions. He slowly pushed open the door to the fourth room.

From her position in the hall, Maureen Bayliss heard her husband scream. A sound which was rapidly choked away as he vomited.

She called his name and raced up the stairs taking them two at a time. As she reached the landing, he staggered drunkenly from the room, waving her back. His face was the colour of cream cheese and thick mucous was dribbling down his chin.

'Jack,' she said, terrified.

'Call the police,' he gasped, struggling for breath.

'What is it?'

'Do it,' he roared at her, dropping to his knees, his entire body shaking. He tried to control his heaving stomach but, as the door swung back gently on its hinges once more, he couldn't. For although he had his back to the horror he had discovered, the thought alone was enough to make him throw up again. He reached back and slammed the door shut, listening as his wife dialled 999 and babbled out her message. He heard her put the receiver down and then he fainted.

Eight

Sergeant Vic Hayes stood in the bathroom of the Mackenzie house and drank down another tumbler full of water. He stood against the sink for a moment, regaining his composure, then, taking one last mouthful of water, he walked back into the bedroom.

At fifty-two, and with more than thirty years experience on the force, he had seen some sights.

Road accidents, industrial accidents, baby batterings. But never anything like this and in Medworth, of all places. He'd been a sergeant here for more than fifteen years and there hadn't been anything worse than a bad case of G.B.H. in all that time. The offender was doing five to ten in Strangeways; Hayes had given evidence at the trial. The man had attacked his girlfriend's father with a spanner. Made a right mess of his face too.

But never anything like this today.

He entered the bedroom and saw Doctor John Kirby leaning over the first of the bodies, just as he had been doing when Hayes had left the room. Hayes didn't care for Kirby much. He was good at his job, but a bit of an arrogant little bastard. He'd come straight from medical school to his position as Medworth G.P. and he also doubled as Police doctor. Not that his services had been needed until now.

Two ambulancemen stood by the door with a stretcher, their eyes looking at the floor. In fact looking at anything other than at what Kirby had at his feet.

Hayes took a deep breath and leaned over him.

'Whoever did this was a very strong man,' said Kirby, matter of factly. 'It's difficult to tell of course without an autopsy, but,

I'd say these cuts are nine or ten inches deep.' He pointed to the throat. 'This particular blow practically severed the head.'

'And the little girl?' asked Hayes, not daring to look behind him. Lying beside the open door was the body of Michelle Mackenzie, her tiny form disfigured by a dozen wounds.

Kirby nodded. 'The injuries are the same, so is the disfigurement.' He stroked his chin thoughtfully. 'Strange.'

Hayes nodded. He knew of which 'disfigurement' Kirby spoke and it was that final touch of horror which had forced him out of the room when he had first seen the two bodies.

Both had had their eyes torn out.

'As I said before,' said Kirby, 'without an autopsy it's difficult to give precise details, but from the scratch marks on both of their faces and...'

Hayes cut him short, 'All right, doc. I'll wait for the reports.' He walked out, leaving the ambulancemen to load the bodies onto their stretchers. Kirby followed them out. Hayes watched him leave. He stood on the deserted landing for a moment then wearily made his way down to the living room. Through the open front door he saw the two bodies loaded into the ambulance which, after Kirby had climbed into the back, drove off. Hayes took off his cap and flopped into one of the arm chairs. Where was Ray Mackenzie? Could the husband be the killer?

'Find anything?' he asked, wiping his forehead.

P.C. Gary Briggs nodded and lifted a plastic bag from the coffee table. It contained the jewel box which had belonged to. June Mackenzie.

Hayes took the box out and opened it.

'We found it upstairs,' Briggs told him, 'under a pillow on the bed.'

Hayes looked into the box and saw the medallion. He studied it a moment then looked up at Briggs. The youngster shrugged. 'It's bloody old, whatever it is.'

Hayes handed it back. 'Take it down to the station. Lock it in the safe.'

Briggs nodded and dropped the medallion back into the jewel box.

'Did anyone talk to the woman who reported this?' asked the sergeant.

'Tony did,' answered Briggs, nodding out of the window, indicating P.C. Walford standing outside the front gate talking to a group of people who were trying to see into the Mackenzie house. 'Her husband found the bodies. She reported it straight away.'

'Poor bastard,' said Hayes, quietly, 'it must have been quite a shock for him.'

Hayes struggled to his feet, feeling more aware of his ample stomach than usual, and replaced his cap on his balding head.

'What do you want us to do, Sarge?' asked Briggs.

'Just keep this quiet. I don't want word getting about, understand? This is a nice town. The people aren't ready for this sort of thing. If any reporters turn up, tell them to fuck off.' He paused as he reached the door. 'I'm going back to the station; I'm going to get in touch with Inspector Lambert. I think we need him on this one.'

He walked out into the fresh morning air and inhaled deeply, allowing the crisp wind to wash the stench of blood and death from his nostrils.

He nodded to Walford as he passed, on his way to the Panda car parked across the street.

Hayes slid behind the wheel and started the engine, picking up the car's two-way radio as he guided it out into the street. He flicked on the transmitter and spoke through the crackle of static, 'Puma One to base.'

The static crackled more fiercely.

'Puma One to base, move yourself, Davies.'

There was a buzz as he flicked to receive and a metallic voice came through, 'Sorry, Sarge, the kettle was boiling, I had to turn it off.'

'Well, put mine out, I'll be back in two minutes and Davies, remember, one sugar, I'm trying to slim. Over.'

'About time, Sarge.' A giggle. 'Over'.

'Fuck off. Over and out.'

Lambert heard the phone ringing as he stepped out of the Capri. He hurriedly locked the door and sped towards the house, wondering who was calling and hoping they wouldn't ring off before he got to the phone. He fumbled out his front door key and dashed in, snatching up the receiver in the nick of time.

'Hello,' he said, breathlessly.

'Hello, sir.'

Lambert recognized the voice immediately as

Hayes. 'Sergeant. What can I do for you?'

'I've rung twice before, I didn't think you were there.'

'I was at the...' Lambert's voice trailed off and Hayes realized that his superior had been to the cemetery. 'What's so important Sergeant?'

'Well, sir, you asked me to tell you if anything happened.'

'Yes' Lambert suddenly felt excited. 'I'm afraid we've had a double murder.'

'Where, for Christ's sake?'

'Elm Street. Number...' Lambert heard the rustling of papers at the other end of the line, then Hayes came back on, 'number twelve. The wife and daughter. The husband is missing. We're treating the husband as prime suspect.'

'What do you make of it?' asked Lambert, scribbling something down on the pad beside his telephone.

'Knifings sir, both of them.'

'Got the weapon?'

'Not yet.'

'What're the names of the victims?'

'Mackenzie. June, that was the wife, and Michelle, the little girl, aged about five we think.'

Lambert wrote the details down on the pad, the receiver cradled between his shoulder and his ear.

'Do you need me down there?' he asked hopefully.

'Not at the moment, sir. I've got some men out looking for the suspect and Doctor Kirby is doing autopsies on the victims this afternoon.'

'Ring me back the moment you get the results of those,' Lambert told him, 'or if anyone sees this Mackenzie, right?' He hung up, a sudden surge of adrenalin firing his body. He had forgotten about Mike for a moment, had managed to push that thought to the back of his mind. He had his work again. Now nothing would stop him from returning. He sat down, his thoughts jumbled, and read what he had written on the pad.

Double Murder. June and Michelle Mackenzie. Husband chief suspect, disappeared. Knifed. No murder weapon found. Autopsies performed.

What was Debbie going to say? He half smiled.

The phone rang again at four twenty-three that afternoon.

The policeman snatched it up. 'Lambert,' he said.

'Hayes here, sir. We've got the results of the autopsy.'

'Go on,' said Lambert, suddenly realizing that he hadn't got a pad or pen. 'Hold it a minute,' he said, retrieving them from the coffee table. 'Right, fire away.'

'Dr Kirby's here, if you want to speak to him, sir,' Hayes told him.

'Put him on,' instructed Lambert, hearing the murmurings at the other end of the line. A second later, he recognized Kirby's voice. They exchanged pleasantries, then Lambert said, 'What's the verdict, John? And keep it simple, please.'

'Messy ones, Tom, both of them. I found traces of skin under the fingernails of the woman.

I would think your suspect is probably walking around with some pretty hefty scratch marks on his cheek. What order do you want them in?'

Lambert was puzzled, 'What do you mean?'

'The mother or the girl first?' Kirby told him.

'It doesn't matter,' said Lambert, impatiently.

There was a pause at the other end and the policeman could hear the sound of papers being rustled, then Kirby again. 'The little girl. I found six separate wounds, mostly around the upper body and neck. The deepest was eight inches, the fatal wound probably, situated just below the larynx. If it's any consolation, I think she was dead before he cut her badly.

Lambert scribbled details, 'And the woman?'

'Twenty-three separate wounds.'

'Shit,' murmured Lambert, still writing.

Kirby continued, 'Mostly in the abdomen, chest and neck as before. The weapon was double-edged, jagged and tapering, which would explain the width as well as the depth of the wounds.'

'What do you think? Butcher's knife, something like that?'

'No. I know what it was, I've got it in my office right now. It was a piece of glass, or mirror to be more precise and the reason your boys couldn't find any murder weapon was because it was still embedded in June Mackenzie's body. I took a piece of mirror nearly fifteen inches long from behind the rib cage. It had been driven in from above, just behind the right clavicle, collar bone to you, and it had punctured the heart. I'd say that was the death wound.'

'Jesus Christ,' said Lambert.

'One more thing Tom,' added Kirby, as if the catalogue of atrocity hadn't quite been enough, 'the eyes were taken.'

'Taken? What do you mean taken?' It sank home. 'Oh God, he didn't cut those out too did he?'

'Well now, that's the whole point. My examination revealed that they were removed without the use of any external implements.'

Lambert's nauseated anger broke forth, 'What the hell are you trying to say? Did he cut out their eyes or didn't he?'

Kirby's voice was low, controlled, 'From the scratches on the cheeks and bridge of the nose, I'd say he tore them out with his bare hands. The fingerprints matched those of Ray Mackenzie.' Lambert tried to write down that last piece of information but, as he pressed down on the paper, the point of his pencil splintered.

'Tom?' Kirby's voice called, 'you still there?'

Lambert exhaled deeply, 'Yes, sorry'.

'Did you get all that?'

'I got it. Put Hayes back on, will you?'

The sergeant's voice replaced that of Kirby, 'Yes sir.'

'Get every available man out looking for Mackenzie. I want that fucking maniac caught before this happens again.' He hesitated a moment then said, 'I'll be in touch. If anything happens in the meantime, let me know.'

He put the phone down. For long moments he stood staring at the pad, the scrawled details of the twin deaths.

Eyes torn out.

Lambert threw the pad down and crossed to the cabinet beside the bay window. He pulled it open and took out a bottle of scotch. He poured indiscriminately, filling the tumbler practically to the brim, then he swallowed half its contents, wincing as the amber liquid burned its way to his stomach. He held the glass, considering it in his hand, then he drained it. Rapidly refilling the crystal tumbler, he wondered how many more of them he'd need before Debbie got home.

She found him sitting in the darkness, only the light from the streetlamp outside illuminating his dark outline. He sat still, the glass still clamped in his hand, staring out of the window, scarcely turning when she entered the room and flicked on the table lamp. The room was suddenly alive with subdued light, changing from the drab place of darkness it had been a second ago into a warm grotto.

He smiled at her.

'Tom, what's the matter?' she asked, crossing to him. Immediately she smelt the drink on his breath.

He lifted the glass in salute and swallowed its contents before setting it down gently on the carpet beside his chair.

'Would you like a drink?' he asked. 'There's plenty more where that came from.'

She took hold of his hand. 'What's wrong?' she repeated.

He looked at her, his smile fading. 'Last night, two people were murdered. A woman and a little girl. Do you know how old that little girl was? Five. Only five years old. They were stabbed and then their eyes were torn out. Bodily.'

Debbie shuddered, 'Oh my God.'

'The crazy bastard who did it is still on the loose.'

They looked at each other, their eyes probing, searching the other's for some sign.

'I'm going back, Debbie,' said Lambert, flatly. He reached out and stroked her cheek, noticing the moisture building within her eyes. She gripped his hand and pressed it to her face, kissing it.

'Tom,' she said, a tear running down her cheek, 'I just want you to be all right. This business with Mike, it's torn you apart and now this on top of it. Please, give it a couple more days, they

71

can manage for a couple more days.' Tears were flowing quickly now and he reached out and brushed them aside.

'I'll be all right,' he said. 'They need me. If this bastard did it once, he might do it again. I can't let that happen. I have responsibilities. I'm supposed to be the law here.'

She stood up, suddenly angry, 'Oh, for Christ sake, you make it sound like a bloody Western. The law. Your responsibilities. You don't have to carry the can for everything, Tom. Not for every bloody cause going. You don't have to feel guilty about all the things you do. You'll be telling me next it was your fault those two people were murdered.' She wiped away the tears, rubbing her eyes when they clouded her vision. 'You know I think you actually enjoy it at times. Being the bloody martyr, shouldering the troubles of the world.'

He watched her, standing before him like some sort of nubile prosecution counsel.

'It's called caring,' he said, softly.

She didn't move, just stood still in the centre of the room shaking gently, tears staining her cheeks. He got up and crossed to her, his arms enfolding her. She tried to push him away at first but, finally, her arms snaked up around his neck and she pulled him closer, tasting the whisky on his breath but not caring. Wanting him near to her, to feel his body next to hers.

They stood there for a long time, locked in passionate embrace, clinging to each other in that twilight room, while outside the dark clouds of night began to invade the sky.

Nine

The photo on top of the television smiled back its monochrome smile at Emma Reece. It showed a young couple on their wedding day, the bride resplendent in her white dress (though now looking somewhat sepia tinted because of the age of the photo). The young man was kissing her on the cheek. She looked across at her husband, slumped in the chair, and smiled.

'It's hard to believe that was twenty-five years ago,' she said.

'What's that, love?' he said, his eyes not lifting from the topless girl in the newspaper he held.

'The photo.'

Gordon Reece put down the paper and looked up, also seeing the picture. He smiled. 'God, I was a handsome bugger in those days.'

Emma snorted, 'And still as modest.'

He winked at her, 'If you've got it, flaunt it, that's what I always used to say.'

'You used to say a lot of things,' said Emma, running a hand through her hair. 'Do you think I should have it dyed before Saturday?' she asked.

'What?'

'My hair. Do you think I should have it dyed before the party on Saturday?'

He shook his head. 'Women. Why the hell can't you just grow old gracefully? If you're grey, you're grey. Who cares? You never hear me complaining about the colour of my hair.'

'It's different for men,' she told him. 'Besides, I want to look my best for our Vera. If she's flying all the way from Australia just for our twenty-fifth anniversary, the least I can do is look presentable.'

'She's coming to see you, not your bloody hair.'

Emma pulled at the greying strands, watched by her husband who smiled benignly and shook his head. He returned to his paper.

'It'll be marvellous to see her again after all these years,' said Emma, wistfully.

'Yes dear,' answered Gordon, his head still buried in the paper.

'I wonder what the little boys will think of England.'

Gordon looked up and grunted. 'They'll probably wonder why it's so bloody cold all the time.'

There was a rustling from behind Emma's chair and their three-year old Labrador bitch, Sherry, emerged wagging her tail frantically. Emma patted the dog and it stretched out in front of the fire. Gordon moved his feet to give the animal more room.

'I think she wants her walk,' said Emma, retrieving the leash from the sideboard. There was a photo of their daughter on it and she paused to study the photo for a moment before handing the leash to Gordon.

'She's all right where she is,' he protested, nudging the dog with his toe. The animal looked round. 'You don't want to go out, do you girl?'

He shook his head vigorously, as if trying to convince the Labrador that he was right.

'She needs it,' persisted Emma.

Gordon grunted and began fitting the leash, glancing up at the clock on the mantelpiece as he did so.

'It's nearly half past ten,' he said.

Emma half smiled, almost knowing what was coming next.

'So?' she said.

'There's a match on after the news. A big game. Arsenal and Liverpool, it's...'

She cut him short. 'Oh all right, I can take a hint.'

Emma went into the hall and pulled down her old navy blue duffle coat and fastened the buttons. She held out her hand for the leash, the dog now excitedly waiting. Gordon winked at her.

'I don't know how I've put up with you for twenty-five years,' she said, trying not to smile. She could hold it back no longer when he blew her a kiss. Laughing, she led the dog out into the hall. Gordon heard her say, 'Back in a bit,' and then the front door slammed shut.

He settled down to watch the game.

As Emma stood on the doorstep, fastening the last toggle of her coat, she shivered. She had not realized just how cold the wind was. Now it lashed her face with icy barbs and felt like a portent of frost or even snow. The sky was clear, the full moon suspended on invisible wires like some huge fluorescent ball. It cast its cold glow over the town, guiding Emma as she walked. The dog tripped along nimbly beside her, its breath forming white clouds in the chill atmosphere.

Lights burned in most front rooms as she walked down the street, and their muffled glow made the night seem a little less forbidding. The estate on which they lived was clean, populated by families well known to one another, and there was a feeling of belonging which Emma had never encountered before. She and Gordon had lived in Medworth for over twenty years, London before that. Both of them found the solitude and peacefulness of country life a positive lift after the hustle and bustle of the capital. Her parents had both come from around this area, so she herself was no stranger to their ways.

She had finished work for good when Vera was born. Gordon had had a good job and his wage was more than enough to keep them comfortably. With their own anniversary due on Saturday, just two days away, things looked rosy. They were only having a small get together, family mainly, and a couple of close friends. But what really made the occasion for Emma was the fact that she would be seeing her daughter again after so long. Suddenly she forgot the cold of the night, instead overcome by that familiar warm glow which comes with expectations.

At the bottom of the street, the road curved sharply away to the right and more houses. Straight ahead lay a large expanse of rough ground and thickly planted trees which locals called The Wasteland. Emma laughed to herself. If old Henry Myers, who owned the land, could hear them, he'd go mad. Myers had a small farm right on the edge of the estate. No livestock, just arable crops like the other small holdings dotted around the outskirts of Medworth. Still, he made a living from it. However, with this particular field, he seemed to have given up. Nothing but stumps of grass and a positive jungle of weeds grew there, the whole thing flanked by a string of cedars. A muddied footpath led to a stile over which one had to climb to get into the field; and it was up this path that Emma led the dog.

The animal scrambled beneath the rotted obstacle while Emma struggled over the top, nearly slipping off. Sherry was panting excitedly as Emma unhooked her leash.

'Off you go, girl,' she said, and the dog bounded away into the field, leaping about like a lamb in spring. Emma leant against the stile for a moment watching the dog, then she began to walk around the perimeter of the field.

The trees crowded in on her from one side, kept back to a certain degree by a high fence of rusty barbed wire. The fence was broken in numerous places, the lengths of wire hanging down in the mud.

The wind combed through the branches creating a sound which reminded Emma of sheets blowing on a washing line.

She jumped back as a low branch, propelled by a gust of wind, snatched at her face. She decided to move further away from the trees, perhaps even to join the dog in the centre of the field.

There was a loud snap as a branch broke behind her.

She spun round, her heart thumping. There were scuff marks around the base of the bushes and beneath her lower strands of barbed wire, which she took to be the work of rabbits.

Or rats?

The idea of being in a field with rats made her shudder and she looked across towards the dog, anxious now to get home. Back to the warmth of the fire and the comforting glare of electric light. She looked up at the moon, suddenly covered by a bank of thick cloud. The field was plunged into momentary darkness and Emma felt suddenly, unaccountably, afraid. She rebuked herself as the cloud cleared and cold white light once more flooded the ground. Nevertheless, she pulled the leash from her pocket and prepared to call the dog.

There was more movement in the bushes behind and she turned, convinced that the creator of the disturbance was much too big to be a rabbit or a rat. Perhaps some kids messing about. She tried to fix that idea in her mind, her eyes glued to the source of the disturbance. She stood riveted for long moments then turned slowly back to call Sherry.

The dog was crouching in the centre of the field, its head resting on its front legs, whimpering quietly. Even from as far away as fifty yards, she could see it was quivering, its eyes fixed on something in the bushes behind her.

She turned, the breath catching in her throat.

The thing that had once been Ray Mackenzie hurtled at her from the cover of the bushes, a shower of leaves accompanying his charge.

Emma opened her mouth to scream, her eyes riveted to the contorted face, now lit obscenely by the moonlight. The feral grin showing discoloured teeth, the three deep scratch marks on one cheek but above all, and this was the last thing she saw before he was upon her, the glowing red orbs that were eyes, burning with the fires of hell.

Mackenzie launched himself at her, cleared the fence and slammed into her, knocking her into the soft mud.

Emma screamed, the sound finally choking away as Mackenzie fastened both talon-like hands around her throat and lifted her off the ground. He held her up at arms' length, her legs dangling uselessly, trying to kick him, trying to ease the grip which was killing her. Through eyes clouded by pain, she saw him grinning, those terrible red eyes burning madly. Then he flung her, as an angry child might fling a rag doll. She crashed into the barbed wire fence, the cruel spikes gouging her flesh and ripping her cheek. She tried to rise but he was upon her again, his weight forcing her down, one hand clamped across her face, pushing her head down as if he wished to drive it into the very earth itself. She struggled vainly, striking feebly at him, her tear-filled eyes catching sight of his other hand. A hand which reached for a length of broken barbed wire. Ignoring the barbs which tore open his palm, Mackenzie snapped the wire free as if it had been thin string. He released his grip, momentarily, on Emma's face, holding the two foot length of barbed wire above her. She made one last desperate attempt to get up and did, indeed, manage to stagger a few feet from him. But her legs gave out and Mackenzie caught her, looping the barbed wire around her neck and using it like some kind of spiked garrotte. He pulled with all his strength, watching as Emma raised one hand to ward off the attack. It was useless.

The barbs tore her flesh, puncturing the twin carotid arteries sending spouting fountains of blood spraying into the night air. Blood filled her mouth and, mercifully, she blacked out. But Mackenzie kept pulling, those insane red eyes glowing like beacons, yellow spittle dribbling down his chin. He jerked the body up, hardly realizing that she was dead, failing to appreciate that the wire was embedded so deep it had practically severed her head. He dropped the corpse and stared down at it for a moment.

The eyes were still open, glazed and wide with terror and agony.

Mackenzie dropped down and bent over the head.

In the middle of the field, the dog watched silently as its mistress was killed. Fear pinned it down as surely as if six inch nails had been driven through its paws. It had seen the man emerge from the woods, seen the awful struggles of its mistress. Then finally it had seen the man bend over her, his hands groping at the lifeless face with frenzied movements before he disappeared once more into the woods.

Only then did the dog wander slowly over to the lifeless body, its nose twitching at the stench of blood and excrement. It whimpered, nuzzling against the corpse as if trying to stir it into life. It stood there for long moments, howling up at the moon, then it scampered off, leaving the body of Emma Reece alone.

'You stupid sod,' yelled Gordon Reece, shaking his fist at the television screen, 'I could have put the bloody thing in from there.' He flopped back in his chair, watching as Liverpool mounted another attack.

'Five hundred pounds a bloody week and he can't score,' grunted Gordon.

It was approaching half time and the scores were still tied at one all. He hoped Liverpool would win. He had a lot of money riding on it, both in the betting shop and at work. Besides, he'd never live it down with Reg Chambers at work, a bloody Arsenal supporter. He'd really rub it in if Liverpool lost. But more importantly than that, Gordon had a fiver bet with him on the result. He didn't tell Emma about his little flutters at work, it would only worry her. She sometimes asked him how he got through his money so quickly. He couldn't tell her it was because he was fond of using that well worn phrase 'Put your money where your mouth is'. Unfortunately, just lately, Gordon's mouth had got the better of his wallet. He'd been losing a lot recently. Still, never mind. The reds would do it in the second half. He hoped.

Half time came and with it the commercials. He pottered off into the kitchen to make a cup of tea. Emma should be back soon. The least he could do was make her a cup after having been out in that freezing wind. He lit the gas beneath the large whistling kettle and retired to the living room.

It was then that he heard the scratching.

At first he thought it was the beginning of rain against the windows, but as it became more insistent he realized that it was coming from the front door.

Emma, he thought. Forgotten her key probably. He flicked on the hall light and opened the front door.

The labrador stood on the doorstep, its baleful eyes dark with the horror it had witnessed. Silent testimony to a secret beyond death itself.

Gordon looked at it, shivering before him. It was only a second before he noticed that the dog held something between its jaws and a second more until he realized what it was.

A blood splattered leash.

Ten

Lambert could hear the persistent ringing and, at first, thought that the noise was in his head. He sighed when it didn't fade and opened his eyes.

The ringing continued.

It was the phone in the hall. He glanced across at the alarm clock on his bedside table and then down at his own watch. No discrepancy between them. It was four-thirty a.m.

He rolled onto his back as the ringing continued, persistent and unceasing. Debbie had one hand across his chest, her fingers nestling softly in the hairs. He smiled and traced a pattern on the back of her hand. She moaned in her sleep and rolled over.

The phone kept ringing.

'Shit,' muttered Lambert and swung himself out of bed, shivering slightly. It was still dark outside and he didn't want to put the bedroom light on for fear of waking Debbie. So he tiptoed across the carpet to the door and, closing it behind him, hurried downstairs to silence the phone.

'Lambert', he said, sleepily, rubbing his eyes with his free hand.

'Sir.'

He recognized the voice at the other end as Hayes, equally weary but with an edge to it.

'There's been another one.'

Lambert shook his head, trying to dislodge the last vestiges of sleep which still clouded his brain.

'Another murder?'

'Yes, sir.'

He exhaled deeply, 'Oh God.' A moment's pause. 'Who?'

'We got the name as Emma Reece. Fifty-two years old, lived up the estate near old man Myers' farm.'

'Who found her?'

'Her husband. Apparently she took the dog out for a walk, across some field at the bottom of the road. The dog ran back to the house carrying its own leash. The husband went looking for her and found her lying in the field.'

Lambert yawned and cleared his throat, 'Where's the body now?'

'Doctor Kirby's got it at the morgue,' Hayes told him.

'I'll be right there.' He hung up. Lambert sat staring down at the dead phone for a second, lost in his own thoughts, then he padded quickly upstairs. Moving as quietly as he could, he pulled his clothes from the wardrobe and crept out again. He dressed in the living room, drinking a cup of black coffee while he did so. Then he found a piece of paper and scribbled a note:

Duty Calls, darling.
Love you.
Tom

He propped the note up on the kitchen table and left by the back door.

The drive to the police station took him less than fifteen minutes and, as he parked the car in its usual position, dawn was beginning to claw its way into the sky. The air felt heavy with dew and the smell of cut grass, and Lambert inhaled deeply as he mounted the set of steps which led to the main door.

The small annexe inside the main door was hung with various crime prevention leaflets, some of which were so old they looked like parchment. Lambert smiled to himself. He had almost forgotten what the place looked like. He walked through the double doors which led into the station proper and found Sergeant Hayes propped up behind the desk with a mug of tea in front of him.

'Hello, guv,' he said, smiling.

Lambert smiled back. Just like old times, he thought. He passed his office, a door to his left marked with his name and thought about going in. But he had no reason to, so he lifted the flap of the desk and walked through into the duty room beyond.

It was a large room, its floor covered by a carpet the colour of rotten grapes. There were three or four worn leather armchairs and a couple of hard backed wooden chairs dotted about. The notice board, which covered the entire far wall, was littered with pieces of paper. Duty rosters, areas to be patrolled, who was due for night beat etc. The paraphernalia of normal police work.

He recognized P.C. Chris Davies, slumped in one of the chairs and nodded at him. Davies, a big man with ginger hair, raised a hand in acknowledgement and stood up. Lambert waved him back to his seat.

'You were first there?' asked the Inspector.

Davies nodded. 'Whoever it was made a bloody mess of her. I've never seen anything like it.'

The constable looked younger than his forty three years, but this particular experience had given him the appearance of a man who had been deprived of sleep for a week. He took a sip of his tea; hands still shaking.

Lambert walked out of the room and back to Hayes.

'Where's Kirby?' he asked.

'Downstairs. I don't think he's finished yet.'

Lambert made his way down the corridor which passed his own office, and headed towards a green door marked private. To his left and right were the cells. The green door was the entrance to the police pathology lab and Lambert hesitated before turning the knob.

The smell hit him immediately. The pungent odour of blood and chemicals which always made him heave. He blew out a long breath and descended the five stone steps which led down to the lab itself.

It was, as seemed common to these establishments, green and white in colour, the floor of shiny white ceramic tiles contrasting with the sea green of the walls and ceiling. A bank of fluorescents threw a cold white light across the grisly proceedings below. In the centre of the room was an aluminium table. The work bench, as Kirby liked to call it. There was a body on it, covered at the moment by a thick white piece of rubber sheeting.

The door to the little bathroom at the side opened and Kirby emerged, wiping his hands with a towel. He was chewing something which Lambert took to be a peppermint. The doctor smiled and offered one to Lambert, who declined.

'Finished?' asked the policeman, indicating the corpse.

'I was just about to start,' said Kirby rolling up his sleeves. He crossed to a closet and pulled out a plastic apron which he quickly put on. 'I can tell you without a post mortem that this woman was killed by the same person who killed that little girl and her mother.'

Lambert looked puzzled. 'How, for Christ's sake?'

Kirby pulled back the sheet and Lambert felt his guts turn a somersault.

Emma Reece's eyes had been torn out.

'Jesus,' gasped Lambert, stepping back, unable to look any longer at the mutilated sockets. 'You're sure it's the same killer?'

'The scratches around the cheeks and nose are identical to those on the first two victims. There's no doubt about it. Mackenzie's marks are all over the body.'

The doctor stood beside the corpse, looking at Lambert, whose own gaze was riveted to the deep, savage gashes in the woman's neck. 'How was it done?' he asked.

'He strangled her with barbed wire,' said Kirby flatly.

Lambert pushed past the doctor and pulled the sheet back over the body. 'Forget the autopsy,' he said.

'Are you sure? I mean it's standard procedure...'

'Fuck standard procedure,' snarled Lambert, loudly. He bowed his head and leant back against the table. When he spoke again his tone was more subdued, weary even.

'What's the motive, John?'

'You're the policeman,' said Kirby smiling.

Lambert grinned weakly and nodded. 'No motive. The bastard hasn't even left us a motive.'

The inspector walked past Kirby. 'I'll be in the office if you want me,' he said and left.

Kirby took off his apron and hung it up again. He looked at the corpse beneath the sheering for a second then he crossed to his bench and began writing his own report.

Lambert had a pad before him on the desk and, on it, he was trying to make a list, but the words wouldn't go down in coherent order. He read back what he had:

No motive. Injuries identical. Ray Mackenzie.

He circled 'No motive' and got wearily to his feet. The wall clock said six-twenty a.m.

Lambert yawned and rubbed his eyes. Debbie would be up by now, she'd have read his note. He wasn't sure what her reaction to it would be. Not that it really mattered.

He thought of Mike.

Should he visit the cemetery today? He sat down on the edge of his desk, reaching for the pad. He reread his notes. Notes. That was a laugh. What bloody notes? A page full of maybes and whys. He read it once more.

No motive.

The words stuck out like compound fracture.

But they carried with them a resonance which Lambert found all the more disturbing. If there had been no motive for the three killings, then Mackenzie could strike anywhere and at anytime.

Christ alone knew who was going to be next. The wife and daughter, perhaps he could understand. Maybe Mackenzie had come home in a drunken rage and killed them both in a fit of temper. But Emma Reece....

And the eyes. Why take the eyes? Was there some significance in that particular mutilation?

Lambert threw the pad across the room in a fit of impotent annoyance. They had to catch Mackenzie, and fast.

He tried to imagine what Gordon Reece must have felt like, finding his wife like that. The poor bastard was under sedation at home. The funeral was tomorrow and he had refused to speak to any policemen until after it was over. Lambert had learned that it was to have been the Reeces' silver wedding anniversary the following day. There was nothing to celebrate now. The family were united to see Emma Reece buried, instead of to celebrate a union which had lasted twenty-five years. Lambert suddenly felt very angry. He wondered how he was going to be able to face Gordon Reece on that coming Sunday. Still, he'd learn to live with it. Everybody had to sooner or later.

Lambert thought about Mike again. Should he visit the cemetery?

He could fight the urge no longer. Telling Hayes where he could be reached, he hurried out of the police station and, climbing into the Capri, headed for Two Meadows.

As he drove, he wondered how much longer it would be before the memory faded.

He wondered, in fact, if that day would ever come.

Eleven

Debbie heard the car door slam in the driveway, followed a second later by footsteps heading for the back door. She turned expectantly towards it as Lambert entered.

He smiled tiredly at her.

'You look wrecked,' she said, quietly.

'That is the understatement of the year,' he said, kissing her gently on the forehead. He walked into the sitting room and got himself a drink. 'Want one?' he called.

She asked him for a vodka and he poured it. His own tumbler full, he drained it quickly, then poured another before returning to the kitchen where he sat at the table.

'You got my message this morning?' he asked.

She nodded, sipping her drink.

Lambert exhaled deeply and took a large swallow of scotch.

'Was it another murder?' she asked.

'Yes. A woman in her fifties.'

'What was her name?' He smiled at her, 'That's supposed to be police business.' There was a moment's silence then he said: 'Emma Reece.'

'Oh my God,' said Debbie, putting down her drink. 'I knew her. And her husband. She was a regular at the library. When did it happen?'

'Last night. She was out walking the dog and...' he drew an index finger across his throat in a cutting motion.

'Was it the same one who killed the Mackenzies?' she wanted to know.

'Yes.' He would say no more.

'What about Mr Reece?'

'He's sedated, apparently. The funeral's tomorrow. I've got to talk to the poor bastard on Sunday.' He finished his drink. 'You know I can understand how he feels. It's like being punched in the guts when something like that happens to someone close, like having all the wind knocked out of you.'

'You went to the cemetery again today.' It came out more as a statement than a question.

He nodded, prodding his food with his fork as she laid it before him. She too sat and they ate in silence. After a while, she looked across at him.

'Want to talk about it?' she said, smiling.

'About what?'

'Anything, I'm game.' They both laughed.

'I'm sorry, love,' said Lambert, 'it's just that, well, this whole business worries me. I feel so fucking helpless. Do you know that in all the police records of this town there's never been one murder, one rape or one mugging? And now, in the space of three days, I've got three corpses on my hands.'

'You make it sound as if it's your fault.'

He shook his head. 'That's not what I mean. I wanted to get back to work, you know that.

But not under these circumstances. Christ, three bloody murders. I didn't think things like that happened in Medworth.' He fetched them both another drink and sat down again, pushing away the remains of his meal.

He looked up to see her eyes on him, something twinkling behind them, the beginnings of a smile on her lips.

'What's up?' he said, also smiling.

She shook her head. 'My old man. The copper.'

He laughed. 'What sort of day have you had?'

'Don't ask.'

She got up and walked around the table. He pushed his chair back from the table and she sat on his knee. He put both arms around her waist and pulled her towards him. She kissed his forehead.

'What do you want to do tonight?' she asked. 'We could drive into Nottingham, see a film, take in a club.'

He shook his head.

'I just thought it would be a break.'

'I don't think I could concentrate on a film tonight. What's showing anyway?'

She giggled, ' "Psycho".' She leapt to her feet and dashed into the living room.

'That's not funny,' he called after her and set off to catch her.

He grabbed her arm and pulled her down onto the sofa beneath him. She was laughing her throaty laugh as he pinned her arms and glared at her.

'That was not funny,' he repeated. Then suddenly, they were kissing, their mouths pressed urgently together, tongues seeking the other. He pulled away and looked down at her, her blonde hair ruffled, her cheeks flushed, her mouth parted slightly and moist with the kiss. She pulled him to her again her left hand reaching further, fumbling for the zip on his trousers. He slid his hands inside her blouse, causing one button to pop off in the process. He felt the firmness of her breasts, kneading them beneath his hands feeling the nipples grow to tiny hard peaks. She squirmed beneath him, fumbling with the button of her own jeans and easing herself out of them. But, as she rolled over to pull them free, they both overbalanced and toppled off the sofa. They lay there, entwined, laughing uncontrollably.

'This never happens in films,' said Lambert, giggling. 'They always do it right.'

She ran a hand through his hair and licked her lips in an exaggerated action of sexuality. She couldn't sustain the facade and broke up once more into a paroxysm of giggles.

'What about the washing up?' said Lambert in mock seriousness.

'Screw the washing up,' she purred, tugging at his belt.

'There are more interesting alternatives,' he said and, once more, they joined in a bout of laughter. Laughter - something Lambert thought he had forgotten.

At roughly the same time as Lambert and Debbie were eating their meal, Gordon Reece was pouring himself his fifth scotch of the evening. He had begun drinking at four that afternoon, large wine glasses full of the stuff, and now, two hours later, the first effects of drunkenness were beginning to descend upon him. The drink brought a kind of numbness with it. But it gave him no respite from the image of his dead wife. Her eyeless, mutilated corpse lying in that field like some discarded scarecrow.

He filled his glass again and stumbled into the living room which was lit by the light of a table lamp. The labrador was stretched out in front of the open fire and the animal turned and licked his hand as he stroked it. Reece felt a tear well up in his eye. He tried to hold back the flood but it was impossible. He dropped to his knees, the glass falling from his grasp, the brown liquid spilling and sinking into the carpet. Sobs wracked his body and he slammed his fists repeatedly against the carpet until his arms ached.

God, he thought, please let tomorrow pass quickly. The funeral was at ten in the morning. There wouldn't be many there: he had specifically asked that it should be a small affair. He had phoned Vera earlier in the day, told her what had happened. He'd broken down over the phone. The doctor had given him some tranquilizers and he knew that he should not be mixing drink with them, but what the hell did it matter anymore.

He looked up at the photo on top of the TV and the tears came again. Gordon Reece sank to the ground, the dog nuzzling against him as if it too could feel his grief.

Twelve

Saturday came and went. The funeral of Emma Reece went off without incident. Father Ridley did his duty as he always did. Gordon Reece wept again, finding that anger was slowly replacing his grief. He felt as if there was a hole inside where someone had hollowed out his body. No feeling any longer, just a void. A swirling black pit of lost emotions and fading memories of things that once were but would never be again.

It had been a beautiful day: bright sunshine, birds singing in the trees, God, that seemed to make it worse.

The guests had gone now. The hands on the clock on the mantelpiece had crawled on to twelve fifteen a.m. and Gordon Reece lay sprawled in his chair with a glass in his hand and the television screen nothing but a haze of static particles. Its persistent hiss didn't bother him because he couldn't hear it. He just sat, staring at the blank screen and cradling the nearly empty bottle of scotch in his lap. He had taken a handful of the tranquilizers. He didn't know how many precisely, a dozen, perhaps more. Washed down with a full bottle of whisky, that should do the trick nicely, he thought and even managed a smile. It hovered on his lips for a second then faded like a forgotten dream.

The doctor had told him not to drink with the tablets. Well, fuck the doctor, he thought. Fuck everything now. He would have cried but there was no emotion left within him, no tears left. All that remained now was that black hole inside him where his life used to be.

His bleary eyes moved slowly from card to card, all put out on the mantelpiece.

'With Regrets.'

'In Deepest Sympathy.'

He looked away and poured what was left of the scotch into his glass. He flung the bottle across the room where it struck the far wall and exploded in a shower of tiny crystals.

In the kitchen, the dog barked once, then was silent.

Reece watched the stain on the wall, the dark patch slowly dripping rivulets of brown liquid. He finished his drink and gripped the glass tight, staring at the photo of his wife on the TV. He clenched his teeth until his jaws ached, his hand tightening around the glass, squeezing.

He scarcely noticed when it broke, sharp needle points of crystal slicing open his palm. The blood mingling with the whisky as it dripped onto his chest. He felt no pain, just the dull throb as his blood welled out of him. He dropped the remains of the broken tumbler and closed his eyes.

Surely it wouldn't be long now.

He awoke at three that morning, aware of the burning pain in his torn hand. His head felt as if it had been stuffed with cotton wool and there was a band of pain running from temple to temple which gripped tighter than an iron vice. He moaned in the depths of his stupor, the noise coming through vaguely as if from another world.

The television was still on, its black face dotted still with the speckles of white static.

The dog was growling.

But there was something else. A noise louder than the others, the noise which had woken him. He listened for a moment.

There it was again. A persistent rattling and banging.

Reece tried to rise and the pain in his head intensified. He almost sank down again but the rattling continued and he hauled himself up, nearly toppling over again from the effort of standing. His clouded brain tried to locate the source of the sound and he finally realized that it was coming from the back door. He grunted and staggered out into the kitchen.

In the darkness he almost stumbled over the dog. The animal was making no sound now, just lying with its head on its outstretched front paws, whimpering. Its eyes riveted to the back door.

Reece stood still for a second, listening. His own blood roared in his ears and he was more than aware of his laboured breathing.

The rattling began again, louder this time. He squinted through the darkness, trying to clear his head, trying to see what was making the noise. He stepped closer and then, in the dull light which was escaping from the living room into the kitchen, he saw it.

The handle of the back door was being moved up and down.

Reece swallowed hard.

Someone was trying to get in.

If he had been sober, perhaps his reaction would have been different. Perhaps he would have noticed the dog, cowering in one corner, perhaps he would have noticed the deep cold which had filled the room. Perhaps he would even have called the police.

As it was, he reached for the handle, his other hand turning the key in the lock.

The rattling stopped and, through clouded eyes, Gordon Reece saw the handle slowly turn as the door was pushed open. He took a step back, rubbing his eyes, his heart thudding against his ribs.

The door swung back gently on its hinges and the room suddenly became colder.

Reece gasped, not sure whether he was asleep or not. Was he dreaming? Perhaps he was already dead and in hell. His dulled brain had no answer to give him this time.

Standing before him, the dirt of the grave still clogging her empty eye sockets, was his wife.

There was a blur of gold as the labrador bolted through the open door into the night and Gordon opened his mouth, not knowing whether to be sick or scream.

The thing which had once been Emma Reece took a step towards him. Her lips slid back to reveal teeth dripping saliva and Gordon saw the savage wounds on her throat which had killed her, the deep scratches around her eyes. Eyes? There was nothing there. Just the torn sockets, black and empty as night.

But there was something more and now Gordon prayed that his mind was playing tricks on him. For in those twin black voids were two pin pricks of red light. Light that glowed like the fires of hell and, in his last moments, Gordon saw that red light fill her empty eyes.

He had no time to scream before she was upon him.

Thirteen

Lambert looked at his watch and then up at the clock on the police station wall. It was nine fifteen, Sunday morning.

'Shit,' he said, 'might as well get it over with.'

Hayes nodded.

'What's Reece's address?' asked the Inspector.

Hayes flicked through the files and found it. Lambert wrote it down. He looked around the duty room. There were only three constables on duty this morning. Three at the station at any rate. The other seven were out looking for Mackenzie.

'P.C. Walford, you drive me,' Lambert smiled. 'Why the hell should I use my own petrol?'

Walford followed him out into the car park and unlocked one of the four Panda cars which the force possessed. Both men got in and Walford started the engine.

'It's a beautiful day,' Lambert observed as the Panda moved slowly through the streets of Medworth. 'Too nice to be doing this sort of thing.'

Walford smiled. 'Where do you reckon Mackenzie is, guv?'

Lambert shrugged. 'He's probably left the area by now. I mean, looking at it logically, if he was still around here we'd have found him by now.'

Walford wasn't convinced. 'There's plenty of places to hide in the hills around town. There's caves that run for miles.'

'Maybe. We'll see what turns up.'

'My Mum's scared about all this, guv.'

'You haven't been talking have you, Walford? I don't want too much of this getting out. In a small town like this panic could spread quickly.' He paused, looking out of the car windows. 'I just wish we could find the bastard before he has the chance to do it again. I'd rather people read about this sort of thing in the paper after we caught him. If there's too much talk before hand, it won't make our job any easier.'

They drove for a little way in silence then Lambert asked, 'You live with your parents then?'

Walford nodded. 'I've been trying to find a place of my own but I can't afford it.'

The Inspector studied his companion's profile for a moment. The lad wasn't much younger than him. He guessed there were three or four years between them.

'I sometimes wonder why I joined the force,' said Walford suddenly, swallowing hard and looking at Lambert as if he had said something he shouldn't. The Inspector was staring straight ahead out of the windscreen. He was silent for a time and the constable wondered if he had heard, then Lambert said:

'It makes me wonder why anyone joins.'

'What about you, sir? Why did you join?' asked Walford, adding quickly, as an afterthought, 'If you don't mind me asking.'

Lambert shook his head. 'Sometimes I wonder. At one time I would have said principles.' He laughed mirthlessly. 'But now, I don't know. I thought at one time that, well, I thought I could better myself. Sounds like bullshit doesn't it?' He glanced across at Walford but the P.C. had his eyes on the road. 'I didn't want to end up like my old man. A nothing for the whole of my fucking life.' His voice had taken on an angry edge. 'This job gave me something I never had before. Self respect. A sense of importance, that what I was doing was making some difference to a tiny part of the world.' He grunted indignantly.

Walford brought the car to a halt.

'That's it, sir,' he said, pointing across the road. Lambert flipped open his notebook and checked the address. He nodded.

The house was the end one of a block of three. Two storey dwellings, the standard, council built red brick structures. Identical to all the other houses in the street. In fact, the same as every one on the remainder of the estate. Lambert noted that the curtains, upstairs and down, were drawn. He inhaled deeply, held the breath then let it drain out slowly.

'You stay here,' he said, opening the door and getting out. Walford watched him as he walked across the street and down the path to the front door of the Reece house.

He knocked twice and waited for an answer. When none came, he walked around the side of the house. There was a purple painted gate barring his way into the back yard but he found, to his relief, that it was unlocked. Perhaps Mr Reece was in the garden.

As he walked around the back, Lambert could see that the garden was deserted. At the bottom was the shattered remnants of a greenhouse, the wooden frame now bleached and bare like the bones of some prehistoric creature. The garden was badly overgrown. He knocked on the back door loudly and called Reece's name.

There was no answer.

Lambert tried the door and found, to his joy, that it was open. He stepped into the kitchen, recoiling immediately from the smell. It reminded him of bad eggs. And, Jesus, it was cold. He pulled the back door closed behind him and looked around. Nothing unusual. A dog basket in one corner near the larder. A calendar which was a month behind where someone bad forgotten to turn the page. Lambert looked down at the floor. There were scuff marks on the lino. He bent to get a closer look, nothing unusual about them. Traces of dirt around too. He stood up and walked into the living room, which was still in darkness because of the drawn curtains. Lambert noticed the shattered bottle of scotch, the broken glass beside the chair and fragments of it still stained with blood. He rubbed his chin thoughtfully and, using his handkerchief, picked up one of the fragments and dropped it into his jacket pocket.

He crossed to the window and pulled back the curtains. Sunlight flooded the room, particles of dust swirling around in its beams. But, despite the warmth of the sun, the room still felt like a fridge.

Lambert went out into the hall and called up the stairs.

'Mr Reece?'

Silence greeted him. He hurried up the stairs and checked the two bedrooms and bathroom.

All were empty.

From the Panda car, Walford saw him emerge from the house and stride down the path of the house next door. He knocked three times, receiving no answer.

'Where the hell is everybody in this bloody street?' said Lambert under his breath.

The front door of the house beside opened and a woman popped her head out. She was in her forties, her hair in curlers and she reminded Lambert of a hedgehog in a dressing gown.

'Do you know Mr and Mrs Reece?' asked Lambert.

'Why?' asked the woman, suspiciously, retreating further behind the half open door until only her head was sticking out.

'I'm a policeman,' Lambert told her. 'I wanted to talk to Mr Reece but there's no one in. Have you seen or heard him around today?'

'Terrible business that,' said the woman, shaking her head. 'And with it only happening down the street too. Makes you scared to go out.'

'Have you seen Mr Reece?' persisted Lambert.

'And what with that other couple being murdered too. I tell you, I don't feel safe, even when my old man's home.'

Lambert was losing his patience. 'Have you seen Mr Reece today?'

'What?'

The Inspector bit his lip. 'Reece. Have you seen him go out, did you hear anything during the night?'

The woman looked horrified. 'He's not dead too, is he?'

Give me strength, thought Lambert. 'No, I just wondered if you'd seen him.'

He turned and set off back up the path, annoyance bubbling within him.

'You'd better hurry up and catch the killer, we could all be murdered in our beds,' called the woman.

'Thank you for your help, madam,' said Lambert and slammed the gate behind him. It was as he looked across the road that he saw Walford climbing out of the Panda.

'Inspector, quick,' he called.

Lambert ran across to the car.

'Message from the station, just come through,' explained the constable.

The Inspector climbed into the car and reached for the two-way radio. He flicked the transmit button.

'Puma Two to base. Lambert here. Come in.'

A hiss of static then Hayes: 'Guv, you'd better come back. We've got Mackenzie.'

There was a grin of satisfied relief on Lambert's face.

'Be right there. Puma Two, out.' He put down the two-way and pointed ahead. 'Let's move.'

With a screech of spinning tyres, the Panda sped off.

Hayes met Lambert at the door of the police station and, together, they hurried down the corridor towards the cell where Mackenzie was being held.

'Where did they pick him up?' asked the Inspector, excitedly.

'He was run down by a car, outside Two Meadows early this morning,' Hayes told him.

Lambert looked puzzled. 'What the hell was he doing up at the cemetery?'

The question went unanswered.

'Who's with him now?' asked Lambert.

'Dr Kirby and Davies and Bell. They brought him in. The bloke who ran Mackenzie down phoned the station, I got them to pick him up.'

'Well done Vic,' said the Inspector. He suddenly stood still. 'You said he was run down.

Is he hurt badly?'

Hayes smiled humourlessly. 'That's the funny thing. There's not a mark on him.'

Lambert pushed open the door to the cell and walked in. Standing on either side of the door were Constables Davies and Bell. Sitting on a chair next to the bed was Kirby and, lying on the bed itself, was the motionless figure of Ray Mackenzie.

'All right, lads,' said Lambert, motioning the two constables from the room. He closed the door behind them and looked at Kirby.

'Well?' he said

Kirby smiled, 'I haven't done a thorough examination yet.'

Lambert walked across to the bed and looked down at the prostrate form, the eyes tightly closed, mouth slightly open. He noted with disgust that a thin trail of saliva was dribbling from it. Kirby got up and crossed to the small wash basin in the cell, splashed his hands and dried them quickly. Then he reached into his black bag for his stethoscope. He pressed it to Mackenzie's chest, hearing at the same time the guttural laboured breathing.

'The heartbeat's strong,' said Kirby.

He checked the blood pressure and found it a little low, but nothing out of the ordinary.

As he rummaged for his pen light, Lambert said, 'Hayes told me a car hit him.'

'Apparently,' said Kirby, still searching.

'Was he unconscious when they brought him in?'

The doctor nodded, finally laying hands on his pen light. He bent closer to Mackenzie and pulled back one closed eyelid.

'Jesus Christ.'

Both men stepped back.

'What the hell is wrong with his eyes?' gasped Lambert.

Kirby, annoyed with himself for having been startled, now leant forward once more and gently pushed back the eyelid. He found himself staring into a glazed orb of blood. No whites, no pupils. Just the fiery red of blood. He exhaled deeply and flicked on the penlight.

'It looks as though there's been some sort of haemorrhage in the vessels of the eye.' He checked the other one and found it was the same. Slowly, he bent forward and shone the tiny beam of light into Mackenzie's right eye.

The man roared a deep, animal bellow of rage and struck out. The powerful fist caught Kirby in the chin and knocked him back against the wall. He coughed, gasping for air.

Mackenzie lay still again.

'You all right?' said Lambert, helping the doctor to his feet.

Kirby coughed again and shook his head. His face was flushed and he rubbed his chest painfully. Only after a minute or so did he find the breath to speak.

'Tom, I want him strapped down before I continue the examination.' He groaned, 'Christ, the bastard nearly broke a rib.' Kirby sucked in air, finding the effort painful but gradually it passed and he retrieved his pen light. Davies and Bell, meantime, had entered and were binding Mackenzie to the bed with thick rope. The Inspector checked that the bonds were secure and looked at Kirby.

'Pull his eyelids up,' instructed the doctor, watching as Lambert moved to the head of the bed. He leant over and gently drew back Mackenzie's thick lids, exposing the red spheres beneath. Kirby, keeping his distance, directed the pen light at them.

Mackenzie roared again and tried to lunge forward but the ropes held him down. Lambert exerted an iron grip on his head giving time for Kirby to get a decent look. Mackenzie's screams of enraged pain echoed around the small cell, nearly deafening the two men. Kirby leaned closer, smelling the fetid breath in his face and nearly wincing away from it. But he kept the beam focused on the red eyes until he was satisfied. Then he flicked it off and Mackenzie's body went limp. The room, silent now, was disturbed only by his guttural breathing.

Kirby shook his head. 'Like I said, I would think it's something to do with the blood vessels in the eye. Possibly a disturbance of the cornea.'

'Would that explain his sensitivity to light?' asked Lambert.

'Not really. If it is corneal haemorrhage then there'd be no sight at all; he wouldn't even have been able to see the light.'

'What do you recommend?' Lambert wanted to know.

Kirby shrugged. 'Leave him for now. I'll come back in the morning and take another look. But Tom, I'd leave those ropes on.'

Lambert nodded and both men walked out, the Inspector being careful to lock the cell behind them. He posted Davies outside, telling the constable to let them know if there was any sign of movement from Mackenzie.

The Inspector looked at his watch. It was ten forty-three. It had been some morning.

'Fancy a drink?' he asked and Kirby nodded.

The snug bar of 'The Blacksmith' was empty when they walked in. The grate, where a coal fire burned at night, was empty. Just a cold black hole and the room itself was chilly but neither of them noticed. Lambert bought the drinks and returned to the table.

'Cheers,' he said, downing a large mouthful of scotch.

Kirby returned the compliment and sipped delicately at his half of lager.

'You realize this is unethical,' said the doctor, smiling.

'What?'

'A doctor and a police Inspector drinking on duty.'

Both men laughed.

'Sod the ethics, John,' said Lambert. 'Right now, I need this.' He took another swig and cradled the glass between his hands.

'I wonder what the local paper would make of this?' pondered Kirby.

Lambert grunted. 'They've got enough to keep them going at the moment without wondering whether you and I are drinking.' He paused for a moment. 'Three murders. Jesus. In a town this size.'

'Just be thankful you've got the killer.'

'I am, don't get me wrong. But there're things about this case that don't add up. And more than that, I've got a missing person on my hands too. Gordon Reece has...' struggled for the word, '... disappeared. I went to talk to him about his wife's death this morning and there was no sign of him. The neighbours haven't seen or heard him about since yesterday morning and I found this in the living room of the house.' He reached into his jacket pocket and pulled out the handkerchief. Unwrapping it carefully he revealed the bloodstained lump of glass.

'Three murders, the victims mutilated, and the husband of the third victim has disappeared without trace. Can you tell me what the hell is going on in this town?' He drained his glass and slammed it down on the table.

'I don't see your problem, Tom,' said Kirby, 'you've got the killer. The missing man probably just left town, couldn't face the questioning or whatever. It's probably quite simple.'

Lambert exhaled deeply, his eyes riveted to the lump of blood-stained glass lying on the table in front of him.

Fourteen

Four fifty p.m. and the purple hues of approaching night were beginning to colour the skies above Medworth. Dusk hovered expectantly, a portent of the dark hours to come. It was the time when working people began to count the minutes to signal the end of the day's labours. A cold breeze had sprung up during late afternoon and there was a promise of frost for the coming night.

Tom Lambert shivered a little in his office and stared down at the solid gold medallion lying on his blotter. He prodded it with the end of a pencil, reading over and over again the strange inscription on it and around its edges. He had scribbled the words down on the edge of his blotter and he determined to look up their meanings when he got home. Debbie might even know. She knew a little Latin. He looked at the pencilled words:

MORTIS DIEI

Below it, the symbols which ran around the edging of the medallion;

UTCON (scratch mark) XER (scratch)

ERATICXE (two scratches)

SIUTROM (scratch) A.

Lambert shook his head. The second set of words didn't even look like Latin.

He'd found the medallion quite by accident that afternoon. Returning from the pub about one, he had gone to deposit the chunk of blood stained glass from Reece's house in the safe where items of evidence were kept. He'd noticed the jewel box which had belonged to June Mackenzie and asked Hayes what it was. The sergeant had explained how they had found the box in the bedroom of the first victim and, upon opening it, Lambert had discovered the medallion.

Now he sat with it before him, wondering how on earth a man like Mackenzie had come to possess an object so obviously valuable. The policeman couldn't begin to guess at the age of the thing but, from the weight of it and the thickness of the chain which supported it, he could at least ponder over its value. It was as he looked closely at it that he noticed the gossamer like strands clinging to the links of the chain. He bent closer and pulled one free. It felt coarse as he rubbed it between his thumb and forefinger. There was more attached to the other links and something else.

It looked like dried mud.

Lambert exhaled deeply. Perhaps a forensic test would establish exactly where the gold circlet had originated. He pulled a few of the coarse strands free and scraped some mud away with the tip of his pen knife. Then he reached into his desk drawer and took out a tiny plastic bag. Into this, he carefully pushed the fibres and mud. He sealed it with a piece of sellotape and left it on his desk, reminding himself to ring Kirby before he went home, perhaps even run the stuff around to the doctor himself.

Once more he looked down at the medallion, the inscriptions causing his forehead to crease as he tried to make sense of them.

MORTIS DIEI

The words had been engraved across the centre of the circlet but the other inscription...

Running around the outside of the medallion, he wasn't sure where the words began and where they ended. He determined to take it home that night, let Debbie take a look at it. The thought of her made him look up at the clock. He smiled when he saw the time and realized that he would set off soon. He was looking forward to getting home. It had been a long day. Every day seemed to be a long one just lately and he told himself it was just a matter of getting back into the swing of things. There was nothing more he could do at the station that night. Mackenzie was still flat out in his cell, tied securely by the ropes. Davies was outside the cell just in case there was any sign of movement from him. The constable had orders to contact Dr Kirby immediately if there was any change.

Lambert pulled another plastic bag from his drawer and slid the medallion into it, then he popped the little package into the pocket of his jacket.

He got to his feet and crossed to the window of his office. Night had descended now, casting its black shadow over the land. Lambert could see the lights of houses in the town twinkling like a thousand stars. The police station was about a mile out of town, built on a hillside which looked over Medworth like a guardian. Far below him, the town lay spread.

Lambert yawned.

The door of his office flew open, slammed against the wall and rocked on its hinges, the impact nearly breaking the frosted glass in it.

Davies stood there panting. 'It's Mackenzie, sir, he's going crazy.'

Lambert dashed past the constable, heading for the cell, aware now of the noise coming from the end of the corridor. Hayes emerged from the duty room and joined the other two men as they reached the cell door. Lambert eased back the sliding flap of the peephole and drew in a quick breath.

Mackenzie had broken his bonds and was throwing himself against the walls frenziedly, every now and then turning towards the open peephole and fixing Lambert in a stare from those blazing red eyes. The Inspector felt the hairs on the nape of his neck rise. Then Mackenzie spun around and hurled himself at the small window at the far end of the cell. It was about half way up the wall. No more than a foot square, it was set at a height which would have made a man of average size stretch to reach it. Wire mesh covered the bars which firmly blocked the narrow opening.

As Lambert watched, Mackenzie leapt at the window, tearing away the wire mesh as if it had been fish netting. Then he fastened his powerful hands around the bars and pulled, roaring in frustration when they wouldn't budge. The darkness outside called him and he would stop at nothing to reach it. Realizing that he could not move the bars, he turned his attention to the cell door. He slammed into it, pressing his face to the peephole and for a split second Lambert found himself staring into those empty crimson eyes. There was nothing there. No emotion registered in them. Nothing. Just the glazed red of two enormous blood blisters. The rage and hatred was registered on Mackenzie's face, the lips drawn back to reveal the yellowed teeth, saliva spattering the room as he spun about in a frenzy.

'How long has he been like this?' Lambert asked Davies, who was white with fear and thankful that a twelve inch thick steel door separated him from the maniac inside.

'A couple of minutes,' he answered, 'as soon as it got dark, he started.'

Lambert looked at Hayes but the sergeant looked blank.

'Get Kirby down here fast,' snapped the Inspector, watching as Hayes scuttled off.

Peering once more into the cell, Lambert said, 'Why isn't the light on in there?' He looked up at the hundred watt bulb, unshaded, in the ceiling of the cell.

'I was just going to do it when I looked in and saw what was going on,' explained Davies.

Lambert stroked his chin thoughtfully, remembering how violently Mackenzie had reacted to light that morning.

'Turn it on,' he said.

Davies flicked a switch and the cell was suddenly bathed in cold white light.

Mackenzie screamed and raised his hands, snatching at the light bulb, trying simultaneously to shield his eyes and to reach the blinding object. His head throbbed as he tried to shield himself from the glare and he backed into a corner like a dog who knows he's about to be beaten. As Lambert watched, Mackenzie slumped to his knees, bowed his head and covered it with his arms. He was growling, the sounds gurgling in his throat. The Inspector watched amazed as Mackenzie slowly raised himself up again, one arm shielding his eyes, and staggered towards the light. Then, with a howl of rage, he leapt and smashed a fist into the bulb, shattering it and ripping the flesh from his knuckles. He seemed not to notice the pain, relieved only that the room was, once more, in darkness. Blood dripped from his lacerated hand but he grunted and raised a dripping fist defiantly towards the peephole.

Lambert slammed it shut and exhaled deeply. 'Jesus,' he breathed, softly.

'What do we do, sir?' said Davies, listening to the sounds coming from inside the cell.

Lambert had no answer for him. He pushed past the constable and headed for his office. Davies squinted through the peephole just in time to see Mackenzie tear the wash basin from its position on the wall. He lifted it above his head and flung it to the ground where it shattered. Large chunks of porcelain flew about the room like white shrapnel. Water from the ruptured pipes jetted into the cell spattering Mackenzie, but he ignored it, turning once more to the tiny window and gripping the bars in a frenzied effort to tear them free.

Davies closed the flap. He swallowed hard and sat down outside the cell, the noises of destruction from inside ringing in his ears.

While he was waiting for Kirby to arrive, Lambert phoned home to tell Debbie that he'd be late, but he got no answer. She couldn't be home yet, he reasoned. He slammed the receiver down and said to no one in particular, 'Where the hell is Kirby?'

Hayes emerged from the duty room carrying a steaming mug of coffee. He handed it to Lambert who smiled.

'I could do with something stronger, Vic.'

The sergeant grinned and pulled a silver flask from the pocket of his tunic. He unscrewed the cap and poured a small measure of brown liquid into the Inspector's mug. Then he repeated the procedure with his own.

'Purely medicinal, sir,' he said.

Lambert smiled broadly and drank a couple of mouthfuls.

From down the corridor they could still hear the frightful noises coming from Mackenzie's cell.

'He's mad,' said Hayes, flatly.

'I hope so,' said Lambert, enigmatically. 'I really do hope so.' Hayes looked puzzled.

The door leading from the annexe opened and both men looked up. It was only constables Ferman and Jenkins arriving for night duty.

'What's all the noise?' asked Ferman.

'Never mind that,' snapped Hayes. 'Just get on with your job.'

Ferman raised two fingers as he walked past, making sure that he was behind Hayes when he did it. The two men disappeared into the duty room.

Kirby walked in, his black bag clutched firmly in his hand. He nodded curtly. ,

'About fucking time,' snapped Lambert, impatiently. He hurried out from behind the enquiry counter and led the doctor down towards the cell.

'My receptionist told me you called,' explained Kirby. 'I'd been out on an emergency.'

'Well, we've got an emergency here, right now,' growled Lambert.

Kirby caught him by the arm. 'Look, Tom, my responsibilities are to my patients. I'm a G.P. first and foremost, a bloody police doctor second. Understand?'

The Inspector held his gaze for a moment.

'Listen to that,' he said, inclining his head towards the cell.

Kirby heard the sounds of pandemonium and frowned. He followed Lambert to the cell door and peered through the peephole. Mackenzie was hanging from the bars with his talonlike hands, blood from his injured limb pouring down his arm.

'He broke the light bulb,' explained Lambert, 'the light drives him crazy. It seems to cause him pain.'

'How long has he been like this?' asked Kirby, not taking his eyes from the hole.

'Since it got dark,' said the Inspector, flatly. 'What can you do?'

Kirby let the flap slide back into position, covering the hole. 'Nothing. If I give him a shot of something there's no guarantee it'll knock him out. That's assuming I can get close enough to administer it in the first place.'

'There must be something you can give him,' snapped Lambert.

'I've just told you,' said Kirby, his tone rising slightly. 'I've got Thorazine in here, but there's no way of knowing if it'll work and I, for one, don't intend going in there with him like that.'

The two men stood silently for a moment, looking at one another. Then Kirby said, more gently, 'Just leave him. I'll look at him in the morning. If he's calmed down.'

'And if he hasn't?'

The doctor peered through the peephole again, 'This will hold him won't it?' He banged on the metal door.

Lambert nodded, 'Yeah.' There was a note of tired resignation in his voice.

'I suggest we both go home, Tom. If anything more happens during the night...' The sentence trailed off and he shrugged.

Lambert touched the metal door gently, listening to the bellowing and crashing coming from inside.

'I just hope it does hold him,' he said, quietly.

Fifteen

Lambert lay on his back in bed, staring at the ceiling. Outside, the wind whispered quietly past the windows. A low, almost soothing whoosh, which occasionally grew in power and rattled the glass in its frame, as if reminding people of its power. But, at the moment, it hissed softly past the dark opening.

The clock on the bedside table ticked its insistent rhythm, sounding louder than usual in the stillness of the night. The luminous hands showed that it was after three in the morning.

Lambert exhaled and closed his eyes. Images and thoughts sped through his mind with dizzying speed.

Mackenzie. The disappearance of Gordon Reece. The medallion.

The medallion.

He had shown it to Debbie earlier on and she had confirmed his own suspicions that the inscriptions were, indeed, Latin. Well, the central one at any rate. The gibberish around the rim of the circlet foxed her too. She said that she would try to find out what the inscriptions meant. There were reference books in the library which might tell them. He had dismissed the idea, telling her that there was probably no significance in it anyway. But something nagged at the back of his mind. Something unseen which had plunged teeth of doubt into his mind and had held on as surely as a stoat holds a rabbit.

He sat up, trying not to disturb Debbie. She was asleep beside him, her breathing low and contented. As regular as the ticking of the clock.

Every minute he expected the phone to ring. To hear Hayes telling him that Mackenzie had broken out. Lambert dismissed the thought. That was impossible. The cell door was a foot thick, the bars of the windows embedded two feet into the concrete. He couldn't possibly get out. Lambert swallowed hard and ran a hand through his hair. He closed his eyes and brought his knees up, resting his head on them.

Again the thoughts came back. Alien thoughts with no answer.

Mackenzie's sensitivity to light. His eyes (if that was the word). The frenzy which overcame him during night-time. The mutilation of the three victims. Why had the eyes been torn out?

'Oh Christ.'

He said it out loud this time, cursing himself as he heard Debbie moan in her sleep. He watched her sleeping form for a moment, worried that he had woken her. When she didn't move he returned to his previous position. Head bowed on his upraised knees.

'What's wrong, Tom?'

Her voice startled him and he turned to see her looking up at him.

'I'm sorry I woke you,' he said, reaching for her hand and squeezing it.

'What is it?' she asked, her voice gentle.

He sighed, 'I can't sleep.'

She snuggled closer to him and he felt the warmth of her body, naked beneath the sheets. 'What were you thinking about?' she wanted to know.

'This and that,' he said, smiling wanly.

'Don't give me that crap,' she said, forcefully, squeezing his hand until he made a cry of mock pain. 'It's this business with Mackenzie isn't it?'

'Debbie, I've never seen anything like it. He's like a wild animal. But it only seems to be at night. Jesus, I don't know what the hell is going on.'

'You know that medallion? I was thinking, why don't you take it to an antique dealer? Old Mr Trefoile in the town would be able to date it for you; he might even be able to decipher the inscriptions.'

Lambert nodded. He was silent for a while, rubbing his eyes. He felt a hand trace its way from the top of his knee to his thigh. Debbie pressed herself closer to him, her hand finally brushing through his pubic hair and closing around his flaccid penis. She looked up at him, surprised.

'You really are worried,' she said.

He grinned and she tried to pull her hand away but he held it there, feeling the warmth of her fingers as they stroked, coaxing him to hardness. When he was fully erect, she ran her index finger from the tip of his penis to the testicles, now drawn up tightly with excitement. She cupped them briefly before returning to his swollen shaft. He moaned softly as she closed her hand around him and began rubbing gently. As her movements became more insistent he lay back, thrusting his hips towards the stroking hand. At the same time, he sought the wetness between her legs, his fingers teasing her clitoris before plunging deeper into the oozing cleft of her vagina. She drove herself hard against him, finally pulling him onto her, his hard organ sliding easily into her.

A moment later they climaxed savagely and clung to one another long after the sensations had died away. He rolled off and lay on his back, both of them panting. She leant across and kissed him, eventually falling asleep with her head on his chest. He stroked her hair with his hand, feeling its soft silkiness beneath his fingers.

He returned to staring at the ceiling, wishing that sleep would come, but the hands of the clock pointed to four-fifteen before he finally drifted off into peaceful oblivion.

Kirby stood up as Lambert entered the room. He had been sitting on a chair next to the cell bed on which Mackenzie lay. Mackenzie was still, his eyes closed, arms by his sides. Sunlight streamed in through the small window in the wall of the cell. Constable Ferman was also in the room, standing at the far end of the bed and looking down at the body of Mackenzie, who was now securely tied down with thick bands of hemp.

'Morning, Tom,' said Kirby.

The inspector nodded a greeting and looked down at the immobile figure of Mackenzie.

'What happened?' he asked in awe.

Kirby motioned to Ferman and the constable coughed, clearing his throat as if he were about to make a public address.

'Well sir,' he began, 'I was sitting out there this morning, listening to all the din going on in here and, well, about five o'clock everything went quiet. I looked through the viewing slot and Mackenzie was lying on the floor.'

'Dawn was at five o'clock,' Kirby clarified.

'I waited for about fifteen minutes,' continued Ferman. 'He didn't move, so I came in, put him on the bed and tied him down again.'

'The light,' said Lambert.

Kirby nodded. 'The darkness triggers him off, the light shuts him down. This man is like a light sensitive machine, only, if you'll forgive the flippancy, his mechanism is working in reverse. He comes alive during the darkness and...' he shrugged, 'switches off during the daylight.'

Lambert looked down at Mackenzie's body, his mouth almost dropping open in awe.

'His vital signs are practically nil,' said Kirby. 'The heart has slowed to less than forty beats a minute, the pulse and blood pressure are so faint I could hardly get readings. He's in a torpor.'

'What the hell is that?' snapped Lambert.

'Coma if you like.'

'What do we do?'

'I wish I knew.'

'You're a doctor for Christ's sake, John; you must have some ideas.'

'Look. During the night, he's fine.'

Lambert cut him short. 'Fine? He's a psycho during the bloody night.'

Kirby waved away the policeman's protests.'What I meant was, his life signs are all in order. There's nothing wrong with him bodily.'

'Apart from the fact that he's a maniac with the strength of ten men,' said Lambert, his voice heavy with scorn.

There was an awkward silence then Kirby spoke again.

'I think the problem is in his brain, not his body. It's psychosis of some sort, but we don't know why it's triggered by darkness.'

'This is getting us nowhere,' said Lambert impatiently. 'I want to know what we have to do. This is going to happen again tonight, right? I want an answer quick, John. I'm asking you for a medical answer to this problem. And keep it simple.'

'You've got a number of alternatives, Tom. I either pump him full of Thorazine now and we wait and see if it keeps him out during the night, we keep him locked in here until someone qualified can look at him, or...' He hesitated.

'Or what?' Lambert demanded.

'We give him an E.E.G.'

Lambert looked puzzled.

'It's an Electroencephalogram. It tests brain waves.'

'I know what it does,' snapped Lambert, 'I don't see how it would help.'

'It might tell us why the darkness triggers off this savagery at night, why he's terrified of light. That's my last theory.'

The policeman nodded. 'Where would it be done?'

'There's a unit in the hospital in Wellham, about twenty miles from here. I know the specialist in charge of it. If I get in touch with him now, we could have this done before nightfall.'

'Do it,' said Lambert and Kirby scuttled out of the room.

The Inspector looked down at the body of Mackenzie and then at the wrecked cell.

Ferman coughed. 'What if it doesn't work, sir?' he asked tentatively.

Lambert looked at him for a moment, searching for an answer, then turned and walked out.

Sixteen

Lambert felt the need to shield his eyes, even though he stood behind a screen of tinted glass. The light inside the examination room was blinding, pouring down from four huge fluorescent banks.

Mackenzie was strapped to a trolley in the centre of the room and, as the policeman watched, two men dressed in white overalls undid the straps and lifted him onto a table. They hurriedly secured him again and one of them, a tall man with blond hair, pulled each of them to ensure they were tight enough. The man turned towards the glass partition behind which stood Lambert, Kirby and Dr Stephen Morgan. The man raised a thumb and Morgan nodded.

He was in his forties. What people like to refer to as 'well-preserved,' for he looked barely older than thirty. He had a carefully groomed moustache which seemed as though it had lost its growing strength when it reached the corners of his mouth and drooped downwards. His blue eyes were obscured somewhat by thin tinted glasses which he removed and began polishing with a handy tissue.

Lambert looked back into the examination room. Mackenzie was now lying, apparently unconscious, on a hinged couch which could be adjusted by a large screw on the side and, as he watched, the intern with the blond hair twisted it so that Mackenzie was propped up slightly. His mouth opened briefly, as if he were going to protest, then it closed tightly. A tiny dribble of yellowish saliva escaped and ran down his chin.

A nurse dressed in a white smock entered from a door which led off to the right. She paused beside the couch, looking briefly at Mackenzie, then she looked at Morgan. He jabbed a finger towards a trolley which stood beside the couch. The nurse reached for a swab and dipped it into a kidney dish full of clear liquid. She dabbed it carefully onto five places on the top of Mackenzie's head.

'What's that?' asked Lambert, fascinated by the ritual which was taking place before him.

'Conductant,' explained Morgan.

The Inspector nodded abstractedly and continued to watch the preparations. Next, the nurse attached five electrodes to the places where she had applied the swab. She looked at Morgan who swiftly checked his readout. The machine which he stood beside looked, to Lambert, rather like a computer. It had a long length of thin paper running through it and, across this, lay a metal arm which would translate into visual terms, by means of lines, the brain waves received from Mackenzie. Lambert almost laughed. It reminded him of a lie detector he had once seen on an American crime film.

Morgan flicked a switch and a red light came on, signalling that the machine was ready for operation. He raised his hand and the nurse and both interns retreated from the room. A second later they joined Lambert and the others in the observation area.

Morgan flicked another switch.

'We'll test the motor impulses first,' he said.

'I thought the machine usually recorded all the waves at once,' said Kirby.

'Most of them do,' Morgan told him. 'This modification, testing each centre of the brain individually, makes it easier to pin down the trouble and it makes things a damn sight easier for me.'

He pressed the green button and the machine whirred into life.

'Here goes,' muttered Morgan.

Lambert didn't know where to look. His eyes flitted back and forth, from Mackenzie to the machine, from machine to Mackenzie. Morgan stood over the readout, a deep furrow creasing his brow. He readjusted his glasses, as if that act would somehow rectify what he was seeing.

'There's no movement at all,' he said, softly. The arm on the paper was immobile, the tiny piece of graphite it held was stationary. Just one continual black line drawn on the paper, unbroken and unwavering. No loops, no zig-zags. Nothing.

'There's no brain impulses at all,' said Morgan, scarcely believing what he saw.

'Perhaps the machine is acting up,' said Lambert hopefully.

Morgan shook his head. He turned to the blond intern, Peter Brooks. 'Turn off the lights.'

Brooks slapped a switch and, immediately, the examination room was plunged into darkness. Two huge shutters had been put up at the vast plate glass windows which looked into the room and not a single chink of light infiltrated the blackness.

'Christ,' whispered Morgan, watching as the needle swung back and forth with a ferocity which threatened to tear it loose. It drew parabolas, pyramids, all with vast savage strokes.

'Lights,' snapped Morgan and, once more, the examination room was filled with blinding white light.

The needle on the readout stopped swinging and settled back into its unerring parallel course, never deviating from the straight line it drew.

'That's incredible,' muttered Morgan.

'You see what we mean about the light?' said Kirby. 'In bright light he's dormant, but in darkness he goes crazy.'

Morgan stroked his chin thoughtfully. He looked down at the readout and then across at the still form of Mackenzie. He'd never seen anything like this before and the discovery sent a thrill of excitement through him. He told Brooks to turn off the lights once more.

It happened again. The needle swung crazily back and forth across the readout sheet, never settling into a pattern, just looping and tearing up and down.

Lambert looked worriedly at Kirby. He had noticed that Mackenzie had moved his right hand, was flexing the fingers.

'Put the lights back on,' he snapped.

Brooks hesitated.

'No, wait,' said Morgan, fascinated by the course the needle was taking. So intent on watching it was he, that he didn't notice Mackenzie raise his head and look up.

The nurse stifled a scream as she saw the twin red orbs which had once been eyes, staring at her through the darkness.

Lambert now crossed to the light switch, seeing that Mackenzie was straining against the straps with a loud crack, one of them securing his arms broke and he began tearing at the broad one which covered his chest and pinned. him to the couch.

Morgan looked into the examination room, horrified as he watched Mackenzie breaking free.

Lambert pressed the light switch. Nothing happened.

Frantic, he pressed it again. Jesus Christ, he thought, what's happened to the fucking lights?

Mackenzie was sitting up now, tearing at the strap which was fastened across his thighs. Another few moments and he would be free.

Lambert slapped the switch frenziedly. For a brief second he thought they were going to work. All four powerful banks flashed with brilliant white light and Mackenzie screamed as the brightness scorched his blazing red eyes. But then, one by one, the tubes blew, exploding in a shower of hot glass, their ends glowing red as they died. Smoke rose from them in silvery wisps.

The darkness was total.

With a last desperate surge of strength, Mackenzie tore free of the final strap and swung himself off the couch. The nurse screamed.

Brooks reached for the door which connected the examination room with the observation booth.

'Get some light in there,' screamed Lambert, following him.

The Inspector stood no more than three feet from Mackenzie, staring into those bottomless red eyes, riveted by the obscene thing before him. Then Mackenzie leapt.

Lambert, with a speed born of fear, threw himself to one side and avoided the rush. Mackenzie crashed into a surgical trolley but was up in an instant and grabbing for the policeman once more.

'The shutters,' screamed Lambert, 'open the shutters!'

Mackenzie was upon him, powerful hands grasping for his throat, forcing him back over the couch. Lambert smelt the fetid breath in his face, disgusted as the yellow spittle dripped onto him. He struck out, his fist slamming into Mackenzie's forehead.

The grip slackened momentarily and Lambert brought his knee up into the man's stomach.

Brooks, meantime, was struggling to tear down the shutters. A chink of light lanced through the blackness and he almost laughed. Another second and the room would be flooded with light. The intern tore at the catches, pulling one of the shutters wide.

Sunlight flooded the room and Lambert suddenly felt the grip on his throat removed as Mackenzie screamed and raised both hands to shield his eyes. The Inspector rolled clear, searching for something to fight back with. It was scarcely necessary. Mackenzie turned towards the window, his red eyes narrowed against the light but fixed on Brooks who was in the process of tearing down the second shutter.

With a roar, Mackenzie ran at Brooks, launching himself at the intern.

He crashed into his prey with the force of a steam train, hurling him backward.

The nurse screamed as both men hit the window.

The glass exploded outward, huge shards flying into the air as Mackenzie and Brooks crashed through the window. They seemed to hang in the air for a second before plummeting the twelve storeys to the ground below.

Lambert scrambled to his feet, hearing the sickening thump as both men hit the ground. Cool air blew in through the broken window and, being careful to avoid the pieces of shattered glass, the Inspector leaned over the sill.

A hundred feet below him, still locked together, lay the bodies of Mackenzie and Brooks. Around them, a spreading pool of blood was mingling with fragments of smashed glass.

'Oh God,' groaned Lambert, bowing his head.

The second intern comforted the nurse who was sobbing uncontrollably.

Kirby and Morgan walked slowly across to the window and also peered down at the smashed bodies.

No one spoke. What was there to say? Lambert ran a hand through his hair and exhaled deeply, suddenly aware of the pain in his neck where Mackenzie had attacked him. He touched a fingertip to it and saw a smear of blood when he withdrew it.

Kirby tilted the policeman's head back and looked at the cut.

'Just a graze, Tom,' he said.

Lambert nodded.

'I don't know what to say,' murmured Morgan. 'I've never seen anything like it. No brainwaves.'

Lambert stood up. 'Is that all that bother s you? Two men have just died, for Christ's sake.'

He sighed and sat down on the edge of the couch.

'It would appear our problems are over, Tom,' said Kirby, trying to sound cheerful.

Lambert regarded him balefully for a second and thought about saying something, but held it back. Kirby was right. He had to admit that. Now the only problem he had was finding Gordon Reece. It seemed petty in comparison to the problems he'd had these last few days. The nurse had stopped crying and the second intern was helping her out of the room. Morgan watched them go.

The Inspector got to his feet and headed for the door.

'Where are you going, Tom?' asked Kirby.

'Back to work,' snapped Lambert and walked out.

Lambert drove back to Medworth alone. He felt as if he needed his own company. He didn't want to talk about what he'd just seen and he drove with both windows open as if the fresh air blowing into the car would cleanse his mind. The smell of damp earth and grass was strong, a welcome contrast to the antiseptic smell of the hospital he had just left. He hated hospitals, always had, ever since he was a child, and what he had just seen had done nothing to change his mind.

The countryside rushed past him as he drove, perhaps a little faster than he needed. He inhaled, held the breath and then let it out slowly, trying to calm himself down. His foot eased off the accelerator and he glanced at the falling needle of the speedometer. Finally, he slowed to about twenty, swung the car into a layby and shut off the engine.

The road was narrow, flanked on either side by tall hedges. To his right lay hillside, green and shimmering in the early morning sunlight. To his left, down the hill, lay Medworth. He could see smoke belching from the foundry on the far side of the town, but from this distance, it looked like nothing more than a grey wisp. Lambert got out of the car, slammed the door and leant on the bonnet, arms folded. He looked out over Medworth.

'Gordon Reece, where are you?' he said aloud, then smiled to himself. The smile dwindled rapidly as he felt the pain from the scratches on his throat. He rubbed them, remembering the power in Mackenzie's hands. If not for Brooks, he wouldn't have had a chance. Fuck it, he thought, Mackenzie had been a powerful bastard. Lambert thought about the three victims he had claimed. He wondered how they had struggled. He dismissed the thought.

There would be a full autopsy on Mackenzie that afternoon and he had been told, before leaving the hospital, that he would be contacted as soon as the results were ready. Lambert shook his head. Four people had been killed, Mackenzie himself was dead. Their knowledge would do them no good now. He sighed, still unable to believe what he had seen that morning, not wanting to believe what had happened in Medworth during the past week or so.

He suddenly thought of the medallion. Could there be a tie up between it, the transformation of Mackenzie, and the disappearance of Gordon Reece? He climbed back into the car and started the engine.

The medallion.

It was time he took a trip to the antique shop.

Seventeen

Howard Trefoile prodded the brown mass of liver and onions before him and plucked up the courage to take a bite. He chewed it slowly. Not too bad, after all. He stirred the brown mass around and continued eating. He would have preferred to have gone out to lunch but that cost money, and the way things had been for the past couple of months he couldn't afford three course meals every day. The business wasn't exactly floundering in the wake of the recession, more like languishing. Things were stable. That, he decided, was the best way to describe them. He comforted himself with the thought that other businesses in the town had gone broke while his still remained on a paying basis.

The antique shop had been left to him by his father when he died, and Howard had run it successfully for the last eight years since that sad event. He and his father had always been very close and it had been more or less preordained that he should take over when his father retired. Unfortunately, cancer had got his father before he could reach retiring age and Howard had been thrown in the deep end, so to speak. But his years of working with his father had stood him in good stead and he found it relatively simple to carry on the business.

His mother had died when he was ten and he could vaguely remember her, but the image wasn't strong enough to cause him pain. He stared across his kitchen table at her photo and sighed quietly. Kitchen. He smiled to himself. It could scarcely be called a kitchen. A small room at the back of the shop which served as dining room, working room, and kitchen. Beyond it lay his tiny sitting room, full of the discarded objects of times gone by. Things which he could never hope to sell in the shop itself, but which he had come to find an affection for. Upstairs was his bedroom and a store room. That was next to the bathroom and toilet.

The building, sandwiched between a shoe shop and grocers, was small, but it was adequate for Howard's needs. He lived and worked alone. There was no one in his life, but he had his work so he needed no one. At fifty-six he sometimes wondered what would become of the shop if anything happened to him, but he knew in his heart what its fate would be. It would be demolished. He felt suddenly sad. Not for himself, but for his departed father. The man had spent his entire life building up the business. The thought that it might someday just cease to exist troubled Howard. Still, he reasoned, what could he do about it now? He couldn't afford to pay staff to carry on running it should he himself pass on, so there seemed no alternative. The shop would become as anachronistic as the things it sold.

He dismissed the thoughts and continued eating. The empty packet which had housed the frozen liver and onions lay on the draining board beside him. Everything for convenience these days, he thought. Speed was of the essence in the modern world. Howard sometimes thought that he had been born twenty years too late.

As he was pushing the last soggy chunk of liver into his mouth, he heard the familiar tinkle of the bell above the door. He tutted. He must have forgotten to put the "Closed" sign up. He often did that. He got to his feet and walked to the door which led out into the shop itself.

The man standing in the shop had his back to Trefoile and, wiping a trickle of gravy from his mouth, the shop owner said;

'Excuse me sir, I'm sorry, but I'm closed for lunch, if...'

The man turned and Trefoile let the sentence trail off as he recognized Tom Lambert.

'Inspector Lambert,' said the antique dealer, smiling, 'I didn't realize it was you.'

Trefoile walked past him and turned the sign on the door around so that it showed "Closed" to the street outside.

'I hope I'm not interrupting anything,' said Lambert, apologetically.

'Just my amateurish attempts at lunch,' said Trefoile, smiling. 'What can I do for you?'

'I've got something that I think you might be able to help me with,' said Lambert, reaching into his pocket.

Trefoile perked up. 'Oh yes?'

The inspector laid the medallion on the counter and motioned towards it with his hand.

'What do you make of that?'

Trefoile looked excited as he bent closer, fumbling in the pocket of his waistcoat for his eyepiece. He stuffed it in and squinted at the medallion.

'Might I ask where you acquired this, Inspector?' he asked.

Lambert sighed. 'Well, let's just say it's part of an investigation I'm working on at the moment.'

Trefoile looked at him for a moment, appearing like some kind of cyclopean monster with the eyepiece still stuffed in position. He bent to examine the medallion once more.

'What exactly did you want to know about it?' he asked. 'The value?'

'Is it valuable?' asked Lambert. 'I mean, it's gold isn't it?'

Trefoile picked up the circlet and hefted it in his hand. He inclined his head and raised his eyebrows. 'This is a very interesting piece of work, Inspector. I can only guess at its value of course, but from the age, weight, and purity of the metal, I'd say its value would run into thousands of pounds.' He took the eyepiece out and handed the medallion back to Lambert who looked at it in awe. He shook himself out of the stupor and gave it back to the older man.

'What period would you think it is?' he asked.

'It's very old. I would say, possibly even sixteenth century.'

Lambert scribbled the words down in his note book.

'I'd need to do certain tests of course to ascertain the exact period,' Trefoile added.

'What about the inscriptions?' said Lambert.

Trefoile bent closer. 'Latin. It's medieval script, I couldn't decipher this on the spot. My Latin isn't up to much anymore.' He laughed and the policeman found himself grinning too, but there was no humour in the smile.

Trefoile frowned. 'You know, Inspector, this might sound ridiculous, but I think I've seen this medallion somewhere before.'

Lambert was instantly alert, his pen poised. 'Where?'

'Not in the flesh, so to speak. But in a book. My father had a large collection of antique books, and this particular object seems to ring a bell.' Trefoile shook his head, as if annoyed at his own loss of recall.

Both men stood in silence, staring down at the circlet of gold on its thick chain.

The antique dealer looked at the inscription around the outside of the medallion and shook his head. 'I don't recognize any of that.'

'Is that Latin?' Lambert wanted to know.

Trefoile shrugged. 'I don't know. If only I could think where I'd seen it before.' He squeezed the folds of skin beneath his chin, plucking at them. Lost in thought. Finally he said, 'Look, Inspector, could you leave it with me? I can make some tests on it, check out its authenticity. Perhaps even decipher the inscriptions.'

Lambert nodded. That would be marvellous. Thank you.' The two men shook hands. Lambert gave him a number to ring if he should come up with anything, then the policeman left.

Trefoile looked at the medallion, the tinkling of the door bell dying away in the solitude of the shop. Something nagged at the back of his mind. He had seen this before. If only he could remember where. And the Latin inscription. He studied it once more, something clicking away in the forgotten recesses of his mind. He looked at the inscription across the centre of the circlet:

MORTIS DIEI

He frowned:

MORTIS

His eyes lit up. He began to remember. Of course, he should have realized. He recognized that word at least.

MORTIS

He smiled to himself, its English meaning now clear. The first word in that central inscription stuck out in his mind.

Death.

Lambert sat in his car outside Trefoile's antique shop but he didn't start the engine. He looked up at the sign outside the shop, blowing gently in the light breeze.

The medallion's value must run into thousands. The antique dealer's words rung in his ears. He drove back to the station where Hayes told him that the results of the autopsy on Mackenzie had come through. There were no unusual features about it. Apart from the eyes, everything was normal. Kirby had been wrong though; it hadn't been corneal haemorrhage which caused the redness in the eyes and nothing had been found to indicate why Mackenzie had become psychopathic during the dark hours. In other words, thought Lambert, the entire damned thing had been a waste of time and they were no nearer finding the motive for the killings.

Still, as he drove home he comforted himself with one thought, Mackenzie was one off the list. Now all that remained was to find Gordon Reece. Men were combing the area under his orders. Maybe he was letting his imagination get the better of him, but Trefoile's words haunted him: the medallion's value must run into thousands.

Lambert frowned as he turned the Capri into his driveway.

Where the hell would Mackenzie get something like that?

PART

TWO

Eighteen

Life in Medworth slipped easily back into the deep groove of normality after the tumultuous events of the previous weeks.

The local paper (on Lambert's orders) kept the details of the Mackenzie killings to a minimum and the residents of the town soon forgot the horrors which had gone before. They found new things to talk about. There were things to moan about. More men made redundant at the foundry, and the heavy showers of rain that had been falling intermittently for the last three days. People began to live their lives normally once more, filing away the recollections of the murders in the backs of their minds.

The killings had been a shock for a place as normally peaceful as Medworth. But the human mind is a resilient thing and forgets easily, especially when tragedy touches others rather than the ones close to the heart. There was that curious kind of emotional limbo which comes from discovering that quiet town, a place where many of the occupants had grown up, could house a killer as maniacal as Ray Mackenzie.

There was small mention of his burial, and that of Peter Brooks. Both men were laid to rest in Two Meadows with a minimum of fuss and a noticeable lack of mourners.

Lambert passed both graves, set side by side, as he continued his visits to the resting place of his brother. He found, with a curious mixture of guilt and relief, that he did not feel the need to visit Mike's grave every day. Two or three times a week and always on a Sunday, seemed to satisfy his conscience. The memory faded slowly, like the afterburn of a flash bulb on the retina. He found that he slept better, no longer waking in the small hours with the vision of the accident screaming before his eyes.

Of Gordon Reece there was still no sign and Lambert was beginning to think that the man had just walked out after the death of his wife, unable to face the house which held so many memories. The forensic test on the piece of glass he had found showed that the blood was indeed Reece's. The Inspector was considering closing the case.

The only question which still remained unanswered was the origin of the medallion.

He had heard nothing from Trefoile for three days. Once he had considered calling into the shop to see how things were progressing but, what the hell, it couldn't be that important and, with Mackenzie dead, the thing didn't seem to have such importance about it anymore.

Medworth was well and back to normal. Lambert had given five of his men leave, secure in the knowledge that his remaining constables could cope with the usual catalogue of shopliftings, bike stealings and complaints about dogs pissing on neighbours' lawns.

As he drove home that Saturday night Lambert felt at ease for the first time in months. He and Debbie were driving into Nottingham that night. Dinner at the Savoy (he'd booked the table a week earlier) and then on to a club or a film. He smiled happily as he swung the car into the drive.

Father Clive Ridley put down his pen and massaged the bridge of his nose between his thumb and forefinger. He shook himself and glanced down at the two pages of notes which lay before him. Tomorrow's sermon. He read quickly through the notes and nodded in satisfaction. It was a job he disliked but, obviously, it had to done. Finding a subject to hold the congregation's interest seemed so much harder now. When he had first become a priest at the age of forty-one, twelve years ago, it had all been so simple. Brimming over with enthusiazm, he had relished his sermons, delivering them with an almost theatrical zest. But lately it was becoming a chore. He seemed to be going over the same ground again and again, and it aggravated him as much as it must have bored the listeners. He looked at his notes again. He had chosen the theme of caring for others, something which he himself knew more than enough about. He had nursed his mother through three years of illness. An illness which had eventually taken her two years ago. She had died peacefully during her sleep and for that, Ridley was thankful. She had suffered a great deal until then, and at one time he had found himself questioning the mercy of a God to whom he devoted his life. For a short time he had begun to question not only his own faith but the wisdom of God. The very memory was painful and he felt almost ashamed to think of it. He looked across his study at the large wooden crucifix hanging on the wall and the silver figure of Christ seemed to stare back reproachfully.

Ridley got to his feet and crossed to the study window, looking out into the gathering dusk. The sky was streaked with brilliant brush strokes of crimson and orange. Colours which signalled the death of daylight and the onset of night. From his window he could see across the road to the cemetery and he decided to take a stroll before he cooked dinner. He often walked through the cemetery during the early evening, in summer particularly he enjoyed his little excursions. The singing of the birds in the many trees which dotted the area, the smell of the flowers in the air. But, as he pulled on his heavy coat and stepped out into the chill evening air, he expected no such sensory feast tonight.

He buttoned the coat, having difficulty with the middle two and promising himself that he would do without potatoes when he cooked his meal later on. He was a big man, tall and thick set. Fat perhaps, at first glance, but on closer inspection it was possible to see that it was only his large stomach which pushed him into the category of obesity. His face, dotted with small warts, was round and red-cheeked, giving him a look of perpetual good health. He blew on his hands, becoming aware of just how cold it was getting, and crossed the road from the vicarage to the cemetery gates.

Despite the chill of the air, the night looked like it would be a still one. The dying sun was sliding from its position in the sky, flooding the heavens with crimson and giving up supremacy to the swiftly gathering blackness. Dusk hung like a blanket over the land, catching it in transition.

A pigeon flew to its nest in the bell tower of the church and Father Ridley watched as it settled on the high sill before disappearing through a gap in the ancient masonry. The weather vane atop the spire twisted gently in the breeze.

He left the gravel drive almost immediately and walked slowly along the muddy footpaths which ran between the rows of graves. Here and there, freshly placed bouquets shone like beacons, their many colours contrasting with the dark earth. Ridley smiled to himself when he saw these, feeling a twinge of sadness when he found plots which bore no flowers or only the dried remains of those left long ago. Perhaps the occupants of the graves had been forgotten. The Reverend sighed. So sad to be forgotten. Death itself was the ultimate horror, but to be forgotten by those who had laid you to rest, that was a tragedy indeed.

He paused at a particularly well kept grave, guarded at all four corners by marble angels whose heads were bent in silent prayer. Engraved on the dark marble slab which covered it were the words:

'I am the Resurrection.'

Ridley smiled weakly and, almost absently, reached for the cross which hung around his neck. He considered it for a second, the tiny figure of Christ seeming to gaze up at him, then he let it slip back into the folds of his clothes.

The breeze had grown stronger now, tugging flowers from their pots and spinning the weather vane atop the spire. The Reverend pulled the collar of his coat up around his neck and decided to return to the vicarage. The sun had almost disappeared now, and besides, he was beginning to feel hungry. He walked quickly, heading for the gravel drive which would take him out through the gates of Two Meadows.

He reached the graves of Ray Mackenzie and Peter Brooks and paused. Such a terrible thing, he thought. He himself had conducted the burial services for all five of the people who had died in Medworth recently, including the entire Mackenzie family, Emma Reece, and Peter Brooks. Ridley shook his head. He noticed that the flowers which covered Ray Mackenzie's grave had been disturbed, scattered across the footpath which ran alongside the plot.

The wind had blown them aside probably, he thought as he stooped to gather the blooms. One by one he retrieved the roses and knelt down to replace them in their position just below the small metal marker which was the only sign that the grave was even there. Its freshly dug earth was already covered here and there with tufts of grass. In a week or so it would be covered completely.

Ridley gently laid the blooms on top of the plot.

A hand shot from beneath the dark earth and fastened iron fingers around his wrist.

The Reverend screamed in disbelieving terror. His eyes bulged and he felt red hot knives of pain stab at his heart. Shaking his head from side to side, he fastened his horrified stare on the earth-covered hand which protruded from the grave, gripping tightly his wrist.

He could not move.

He tried to rise but his legs wouldn't support him, and all the time the grip on his wrist tightened until he was sure it would snap the bone.

The hand thrust forward, followed by more arm.

The grip loosened and Ridley pulled free, his breath coming in gasps, his head spinning, the pain still stabbing through his heart. He backed off, his eyes threatening to pop from the sockets as he watched the movement from beneath the earth of the grave.

The arm seemed to sway in the air for a second, then, the earth slowly rose and, from below, Ridley saw a face.

The face of Ray Mackenzie.

He was grinning, the blazing red eyes fixing the priest in their unholy stare.

Ridley slipped in a patch of mud and staggered back against a stone cross, hanging onto it for support as he watched Mackenzie drag himself from the grave to his full height. He stood there, the dirt and mud caking his clothing, his eyes (if those two virulent blood blisters could be called that) turned on the cowering cleric.

Ridley was panting, the pain in his chest spreading inexorably to his left arm and up into his jaw. White stars danced before his eyes but he held on to consciousness just a little bit longer.

He might have wished he hadn't, for in his last agonized minutes, he saw the ground which covered the grave of Peter Brooks erupt and, a moment later, the intern stood next to Mackenzie.

Through eyes blurred with pain, Ridley saw that Brooks too had no eyes, just the hellish red orbs.

A final wrenching spasm of agony racked his body and he crumpled, the sound of his own breathing rattling in his ears.

They were advancing towards him, and, as he lost consciousness, he was grateful for one thing.

He would be dead before they reached him.

Nineteen

Lambert stared down at the fried egg on his plate and groaned.

There was a loud crack as the pan spat fat at Debbie who jumped back, brandishing the fish slice at it defiantly. She peered across at her husband who was still considering the egg. He cut into the yolk, watching as it gently spilled its colour onto the plate.

'I don't think I can face this,' he muttered, pushing the plate away from him.

'After three bottles of Beaujolais, three scotches and a brandy, I'm not surprised,' said Debbie, trying to sound stern but fighting to suppress a grin. Her stomach too felt as if it were on a trapeze. As she looked down into the bubbling pan she shook her head and switched off the gas flame beneath it. She had drunk more than usual the night before and she smiled as she remembered how they had tried to undress one another, giggling when they accidentally tore buttons off in their clumsy attempts. They had managed it eventually and slumped into bed, both of them dropping off to sleep before they could even embrace each other.

She crossed the kitchen and sat on Lambert's knee. He put his arm around her waist, drew her to him and kissed her gently on the cheek.

'Did you have a good time last night?' he asked.

She nodded smiling. 'Fantastic.'

He groaned and put a hand to his forehead. 'I wish my brain would stop trying to climb out of my head; it's using a pickaxe to make its escape.'

Debbie laughed and hugged him and they sat in silence for a moment. Then Lambert looked up at her. 'You know, last night I managed to forget what's happened over the last month or two. It was as if it never...' He struggled for the words, '... as if it were all unreal.'

She kissed him. 'That's good.'

'Even about Mike,' he elaborated. 'The memory is there, it'll always be there, but not so strong now. I don't want to forget though, Debbie. I won't torture myself with it, but maybe I need that memory.'

She looked at him for a second, puzzled, then said:

'Do you want to drive up there this morning?'

He nodded.

'Mind if I come?'

He pulled her close. 'I think the fresh air will do us more good than this bloody stuff.' He pushed the plate away and imitated the noise of vomiting. They both laughed.

The watery sun had settled in a cloud streaked sky as Lambert guided the Capri along the roads and twisting lanes which led out of Medworth and up towards the cemetery. Sitting alongside him, Debbie clutched a bunch of roses which she sniffed occasionally, enjoying the sweet odour.

'Who'd live in a city?' said Lambert, looking out over the rolling green hills.

'Someone's got to,' Debbie said.

They drove a little way in silence, windows open, enjoying the sight of the countryside around them. The near naked trees added a contrast to the richness of the grass. Here and there a blaze of colour would erupt in the hedgerows where a clutch of wild flowers grew. Above them, where the hillside sloped up gradually into woodland, birds hovered above the trees and Debbie actually caught sight of a kestrel as it glided about looking for prey. The magnificent bird seemed to be suspended on invisible wire as it swung back and forth before finally disappearing from view.

'Are you going into the station today?' she asked, looking at him.

Lambert shook his head. 'Nothing to go in for. The Mackenzie case is closed. Gordon Reece seems to have cleared out. It's back to the normal routine from now on.' He smiled.

'What about the medallion?'

'I haven't heard anything from Trefoile yet, but I doubt if it'll be important. Mackenzie probably just found it somewhere. Maybe he dug it up in his back garden.' Lambert grinned.

'You know better than that,' she rebuked him, letting one hand stray across his thigh.

He swerved slightly and she jumped.

'See what you do to me,' he said, leering exaggeratedly.

They both laughed as he pulled up across the road from the cemetery gates. Debbie squeezed his hand as they sat for a moment, then they both climbed out. High up on the hill top, where Two Meadows was situated, the wind seemed to blow stronger, and Debbie brushed her hair from her face as the breeze whipped silken strands across it. She shivered slightly but relaxed as Lambert put his arm around her, and locked together they walked in.

'Father Ridley's usually around at this time,' said Lambert, peering over his shoulder towards the vicarage.

'Perhaps he's in the church,' she offered.

'Maybe he's having a lie-in.'

She punched him playfully on the arm. 'Priests don't lie-in on Sundays, you heathen.'

She reached for his hand and found it, their fingers intertwining. As they walked, Debbie found herself prey to that mixed emotion which comes so frequently in a cemetery. The uneasiness mixed with the feeling of almost idyllic peacefulness.

'It makes you aware of your own mortality,' said Lambert, looking at the rows of graves: the ornate, the unkempt, the welltended.

Mike's grave.

They stood beside it for a second before Debbie knelt and gently laid the roses on top of the marble slab. Lambert smiled as he watched her do it, drawing her close to him as she stepped back. They stood for long moments beside Mike's grave, gazing down at it, aware only of one another and of the wind rustling in the tree which hung above them. Finally, Lambert, squeezed her gently and said, softly:

'Come on.'

They turned and headed back towards the gravel drive.

As they reached the small kerb which edged the drive, Debbie stopped and pointed to something lying no more than ten feet away from them. It was glinting in the sunlight and that was what had attracted her attention.

She pulled away from Lambert and picked the object up.

It was a crucifix.

'Tom,' she called, 'look at this.'

He joined her and peered at the small silver cross which lay on her palm.

'Somebody must have dropped it,' he said, taking the object from her and holding it between his thumb and forefinger.

He dropped the crucifix into his jacket pocket and looked around, searching the ground for something else.

He found it.

A few yards up the path which ran between two rows of graves lay a pile of clods. Lambert hurried to them and kicked at them with his shoe. Then he noticed the flowers scattered around like shredded confetti and trodden into the mud.

'What the hell is this?' he said under his breath.

He took a step closer to one of the graves, noticing that a marble angel had been smashed from its position at a corner of the plot. There was a dark stain splashed across it which Lambert recognized immediately. He knelt and ran his finger through the stain, sniffing the red liquid on his finger tip.

It was blood.

He noticed more of it splashed up the headstone next to the other grave. He read the name on the headstone.

Peter Brooks.

The earth was piled up around the grave and a hollow had been formed in the centre, as if someone had begun digging and then given up half way.

Lambert stood up, his breath coming in gasps. 'Tom, what is it?' called Debbie, advancing towards him along the path.

He ignored the question, looking instead at the small metal marker on the grave next to that of Brooks. Barely readable was the name: Ray Mackenzie. The earth was strewn for many feet around it. Dark, wet earth. Lambert turned and waved Debbie back.

'We've got to find Father Ridley,' he said, tersely.

'What's wrong?' she asked, puzzled.

'I think some sick bastard has been mucking about with Mackenzie's grave.'

He walked past her, then suddenly hesitated.

'You'd better come with me,' he told her, and the two of them hurried across the road to the vicarage.

The curtains were open, and as he headed towards the front door, Lambert hoped that Ridley was in. He rapped hard, three times on the front door, and when he got no answer, went round the back.

'Damn,' he growled. 'He must be in the church.'

Debbie found that she almost had to run to keep up with him.

'Tom, what's going on around here?' she demanded.

'I wish I knew,' he said.

They reached the broken path which led up to the church door and hurried towards it, Debbie's high heels clicking noisily in the silence.

The church towered above them and Lambert pushed the door, noticing, as he did, that there was more blood on the great brass handle of the door. He swallowed hard and popped his head around the door.

'Tom.'

Her single word hung in the air as the policeman stepped cautiously into the great building. His footsteps echoed on the cold stone floor and he shivered at the coldness of the place.

Debbie stepped in behind him, pushing the door closed.

The church ran a good fifty yards from door to altar. Pews arranged with soldierly precision on either side formed a narrow aisle down the centre which led straight to the altar. Dust particles danced in the light shining through the stained glass windows on both sides of the building. It smelt musty in there, a smell which reminded Debbie of Madame Tussaud's Chamber of Horrors. She quickly dismissed the thought, making sure she kept close to Lambert as he advanced down the central aisle. To the left stood the pulpit with a huge Bible open on it.

There was no sign of Ridley. Lambert called him, his voice echoing off the walls and ceiling, turning the huge room into a vast stone echo chamber.

'Father Ridley,' he called again.

Silence.

It was then that he noticed the pieces of earth scattered around the base of the altar. The Inspector crossed quickly to them and prodded a large lump with his index finger. He exhaled deeply. Where the hell was Ridley? There was one place left in the church he hadn't looked. The bell tower. A flight of stone steps ran up to the belfry from just behind the altar. Lambert looked up. A wooden floor hid the belfry itself from view below. He would have been able to see from where he stood whether or not the priest was up there, but the wooden slats obscured his view. He would have to go up and take a look for himself. He was suddenly filled with a feeling which he took to be fear, but why such a feeling should take hold of him, he didn't know.

'Wait here,' he told Debbie, and set off up the stone steps which would take him into the belfry.

Debbie nodded and watched him go, edging back so that she leant against the altar, looking out into the church. Hundreds of invisible eyes seemed to be fixed on her and she shuddered involuntarily.

Lambert, meantime, found that the staircase spiralled as it rose. The walls on either side hemmed him in so that he could not even extend his arms without touching them.

He slipped and nearly fell, but regained his footing cursing, and looked to see what had made him stumble.

There was a slippery streak of blood on the step on which he stood. And the one above it. Lambert gritted his teeth. The cold seemed to have intensified and he was also beginning to notice a strange smell which grew stronger as he neared the top of the stairs. Mixed with the cloying odour of damp wood was something more pungent. A coppery, choking smell which stung his nostrils and made him cough.

He reached the top of the stairs and peered round into the belfry.

It was small. No more than ten feet square and Lambert felt as if the walls were closing in around him. The bell, a large brass object, lay discarded in one corner, torn from the thick hemp which secured it.

Lambert gasped and backed against the wall, his heart thumping.

Dangling from the bell rope, the hemp knotted tightly around his neck, was Father Ridley.

His face was bloated, the blackened tongue protruding from his mouth. Blood had splashed down his chest, turning his coat red and the rope which supported him had cut deeply into the thick flesh of his neck, drawing blood in places. He hung like some obscene puppet, his own blood puddled beneath him, soaking into the ancient timbers of the belfry floor.

But, the thing which finally made Lambert turn away in horrified disgust was the face. Splattered with gore, it seemed to glare mockingly at the policeman who noticed with mounting terror that there was something horribly familiar about it.

Both the eyes had been torn out.

Lambert turned and raced down the stairs, almost running past Debbie who caught his arm. Her eyes searched his, looking for an answer which she already suspected.

'He's dead,' said Lambert flatly. 'Come on.'

They ran from the church, chased by a fear beyond their understanding.

They ran to the car and climbed in. Lambert burned rubber as he spun the Capri round. The needle on the speedometer touched sixty as he drove for Medworth, his face set in an expression of fearful resignation. Debbie studied his profile.

'Tom.'

'What?' His voice was tense, sharp.

'What's happening?' There was a note of something near to pleading in her voice.

'The graves,' he snapped, 'the graves of Mackenzie and Brooks were disturbed. It looked as if someone dug them up.' The words trailed off. 'Oh Jesus,' he said, his voice catching.

She reached out and laid a hand on his shoulder.

'What are you going to do, Tom?'

'Open the graves.'

'What?' She swallowed hard, not quite believing what she had heard. 'But you can't. I mean, why?'

'Someone tampered with those graves, Debbie. There must be a reason for that. I want to know what it is.'

'But don't you need an exhumation order?'

'Why?'

'It's the law.'

He looked at her. 'I am the law.'

Lambert stood beside Sergeant Hayes, watching as Davies and Briggs threw shovelfuls of earth into the air in an effort to reach the coffin of Ray Mackenzie.

Lambert was smoking. His third that morning. He'd been trying to give up just lately, but the events of the day so far had suddenly persuaded him that he needed something to calm him down. He sucked hard on the cigarette, holding the smoke in his mouth for a second before expelling it in a long grey stream which mingled with his own frosted breath in the crispness of the morning air.

He had driven home after finding Ridley's body, left Debbie there and told her he would be in touch. At first he had been reluctant to leave her alone, a fear which he couldn't understand nagging at the back of his mind. She had assured him that she would be all right and he had driven to the station. Taking a Panda, he, Hayes and the two constables had driven back to the cemetery armed with shovels. As Davies drove, Lambert recounted what he and Debbie had found that morning and when he got to the part about the eyeless corpse of Ridley, Briggs had found himself struggling to keep his poached eggs down. Hayes had said nothing, only looked questioningly at the inspector as if the description of the injuries inflicted had stirred some horrific memory within himself.

The ambulance which removed the vicar's body had been pulling out as the Panda swung into the driveway. Kirby was to do an immediate autopsy on it and ring Lambert with the results as quickly as possible.

Now the Inspector leant on a stone cross and dropped his third butt to the ground, crushing it into the earth with the toe of his shoe.

There was a scraping sound as the shovel Davies was using ran along a wooden surface.

They had reached the coffin.

Lambert stepped forward and watched as the two men scraped away the remaining earth with their fingers. As the last sticky clods were removed, all four policeman noticed the large hole about two feet from the head of the coffin. Splinters of wood were bent outward from it, some mingled with the dark earth.

The Inspector sighed and rubbed his chin.

It was scarcely necessary, because all of them could see through the holes that the coffin was empty, but Lambert gave the order nonetheless. 'Open it up,' he said, jabbing a finger towards the splintered box.

Davies wedged the corner of the shovel underneath one edge of the lid and pushed down. It came free with a shriek of cracking wood.

White satin greeted the men. A few specks of earth had fallen onto it but, apart from that, it was untouched.

No corpse. Nothing.

'Jesus,' said Briggs under his breath.

Lambert noticed some tiny dark specks of colour on the satin of the lid and jumped down into the hole alongside the two astounded constables. Leaning close he saw that the stains were dried blood. There was more smeared on the inside of the coffin. He straightened up and looked up at Hayes. The sergeant was expressionless, his lips and face white, bloodless.

'And the other one,' said Lambert, pointing to the grave of Peter Brooks. 'We've got to be sure.'

Davies groaned and wiped the perspiration from his brow. He gave Briggs a helping hand up from the hole and the two of them set to work on the second grave.

That too was empty.

Lambert bowed his head and, for long moments, no one spoke. Then Briggs said, nervously, 'What's going on, sir?'

'You tell me,' said Lambert, reaching for another cigarette.

Lambert drove home with his mind in turmoil. He told the men to keep quiet about the empty graves until they all had a better idea of what was happening. Probably someone having a sick joke, thought the Inspector. He hoped to Christ he was right. The men were edgy, Hayes too. Lambert had never seen the old sergeant like that. Usually nothing could get him rattled, but this time he strutted around the station trying to find jobs that didn't exist and snapping at the younger constables and making everyone feel all the more uneasy.

Lambert had left them sitting around in the duty room drinking cups of coffee. He had given them no orders. After all, he would have felt slightly foolish asking his men to keep their eyes open for two missing corpses. If the situation had been different he might have laughed about it. 'Just keep on the look out for the missing bodies. They'll turn up somewhere. Probably just been misplaced.' He could hear himself saying it.

He had no answers as yet. No theories floating about in that supposedly logical mind of his. On the other hand, what he had seen that morning defied logic. A priest murdered and hung from the bell rope of his own church. Two empty graves, one of them formerly belonging to a mass murderer, and the last and most disturbing thing, holes in the tops of both coffin lids.

Lambert had no theories but what did make him shudder was the fact that the wood was bent outward in both cases. As if some powerful force had stove it out... FROM THE INSIDE.

He was shivering as he swung the Capri into the driveway of the house. He left it in front of the garage and went in the front door.

He found Debbie sitting in the lounge, a steaming mug of tea cradled in her hands. She got up and crossed to him, setting the mug down on the small table beside her chair.

'I could do with one of those,' he said, embracing her and nodding towards the mug of tea.

She hurried into the kitchen to fetch him one and returned to find him slumped on the sofa, head bowed in thought. He smiled up at her as she handed him his tea.

'You all right?' he asked.

She nodded. 'What happened?'

He sighed, staring down into the steaming brown liquid as if an answer lay there. 'Both the graves were empty.'

'Both?' She seemed puzzled.

'Mackenzie and Brooks.' He took a sip of his tea. 'I'm waiting for the autopsy results on Ridley.'

She sat beside him and reached for his hand, squeezing it. 'How about dinner?' she said.

'Not for me, love,' he said, smiling. 'I seem to have lost my appetite.' He took another sip of his tea, watching a tiny brown tea leaf floating on the surface.

Debbie went to the record player and turned it down. Elton John faded into the background.

Lambert hardly noticed and, when the record finally came to an end, neither of them got up to take it off the turntable. It stuck in the runoff grooves, the steady click-click the only sound in the room.

When the phone rang it seemed to galvanize them both into action. Debbie snatched the record up while Lambert grabbed the receiver.

'Hello,' he said.

'Tom.'

He recognized the voice as Kirby.

'John, what have you got?'

'Well,' Kirby sounded tired. 'Not much really. Ridley died of a heart attack.'

'What caused it?'

There was silence on the other end and Lambert repeated his question before Kirby finally, and falteringly, said:

'It's hard to say. He was overweight, anything might have triggered it. I can't be sure, Tom.' A long pause. 'But, from the condition of the arteries around the heart and the condition of the heart itself there would appear to have been massive cardiac failure. His heart burst, to put it simply.'

'You're hedging, John.'

'He died of fright.'

The words came out flatly. No inflection to soften the statement. Cold hard fact. Simplicity itself.

Lambert swallowed hard. 'The other injuries?'

'I compared the scratch marks on the cheeks with those on the faces of Emma Reece and the Mackenzies.'

'And?'

'They match up.'

Lambert inhaled quickly. 'So what does that mean?' His own mind was telling him an answer which he could not, dare not, accept.

'Ridley was killed by the same man who killed the other three. Or so it would appear. That, of course, is impossible.'

There was a long silence. Lambert held the phone down, Kirby's voice seeming far away as if it were in a vacuum.

'Tom? Tom!'

Finally, the Inspector raised the receiver to his ear.

'Sorry, John.' His tone changed. 'Look, can you come over here tonight?'

'To your house?'

'Yes. About seven?'

'Yes. Tom, what is it?'

'Bring all the papers relating to the previous victims, and those on Ridley. And the autopsy reports on Mackenzie and Brooks.'

'Sure, but...'

Lambert cut him short, his voice edged slightly with worried impatience. 'Just do it, John.'

They said their goodbyes and Lambert dropped the phone back onto its cradle. Debbie looked at him and he returned her gaze, their eyes locked together. He sat down beside her and reached for his tea. He took a mouthful and winced. It was stone cold. He put the cup down and crossed to the drink cabinet.

Right now he needed something stronger.

Twenty

It was a minute before seven that evening when there was a sharp rapping on the front door of the Lambert household. The Inspector checked his watch as he crossed to the door. Punctual as usual, he thought smiling. He opened the door to find Kirby standing there, a briefcase in his hand. The policeman ushered him in, his eyes gazing out into the night. The darkness was broken only here and there by the glow of street lamps. He closed the door and led Kirby through into the living room.

There was a pleasing warmth within the room which Kirby enjoyed, and he loosened his tie.

'Sit down,' said Lambert, and the doctor gratefully accepted, placing himself at one end of the sofa.

Debbie emerged from the kitchen. She was wearing a faded old blue blouse and jeans and Kirby ran an appreciative eye over her figure.

'Hello,' she said, gaily.

The doctor tried to rise but she waved him back. 'Would you like a drink? Tea, coffee or something stronger?'

'Tea is fine,' said Kirby, smiling.

She retreated into the kitchen and Lambert pointed to the briefcase lying beside Kirby. He flipped it open and took out a number of manilla files, each stamped with a number and name. He laid them on the coffee table before him and opened the first one.

'Ridley,' he announced. 'Like I told you over the phone, Tom, it was heart failure. The rest...' he hesitated, '... was done afterwards.'

There was a long silence as the policeman flicked through the slender report. He closed the file and looked at Kirby. 'You said over the phone that the scratch marks on Ridley's face matched those on the other three victims.'

Kirby nodded.

'What conclusions would you draw from that?'

The doctor shrugged. 'I'm not a policeman, Tom.'

'Imagine you were. What would you think?'

'I would say, against my better judgement, that Ridley was killed by the same man who killed the other three.'

'Which of course is impossible,' said Lambert, something mysterious dancing behind his blue eyes.

'Well of course it's impossible. Mackenzie's dead,' said Kirby, almost smiling.

Lambert got to his feet and crossed to the drinks cabinet. He poured himself a large scotch and downed a sizeable gulp before continuing.

'John, there was another reason I wanted you here tonight. I think it might be linked with Ridley's murder.'

Kirby interrupted him. 'He wasn't murdered. He died of a heart attack.'

'He died of fright,' said Lambert, his voice rising in volume slightly. 'Besides, some mad bastard did that to him. Some fucking headcase tore out his eyes and hung him up.' There was anger in his voice, tinged with something else which seemed, to Kirby, like fear. The policeman drained his glass. 'Look, as I was saying, something else happened up at the cemetery. The graves of Mackenzie and Brooks were tampered with.'

Kirby looked vague.

'Dug up. Desecrated. Call it what you like. The bodies were taken.'

'How do you know?' Kirby swallowed hard.

'I ordered the graves to be opened. Both bodies were gone.'

'So how does this tie up with Ridley?'

Lambert poured himself another drink and inhaled slowly.

'What would you say if I told you I think Ridley was killed by Ray Mackenzie?'

Kirby almost smiled. 'I'd say you should consider visiting a psychiatrist.'

'You said the marks on the faces of all four victims matched.'

'Tom, he's dead. I did the autopsy myself,' said Kirby incredulously.

Debbie emerged from the kitchen carrying a cup of tea which she handed to Kirby. He thanked her and sipped tentatively at it. She got one for herself and joined them, curling up in one of the armchairs beside the fire. Lambert too, sat down, his third glass of scotch cradled in his hand.

Kirby smiled. 'You do realize, Mrs Lambert, that your husband is a total lunatic?'

'This is no joke,' snarled Lambert. 'What's your explanation?'

Kirby eyed the Inspector warily and stirred his tea needlessly. 'Tom, there must be a logical explanation for what happened. It's some sort of sick imitator. They must have read about the other murders in the paper and well...' He let the sentence trail off.

'No details of the murders were published in the paper,' Lambert corrected him, 'especially the taking of the eyes.'

'Coincidence,' said Kirby.

'Bullshit,' snapped Lambert. He took a sip of his drink. 'Look at what we've got here. A man is murdered, or mutilated anyway, in exactly the same way as three previous people. We've got two empty coffins, one of which belongs to a killer. Now, you tell me why anyone would want to steal those bodies and kill Ridley.'

There was silence in the room. The glow of the fire and single table lamp which had at first seemed so comforting now became almost oppressive. Shadows in the corner of the room were thick, black, almost palpable, and Debbie drew her chair closer to the fire.

'Tom, you're a logical man, for Christ's sake,' said Kirby.

Lambert held up a hand. 'O.K., let's look at it logically. God knows I want to find a logical explanation for all of this. Both coffins were empty, right? Both had large holes in the lids. The wood was bent outward.' He paused. 'Any theories?'

Kirby shrugged. 'Body snatching.'

'But why? Who'd want to steal two corpses? What are you going to do with them? Hang them over your fireplace?'

Debbie suppressed a grin, especially when she saw the pained expression on her husband's face.

'There is another explanation,' said Kirby.

'I'm waiting,' Lambert said, impatiently.

'Have you ever heard of catatonia?'

'I've heard of it, but I don't know exactly what it is.'

Kirby put down his tea. 'It's very rare now; it was quite common at one time but, what with advanced examination procedures it's become more or less obsolete.'

'Get to the point, John,' demanded Lambert, quietly.

'In a catatonic state, sometimes called a catatonic trance, the patient displays all the appearances of death. The bodily functions slow down, sometimes even stop altogether. It can last for seconds or hours.'

'So what are you saying?'

'That Mackenzie could have been in a state of advanced catatonia when he was buried.' A pause. 'He could have been buried alive.'

Lambert shook his head. 'John, he fell over a hundred feet from that hospital room. That's what killed him. He was dead. Dead as a bloody doornail and to hell with your scientific explanations. Besides, the grave of Brooks was empty too. Even if this crap about catatonia was right, the chances of it happening to two men at exactly the same time are millions to one.'

'What else do you have?' said Kirby, wearily.

Lambert shook his head. 'Nothing. Not a goddam thing.'

The three of them sat in silence. Outside, a motorcycle roared past, breaking the solitude for a second before the harsh sound gradually died away. Kirby sipped his tea but found that it was cold. He winced and put the cup down again, declining when Debbie offered him another.

'All right,' began Lambert, 'sticking with this idea of catatonia, how do you explain the holes in the lids of both coffins?'

Kirby shrugged. 'They were trying to get out.'

Lambert shook his head. 'Have you ever felt a coffin lid? It's about two inches thick. Solid oak. You'd need to be bloody strong to punch a hole in that. And then, assuming they managed that, they clawed their way up through six feet of earth?'

'Tom, you've just defeated your own argument. It's impossible. It had to be body snatchers, there's no other logical explanation for it.'

Lambert shook his head. 'Why does the answer have to be a logical one? There's been nothing logical about this whole bloody case ever since it started; why the hell should we start worrying about it now?' He took another hefty swallow from his glass before continuing. 'Look at the facts, John. An ordinary man in an ordinary job with an ordinary family suddenly goes crazy. Butchers his family, tears out their eyes then kills another woman, tears out her eyes. During the day he's in a torpor. At night he's like a wild animal. A brain test shows that, to all intents and purposes he's dead, but what happens when the lights go out - he gets up and kills himself and another man. Now, two weeks after he's buried, our vicar is found hanging from his own bell rope, both eyes torn out after having died of fright and the grave of the murderer is empty.' Lambert's voice had been rising steadily as he spoke but now he was almost shouting, his breath coming in quick gasps. Now, the veins on his forehead standing out angrily, he slammed his fist down on the coffee table and shouted:

'Now you tell me that's logical.'

He slumped back into his chair, hands covering his eyes, totally drained. No one spoke, then, after what seemed like an eternity of silence Lambert said, 'And there's another thing.' His voice had regained its composure; it was low, resigned almost to the horrors he had just described.

'Mackenzie had a medallion with him. It was old, very old. There was inscriptions on it, in Latin. I think that is the key to all of this.'

'Where is it now?' asked Kirby.

'Trefoile, the antique dealer in town, has got it. He said he recognized it from somewhere.'

'What makes it so important, Tom?' Kirby wanted to know.

Lambert smiled humourlessly. 'Maybe I'm wrong. Perhaps this is what's known as clutching at straws but, right now, it's all I've got.'

'What are you doing about Mackenzie and Brooks?'

'What can I do? Tell my men to be on the look out for two of the living dead? Report in lads, if you happen to bump into anyone who was buried recently, that sort of thing? Frankly, John, I don't know what the fuck to do.' He looked long and hard at the doctor. 'All I know is, it must be kept out of the papers. If the press get hold of this, we'll have half the country crawling over Medworth trying to find out what's going on.'

'Call in help.'

'Where from?'

'Tell your superiors what's going on.'

Lambert laughed bitterly. 'Can you imagine what Detective Inspector John Barton would make of this? He'd have me locked up. No, I can handle it for now.' He exhaled deeply. 'Christ, if only we had a motive. I mean, what kind of person steals corpses?'

The Inspector's eyes suddenly flared. He pointed an inquisitive finger at Kirby.

'Assuming, just assuming, that someone is trying to imitate Mackenzie's crimes and also working on the assumption that that same person stole the bodies, then surely they would have taken the corpse of Emma Reece as well.'

'Why?' Kirby wanted to know.

'Because she was one of his victims.'

'Was her grave tampered with too?'

'I don't know, I never thought about her at the time.' The Inspector got to his feet. 'We've got to find out now.'

Debbie looked worried. 'Tom, what are you going to do?'

'We have to see if her body has been taken as well,' he said flatly.

'You mean dig her up?' gasped Kirby.

'We've done it twice today already,' said Lambert.

Kirby lowered his head. 'But...'

Lambert's tone was soft, but stern. 'We have to know.'

The doctor swallowed hard and looked up at Lambert. He nodded almost imperceptibly. A thin smile creased the policeman's face, and he hurried out of the house to fetch the tools. Debbie and Kirby stared at one another, neither of them able to speak. The cold draft from the open back door blew into the room, temporarily driving away the warmth and making them both shiver.

Lambert returned a second later with a spade and a garden fork. He held them out in front of him.

'Ready?' he said.

Kirby nodded. 'We'll take my car.' He took the tools from Lambert and walked out to his car. Inside, Debbie and the Inspector heard the sound of the engine being started. She pulled Lambert close and he held her head on his chest.

'Lock all the doors,' he said quietly and kissed her on the forehead. He turned quickly and ran out to the waiting Datsun. Debbie, watching from the front window, saw him slide in beside Kirby, and a few seconds later the car disappeared into the darkness.

She hurried to the back door and drew the bolts across then repeated the procedure at the front. Then she walked back into the living room and crouched in front of the fire, suddenly gripped by an icy chill which seemed to cling to her like frost to a window pane.

It was a long time before she was warm again.

Twenty-One

The drive to the cemetery took less than twenty minutes. Kirby brought the Datsun to a halt and switched off the engine. Both men got out, their breath forming clouds in the cold night air. The doctor unlocked the boot of his car and took out the spade and fork. The latter he kept for himself, the other implement he handed to Lambert. The Inspector reached into his pocket and pulled out a torch and flicked it on, checking the power of the beam. Satisfied, he nodded and the two men set off up the gravel drive which led them into the cemetery. The noise of their shoes on the rough surface sounded all the more conspicuous in the silence.

To their right, the church. A dark mass, the huge black edifice stood surrounded by a sea of shadows. Lambert shuddered as he looked at it, remembering what he had found in there the day before.

'Where is the grave?' asked Kirby, whispering.

'Over near those trees,' said Lambert, motioning with the torch.

They continued up the gravel drive, turning with it as it curved around to the left. Finally, they left the gravel drive and took one of the muddy paths which ran between the rows of plots. It was at this point that Lambert flicked on his torch, sweeping its broad beam back and forth over the marble headstones and crosses. The mud squelched beneath their feet, and once Kirby almost slipped over. Lambert held out a hand to steady him and the two men continued on their way. A row of poplars grew with military precision along the edge of one of the paths, and it was beneath the shade of one of the trees that Lambert's torch beam picked out the chosen spot. In the cold white light, both men read the name on the headstone.

Emma Reece.

There was an urn on top of the grave, withered carnations drooping impotently over the edges. The Inspector removed it, laying it gently to one side. He rested the torch on the headstone itself, the beam giving them a little light to work by.

Standing one on either side of the grave, the men looked at each other and Lambert noted how pale Kirby looked. His face was dark with shadow and, despite the cold, the Inspector could see that there were tiny beads of perspiration on his forehead. They held each other's gaze for a second, then, with a grunt, Lambert drove his spade into the dark earth. The doctor watched him for a second then followed his example, using the fork to tear up large clods which he flung to one side.

In the beam of the torchlight they worked, tearing away more and more earth until mounds of it began to accumulate on either side of the grave.

Lambert felt the perspiration seeping through his shirt and, twice, he had to stop to wipe it from his forehead. He leaned back, using the handle of shovel as a kind of stool. Kirby too, stopped for a moment and wiped his brow.

'Four hundred years ago we'd have been burned at the stake for this,' he said with a grim humour in his voice.

Lambert nodded and smiled weakly.

They continued with their digging, aware of nothing but the sounds they made as they turned the dark earth and the gentle rustling of the wind in the trees above them. Both men were stooping now to get at the fresh earth.

'Nearly there,' said Lambert, quietly. Almost triumphantly. He felt his heart quicken a little bit.

The earth was piled high on either side of the hole and both men found that it was sticking to their clothes. Kirby tried to pull the clods from his shoes but it was useless. They stuck like lumps of thick brown glue. The prongs of the fork, too, had become encrusted with the wet ground.

There was a dull scraping sound as Lambert's spade struck wood.

He pulled away the remaining clods with his hands, baring the brass plate on the coffin lid. He reached up for the torch and shone it on the plate.

'This is it,' he said.

'How do we get the lid off?' said Kirby, noticing the thick screws which held it firmly in position.

Lambert produced a penknife from his trouser pocket and, tossing the spade aside, pulled the blade up into position.

'Shine the light here,' he snapped, handing the torch to Kirby who put down his fork and held the beam over the place where the Inspector was indicating. Inserting the wide edge of the blade into the groove in the screw head, Lambert began to loosen it. It turned easily and he grinned triumphantly up at Kirby.

One by one, the screws were removed and Lambert slid his fingers beneath the lid to ease it free. He swallowed hard, not knowing what he was going to find beneath the heavy lid.

'Keep that bloody light steady,' he whispered.

Heart thudding against his ribs, he pushed the lid to one side.

Lying in the coffin, arms folded sedately across her chest, was Emma Reece.

Lambert looked at Kirby who shrugged with the sort of gesture that says 'I told you so.' The Inspector stood up, wiping a hand across his forehead, his eyes riveted to the two empty sockets in Emma Reece's face which had once housed eyes. Gaping black maws now filled with the dirt of the grave. And yet, there was something else...

Kirby stepped forward, handing the flashlight to Lambert. He knelt beside the corpse and touched a hand to the face. It was ice cold.

'Curious,' he said, abstractedly.

'What is?' Lambert wanted to know.

'She was buried three weeks ago. The skin usually begins to undergo some minor deterioration within a matter of days. Her skin is still supple.' He prodded it again. 'No deterioration at all.' He reached for the right arm and lifted it a few inches. 'Not even evidence of rigor mortis.' Kirby straightened up, rubbing his chin thoughtfully. 'It must be something in the soil.' He felt a lump between his fingers. 'It is very moist, that could account for the preservation.'

Kirby knelt once more, shining the torch into the face of the corpse, bending close until the putrid smell finally drove him back. He shook his head and straightened up again, turning towards Lambert.

'Well, Tom,' he said, brushing the dirt from his hands, 'that seems to put pay to your theory.'

The thing which had once been Emma Reece leapt from the coffin with the speed of an arrow.

Kirby had no time to move and Lambert was momentarily frozen by the sight before him.

The living dead thing fastened both hands around Kirby's neck and pushed him forward, grinding his face into the mud wall of the grave. He struck blindly at it, trying to shake himself free of the vicelike hold. Lambert struck out madly with the torch, shattering the bulb as it crashed against the top of Emma Reece's head. The place was suddenly plunged into darkness, only the vague light from the street lamps outside the cemetery illuminating the unholy scenario.

Kirby was clawing at the bony fingers which encircled his throat, the dirt now beginning to clog his nostrils. He was fighting for breath, his throat being blocked by the crushing fingers while the stinking dirt of the grave filled his nostrils. He felt unconsciousness wrapping its dark blanket around him and his efforts to break free grew more feeble.

Frantic, Lambert drove a fist into the side of Emma Reece's face, hearing bone splinter beneath the impact. It was enough to make her loosen her grip on Kirby, who slumped to the ground sprawled half in and half out of the open coffin.

The living dead thing turned towards Lambert, and he saw with horror the blazing red pinpricks deep within the gaping empty eye sockets. Saliva dripped from her open mouth and he noted, with disgust, that her false teeth were dangling pathetically from her top jaw. Emma Reece leapt at the Inspector across the narrow hole but he caught her by the wrists and held her, surprised at the strength of those apparently frail arms. Her face pressed close to his and he was splattered with the yellowish mucous. A hideous grin began to spread across the creature's face as she forced Lambert back, her talon-like hands reaching for his throat. He stared into those bottomless pits of blackness that had once been eyes and, with a surge of strength aided by fear, forced her back. They both fell, still locked together, Lambert not daring to relinquish his grip on those arms. But now he was on top of her. Still that feral grin sneered up at him.

Kirby, meantime was dragging himself to his feet, his head spinning.

'Kill it,' screamed Lambert, realizing that the Reece thing was squirming free. But Kirby could only stagger against the wall of the open grave, watching the life and death struggle before him. Paralysed with fear he saw Lambert jump back, his hand groping behind him to the lip of the hole.

His hand closed around the spade.

The living dead thing raised both arms and launched itself once more, but this time at Kirby, who, in his dazed condition, went down under the rush.

Eyes wide with horrified revulsion, Lambert saw the thing throttling the doctor, pressing its vile body against him in a manner which made Lambert want to vomit.

With a shriek of rage he swung the spade and slammed its edge into the spinal area just above the pelvis. There was a loud snapping sound, like a branch being broken, and the thing stepped back. Moaning in agony, it stepped away from Kirby, both hands elapsed to the rent in its back. Lambert lashed out again, the powerful stroke catching Emma Reece just below the chin.

The head, severed by the blow, rose on a fountain of dark blood and thudded to the ground several feet away. The living dead thing remained upright for a second, blood spurting madly from the severed arteries, then pitched forward into the coffin. The white satin rapidly turned vivid crimson.

Lambert dropped the spade and crossed to Kirby who was slumped against one of the grave sides coughing. Even in the darkness, Lambert could see the savage cuts around the doctor's throat, bruises and lacerations that would have been normally credited to a garotte. He tried to speak but could only cough, a string-thin trickle of blood running down his chin. Lambert helped him to his feet and then vaulted up out of the dark hole, taking Kirby's hands and pulling him up, supporting him when he was clear.

The Inspector looked down and saw the head of Emma Reece lying nearby. He rolled it gently with his foot, tipping it into the grave where it landed with a thud, the black, empty, eye sockets gazing up at the night sky. He shuddered and turned away, supporting Kirby until they reached the gravel drive. The doctor stood alone for a second then nodded that he was all right. His voice, when he spoke, was dry, like old parchment and every syllable brought a new wave of pain.

'It looks like you were right,' he croaked, touching his throat. 'Drive me to my surgery.'

Lambert nodded and the two of them made their way back to the waiting Datsun.

Kirby collapsed into the passenger seat and gently touched his injured neck. He wound down the window and spat blood onto the road.

'You need hospital,' said Lambert.

Kirby shook his head and extended his tongue to reveal a deep gash where he had bitten into it. That was the source of the blood, not his throat. Lambert had thought that he might be bleeding inside the throat itself but now he was reassured.

As they drove, Lambert's face was set in an expression of grim resignation.

'Like I said,' gasped Kirby, 'it looks as though you were right about where the bodies of Mackenzie and Brooks went.'

Lambert nodded. 'This is one time I wish I'd been wrong. How the hell are we going to get anyone to believe this?'

They drove the rest of the way in silence. Kirby concerned with his own pain, Lambert tormented by the obscene spectre of Emma Reece. His mind was not quite able to come to terms with the fact that he had just fought a woman who had already been dead for three weeks. He shuddered.

The street lamps had gone out in a number of streets in Medworth that night. The local power station had been inundated with complaints and every caller had been assured that everything was being done to rectify the fault.

Not everyone complained though.

The darkness was a welcome companion to some who walked that night.

To two men in particular.

Emma Reece had been destroyed, true enough. But there were others abroad that night more powerful.

It was eight-twenty. A long time before dawn. There was nothing but darkness.

Darkness.

Twenty-Two

Bob Shaw peered out into the blackness of the night and tried to make out the shape of his Suzuki 750 parked in the road outside.

'All the bloody street lights are out,' he muttered.

He tried one last time to catch a glimpse of his motorbike but gave it up to the all enveloping darkness. Christ, he hoped no bastard pinched it. It had taken him nearly two years to pay for it, fifteen quid a month until he'd paid the five hundred. Still, it was worth it. He was the envy of all the blokes he hung around with. He laughed as he thought of them puttering around on their poxy little 250's. At nineteen, with a stable-job as a garage attendant and, most importantly, the bike of his dreams, he was reasonably content.

There was one thing which bugged him.

She was lying on the sofa now. One leg drawn up provocatively, revealed by the split in her skirt.

Kelly Vincent was a month or two younger than Bob. She'd made quite a name for herself within the confines of Bob's little circle. Most of his mates had shafted her at one time or another.

Bob seemed to be the only one who hadn't. She hung around with them, she said, because she liked the motorbikes. Bob and his mates liked to think it was for other reasons. After all, as the others had told him, she was a right little nympho. She'd do anything. Even take it in the mouth.

Just the thought made Bob break into a sweat. He stood behind the sofa for a moment, watching her, running his eyes up and down her body: the long, curly hair and full lips, eye make-up which looked as though it had been applied with a trowel. She wore a tight fitting red blouse, undone to the third button.

Just far enough to stretch the imagination and whet the appetite. She wore no stockings but her legs were smooth and shapely. As he watched, she scratched the inside of her thigh, revealing just a hint of white knicker.

She looked up and saw him standing there.

'Are you going to stand there all bloody night?' she said.

Bob shook his head and hurried round to join her. She raised her head so that he could sit, then she rested it in his lap. He felt a warm thrill run through him and tried to control the erection which threatened to run riot at any minute. Bob glanced up at the TV screen. There was some crap on about the war. Kelly's old man was always on about the war. Boring old bastard. That was all he ever talked about. Bob hated coming round when he knew Kelly's parents were going to be there. But tonight was different. They were out, possibly for the night. They never moved out of the house usually, that was why it had taken Bob so long to get round to this. His own parents went down the local boozer but he couldn't take Kelly back to his place because his little brothers were always in. Little bastards. He could imagine the cries of derision from them if he arrived home with a girl. They took the piss out of him now which was as much as he could stand. He didn't fancy having one of them walking in while he was shagging Kelly.

But tonight it was going to be different. Her parents had gone to a party. Something like that, he couldn't remember exactly what it was. All that concerned him was, they would be out of the way for a few hours.

He looked around the room. A posh place really, he thought. Fitted carpets, brand new wallpaper, colour television. They even had a stereo. Bob compared it to his own house. The threadbare rugs which barely covered the floor in the living room, peeling wallpaper. The stink of damp which seemed to hang in every room. God he hated his home, but as yet he could see no way out. No respite from the rows between his mother and father, the squabbles with the kids. He didn't earn enough to buy a flat of his own, not even to rent one. Property was scarce in Medworth and he didn't fancy moving out of the town and leaving his mates. Bob realized that he was just going to have to learn to accept things as they were. After all, that was life for people like him. He knew it and he also knew that there was nothing he could do about it. It was like having your life mapped out for you, following the same routes as your parents. Only his route led to a dead end. He tried to push those thoughts to one side and concentrate on the matters at hand. He let his fingers stray to Kelly's breast and he managed a quick squeeze before she knocked it away.

'Get off,' she bleated.

He sighed. He hoped tonight wouldn't be a waste of time. If he didn't get to screw someone pretty soon, his mates would know. They were starting to get suspicious already. Bob shuddered as he thought of their derision if they did ever discover he was still a virgin. Of course he had boasted conquests, as do all young men, but he was getting worried. What would they think of him? Some blokes in his gang had fucked more than ten girls. He hadn't even got as far as kissing one yet. Bob was a master of bravado but his facade was beginning to crack. If he didn't score tonight he'd be a laughing stock.

He slid his hand once more to her breast and, once again, she knocked it away.

He gritted his teeth and a secondary thought passed through his mind. What if he fucked it up? Kelly would be sure to tell his mates. Bob began to become more nervous.

'Get us another drink,' said Kelly, reaching for the cigarette packet on the coffee table beside her.

Bob got to his feet and scurried across to the drink cabinet. He poured a large measure of vodka into Kelly's glass, hesitated a moment, then filled it right up, adding just a touch of lemonade. Perhaps if he could get her pissed it would improve his chances. He poured himself another beer and returned to the sofa.

She blew a stream of smoke into his face and giggled.

He waved it away with his hand and tugged on her hair. She squirmed.

'You bastard,' she said, smiling, 'don't be so rough.'

'I thought you like it rough,' said Bob, trying to sound experienced.

'Who told you?'

'A few people.'

She giggled and took a large gulp of her drink.

'Are you sure your parents aren't going to get back early?' he asked agitatedly.

She put down her drink and slid her arms around his neck, pulling him towards her. He felt her mouth against his, her tongue pressing against his lips. He opened his mouth a little but she pulled away, a grin hovering on her lips.

'You do know how to kiss, I suppose?' The question was heavy with scorn.

He grabbed her, more assured now, pulled her towards him and pressed his mouth to hers, his tongue probing. After a moment he pushed her away.

'That better?' he said, smugly.

She giggled. 'What have your mates told you about me?' she wanted to know.

'This and that,' he said.

'What does that mean?'

He felt her hand on his thigh and he swallowed hard, his penis growing swiftly within the tight confines of his jeans. She noticed the bulge and allowed her hand to stray to it, stroking it through the thick material.

'You like sex,' he told her.

'Who told you?' She giggled again, her movements becoming more urgent.

Bob shuffled uncomfortably, aware of his swiftly growing excitement.

'Your mate Dave,' she began, 'he's got a big cock. One of the biggest I've seen.'

'What are you? Some kind of expert?' he said.

She giggled again. 'I've seen enough to know.'

He felt her hand fiddling with his zip, easing it slowly down and he had to grit his teeth to control himself. She gazed at the bulge in his underpants and smiled, holding it firmly in her expert hand. Then, smiling, she backed off and unbuttoned her blouse. Bob never took his eyes from her large breasts, especially when they spilled forth as she unhooked her bra. The nipples were already erect. Bob didn't think he could control himself much longer, but the thought of what his mates would say gave him that extra bit of control that he needed.

Kelly eased herself out of her skirt and stood before him, just the white of her knickers covering that part which Bob sought so desperately. Through the thin material he could see the dark curls of her pubic hair. Swiftly he whipped off his tee-shirt and flung it to one side, kicking his jeans off simultaneously. For one ridiculous second, he realized that he still had his socks on. Hurriedly he pulled them off and knelt on the floor beside her. She pushed him back and tugged his underpants down, revealing his rampant organ.

At first he thought she was going to laugh, but she nodded admiringly and ran her fingers along the hard shaft, pausing for a moment at the swollen, bulbous tip. Bob closed his eyes. He didn't think he could hold back any longer. He thought about anything to distract him from the sensations. West Ham losing the cup final, death, unemployment.

She stopped stroking him and he relaxed, watching as she removed her own knickers. She lay back, waiting for him. Bob hesitated, the uncertainty returning. What if she did tell the others?

'Well, come on,' she said. 'I mean, you do know what to do?'

He clambered on top of her, trying to force his erection between her thighs.

'Careful,' she said, becoming agitated by his clumsy efforts.

He repositioned himself and tried again. This time she grunted angrily and rolled to one side. 'I don't think you know how to do this,' she chided. 'I think you're a bloody virgin.'

The word stuck in his mind and he could feel himself turning scarlet.

'I know what I'm doing,' he lied, trying to sound forceful.

'Dave knew what to do. He gave me a good fuck. So did Paul.'

'Fuck Dave,' he growled, 'and bloody Paul. I know what I'm doing.'

She rolled onto her stomach and looked away from him. Bob felt the tension growing. He swallowed hard. What were the others going to say? The mouthy little whore was bound to tell them. In a last desperate attempt to save face, Bob grabbed her hips, raising her bottom into the air. Then, with a finesse which he didn't realize he possessed, he slid into her from behind. She moaned pleasingly and pressed back to meet his urgent thrusts.

Bob was ecstatic. He knew it wouldn't be long before he reached his climax but he didn't care. He felt like shouting it out:

"Goodbye, virginity!"

There was a scratching at the front door.

Both of them froze, locked together like some kind of surreal statue.

The scratching came again, louder this time. There were footsteps on the front path.

'Oh God,' gasped Kelly, 'it's my Mum and Dad.'

'I thought you said they were going to be late,' Bob blurted, hastily withdrawing and snatching up his jeans. Both of them pulled on their clothes as best they could, expecting the door to open at any moment and to see Mr and Mrs Vincent standing there. Kelly couldn't begin to imagine their reaction. Bob, gasping for breath, tried to force his erection back inside his jeans while pulling on his t-shirt. In his haste he forgot one sock. Kelly stuffed her knickers and bra beneath a cushion, taking care to remind herself to remove them later.

Finally, the two of them threw themselves back onto the sofa, red in the face, waiting for the door to open.

There was no sound.

'I thought that was them,' whispered Kelly.

Bob exhaled deeply. If he'd lost his chance because of a false alarm he'd leave right now. He began to wonder if it was all a set-up. Were Kelly, Dave and the rest of those bastards he called mates playing a bloody joke on him? The thought stuck out strongly in his mind and, when he saw Kelly begin to giggle, his suspicions were confirmed. He got to his feet, pushing her to one side and made for the door.

'You set this up,' he shouted, 'you fucking scab.'

Kelly shrugged, her grin fading.

'I'm going to kill those wankers when I get hold of them,' he snarled. This was it, this was the bloody limit. He wrenched open the hall door, flicked on the light and tore open the front door.

'Right, you cunts...'

The words were cut off as powerful hands fastened themselves around his throat.

Bob was driven back into the hall, propelled by the force of his assailant. He slammed into the wall, cracking his head and, for a second, everything went black. But he recovered and grabbed for the hands which were throttling him. He caught sight of the face of his attacker and his stomach contracted. The mouth drawn back in a deathly grin to reveal yellowing teeth, the scratch marks and cuts on the cheeks and forehead and, worst of all, the blazing red eyes of Ray Mackenzie.

The pressure on his throat increased and he felt spittle froth on his lips as he fought for breath. Mackenzie had him against the white wall, slamming his head repeatedly against it until the white paper began to sport crimson smudges. Bob knew that he was blacking out. In his last moments of consciousness he saw another man dart towards the living room. He too had those same burning red eyes.

Kelly heard the struggles from the hall and got to her feet, suddenly frightened. She screamed as the thing which had once been Peter Brooks entered the room. The living dead creature fixed her in that red stare and advanced towards her. Kelly screamed Bob's name. He could not help her. Already lying dead in the hallway, his lifeless form was jerked savagely about as Mackenzie tore his eyes from their sockets, ignoring the blood and vitreous liquid which splashed onto him.

Kelly was weeping with terror, big salt tears pouring down her cheeks. But, with a final surge of strength, she leapt for the kitchen door, vaulting the coffee table in the process. The Brooks thing lunged after her and caught her arm, raking it with broken nails. The girl screamed again but shook free and flung herself through the open door, forcing it shut behind her. Even with her back pressed against it, she knew she would never keep Brooks out. He punched at the door, denting it.

Tears clouding her eyes, she scanned the kitchen for a means to defend herself. She had a choice to make and she had to make it fast.

To try and make it to the back door or to grab the carving knife from the drawer beside her. Her mind spun. It would not give her an answer and the indecision brought fresh tears.

She heard the angry roar from the other side of the door and, a second later, Brooks charged, crashing into it shoulder first. The impact knocked Kelly across the room where she smashed into a chest of drawers. Dazed, she clambered to her feet, sidestepping the living dead thing's lunge and grabbing for the carving knife.

Screaming, she brought it down in a swatting action. The heavy blade caught Brooks on the point of the shoulder and sliced away a large chunk of his coat. He grinned and Kelly swung the knife again, this time scoring a line across his cheek. The Brooks thing roared and put a hand to the wound, blood pouring through his fingers and he backed off. Sobbing uncontrollably, Kelly edged her way towards the beckoning back door. Brooks stood still, watching her.

Praying, she dived for the door, finding to her horror that it was locked. In the split second it took her to turn the key, Brooks leapt at her. The two of them crashed to the ground, his weight pinning her. The knife skidded away.

Kelly screamed, again and again until the sound seemed to merge into one unending caterwaul of terror.

She knew she was going to faint.

Mackenzie appeared in the doorway, that familiar feral grin smeared across his face, his hands dripping blood. And beside him stood another man...

Not man so much as youth. Both of them were grinning.

Kelly stopped screaming for a second, the sobs choking away as she turned her head to look at the two onlookers. The first of them tall, his blazing red eyes like those of the thing which held her down. But beside him, and this was what started her screaming again, stood Bob Shaw.

Where there should have been eyes there were just bloody holes, still weeping crimson. Open sores with pits of congealing gore and yet, somehow, he could see her. Somehow he knew. And he was grinning.

Kelly managed one last scream before all three of them fell on her.

Eight more people were killed that night.

Twenty-Three

There was an expectant hush inside the duty room of the Medworth police station.

Outside a light drizzle was falling, casting a haze over everything and spotting the windows of the room. The windows on the inside were steamy and the place smelled of stale cigarettes and coffee.

A blackboard had been set up at the far end of the room and there was a chair in front of it. The leather chairs which normally were dotted around the edges of the room had been drawn up into two rows, and on these chairs sat the ten men who made up the Medworth force. Facing them was Lambert. To his left, on the other side of the blackboard, sat Kirby, his neck still heavily bandaged from his encounter with Emma Reece a week earlier. He pulled irritably at the bandages every so often and sipped at the lukewarm coffee which Sergeant Hayes had given him earlier.

Lambert lit a cigarette and took a drag, finally expelling the smoke in a long stream. He sighed and turned to the blackboard. There were several names written on it in yellow chalk. He turned his back on the waiting men for a second, reading the names and breathing quietly. The knot of muscles at the side of his jaw pulsed. He felt like a schoolmaster. Finally, he turned.

'Twelve people,' he said quietly, 'have disappeared in the last three days. We can't find a trace of one of them.' He hooked a thumb over his shoulder at the blackboard. 'The pattern is the same in every case. All we ever find at the scene is a lot of blood, scraps of clothing if we're lucky, and other little clues. Never any sign of a body, even though all the indications are that there has been a violent struggle.'

The Inspector took another drag on his cigarette, held the smoke in his mouth for a second then blew it out in a long stream. He pointed to the names at the top of the list.

'Bob. Shaw and Kelly Vincent. Reported missing by the girl's parents. We found blood in the hall, in the kitchen, on a knife. The blood matched the known groups of the two missing people. Except the blood on the knife. That belonged to a third party, I'll explain more about that at the end.' He pointed to the second name. 'Ralph Stennet. Attacked on his way across a field after leaving a pub. Reported missing by his wife.' Lambert scanned the faces of the watching men. 'Who found the evidence on this one?'

Constable Ferman raised a tentative hand. Lambert nodded.

Ferman coughed, coloured slightly and began. 'I visited the pub where Stennet was last seen and then followed a set of footprints which I thought to be his, across a field. I found blood.' He swallowed hard. 'Lots of it.'

Lambert nodded, and pointed out the next on the list.

'Janice Fielding. Attacked in her own back garden.' He exhaled deeply, finally turning his back on the blackboard. 'There's no point in going on. As I said before, it's the same in every case. The victims are attacked, from the evidence we found, badly assaulted, and then they disappear.' He looked from face to face. 'Any theories?'

A muted silence greeted his enquiry.

'Guv.' It was Hayes. 'You said something about the blood on the knife in the first case belonging to a third party. What do you mean?'

Lambert almost smiled. 'What I'm going to tell you now will probably confirm some suspicions which a few of you have had ever since you've known me. Namely, that I'm a lunatic.'

A ripple of laughter ran around the room.

The Inspector paused, searching for the words. 'Well, maybe that's right. In this case I wish it was.' All the humour had left his voice, his tone now flat, clinical and the men in the room sensed it too.

'The blood on that knife belonged to Peter Brooks.'

There was a moment's stunned silence. Someone laughed, the sound choked off abruptly. No one knew what to say. Hayes found the words.

'But, guv, Brooks is dead.'

Lambert nodded almost imperceptibly and motioned towards Kirby.

'Doctor Kirby,' he continued, 'who, you can see, suffered some injuries the other night, will verify the fact that it was Brooks' blood on the knife.'

Kirby nodded and, as the men watched, he slowly began to unravel the bandage around his neck, finally revealing the scars and bruises beneath. The area around his Adam's apple and below the ears was a patchwork of black and purple welts and angry scabs.

'Jesus Christ,' murmured P.C. Briggs.

'The doctor's attacker was Emma Reece, Mackenzie's third victim. Father Ridley, who was found hanging from the bell rope of his own church with both eyes torn out, was murdered by Ray Mackenzie.'

The watching men were silent. They heard but could not, dare not, believe.

'All the attacks which have taken place over the last three days,' said Lambert flatly, 'have been carried out by people who were thought to be dead.'

That was it. As simple as that. Lecture finished. Lambert dropped his cigarette butt and ground it into the carpet. He exhaled slowly, as if the movement was painful.

'I don't believe it,' said Constable Davies, flatly. 'It's impossible.'

'It happened, man,' shouted Lambert. 'Look at the marks on his neck.' He pointed to Kirby, his temper now gone. 'They were put there by a woman who'd been buried three weeks before.' He gritted his teeth, his breath coming in short, rasping hisses.

Davies lowered his voice a little, some of the cynicism draining from it. 'Where is she now?'

'She's dead. I cut her head off with a spade.' Lambert raised a hand to his head and ran it through his hair. He exhaled deeply. 'These... things, whatever they are, they're strong.' He could say no more. Kirby stood up, seeing that the stress of the situation was beginning to affect Lambert.

'The Inspector and I exhumed the body of Emma Reece; that was when the attack took place,' he said. The doctor smiled weakly at Lambert who nodded and began again.

'At the moment we don't know how many of them there are. The fact that the corpses of each victim disappear would seem to indicate...'

Hayes cut him short. 'But how can you be sure that these people have been killed if we've found no bodies?'

'I'm assuming, Vic,' said Lambert, calmly. 'Assumptions are the only thing I've got at the moment. Assumptions and twelve missing people.' There was a long silence, then the Inspector continued, 'As I said, there's every reason to believe that the missing victims are now in the same condition as Mackenzie and Brooks.'

'Does that mean they're alive, sir?' said P.C. Briggs.

'I don't know what it means,' said Lambert.

'Alive, undead, living corpses.' He slammed his fist against the blackboard and growled, 'This case gets more insane the closer you look at it.'

'Are you discounting the theory of body-snatching?' wondered Hayes.

Lambert's reply was emphatic. 'Yes. After what happened with Emma Reece, there's no question of it having been that.'

The men shuffled uncomfortably in their seats and an almost palpable silence began to fall over the room.

'Any questions?' said Lambert.

'Do we get any help on this, guv?' asked Hayes.

Lambert shook his head.

Hayes looked put out. 'But surely H.Q....'

Lambert interrupted, 'And what the hell am I supposed to tell them? Please could I have some reinforcements here as we've got several living corpses walking around? They'd find me a nice cell with padded wallpaper.'

A ripple of nervous laughter broke up the tension. It quickly vanished as Lambert continued. 'No. For the time being, it's up to us. Now, these things only seem to come out at night which gives us a bit of breathing space at least. I want full patrols tonight, no man walking a beat is to be alone. Radio in if you see anything suspicious. Don't go near one of them alone. Understand?'

The men nodded. Lambert stood for a moment, trying to think if there was anything he'd left out. Finally deciding that there wasn't, he dismissed the men. As they filed out he heard young Briggs mutter to Walford, 'It's like something out of a horror film,' and he guffawed as he said it.

'I wish it was,' Lambert called after him, then, softly, 'I wish to God it was a bloody film.' He turned to Kirby, 'There's always an expert in a horror film, isn't there? You know, some smart-assed bastard who knows how to deal with things like this.' He almost laughed.

Kirby shook his head. 'Let's not get too paranoid about it, Tom.'

Lambert looked at him for a second, then he headed for the door. When he reached it he turned. 'I'll stop being paranoid when all this is over.' He walked out, leaving Kirby sitting alone in the room gently rubbing the scars on his neck.

Lambert drove home slowly that night, taking a route directly through the centre of Medworth, something which he usually avoided doing. He didn't know why, but the sight of people milling about the town centre reassured him. He drove in silence, not bothering to switch on the radio. He had enough on his mind as it was. The clock on the Capri dashboard showed five o'clock and the shops were beginning to close. Dusk hovered on the horizon, a portent of the darkness which would envelope the land in the coming hours. Lambert wondered what this particular night would bring with it. More deaths perhaps? He pushed the thought to one side and brought the car to a halt at a crossing. He tapped agitatedly on the wheel as the two women crossed, nodding affably to him. He lifted a weary hand in acknowledgement and drove on.

A motorcycle passed him, the driver wearing no crash helmet. Ordinarily, the Inspector would have driven after the youth and maybe even cautioned him, but this particular evening he let the incident pass. He watched as the bike roared away out of sight.

The drizzle which had blanketed the town for most of the day had finally given way to heavier rain and, as large spots of moisture began to splatter the windscreen, Lambert flicked on his wipers. The rubber arms swept away the rain, momentarily blurring his field of vision. By the time he reached home, it was pouring down. He locked the car door and bolted for the house, careful to remove his shoes when he got into the hall. He stood there for a moment then swiftly slid both bolts across, securing the door. Satisfied, he walked into the living room. The smell of cooking beef wafted out of the kitchen to greet him.

'Jack the Ripper's home,' he called, reaching for the local paper.

'Oh good, I thought it might be someone dangerous,' Debbie called from the kitchen.

Lambert took off his jacket and draped it over the back of his chair, his eyes fixed to the column of newsprint beside the headline. The policeman sat down and scanned the small article headline Police Baffled Over Disappearances.

'That bastard,' he snarled and threw the paper down.

Debbie appeared in the doorway. 'What's wrong?' she asked.

'Have you seen the local?' said Lambert, motioning to the discarded paper on the coffee table. 'That bastard Burton, I told him not to mention this in the paper. He's called me three times in the past week to ask what's going on. I said I'd issue a statement when the time was right.'

Debbie picked up the paper and read the short column which told of the disappearances of a number of people in Medworth. No names mentioned, though.

'It doesn't seem to give too much away, Tom,' she said.

'That's not the point,' snapped Lambert. 'I told him. Nothing to be printed until I found out what was going on. It's bloody scare mongering, that's all it is. If people read this it won't make the investigation any easier.'

'It'll get round by word of mouth,' said Debbie, returning to the kitchen. 'People are talking about it now.'

'What people?' Lambert wanted to know.

'Come on, Tom, it's a big talking point in the town. After all, it's the most exciting thing that's happened here for years.'

'I'd hardly call five murders and twelve disappearances excitement, would you?' He sighed. 'Christ, if they knew the truth they'd shut up.'

He flicked on the television and watched the news. The same old stuff. Strikes, Government upsets, the usual batch of robberies and murders. He picked up the local newspaper and read the column again, wondering if Detective Chief Inspector James Baron had seen it. If he had, it would be odds on he'd be on Lambert's back the following day wanting to know what was happening. The Inspector dropped the paper again. How the hell was he supposed to explain if Baron did call? Debbie's shout to tell him that dinner was on the table interrupted his chain of thought and be trudged out into the kitchen and sat down. He ate in silence for a time with Debbie watching him. 'I had a lovely day, thank you dear,' she said, sarcastically. 'Oh did you, dear, fine.'

Lambert looked up and smiled. 'Sorry.'

'Welcome back to planet Earth,' said Debbie, softly.

'I was thinking,' he said.

'You always are.'

'I mean, what do you call this? This state that Mackenzie and Brooks are in? How do you rationalize what Kirby and I saw the other night?'

'You can't rationalize it, Tom. It happened, that's all there is to it.'

'But, Mackenzie. I mean to say, it's not life after death in the sense we know it. It's living death. He's dead but he's walking around.' Lambert began to laugh, quietly at first and then more heartily. Debbie swallowed hard as she watched him. He smiled and shook his head, the spasm subsiding.

'I think I'm going insane,' he said, looking at her. 'None of this can be happening. Things like this only happen in bad horror films.' His tone darkened once more. 'And yet I saw Emma Reece get up out of that coffin. I saw her attack Kirby, I felt her strength. I saw that, Debbie. My eyes saw something which my mind can't accept. I saw a dead man walk.' He pushed his plate away from him and rested his head on his hands which he had clasped before him.

'Do you think I'm insane?' he asked.

She shook her head.

'What's happening now, it goes against everything I've ever believed in. Right from the start of your training, they teach you to keep an open mind about things. Never make hasty decisions, Always weigh up all the evidence before making your judgement.' He smiled humourlessly. 'The trouble is, I've made up my mind. All the evidence points to something which, by all the laws of nature, is impossible. The dead are coming back to life.' He paused. 'All those who are victims, in turn, become living dead themselves. Even Brooks, Mackenzie killed him in the fall.'

'But what about the first two victims,' asked Debbie, 'and Father Ridley?'

'June and Michelle Mackenzie were cremated. Ridley died of a heart attack. He wasn't actually killed by the living dead. It's only those who are murdered by them that return.'

'Like vampires,' said Debbie, flatly. 'Their victims always become like them.'

Lambert shook his head. 'This is different. There's a pattern, a reason for it. It's almost as if there's a force behind it. Something more powerful than the creatures themselves. Something... something that's guiding them.' He rubbed his chin. 'There's a key somewhere, Debbie, a key that will give us the answer. It's just a matter of finding it. I hope to God I can find it in time.'

The phone rang. Debbie got up but Lambert waved her back.

'I'll get it,' he said.

He walked wearily into the living room and picked up the receiver.

'Hello.'

The line was crackly, thick with static and he repeated himself.

'Inspector?' he heard through the hissing. 'It's Trefoile.'

Lambert perked up. 'What have you got?'

'It might be easier if you come to the shop,' said the antique dealer, shouting to make himself heard above the roar of static. 'I was right about...'

The phone went dead.

'Trefoile!' Lambert flicked at the cradle. There was no sound. Nothing. The Inspector repeated the antique dealer's name.

He held the silent receiver in his hand for a second then gently replaced it on the cradle. His forehead was heavily creased.

'Who was it?' asked Debbie.

'Trefoile,' he told her, then he added, more urgently, 'Come on, let's go.'

She looked bewildered. He explained that they were to visit the antique shop immediately and, from the force with which he gripped her hand, she knew it must be important. Grabbing their coats, they hurried out to the car, and in minutes were speeding towards the shop. Lambert could feel his heart thumping faster as he drove and he pressed down just that little bit harder on the accelerator. .

'A key.' His own words echoed in his mind.

Was the medallion the key?

He thought of the phone going dead and shuddered. Perhaps his imagination was running away with him, but, as he swung the car into the main street of Medworth, he prayed that Trefoile would be the only one waiting for them in the antique shop.

Lambert stopped the car and the two of them sat for a moment, watching the sign above the door which was swinging back and forth in the wind. The shop was in darkness, not a light to be seen anywhere. Lambert scanned the other shops along the street. Many had residential flats above and, in most of these, lights were burning. Trefoile's shop, though, was a stark contrast and the Inspector felt an involuntary shudder run through him as he opened the car door. Debbie moved too, but he put a hand on her arm and shook his head.

'Stay here,' he said, softly, reaching for the flashlight on the parcel shelf. He flicked it on, testing the beam, and then stepped out onto the pavement. Debbie leant across and locked the door behind him, watching as he walked briskly to the front door of the shop. Lambert's anxiety was beginning to reach her and she anxiously scanned the street from end to end. Not a living soul to be seen. The light from the dull yellow of the streetlamps reflected back from the wet pavement like pools of liquid gold. The rain bounced hard against the car roof, beating out a tattoo.

Lambert knocked twice on the front door and, when he received no answer, tried the handle.

It opened.

He held up a hand to Debbie to signal that he was going in. She watched as he closed the door behind him.

He flicked on the flashlight and swung it back and forth across the room, aware of the musty smell of the place.

Two gleaming eyes shone at him from a corner and he gasped, suddenly angry with himself as he saw that they belonged to the head of a stuffed fox. He walked behind the counter towards the back room which served as a dining room, workshop, and kitchen

'Trefoile,' he called.

No answer. Lambert reached for the light switch to his right and flicked it down. Nothing happened. He tried again. The darkness remained. His beam picked out a plate of unfinished mince lying on the table beside it was a large book which, upon closer inspection, was revealed as a ledger of some sort. He walked to the back door and tugged at the handle. It was firm, the door securely locked and bolted. The Inspector swung the light around once more and found that there was a door which led out of the room. It was ajar. He crossed to it and cautiously peered round, shining the beam inside. It illuminated a narrow flight of steps which led up into even more impenetrable darkness.

'Trefoile,' Lambert called again, suddenly, and for no discernable reason, wishing he was armed.

Again he received no answer and, slowly, he began to ascend the staircase, finally reaching a small landing which had two doors leading off from it. He shone the flashlight onto each one in turn then made for the nearest one. He opened it quickly and found himself looking into a cramped toilet and bathroom. He closed the door and walked towards the second room.

Something moved above him.

Lambert froze, the breath trapped in his lungs. He shone the beam upwards and saw a trapdoor which he assumed led up into the attic.

Another movement. Heavy footsteps from above. He edged back towards the head of the stairs, beam pointed at the trapdoor as if it were a weapon. He wished it were a gun he was holding.

The trapdoor opened and Lambert stepped down one stair. Copper he might be, hero he wasn't. If there was something in that bloody attic he didn't intend tackling it alone.

A face appeared in the opening.

It was Trefoile. He smiled affably. Lambert exhaled deeply and almost laughed.

'Bloody fuse blew,' the antique dealer explained. 'I don't know why the hell they had to put the box up here. Won't be a moment.' With that, he disappeared back into the attic and, a second later, the place was bathed in welcoming light.

The antique dealer jumped expertly from the attic and brushed himself down. He smiled at Lambert and said, 'The phone call, it was about the medallion.'

'I thought it might be,' said the Inspector. He explained that Debbie was waiting in the car.

'Bring her in,' said Trefoile. 'We'll have a cup of tea. I think she'll be interested in what I've found too.'

The three of them sat in Trefoile's back room with cups of tea before them. Lying on the table were two huge, leather-bound books. Their pages were yellowed and crusty with age, and one had gold leaf words upon its cover, written in Latin.

Between them lay the medallion.

'As I said to you before, Inspector, this is a most remarkable piece of work,' said Trefoile, prodding the circlet with the end of his pen. 'I sent it to a friend of mine who works in a museum and he verified the fact that it was sixteenth century. He couldn't pinpoint the exact time though.'

'That doesn't matter,' said Lambert, reaching to his coat pocket for his cigarettes.

'You may remember me telling you,' began Trefoile but he broke off as he saw Lambert lighting up the cigarette. 'Would you mind not smoking, please, Inspector? My father never did like it in the house. You understand.'

Lambert shrugged and looked for somewhere to stub out the freshly lit cigarette. Trefoile took it from him and dropped it into the sink where it hissed.

'Sorry,' said the antique dealer, returning to the table.

Debbie suppressed a grin.

Trefoile continued. 'As I was saying, I did mention to you when you first showed me the medallion that I recalled seeing it somewhere before.'

Lambert nodded, watching as Trefoile flipped open the first of the mammoth volumes. He found what he wanted and turned the book so that Lambert and Debbie could see the picture he was indicating. It was an early woodcut of the medallion. Beneath it was a caption in Latin which Lambert pointed to.

'What does it mean?' he asked.

'It doesn't mean anything,' Trefoile said, enigmatically. 'It's a name.'

Lambert read it again, the letters standing out darkly against the yellowing paper.

Mathias.

'I still don't get it,' said the policeman, a slight edge to his voice.

'Mathias was the owner of the medallion. That very medallion which came into your possession.' He paused, watching' their reaction carefully to his next words.

'Mathias was a Black Magician. Said, at the time, to be the most powerful ever known.'

Lambert snorted. 'So you're telling me that this,' he poked the medallion, 'belonged to a witch?'

'A Black Magician,' repeated Trefoile, 'a High Priest if you like, a Druid. Does it matter what the name is? It all amounts to the same thing.'

There was a moment's silence then the Inspector said, 'What about the inscriptions? Could you decipher them?'

Trefoile sighed. 'The one across the centre of the medallion was pretty simple. It means Deathday.'

Lambert shrugged. 'The other one?'

'That was trickier, much trickier. You see, it's not like the central one. The inscription around the outside of the medallion is written in reverse.'

'A sort of code?' asked Lambert.

The antique dealer nodded. 'When the letters are transposed, that's when it begins to make a bit of sense.' He pushed the gold circlet towards Lambert, pointing out the letters with the tip of his pen. 'These two words,' he wrote them down on a pad, 'as

they are, make no sense. Transposed, they read REX NOCTU.'
He paused. 'It means, King of the Night.'

'What about the other words?' Lambert demanded.

Trefoile swallowed hard: 'Inspector, don't think me a fool, a coward even, but, if I were you, I'd get rid of this thing now.'

'Why, for Christ's sake?'

'Because it's evil.'

Lambert half smiled. 'Evil.'

'Take these books,' said Trefoile, 'you'll find your answers in there. I want no part of this.'

The Inspector's expression changed when he saw how pale the antique dealer had become. The older man's hands were shaking visibly as he wiped a bead of perspiration from his forehead.

'Trefoile,' he said, 'what the hell is it with this bloody medallion? It's important. People could have died because of this.'

'Does it have anything to do with what's happening here at the moment?' The question hung in the air.

'What makes you think that?' demanded Lambert.

'As I said, it's evil. I can't help you anymore, Inspector.' Trefoile's voice had dropped to a low whisper. 'Just take the books and go. Please.' There was a hint of pleading in that last word.

Lambert looked stunned. He looked at Debbie and shook his head before gathering up the two books and the medallion. He thanked the antique dealer for his help and told him that they would find their own way out. He nodded abstractedly, gazing into the murky depths of his cup, aware only of their departure by the soft tinkling of the bell over the door, lingering like some unwanted nightmare.

Lambert and Debbie hurried to the car and climbed in, placing the two huge volumes and the medallion on the back seat. The Inspector started the engine immediately and drove off.

'Tom, he was really frightened,' said Debbie, softly.

'Drive me to the library,' she told him.

'Now?'

'We'll need a dictionary to translate the Latin; there's two or three in our reference section.'

Lambert nodded and swung a right at the next junction. As he drove he noted how few people were on the streets. A couple of lads in leather jackets smoking, standing in a shop doorway. One or two in the fish and chip shop but, apart from that, they hadn't seen above five people since leaving the house two hours earlier.

He brought the car to a halt outside the library and both of them got out. Debbie was first up the stairs, fumbling in her jacket pocket for the master key. Cursing the cold weather, she finally found it and there was a loud click as the heavy lock opened. They stepped in, Debbie slapping the panel of switches near the door. The powerful banks of fluorescents blazed and the library was filled with cold white light. Lambert shivered as he followed her through the maze of shelves towards the reference section.

'Don't you have any bloody heating in here?' he said. He passed a radiator and pressed his hand to it, withdrawing it quickly as it singed him.

'Shit,' he grunted. The radiator was red hot.

Yet still he could feel that penetrating cold, an almost palpable chill which encircled him with icy fingers.

Debbie found the dictionaries and hurried out again, turning off lights as she went. Once outside, she locked the door and the two of them hurried back to the car.

Lambert put his foot down and they were home in under twenty minutes. He put the car in the garage while Debbie carried the heavy volumes indoors where she laid them on the coffee table. Once inside, Lambert locked and bolted every door and window in the house then retreated to the comforting warmth of the living room. Debbie already had the books spread open, a notepad by her side.

It was going to be a long job and, as he looked at the first page, Lambert wondered what they were going to find.

The entire book would have to be translated, word for word. They would find one word and, immediately, be forced to look it up in the dictionary. The meaning clear, it would then be transcribed onto a fresh piece of paper.

Lambert looked at his watch as they began. It was eight fourteen p.m.

It took them three hours to do the first page. Outside, the rain lashed down, the darkness covering the town and countryside like an impenetrable blanket.

Twenty-Four

Charles Burton stubbed out his third cigarette and checked his watch against the wall clock above Lambert's desk. He exhaled through clenched teeth and pulled open the office door.

'When the hell is he getting here?' said Burton.

Sergeant Hayes, who was making out a duty roster, looked up and smiled.

'He shouldn't be long, Mr. Burton,' he said.

Burton slammed the door and Hayes raised two fingers at it. Miserable bastard, he thought, and carried on with the roster. Burton had never been a patient man, but, at this precise moment in time, seated in Lambert's office, he was on the point of blowing his top. He'd been waiting for the young policeman for more than thirty minutes and he wasn't going to wait much longer. As editor of Medworth's newspaper, he deserved prompt attention. He never had liked Lambert. Cocky young sod, he thought. Burton, approaching his fortieth year, wondered how someone as young as Lambert had ever been put in charge of the Medworth force in the first place. He was never very cooperative, but, regarding recent events, he'd been downright secretive. Burton was determined to get to the bottom of things. It was his right as a newsman, and the people of Medworth had a right to know too. He resolved not to leave until Lambert had told him what was really happening in the town. Burton checked his watch again. That was if the young bastard ever arrived.

Burton felt quite exhilarated. He'd never had anything quite this big to write about since becoming editor of The Medworth Herald, but what with a number of deaths and disappearances over a matter of weeks, this was something new. Usually it was all jumble sales and tedious local events and he allowed his own meagre staff to deal with those trivialities. But this one he wanted for himself. He didn't trust one of his three reporters to cover it adequately. They'd probably miss some important detail here or there. Besides, Lambert would be able to brush them aside easily. Burton was determined not to be pushed away with excuses and half-baked explanations.

He checked his watch again and lit another cigarette. The room was already heavy with the smell of stale smoke and Burton added to it, blowing out a long stream as he dropped the lighter back into his pocket.

His wife had bought it for him for their tenth wedding anniversary. He half smiled, thinking about her. She'd be at home now, up to her elbows in washing up or vacuuming. She was always doing something. Cleaning up, rearranging the furniture. He wondered if there was a medical term for it. Compulsive house cleaning or something like that. She went mad if he even so much as dropped a speck of ash on the carpet. Out came the Hoover straight away. Burton had put up with it for the first couple of years, but, gradually, her mania for neatness had begun to annoy him. He stayed at the office later each night. She never complained about that, though. As long as their house was neat and tidy, she was happy. He often thought that she wouldn't mind if World War Three broke out tomorrow, as long as the house was in good shape. He stayed out until all hours, boozing, sometimes just driving around, even screwing other women, but when he finally got home, she would never question him. Just peck him lightly on the cheek and ask him if he had a good day.

There was a girl at the moment. She worked as a barmaid in 'The Bell,' a pub on the outskirts of the town. Her name was Stephanie (he called her Stevie) Lawson and, although she had never told him, he guessed her age to be around twenty. Only once did it occur to Burton that he was old enough to be her father and that once was after their first bout of lovemaking. Even the recollection exhausted him. Christ, she was a bloody animal he thought, smiling. She was cooking him dinner tonight at her place. It was her night off and Burton was looking forward to it.

His train of thought was broken as he heard footsteps outside the door.

Lambert walked into the station and smiled at Hayes. He held up two, grimy, oil-covered hands.

'Would you believe it,' he said, 'I had a bloody puncture about ten minutes from home. Changed that, and then found out my oil was low so I had to top up with that too.'

Hayes pointed to the closed door of the office. Lambert looked around.

'You've got a visitor, guv,' said the sergeant.

'Who is it?' asked Lambert, lowering his voice.

'Charlie Burton.'

Lambert sighed. 'Christ, I'd forgotten. How long's he been here?'

'Half an hour.'

Lambert nodded and pushed open his office door. Hayes heard the initial greeting then the conversation was cut off as the door closed once more.

'I've been waiting nearly forty minutes for you,' said Burton, irritably.

'Sorry,' said Lambert, smiling, 'I had a blow out.'

He crossed to the sink in one corner of the room and began scrubbing his hands.

'You said nine o'clock,' persisted the newsman.

Lambert gritted his teeth. 'I can't help it if my bloody car gets a flat, can I?' he said, drying his hands. He turned to face Burton, wondering why he ever agreed to meet the man in the first place. If Burton disliked the Inspector then the feeling was more than mutual. Lambert tried to be pleasant. Smiling, he sat down.

'What can I do for you?' he asked.

'You know what I want,' said Burton, impatiently. 'Some information about what's been going on around here during the last few weeks.'

'I told you over the phone that no information would be given until the investigation was over.'

'That's bullshit,' snapped Burton. 'You said there would be press releases.' He emphasized the last two words with scorn. 'Some sort of statement and yet every time me or one of my reporters rings up, you're either not here or you won't tell us anything.'

Lambert picked up a pen which was lying on his desk and began toying with it.

'Like I said,' Lambert said softly, 'I don't want any of this in the papers until the investigation is over.'

'Any of what, for Christ's sake?' said Burton, angrily. 'Just what is going on, Lambert? People have a right to know.'

'It's classified.'

'Don't give me that shit. Come on, divulge.'

Lambert sat forward in his chair, the pen pointing at Burton.

'Look, Burton, none of this has anything to do with you or your blasted paper. If I say there'll be no information given about this case, then that's how it'll be.'

Burton smiled cryptically. 'You're a jumped up little bastard, Lambert, you know that? Just who the hell do you think you are?'

'I'm the law. Who are you? Some glorified bloody paper boy who wants to find out some details so he can stick them in the local rag. I told you, there'll be no info given on this case until it's all wrapped up.'

'So what's all this crap about "Police statements"?' the newsman demanded.

'You'll get them in time,' Lambert told him.

Burton laughed. 'I know why you won't tell me anything. It's because you can't. You don't know what the hell is going on either. Lambert, you couldn't figure out a fucking crossword puzzle, let alone what's happening here.'

'It's police business. It's none of your concern.'

'People are dying, disappearing in this bloody town. We all have a right to know what's being done about it.'

Lambert reached into the drawer of his desk and pulled out a copy of the previous night's paper. He hurled it down.

'You don't have a right to print that,' he snarled, pointing to the column headed, 'Police baffled over disappearances.' 'And, another thing, if you print anything else about this case without my say so, I'll close your fucking paper down.'

'You bastard.'

'Welcome to the club,' said Lambert, angrily.

The two men regarded each other for a moment, the tension between them almost visible. Then Lambert said:

'I mean it, Burton. I want all details, all speculation, kept out of the paper.'

The newsman was unimpressed but, his tone softened slightly.

'Off the record, what is going on?'

Lambert smiled at him. 'Off the record?'

Burton sat forward eagerly.

The Inspector pressed his fingertips together and sat back in his chair. 'I don't know.'

'Come on, Lambert, I said off the record.'

'I'm telling you,' the policeman continued, 'I don't know.'

'But it is true that twelve people have disappeared during the last couple of weeks?' asked Burton eagerly.

'Where did you get that information?' the Inspector wanted to know.

Burton was losing his temper. 'People talk. That's the only thing they are talking about at the moment. Nothing's happened in this place for fifty years. The biggest event of the year is the bloody Church social. What the hell do you expect them to talk about? It's common knowledge.' He paused, waiting for the Inspector to speak but he remained impassive.

'So, is it true?' he asked again.

'Off the record?'

Burton nodded.

'It's true,' Lambert said, 'but if you print that, I'll have you for disclosure of evidence.'

'What's happened to them?' asked Burton.

'Maybe they just left town.'

'Come on, Lambert, I said this was off the record,' said the newsman, becoming irritable again.

'You want a comment, right?' Lambert said. 'Something to print. An official police statement?'

Burton looked eager, nodding frenziedly.

'All right,' said Lambert, 'got a pen?'

Burton pulled out a notebook, flipped it open and waited expectantly.

'My official statement regarding this case,' began Lambert, 'is simple enough.' He paused. 'No comment.'

'You bastard,' snarled Burton.

Lambert had to fight to suppress a grin as he watched the editor turn scarlet with rage. He stood up, slipping the notebook back into his pocket. The newsman headed for the door, turning as he reached it.

'This case will beat you, Lambert, and I'll be the first one to wave goodbye when they wheel you out.'

Burton had the door half open.

'Hey, Charlie,' called Lambert, half smiling, 'for the record.'

'What?' snapped Burton.

'Fuck you.'

The editor slammed the door as he left. A moment later Sergeant Hayes popped his head round the door.

'Everything all right, guv?' he asked.

Lambert smiled, 'Yes thanks, Vic. Just Mr Burton blowing his top. Nothing to worry about.'

Hayes nodded. 'Anything else, guv?'

Lambert smiled, 'Yes. I could murder a cup of tea.'

Hayes scuttled off to make it, closing the door behind him. Lambert exhaled deeply, his forehead creased heavily. He thought of Debbie, at home at this very moment, trying to decipher the two huge volumes which Trefoile had given them. She had taken a few days off so that she could work on them and perhaps find an answer quickly. Time suddenly seemed very important.

Lambert just hoped that it wouldn't run out for him. Or for the whole town, come to that. He looked out of the window, pleased to see the sunlight.

He was beginning to dread the night.

Twenty-Five

The wind had grown steadily as the evening wore on. As the sun sank, it had been little more than a gentle breeze, but now, just after midnight, it had grown in ferocity to almost gale proportions.

Charles Burton lay in bed listening to the gate slamming repeatedly in the passageway below. The narrow entrance and stone corridor separated the house from the one next door and it was the wooden door at the head of the passage that was being buffeted by the wind. It smashed sporadically into the lintel, each fresh impact jarring Burton and making him more irritable. If it went on much longer he would have to get up and close the bloody thing. It had a latch but the people next door usually forgot to put it on. That was why the door was slamming now.

Burton exhaled deeply, closed his eyes and tried to sleep, but the insistent banging of the gate disturbed him. Finally he swung himself out, pulled on his trousers and slid his sockless feet into his shoes.

'What's up?' croaked Stevie Lawson, sleepily. She looked up and saw, through blurred eyes, Burton trying to zip up his trousers. He caught a pubic hair in the zipper and yelped in pain.

'Shit,' he snarled.

Stevie smiled. 'What are you doing?'

'It's that bloody gate,' said Burton, inclining his head. As if to add weight to his statement, there was an almighty crash as it cracked into the jamb once more.

'They must have forgotten to lock it, next door,' said Stevie, yawning. 'Can't you leave it?'

'It's getting on my nerves,' he snapped, heading for the bedroom door. He pulled it open and fumbled for the landing light which he slapped on.

'Come back to bed,' purred Stevie, allowing the sheet to drop, revealing her breasts. 'Forget about the gate.'

Burton felt a stirring in his groin at the sight of those firm mounds and he almost hesitated, but the gate slammed again and he was off down the stairs.

Stevie heard him open the hall door and blunder through the living room. She rolled onto her back and stretched beneath the sheets. Burton might be getting on a bit, she thought to herself, but he certainly knew how to treat a woman. Their lovemaking had been even more abandoned that night, animalistic almost, and the thought of it made her tingle. She'd hang onto him for a couple more weeks. He bought her flowers and perfume, anything she wanted really. She only had to ask and he'd get it for her. Silly old bastard, she thought. Couldn't he see she was using him? She'd cooked him dinner that night, listened disinterestedly as he'd prattled on about his day's work. She fussed him, teased him, and finally they had climbed into bed. To her it seemed like a fair deal, he got what he wanted from her, she got what she wanted from him. Sometimes it was difficult to tell who was using who. Still, she thought, next time she'd pick up a younger bloke. Burton had the money and he was good in bed, but she wanted someone nearer her own age. He could only manage it twice in a night and sometimes that wasn't enough for her. Her husband had been the same. She almost laughed aloud as she thought of him. Poor old Ron. He'd joined the army a year before they got married. He was a sergeant in the Signals. Out in Ulster at the moment. She'd had no letter from him for over a week. For all she knew, or cared, he could be lying in some Belfast gutter with an I.R.A. bullet in him. He usually wrote to her once a week to ask how she was, how the family was, and his little joke at the end, to make sure that she was behaving herself. Ha bloody ha, she thought. Dutifully she wrote back, always telling him that she missed him and couldn't wait for him to get home. She smiled to herself. Fucking idiot he was, probably believed her too. She was toying with the idea of moving away from Medworth. It was boring. She wanted to see some life. Ron was happy there, but, of course, he never did have any ambition. London was the place for her. The nightlife. The men. Beneath the sheets she ran both hands over her body, satisfied that she would have no trouble finding someone dumb enough to keep her if she ever should make the trek down there. Any bloke, anywhere, would give his right arm to have her. She was one of that rare breed of women who were not only aware of their good looks but also knew how to use them to get what they wanted. She heard Burton open the back door and wished he would stop farting about and hurry back to bed. She was beginning to feel horny again.

The wind hit him like a cold hammer when he opened the door and the newsman shivered, wishing he'd put on a coat. He stepped out into the darkness and hurried around the corner to the passage. Peering up it, he could see the gate slightly ajar. As he started towards it, a gust of wind blew it shut; plunging the passage and back yard into total darkness. Burton placed his hands on one wall and groped his way towards the door.

He cracked his leg on something which was standing in the darkened passage.

'Jesus,' he groaned, rubbing his injured shin. The object which he'd collided with was a motorcycle. The lad who owned it lived in the next house and he always put it in the passage on bad nights. Burton cursed under his breath and edged past the bike. He reached the gate just as a gust of wind sent it hurtling back. It slammed into the rear wall with a loud thud and momentarily gave the newsman a view of the street outside. All the lamps were out. It was like a bloody coal mine out there. Burton thought he saw something move at the end of the pathway which led out from the gate, but he dismissed it and fumbled with the latch on the gate, finally dropping it into place and tugging on the metal handle to ensure that the wind wouldn't blow it loose again. Satisfied, he turned and groped his way back down the passage, careful to avoid the motorcycle this time. He edged around the corner into the back yard of Stevie's house and smiled at the sight of light flooding from the open back door. He paused for a moment. He didn't remember leaving the door open when he came out. Burton shrugged. The bloody wind had probably blown that open too.

He heard a scratching sound close by and spun round, trying to make out what it was in the light from the open back door.

A dark shape was moving at the bottom of the garden. Hidden by the large hedge, it was difficult to make it out. The newsman hesitated, squinting into the gloom, trying to distinguish shape from shadow. A particularly strong gust of wind rocked him where he stood and he shivered, bringing both arms up and trying to cover himself while still attempting to make out what exactly was moving about at the bottom of the garden. There was another sound, like that of sticks being broken. Finally, his curiosity getting the better of him, Burton strode off down the garden to find the source of the noise.

Stevie sighed. What the hell was Burton playing at? Surely it didn't take that long to lock a gate? She hadn't heard it banging for the last couple of minutes so she assumed that he had closed it. What the bloody hell was he pissing about at?

She heard footsteps on the stairs and smiled, deciding to play a joke on him. She rolled onto her side, pretending to be asleep. The landing light went off and she heard movement outside the door. She'd frighten the bastard when he came back in. She'd wait until he was leaning right over her then jump up. Stevie suppressed a grin.

Her back was to the bedroom door when it opened.

Burton reached the bottom of the garden, the wind now drowning out all other noises. It gusted around him, roaring in his ears and he began to wish he'd gone straight back into the house. He could hardly see in the darkness and he was freezing but he was determined to find out what it was that was making the scratching noise.

He peered over the top of the hedge, scanning the ground for some sign of movement.

Nothing in sight. He sighed.

Something touched his foot and he jumped back, almost shouting in terror. Controlling the urge to run, he looked down to see a hedgehog scuttling past. It hurried past him and disappeared beneath the wire fence which separated Stevie's garden from the one next door. Burton smiled, amused and angry with himself for his exaggerated reaction. He turned and trudged back towards the house.

He was pleased to regain its warmth and light and he hastily locked and bolted the back door, shivering. Then he made his way back through the darkened house until he reached the hall. Here he paused. The landing light was out, the staircase in darkness. Burton flicked the switch in the hall which also controlled the landing light and the place was illuminated once more. He started up the stairs, slowing his pace as he noticed a strange odour. It reminded him of bad fish and he wrinkled his nose as it became stronger. By the time he reached the landing itself, the stench was almost overpowering. The door to Stevie's bedroom was closed tightly and Burton found that he had to use unexpected force to open it. He stepped inside, reaching for the light switch, the smell now so strong he wanted to vomit. He called her name once and turned on the light.

There were three of them in the room.

Burton froze in the doorway, not quite able to accept what he saw.

The living dead creatures were huddled around the bed like worshippers at an altar, As the light went on, two of them cowered down, trying to hide their blank eyes from the brightness.

Eyes?

It was with mounting revulsion that Burton realized they didn't have any eyes. Just black, empty holes, dark with dried and caked blood.

The third of the trio, a man in his thirties, had one hand on Stevie's face, and the newsman saw that one of his bony fingers was still embedded in her, now empty, eye socket. Blood from the torn cavity had run down like crimson tears, staining the sheets. In other places it had splashed over her chest. He noted the wounds around her throat, the bruising and red welts where she had been throttled to death, the numerous other abrasions on her body where the trio of living corpses had attacked her.

Burton couldn't move. All he could do was shake his head slowly back and forth, his eyes gaping wide at the scene before him. Had his mind been functioning properly he would have realized that it was the light that was keeping the things still, but, in his present state, nothing registered. Just the obscene image of those creatures, crouched around Stevie's body like eyeless vultures.

Then, when he seemed beyond horror, something happened which finally galvanized him into action.

Stevie sat up.

Very slowly she turned her head, the bleeding holes which should have been eyes fixing him in a blazing stare.

She was grinning.

Burton screamed and reached down, his fist closing around a hand mirror which lay on the dressing table beside him. He took a step forward and, with all his strength, smashed it into the face of the first living corpse. The impact shattered the mirror and long shards of razor-sharp glass shredded the man's face. So powerful was the swing, it knocked the thing off its feet and it toppled onto the second of the living dead creatures, a woman no more than twenty-five. The third, another man, leapt across the bed at Burton and grabbed him by the throat. Roaring with rage, the newsman pushed the creature away, bringing his foot up. It connected savagely, just below the ribcage and the thing crumpled up. Burton aimed another kick at its head, gratified by the sound of snapping bone as he shattered a cheekbone with the force of his blow.

He staggered for a second, his mind frozen, filled only with one thought. Hatred for the things that had killed Stevie. But now she was upon him, her sharp nails tearing at his face, raking his cheeks. Aiming for his eyes. He punched her hard, the blow splitting her bottom lip, but she staggered a moment then was at him again. They fell back against the wall, her hands reaching for his throat.

The second creature, the woman, clambered over the bed and joined in the attack and Burton felt more sharp nails tearing at his face. Blood spurted from three deep gashes and he lashed out, catching the creature in the throat. It made a gurgling sound, yellow mucous spilling over its lips but it continued with its attack and Burton now noticed that the second woman too, was grinning.

They were all grinning.

Even the first of them, staggering towards him with splinters of glass protruding from his torn face where the mirror had cut him.

Burton screamed once more and, with a last desperate surge of strength, hurled Stevie away. She toppled over the fallen creature and the newsman bolted for the door, slamming it behind, him and racing for the stairs. The second woman was after him, catching his arm as he reached the top step. He spun around, the momentum of his swing aided by the turn, and slammed both fists into her face. The nose crumbled beneath the impact and bright blood spurted into the air, some of it onto Burton. He grabbed the woman by the hair and hurled her down, watching with something approaching insane joy as she tumbled down the stairs, finally crashing into the table at the bottom. He almost shouted in anguish as he saw her get up, starting towards him once more.

And now the others were spilling onto the landing, all of them sporting that hideous feral grin. Headed by Stevie they lunged at him but he ducked back into the bathroom, slamming the door and sliding the tiny bolt.

One of the living dead men crashed into the door and Burton knew that it wouldn't hold them back for long. His breath coming in gasps, he looked frantically around the tiny room which had become a prison. There was nothing to defend himself with. He couldn't hope to fight off four of them.

There was one chance....

If he could climb out of the window onto the window sill, he might be able to hoist himself up onto the roof of the house. They'd never be able to reach him up there and, even if they did succeed in climbing up, it could only be one at a time. He'd kick the fuckers off as they reached the top.

The bathroom door rocked once more and the bolt began to bend. Burton crossed the room, opened the window and clambered up onto the sill, using the sink as a foothold.

He could hear them moving about outside the room.

Twenty feet below him was a mass of solid concrete and he was thankful he couldn't see it as he scrambled out onto the sill. The powerful wind tugged at him and, for a second, he tottered but he grabbed at the guttering a foot or so above his head and steadied himself. He prayed that it would take his weight.

There was an almighty crash as the bathroom door was smashed in. The living corpses crowded into the room, the first of them rushing to the open window, grabbing for Burton's exposed legs. He shrieked and kicked out at the grasping hand, trying, simultaneously, to hoist himself up. The wind roared in his ears, the hands of the creatures tore at his legs. With almost tired resignation, he realized he wasn't going to make it.

He groaned and tried to pull himself up but the guttering buckled under his weight. For precious seconds it held and he actually managed to hook one leg up onto the slates of the roof, but, with a sickening creak, it gave way.

Burton uttered one mournful cry and plummeted to the concrete below.

The impact broke his back and most of his ribs on the left side, one of which tore through his lung. His head slammed down. Blood burst into his mouth and he sensed a feeling of total awareness before he blacked out. The last thing he saw was the living dead things peering out of the bathroom window, as if, somehow, they could see his shattered body. Even though he couldn't see them clearly, he could sense that they would be grinning.

Twelve more people were to die that night.

Twenty-Six

The night was alive with a kaleidoscope of flashing blue lights as Lambert swung the Capri into Victoria Lane. There were two squad cars and an ambulance, all with their lights spinning, parked in the road outside a house about half way down the street. One of the Pandas was parked on the pavement.

The Inspector rubbed his eyes as he switched off the engine. The clock on the dashboard glowed one-thirty a.m. and Lambert yawned as he stepped out of the Capri and walked hurriedly towards the group of vehicles. There were lights in the windows of houses next door and across the road and he could see people peering out to see just what the hell was going on at this ungodly hour of the morning.

The wind had dropped but there was a biting chill in the air and the Inspector pulled up the collar of his coat, digging his hands deep into the pockets. He recognized Constable Bell, and the policeman smiled grimly as he saw Lambert approach.

'What happened?' asked the Inspector, yawning.

Bell reached for his notebook but Lambert waved it away. 'Just the shortened version,' he said.

'Well, the house belongs to a Mrs Stephanie Lawson, her husband is in the army, he's away at the moment...'

Lambert cut him short. 'I said the short version.'

'Sorry, sir,' said Bell and continued, 'a neighbour rang up about an hour ago to complain about some noises she heard coming from the house. The sarge radioed me and P.C. Jenkins and we came straight over. I knocked on the door but I couldn't get any answer. When I went around the back I found...' he hesitated.

'What?' demanded Lambert.

'A body.'

He was about to walk away when Bell called him back. 'He was still alive when I reached him.'

Lambert nodded.

'Dr Kirby is in the ambulance with him now.' Lambert turned and hurried across to the parked emergency vehicle, its two back doors still open. The Inspector assumed that Kirby must have been summoned at roughly the same time as himself. Hayes had called him ten minutes earlier and told him that there was trouble in Victoria Lane. Now he peered into the ambulance and saw a worried looking Kirby bending over the covered form of a man. There was a red blanket pulled up to his neck but its colour did little to mask the dark stains which had seeped through the thick material in several places.

'John,' said Lambert, climbing up into the ambulance.

'He's dying,' said Kirby flatly.

It was then that Lambert looked down at the prostrate form and saw that it was Charles Burton.

'Jesus Christ,' gasped the Inspector.

At the sound, Burton opened his eyes slightly. When he saw Lambert, they widened to huge orbs, filled with pain and something more. Fear perhaps. The newsman lifted one bloodstained hand towards Lambert and croaked, 'Lambert.' Blood dribbled over his lips and he winced, as if the effort of talking were too much, but he drew in a painful breath and continued. The policeman leant closer.

'What are they?' gasped Burton, his wide eyes fixing the Inspector momentarily in a piercing stare. Then, slowly, he closed his eyes. Lambert looked down at the torn face, the blood-matted hair, a portion of skull shining white amidst the clumps of congealing gore. Kirby pushed him aside and laid his stethoscope on Burton's chest. He felt for a pulse, digging his fingers almost savagely into the wrist. He shook his head angrily.

An ambulanceman appeared in the doorway and looked at Kirby.

'Will you be travelling to the hospital, doctor?' he asked.

'No need,' said Kirby and stepped down, followed by Lambert.

They heard the doors being slammed and, a second later the ambulance pulled away. Its blue light was extinguished. There was no longer an emergency. No hurry to reach the hospital. Not any longer.

Constable Bell appeared again.

'There's blood all over the house, sir,' he said, swallowing.

Lambert nodded. 'What about Mrs Lawson?'

'No sign of her anywhere.'

Bell wandered off again, leaving the two men alone outside the house. Lambert looked up into the dark sky, flecked with hundreds of silver pinpricks of stars. He sighed then looked at Kirby.

'This has gone far enough, John,' he said, flatly. 'We need help.'

Twenty-Seven

Lambert and Kirby spoke little on the journey to Divisional Headquarters in Nottingham. Almost against his better judgment, the Inspector had finally decided that he needed reinforcements to deal with the growing threat which hung over Medworth like some supernatural cloud. He was perspiring slightly although the early morning sun had not yet reached its full power and the last vestiges of dawn mist still hung, wraithlike, in the hollows and woods which dotted the route. There wasn't much traffic on the road and for that Lambert was thankful. He cruised, doing an even fifty for most of the journey, causing Kirby to glance down at the speedometer every now and then. But he said nothing. He too realized the importance of their journey, and as far as both of them were concerned, the sooner it was over, the better.

On the back seat of the Capri was a leather attaché case, filled to bursting point with every detail they could lay their hands on concerning the horrors which had taken place in Medworth over the past month or so. Coroner's reports, backgrounds of victims, what scant details they had of the disappearances (there had been twenty-four up to date) and full reports by Lambert on what was happening.

As they sat in silence, watching the countryside speeding by, both men had the same thought. How the hell were they going to convince Lambert's superiors of the truth of what was going on in the little town?

The journey took less than forty minutes and, at around nine-thirty, Lambert was guiding the Capri through the busy streets of

Nottingham, blasting his horn angrily at a cyclist who hesitated too long at traffic lights. The poor woman was so unnerved by the sudden sound that she nearly toppled off into the path of a passing jeep. Lambert swung the car past her and asked Kirby to check just exactly where they were.

'Take a left at the next crossroads,' said the doctor, running his index finger over the inner city map.

The Inspector obeyed, and within minutes they found themselves in a huge car park which fronted the main building, a massive edifice of glass and concrete which seemed to tower up into the very clouds themselves. Sunlight glinted off the many windows which winked like myriad glass eyes, peering down on the tiny car as the Inspector parked it and they both got out. They walked swiftly across the paved area, Lambert looking in awe at the seemingly endless lines of parked Pandas.

They reached the main entrance and climbed the flight of broad stone steps until a row of wire meshed glass doors confronted him. Lambert pushed the first of these, holding it open for Kirby to pass through. They found themselves in a huge reception area with what looked like a gigantic duty desk at one end. Lambert crossed to it and asked the sergeant on duty where he could find Detective Chief Inspector Baron. The sergeant asked who the Inspector was and Lambert produced his own I.D. card to prove his validity. The sergeant nodded and directed the two men to a lift across the entrance way and told them to take it to the fifth floor.

There was a loud ring as the lift arrived and three uniformed men stepped out, pushing past Lambert and Kirby as if they were in a hurry. The two men stepped into the lift and Lambert jabbed the button marked '5.' There was a humming sound as the lift ascended. It reached five and, with a loud ring, the doors opened. The two men stepped out, feeling the thickness of lush carpet beneath their feet. The corridor was silent, all sounds muffled by the thick cloth on which they walked. At the far end was a desk behind which sat a woman in her thirties. She was reading and, as Lambert drew closer, he could see that the book was called 'Hot Lips.' He suppressed a grin as the woman put the book down and smiled politely up at him.

'Good morning, sir,' she said.

'Good morning,' replied Lambert, 'I'd like to see DCI Baron please. My name is Lambert.' He reached for the plastic card again and showed it to her, 'Inspector Lambert.'

'Just a moment, sir,' she said and flicked a switch on the panel before her. There was a loud buzzing noise and then a metallic voice came through the speaker;

'Yes.'

'Carol. There's a...' she hesitated, looking at the name on the card, '... Inspector Tom Lambert out here. He wants to see Mr Baron.'

'Send him in,' instructed the voice. 'But Mr Baron is busy at the moment, he might have to wait.'

'That's O.K.,' said the Inspector.

The receptionist showed them a door off to the right and the two men nodded as they walked in.

'It's more like a bloody hotel,' said Lambert under his breath, walking into another office. It was decorated in a lemon yellow, the walls hung with a number of paintings. The area to their left was one huge plate glass window through which the early morning sun was streaming, dust particles swirling in its powerful rays. There were five leather chairs along the opposite wall and an ashtray beside each one. At the far end of the room was a desk and, on either side of the desk, a door. As Lambert approached the desk he could see the two names, which were fastened to the dark wood of the doors, in gold letters. The name on the right hand door was Chief Inspector Mark Dayton. The one on the left read Detective Chief Inspector James Baron.

'Inspector Lambert?' said the receptionist, a woman with a round face and large glasses.

Lambert nodded.

'You'll have to wait, I'm afraid. Mr Baron is busy at the moment.'

'How long will he be?'

The woman smiled, an efficient smile practised over the years. 'I can't say for sure, but if you'd like to take a seat I'll send you in as soon as I can.' She motioned to the leather chairs and the two men sat down. The wall clock said nine forty-five. Lambert lit up his first cigarette of the day.

The hands of the clock had crawled on to ten thirty and there were seven butts in the ashtray before Lambert when the buzzer finally sounded and a little red light flared on the panel before the receptionist. She leant forward and spoke into the intercom.

'Yes, sir,' she said.

Lambert heard something babbled but couldn't understand what it was. He gritted his teeth and exhaled deeply. If there was one thing he hated, it was being kept waiting. He ground out his cigarette angrily and looked across at the receptionist who still wore that perpetual grin.

'There are two gentlemen to see you, sir. An Inspector Lambert and...' she looked up, realizing that she didn't know the other man's name.

'Dr Kirby,' he said.

'Dr Kirby,' she repeated.

There were more metallic babblings from the other end and then she nodded and flicked the switch back to 'Off.'

'You can go in,' she said.

'Three bloody cheers,' muttered Lambert. He knocked once and a voice from inside told him to come in. The two men entered the office. It was small, not the grandiose abode which the Inspector had imagined. There were several banks of filing cabinets, a rubber plant on one window sill, and of all things, a tropical fish tank set on a table beside one wall. Baron himself was bending over the tank when the two men entered. He looked up and smiled, extending a friendly hand which they both shook.

'Fascinating things, fish,' said Baron, cheerfully and sat down behind his desk. He pointed to two plastic chairs upon which his visitors seated themselves. So, thought Lambert, this is the great James Baron? The man who had solved more murder cases in this area than he'd had hot dinners? Baron's reputation was a formidable one and well known to all those under him. He'd been a colonel in the Chindits during the war and still bore a scar, running from the corner of his left eye to his left ear, as a legacy of those days. Two broken marriages and countless affairs had charted his rise to the very top of his profession, a position which he intended holding until he retired. Another eight years. There was, Lambert had been told by men who had worked directly under Baron, a feeling of ambivalence towards the man. On the one hand he was respected for his abilities as a policeman, but on the other hand he was hated for his hardhearted cynicism, the latter being something that Lambert was all too aware of as he tried to figure out what he was going to say to his superior. Baron was not a favourite with the media either. His policy of releasing only tiny pieces of information had led to him being regarded as uncooperative and rude. That at least, was something Lambert could respect about him. Baron had been in the force for nearly thirty years and had held the rank of D.C.I. for fifteen of those. During his term in command, the force in that area had undergone a radical change, dealing with troublemakers in a tougher way which had many crying police brutality, But Baron cared nothing for the reactions of the press and television. As far as he was concerned he was there to do a job and he would do it as he thought best and the way he could best achieve results.

Now, as he sat back in his seat, Lambert studied this powerful man. Well preserved for his age and, considering the responsibilities which he carried, remarkably untouched by the rigours of worry. No wrinkles or grey hairs here. Just the slightest hint of a paunch, visible as it strained against the tightly buttoned waistcoat which he wore. His jacket was hung up behind the door along with his overcoat. Neat.

Baron looked at Lambert and smiled.

'Inspector Lambert, eh?' he said, his voice gravelly.

'Yes sir.'

'You're a young man to hold such a responsible position. You must be good at your job.' He smiled warmly. 'Would you like a cup of coffee?'

'Yes, please,' said Kirby and Lambert too, agreed.

Baron flicked a switch on his intercom and spoke rapidly into it, telling his secretary to fetch three coffees. He sat back in his chair once more, hands clasped across his broad chest.

'Which area are you from?' Baron asked.

'Well, we're based in Medworth, but we cover, most of the area round about,' Lambert explained.

'How many men are under you?'

'Ten.'

Baron nodded.

'Married?' he asked.

Christ, thought Lambert, it's like a bloody interview.

'Yes, sir.'

'And you doctor?' Baron wanted to know.

Kirby shook his head. 'No, I'm still a free agent.'

'And quite right too,' said Baron laughing. 'They're more trouble than they're worth, women.'

The other two men laughed nervously. There was a knock on the door and the coffee arrived. Carol set it down on the edge of the desk and left. The three men helped themselves to milk and sugar and Baron sat back in his chair, stirring slowly.

'Well, Inspector, what exactly can I do for you?' said the older man. 'It must be important for you to come all this way.'

Lambert and Kirby exchanged brief glances and the Inspector coughed nervously. He put his coffee cup on the corner of the desk.

'I need your help, sir,' he said. 'I need some of your men.'

Baron took a sip of his coffee and regarded Lambert over the rim of the cup.

'Why?' he wanted to know.

Lambert opened the attaché case and fumbled inside until he found what he was looking for. It was a photograph of the body of Father Ridley, hanging from the bell rope. Baron took it and studied the monochrome print, his eyes coming to rest on the damage done to Ridley's face. He nodded gently, looking at the second photo which Lambert handed him. It was of Emma Reece.

'Both the work of the same person?' mused Baron, his gaze settling on the torn eye sockets of both victims.

Kirby reached for two of the manila files in the case with Lambert watching him anxiously.

'The marks on the bodies of the first victims match those on the bodies of the latest ones,' said the doctor, pushing the files towards Baron.

The D.C.I. peered briefly at the files, shaking his head.

'Twenty-four people have disappeared inside a month,' Lambert told him. 'We can't find a trace of them. All we ever find at the scene of the assault is lots of blood.'

'That proves nothing,' said Baron flinging the files back onto the desk.

'People don't just disappear,' said Lambert, his voice rising in volume, 'there's a pattern to it.'

Kirby pointed to the marks on his neck.

'These wounds were inflicted by a woman who had been buried for over a week.' There was a long silence as Baron regarded the two men suspiciously.

'You're both bloody crazy,' said Baron, smiling.

'Sir, for God's sake, can't you at least offer an explanation? We've tried every possible avenue to find a plausible answer. There is not a plausible answer,' said Lambert, barely able to control himself.

Kirby returned to the wounds on his neck. 'This woman attacked me. She rose from the grave and attacked me. I was as sceptical as you until that happened but I'm telling you, I was attacked by a living corpse.'

There was a moment's silence, during which time Baron's smile faded. He leant forward, his voice now hard-edged and emotionless.

'Now you listen to me, both of you. I'm a busy man, I've got lots of responsibilities and I haven't got the time to sit around listening to two raving lunatics trying to tell me that they've got a town full of living corpses.' He pointed a stern finger at Lambert. 'If you were a man off the street I might find this whole thing amusing. But you're not, you're an Inspector in Her Majesty's Police force and, listening to what you've just told me, you make me wonder how you ever got past the cadet stage, let alone become an Inspector.' The older man's face was going scarlet with rage. 'How old are you, Lambert?'

'Twenty-two,' he replied, the fury likewise building within himself. He felt like dragging Baron across the desk, strapping him in the car and driving him back to Medworth to leave him at the mercy of the things which roamed the town at night. Perhaps then the old sod would begin to understand.

'Well, when you've been in this bloody game as long as I have perhaps you'll have the sense to keep your idiot fantasies to yourself instead of wasting my time with them.'

Lambert clenched his teeth, the knot of muscles at the side of his jaw pulsing angrily. He gripped the sides of his chair until he threatened to tear them loose.

'All I want is half a dozen men to back up my boys,' he said quietly, the anger seething behind his words.

'Forget it,' snapped Baron, returning to his coffee and looking out of the window as if the two men didn't even exist.

'We can't manage on our own,' snarled Lambert, his voice rising in volume.

Baron swung round. 'Get out of here before I have you both thrown out,' he shouted.

Kirby gathered the photos and files and dropped them into the case.

The D.C.I. hadn't finished: 'Another thing, Lambert. If I hear anything more about this... ridiculous affair, if I see anything in the paper about it, I'll tell you this now, sunshine, within a week, you'll be back walking a damned beat.' He paused a second: 'Now get out before I have you both locked up.'

Lambert hesitated. 'All right, if you won't give us men at least give us guns.' That was it. The words hung in the air. Make or break.

Silence reigned supreme in the sunlit office. There was a high pitched squeaking sound as Baron leant forward in his chair. The Inspector wasn't sure whether or not a smile was hovering on his lips, and when he finally spoke, his tone was soft, gentle even.

'You know something, Lambert, you really have got nerve, haven't you?'

Lambert swallowed hard. 'The guns sir. Please.'

Another long silence followed then. Baron reached forward and flicked a switch on his intercom.

'Carol,' he said, 'have Dayton come in, will you?'

He sat back again, gazing at the two men who stood before him like naughty children in front of an angry headmaster. A second later the door to Barton's office opened and Chief Inspector Mark Dayton walked in.

'You wanted something, guv?' he said, without looking at either Lambert or Kirby.

'Take Inspector Lambert here down to the basement. Issue him with all he wants.'

Dayton looked puzzled, he raised one eyebrow and looked quizzically at the two men then he said, 'Come on, follow me.' The trio turned but, as they reached the door Baron called:

'Lambert.'

The young Inspector turned. 'Sir?'

Baron's voice was low, soft with menace. 'If this turns out to be bullshit, I'll have your fucking head.'

Lambert closed the door gently behind him. 'Cunt,' he muttered under his breath and hurried off to catch up with Kirby and Dayton who were already half way down the corridor.

Dayton leant up against one corner of the lift as it dropped the six floors to the basement. He regarded the men opposite him with indifference. Lambert guessed that the policeman must be ten, perhaps fifteen years older than himself. Dayton was tall but in an ungainly way and his feet seemed to have been designed for someone much smaller than him. That would probably account for his shuffling walk. He had thick eyebrows which snaked upwards giving him a look of perpetual surprise.

The lift came to a halt and the doors slid open. Both Lambert and Kirby were immediately taken aback by the overpowering smell of oil and cordite, an odour which the Inspector rapidly recognized as gun oil.

They walked across the stone floor of the basement, their footsteps echoing on the hard surface and the sounds reminded Lambert of an underground car park. They came to a heavy iron gate which Dayton unlocked. He ushered them in.

The room was small but all four walls held racks which sported row upon row of rifles, shotguns and pistols. There was what looked like a counter over by the far wall and a man in a white smock was cleaning a revolver behind it. He looked up when he saw the trio enter, then looked down again, returning to his task.

'Pete,' called Dayton, 'we want some stuff.'

Peter Baker put down the pistol and nodded. He wiped a hand across his forehead, forgetting it was still smeared with grease, and left a black mark from temple to temple. Lambert looked up at the rows of guns.

'How many in your force?' asked Dayton.

'Ten,' Lambert told him.

'What are they like with weapons?'

Lambert shrugged, 'God knows. I doubt if any of them have even touched a gun let alone fired one. I haven't myself.'

Baker grinned and reached to the rack behind him. He pulled the gun down and handed it to Lambert who was surprised by its weight.

'What is it?' he asked, hefting it back and forth.

'An automatic shotgun,' Baker told him. 'The Yanks call them pump guns.' He looked at Dayton and both men laughed. Lambert couldn't see the joke. He held the gun up to his shoulder and squinted down the sight.

'No need for that,' said Baker, smiling, 'it isn't a hunting rifle. Just make sure you're on target when you pull the trigger and hang onto it tight. Whatever you hit with that won't get up again.'

'Let's hope not,' said Kirby, cryptically.

'With just a bit of practice you'll be able to handle it,' Baker assured him. 'But like I said, hang on tight when you pull the trigger, it's got quite a recoil. You could blow a hole in a house with one of those.'

'Give him ten,' said Dayton.

'What about pistols?' Lambert asked.

Dayton looked aghast. 'Are you planning a commando raid or something? This is England. Not bloody New York.' He shook his head. 'Pete, give him a couple of Browning's too.'

Baker nodded and laid down two automatic pistols beside the stack of shotguns and ammunition.

'Bring your car round to the back of the building,' said Dayton. 'We'll have this lot sent up and you can load it straight in.'

By one that afternoon, Lambert and Kirby were on their way back to Medworth, the guns safely stored in the boot of the Capri. Neither of them spoke.

The Inspector put his foot down, anxious to get back. He had to tell his men what had happened, tell them that from now on they were on their own. He realized too that he and the rest of the small force would have to practise with the weapons if they were to be any use.

He sighed. They didn't even know if guns would stop the creatures. Baker's words passed fleetingly through his mind:

'Whatever you hit with that won't get up again.'

Lambert prayed to God he was right.

PART

THREE

'Hast thou found me,
O mine enemy?'

- 1 Kings; 21:20.

Twenty-Eight

Dawn rose grey and dirty over Medworth and Tom Lambert shivered as he tugged back the bedroom curtains. He stood in the window for a moment, gazing out into the street below. There were one or two people on the street, on their way to work probably. He wondered if they realized what was going on nightly around them. Shaking the thought from his mind he washed and dressed quickly and hurried downstairs, the smell of cooking bacon meeting him as he reached the living room.

Debbie stood over the pan, stirring with a wooden spatula. He kissed her gently on the lips and ran a hand through her uncombed hair before sitting down. There was mail, a couple of letters, but he didn't bother to read them. He glanced briefly at the paper, setting it aside as Debbie laid his breakfast before him.

'How long have you been up?' he asked, taking a mouthful.

'Since about five.'

He looked surprised.

'I couldn't sleep, and besides, I thought I'd try and get a bit further through those bloody books that Trefoile gave us.'

Lambert nodded. He had read through her transcriptions the night before and, although she was almost half way through the huge volumes, nothing of any importance had turned up yet. Anything of note she had ringed in red marker but, as yet, there were precious little pieces of information to be had. However, on one sheet, one of the most recent ones, the name had appeared for the first time. That name which had caused Trefoile so much distress.

Mathias.

Lambert had studied the name over and over again, finally discarding the piece of paper.

Debbie sat opposite him and sipped her coffee. He looked up at her, concern in his eyes.

'Do you think Trefoile was throwing us a line about the medallion?' he said.

'What do you mean?'

'The secret,' he emphasized the words with scorn. 'I wonder if the answer really is in those bloody books.'

'What reason would he have to lie?' asked Debbie, stifling a yawn.

Lambert shrugged. Now it was Debbie's turn to look at him. She warmed her hands around her mug and watched him as he ate. He had come home late the previous night, looking pale and drawn, as if he were in need of a good night's sleep. They had lain together on the sofa while he told her of what Baron had said. How there was to be no help for them, and she had shuddered involuntarily when he had said that. Lambert had received much the same reaction when he told the men at the police station of Baron's words. A feeling of isolation, but something more, foreboding, had greeted the declaration that they were to fight the menace alone. The guns had given little reassurance to most of them; but the older members of the force, Hayes and Davies in particular, had listened to Lamberts words with grim resolution etched on their faces. Both, fortunately for the Inspector, knew how to use guns. Davies had done National Service and Hayes informed them all, to a great peal of laughter, that his father had been a poacher, and consequently he himself had grown up with guns. Upon hearing this, the tension amongst the men slackened off a little. Briggs and Walford, youngsters that they were, seemed anxious to use the weapons and were positively delighted when Lambert announced that they would all have to practise. They must all become proficient with the weapons. It could, he had told them, save their lives. They were probably all out now in the field at the back of the station blasting away at the targets, under the watchful eyes of Hayes and Davies. Lambert had given the other Browning to Hayes, keeping the first for himself.

The sight of the guns frightened Debbie and she shuddered when she thought to what use they were to be put. Even now, the shotgun stood propped up against the far wall of the kitchen, the Browning hanging in its shoulder holster from the back of the chair on which Lambert sat.

He finished eating, leaving sizeable portion on his plate, and pushed the remains away from him. They regarded one another across the table, their eyes locked together like magnets. She finally got to her feet and walked around the table to him, reaching for him. He drew her close, squeezing her hard and he could hear her weeping softly. Lambert swallowed, his fingers tracing patterns in her hair. When she sat back, propped on his knee like some little child, tears stained her cheeks and he wiped them away with his finger.

'I love you,' he said, quietly and she smiled a little, fighting back the tears which threatened to spill forth once more.

'Tom,' she said, her voice catching, 'I don't understand any of this.'

He smiled humourlessly. 'Join the club.'

'I don't know why it's happening here. Not here in Medworth. I don't understand why it's happening at all.' Now the strength was returning to her voice and he felt a new power in the soft hands which gripped his.

'Perhaps the answer is in the books. Maybe that's the only explanation.' He peered past her into the living room to where the books lay open on the coffee table. Beside them was the medallion. Was it indeed as important as he suspected in getting to the bottom of this horror? Would the inscription finally reveal something of value? Something which they could use to aid them in the coming fight?

He exhaled deeply and kissed Debbie on the forehead.

'I'd better get moving,' he said and she slid from his knee, watching as he strapped on the shoulder holster, finally pulling on his jacket to cover the weapon. He held her close once more, not wanting to let her go. He closed his eyes and felt her arms grip him tight around the waist. Finally he stepped back, still resting his hands on her shoulders.

'As soon as it starts to get dark,' he began, 'lock and bolt all the doors and windows. Don't open them to anyone but me.' He swallowed hard, the next set of words coming out in fits and starts. 'If anything happens, get in touch with the station. Someone will be able to reach me wherever I am.'

'What do you hope to do, Tom? How can you fight them?' she asked, a note of tired desolation in her voice.

He picked up the shotgun, taking a box of shells from the drawer nearby. 'We'll cruise the streets, pick them off as they come out.' She noticed that he was shaking. He saw too, that his hands were quivering and he tried to laugh.

'I don't think there's anything in the rule book about this.' He was scared and he didn't mind admitting it. They kissed a last time and then she closed the door behind him, listening as the Capri started up, its wheels crunching gravel as Lambert reversed out into the street, did a quick three point turn and drove off.

Debbie felt more alone than she ever felt in her life.

She drank another mug of coffee and retreated into the living room. Back to the books. She continued deciphering.

Lambert drove slowly, the shotgun propped up on the passenger seat beside him. He looked at the weapon, its shiny blue-black colour contrasting with the light wood of its stock, the ribbed slide set firmly beneath the huge barrel. The box of cartridges bounced about beside it as he swung the car into a street, gazing out at the houses on either side of him, many of them now empty. Whether their occupants had been killed to join the ranks of the living dead, or simply just left town, the windows of the houses were as blank and vacant as blind eyes. The toll, both of murders and departures, had been mounting daily and the Inspector wondered how long it would be before there was no one left.

He drove through the centre of town, reassured by the sight of a few more people. By day things were not so bad, but once darkness descended the town became deserted. A ghost town. It was possible, if anyone were foolish enough to do so, to walk the centre of Medworth, in fact the entire town, without bumping into a single living soul. Everyone was secure inside their houses. At least that was what they thought. The only person who didn't mind the current wave of devastation was Ralph Sanders, the local locksmith. He had a little shop in the main street of Medworth and he had virtually sold out of door and window locks and bolts. Those people who had decided to stay seemed intent on keeping out anything that tried to enter their homes. Lambert wondered how many of them had been successful. Hayes would probably have new figures waiting for him when he reached the station but, at the present time, they knew for certain that there were ninety-three people missing. Probably more and, when totalled with the number that had just upped and left, he was staring at a figure closer to three hundred. But, as yet, ninety-three was the figure they had. A question stood out vividly in the Inspector's mind and it was one which was to plague him for a long time to come.

Where the hell did that many people disappear to during the day?

He tapped absently on the wheel as he drove, his mind elsewhere. He was so absorbed in his own thoughts that he almost ran into a woman as she was crossing the road. He braked sharply, making the woman jump back in shock. Lambert raised a hand in a gesture of apology and drove on.

'No, no,' shouted Hayes, 'squeeze the bloody thing.'

P.C. Ferman jerked his finger around the trigger of the shotgun, groaning as the recoil slammed it back into his shoulder, the roar of the discharge deafening him. He worked the pump action, ejecting the spent shell and lowered the weapon, rubbing at his bruised shoulder.

Beside him, Bell was squinting down the narrow sight, trying to line up the bottle before him. He fired, the savage blast nearly knocking him over. The shot missed wildly, leaving the bottle unscathed but peppering the wall above with pellets. Davies groaned and took the weapon from him, demonstrating how it should be used. He swung the shotgun quickly onto its target and fired, smiling as the bottle exploded, showering glass everywhere.

Briggs was having a little more luck. He'd managed to hit two of the bottles lined up before him and was beginning to feel proud of himself. He worked the pump action vigorously and sent three expert blasts tearing into the wall behind, each punching football size holes in the concrete.

'Very flashy,' said Hayes, appearing at his side, 'but let's see you hit the bloody bottles.'

Briggs coloured slightly and returned to the smaller targets, missing twice. He pushed in five fresh cartridges and worked the pump action, chambering one.

'But Sarge,' he protested, 'why do we have to shoot at bottles?'

Hayes shook his head. 'Because, mastermind, if you can hit something that small then you shouldn't have too much trouble hitting a body.'

Both men looked at each other for long seconds, the words hanging on the air. Hayes shuddered. By God, that didn't sound right. Hitting bodies. He coughed awkwardly and rested a hand on Briggs' shoulder. When he spoke again, his tone was softer.

'Come on, lad, keep at it.'

Hayes walked up and down the short line. There were only six of them out there but, even so, in the still morning air, the sporadic explosions of fire from the shotgun muzzles were thunderous. The sergeant remembered the first time his Dad had taught him how to shoot. An old .410 it had been. Hayes had been twelve at the time and he could still remember the clouds of black smoke which belched from the twin barrels as he fired. His Dad had loved that gun, just like he had loved all his other weapons. Particularly the special weapon he had made. A single barrel rifle which, when unscrewed and disassembled, could fit into its own stock. Hayes had that gun at home now, along with the old .410 and his own under-over shotgun. He had been brought up with guns but never did he imagine that he would need to call upon that experience in a situation like this. He stood still and watched as the men fired, and as he stood he shivered, trying to convince himself that it was the coldness of the wind which caused it.

Davies joined him, his own shotgun still smoking from recent fire.

'Have you tried out the pistol yet, sarge?' asked the constable.

Hayes shook his head and fumbled in his jacket for the Browning. It felt heavy, its thirteen shot clip snug in the butt. He'd only fired pistols a few times and never anything as powerful as this. He drew the weapon and, steadying it with both hands, fired.

There was a loud retort and the pistol bucked in his grasp, the golden cartridge case spinning from the weapon, the bullet tearing a hole in the wall beyond.

'Christ,' muttered Hayes and, excited by the power of the thing, squeezed off two more rounds. Both missed the bottles but he was beginning to get a feel of the thing.

'I hope it's enough,' he said under his breath. And both men looked at each other.

Neither saw Lambert approaching. The Inspector had heard the sporadic gunfire as he had parked his car outside the station. He'd popped inside and found Walford behind the desk. There'd been a couple of calls from people outside the town asking about relatives who they couldn't contact. Walford told the Inspector that he'd informed the callers that inquiries were being made.

'Good lad,' said Lambert and hurried off towards the field behind the station, the shotgun gripped firmly in his grasp, a box of shells in his pocket. That was one thing he was thankful for, at least they had plenty of ammunition. The sound of the savage discharges grew in volume as he neared the line of men.

Davies was the first to see him. The constable nodded and Lambert smiled in return.

'Morning guv,' said Hayes.

'How's it going?' asked Lambert, watching more holes being blown in the wall.

'Not too bad,' said Hayes, trying to smile. 'With a little time...'

Lambert cut him short. 'That's one thing we haven't got.'

He strode past the sergeant and Davies and pushed cartridges into his own shotgun before raising it to his shoulder and firing. The recoil cracked savagely against his shoulder.

'Shit,' muttered the Inspector under his breath.

'They're powerful.' Hayes said it as if he were telling Lambert something he didn't know.

The Inspector worked the slide, fired, pumped, fired. The third shot hit a bottle and shattered it. He lowered the weapon and rubbed his bruised shoulder. Hayes was grinning. Lambert felt somewhat reassured, having seen the power of the weapon. He handed the shotgun to Davies and drew the Browning, trying, at first, to sight it with one hand. When he fired, straight armed, the recoil nearly threw the gun from his grip.

'Jesus Christ,' said Lambert aloud and now the other men laughed too. The bullet sped past the wall and disappeared into the distance.

'Two hands, guv,' said Hayes, grinning.

Lambert steadied himself and fired, still surprised by the force of the recoil. He sighted carefully and squeezed off five rounds in quick succession. When he finally lowered the pistol, his ears were ringing and the palm of his right hand felt numb. He exhaled deeply and bolstered the pistol. The other men began firing once more and again the morning air was filled with the roar of shotguns, occasionally accompanied by the strident explosion of a shattering bottle.

Hayes and Lambert stood together, watching. The Inspector was pushing more shells into the weapon, hefting it back and forth before him.

'Keep them at it for a couple of hours,' he said. 'No one's asking them to be bloody marksmen, I just want to be sure they hit what they aim at.'

Hayes nodded, watching as Lambert turned to the wall once more and fired the five shells in rapid succession, each one smashing holes in the concrete, two of them even hitting bottles. The Inspector watched as the last empty case fell to the ground, aware finally of the stink of cordite in the air. Then he strode past the sergeant, slapping him on the shoulder as he did so.

Hayes watched the young Inspector leave the field then turned back to the bruised constables before him.

'Well, come on then,' he shouted, 'let's see those bloody bottles get hit for a change. Many more shots off target and you'll have that fucking wall down.'

The intermittent roar of fire continued.

Debbie Lambert reached for the coffee mug and took a sip. Wincing, she noted that it was stone cold. She put the mug down and returned to the two books spread out in front of her. She swallowed hard and scanned the notes she had made. The name Mathias was beginning to crop up with surprising regularity. Debbie felt a twinge of something which she likened to excitement run through her and she almost forgot the steadily growing ache at the back of her neck. She massaged the stiff muscles with one hand, scribbling away frantically with the other. She reached the bottom of another page and turned it, the musty smell of the old book making her cough. She closed her eyes and massaged the bridge of her nose between thumb and forefinger.

'Enough for a minute,' she said aloud and got to her feet, padding into the kitchen where she switched on the kettle. More coffee. She ached all over her body but, somehow, she sensed that she was near her goal. A quick glance up at the wall clock told her it was approaching three thirty in the afternoon.

Lambert stood alone in the field, ignoring the spots of rain which bounced off him. He looked up at the sky, already dark with storm clouds. It would soon be dusk and he felt a shudder run through him. He looked into the box of shells at his feet. Nine left. He'd use them up then go back in. The men were waiting. He raised the shotgun and fired, watching with satisfaction as a bottle exploded under the impact. Again he fired, blasting a huge hole in the wall. His hands and shoulders ached but he kept up the steady fire until the shotgun was empty, the final spent cartridge spinning away as he worked the slide. He laid the weapon gently on the grass and reached inside his jacket for the Browning. He studied the pistol for a second before raising it with both hands and fixing one of the remaining bottles in his sights. Closing one eye he fired. He smiled weakly as he saw it shatter. The grass round about was littered with empty shell cases. It looked like a bloody battlefield. Lambert bolstered the pistol and picked up the shotgun before trudging wearily down the hill to the station. He glanced at his watch. Four-fifty. It would be dark in an hour.

Debbie looked down at the medallion. The inscription stood out defiantly, as if challenging her to decipher it. She studied it against the woodcut on the page of the book before her. Beneath it, as Trefoile had shown them, the single word;

MATHIAS.

Owner of the medallion.

She looked at her notes, at the words which she already understood.

MORTIS DIEI - DEATHDAY

REX NOCTU - KING OF THE NIGHT

The inscription around the outside of the medallion still eluded her then, suddenly, she remembered what Trefoile had said, that the words were transposed. The inscription could only be understood when read from back to front. She took the words one at a time:

A

She looked it up in the dictionary. It meant 'to.' Simple as that. She smiled to herself. Now she took the next word. On the medallion, engraved in reverse, it appeared as SIUTROM. She quickly transposed the letters to form the word as recognizable Latin. It came out as:

MORTUIS.

She hunted through the dictionary for that one. Something jumbled here. Not quite right.

There were several meanings. Death. Dead. Die. She put a question mark next to the word and looked at the last of the three reversed inscriptions. In its present form it appeared as ERATICXE. She transposed and found that it came out as something more accessible:

EXCITARE.

Another run through the ever present dictionary. Her finger sped over the entries, searching, probing like a doctor in search of some malignant growth. She found it. 'Awake.' She wrote it down then went back to check the second word once more. Perhaps if she could put it into context she could understand. She read her notes, the transcriptions.

A MORTUIS EXCITARE - TO (something) AWAKE.

She frowned. No. That wasn't it. The structure was wrong. The words were in the wrong order. Heart pounding she wrote it out again.

A MORTUIS EXCITARE - TO AWAKE (something).

She re-checked her definitions.

MORTUIS - DEATH. DIE. THE DEAD.

It struck her like a physical blow and she exhaled deeply, quivering slightly as she finally understood. With shaking hand she wrote down the finished translation then transcribed the entire thing onto a fresh piece of paper. When she had done that she read it back, not daring to speak the words aloud. But they were there before her and she was gripped by a strange contradiction of feelings. A feeling of triumph for having deciphered the inscription but overwhelmed by an icy fear which gripped her heart in a vice-like hand and would not let go. She studied the words on the paper. The answer:

A MORTUIS EXCITARE - TO AWAKE THE DEAD.

And beneath that:

REX NOCTU - KING OF THE NIGHT.

Finally:

MORTIS DIEI - DEATHDAY.

Deathday.

And the single word that summed up all that evil.

MATHIAS.

She turned to the second book, searching its age-crusted pages for the information she sought.

She looked at the medallion, suddenly distracted from her task. It seemed to glow dully in the dimly lit room and it was a moment or two before Debbie realized that it was nearly dark outside.

She crossed to the big bay window at the front of the house and peered out. The street lamps were, as yet, unlit. They didn't come on until six. Another ten minutes. She hurriedly switched on the lamp which perched atop the TV, repeated the procedure with the one on the coffee table and also the taller standard lamp which was propped behind Lambert's chair. The light gave her a measure of reassurance but she found herself still shivering. She hurried upstairs and checked that all the windows were securely closed, particularly the one which looked out over the flat garage roof. She double-checked that one. Satisfied, she sped downstairs and slid the bolts on both front and back doors before retreating into the living room. She sat in silence, curtains drawn against the darkness outside, surrounded by the paraphernalia of ages gone by. Her nostrils were assailed by an odour of dampness, mustiness.

The medallion glinted wickedly and Debbie found herself staring at it with the same horrified fascination with which a mouse watches a snake. She finally managed, as if it were an effort of will, to tear her gaze from it. She scanned the large yellowed page before her, dictionary at the ready. The page had the name of Mathias at its head and she began to read, intrigued and alarmed in equal proportions. Maybe by the time she finished she would know who this man really was.

She set to work.

The three Pandas were parked outside the station, all facing in the direction of Medworth town centre. From his position in the duty room Lambert could see them, just about. The darkness which had descended was total, almost palpable. He tore his eyes away and looked at the rows of sanguine faces arrayed before him. Each of the men sat with shotguns across their laps. If not for the circumstances, Lambert could have laughed. It looked like a scene from some bloody western. He cleared his throat and stepped forward. All eyes focused on him.

'Right,' he began, 'I'll keep it simple. Two men to a car, three where possible. Grogan will stay here to take any calls. Bell, Ferman and Davies in Puma One. Vic,' he nodded towards Sergeant Hayes, 'you take Greene and Walford with you in number two. I'll take Puma Three. Briggs and Jenkins, you're with me.' The men didn't speak. Lambert waited, almost hoping for a question but none was forthcoming. He continued, 'Cruise around, that's all you've got to do. If you see anything moving about, anyone...' he searched for the word, 'suspicious, don't waste time finding out details, just shoot.'

A hand went up. It was Greene. He was in his early thirties, a capable lad who just happened to be as pale as death at the moment.

'How do we know the guns will work, sir?' he asked.

'We don't,' said Lambert, flatly. 'Try praying when you pull the trigger.' He tried to smile but it faded, washed away like chalk in the rain.

Another hand. This time it was Walford.

'Sir,' he said, 'how do we know that these... things will be all that's on the streets tonight? I mean, we might kill innocent people.' He swallowed hard.

Lambert nodded. 'Look, at the risk of sounding melodramatic, anything that's walking those streets tonight won't be human.' He became aware that his own hands were shaking and clenched them into fists. 'Whatever you see, blow the fucking thing to pieces.' There was a note of anger in his voice. He scanned the faces once more. Silence hung over the room like some huge invisible blanket. Lambert continued. 'All right, the cars are full of ammunition, you'll have no problems there. It's in the glove compartments, on the parcel shelves, everywhere we could find to put it, it's there.' He tried to smile again. 'One more thing, I want all the cars to keep in touch. Retain contact at all times and radio in to base every thirty minutes. No more than two men are to leave a car at one time. Understood?'

Nodding. Murmurs of approval.

'Right,' he checked his watch, 'it's seven fifteen now, I want this town patrolled until morning.' He finally found the note of humour he'd been looking for: 'Don't worry, you'll all get paid overtime for this.'

A ripple of laughter.

The men rose to their feet and were filing out of the room when Davies turned and raised his hand.

'What is it, Chris?' asked Lambert.

'These...things,' said Davies, 'they're living corpses, right?'

Lambert nodded.

'Well, then how the hell do you kill something that's already dead?'

The Inspector had no answer and the words hung in the air.

Twenty-Nine

It seemed like they were driving into a huge black pit. That, at any rate, was how young Gary Briggs viewed the slow descent into Medworth. The town was in almost total darkness apart from the time switch lights which illuminated shop windows and a sparkling of house lights, most of which were subdued behind drawn curtains. Beside him sat Lambert, the shotgun cradled across his lap. He was stuffing handfuls of cartridges into his pocket. There was a sudden metallic click from the back seat where Dave Jenkins sat and Briggs felt his heart leap. He realized that it was only the older constable cocking his weapon. The youngster tried to relax, attempting to find some comfort in the fact that, if they did sight any of the things, he would be the one to remain in the car. His own shotgun was propped against the dashboard beside him. Even in the chill of the night air which was flooding in through a partially open window, he could feel the perspiration forming on his back.

Dave Jenkins, the oldest of the trio in the Panda, swallowed hard and ran his hand absentmindedly up and down the sleek barrel of his own shotgun. He peered out into the night, squinting into hedgerows, trying to see through the all enveloping gloom. His mind was elsewhere though. It was with his wife, Amy. He'd packed her off to her mother's when this trouble first began, fearing that it could escalate and he had been disturbed to find that it had. But, besides that, she was pregnant. Near her time by now. Jenkins was overcome by a great feeling of helplessness. Even now it could be happening, she could be having the child. He just prayed that he lived to see it.

Inspector Tom Lambert sat back in his seat and scanned the road ahead, lit only by the twin powerful headlamps of the car. The road which led down from the police station into town was a series of sharp curves and bends and Briggs was constantly braking in order to steer the vehicle safely onward. The car they occupied, Puma Three, had been the last of the three to leave. Lambert had watched the other two drive off, then, after all the men had checked their ammunition, he had climbed into the Panda beside Briggs. They were to patrol the Eastern part of the town, the area which took in the small industrial estate, one or two of the housing areas and Lambert's own home. The other two cars had their designated sectors as well. As he watched the darkened countryside drifting by, Lambert's face was etched in an attitude of grim determination. An act he hoped was working. He'd never been so bloody scared in his life. Frightened not just for himself but also for Debbie, but he drove her fleeting image from his mind and concentrated on the road ahead. It was beginning to straighten out.

Paul Greene sat in the back seat of Puma Two and shivered. He felt sick and could scarcely control his rapid breathing. Once already, Sergeant Hayes, seated in the front beside Walford, who was driving, had looked round at him and asked him if he was O.K. Greene had nodded and clutched his gun tighter as if trying to find some comfort in it. He wondered what his mother was doing. He had personally fitted the locks and bolts to her doors when she had decided to stay in Medworth. He had pleaded with her to go but she had refused. The least he could do now was to make sure she was adequately protected. If indeed, that was possible. They had lived together in that little house just outside the town centre for the last twelve years. Ever since Greene's father had left. In his late twenties now, the young P.C. could still recall the vision of his father standing in the doorway of the house, the night he had left, the car of his 'fancy woman' outside, waiting. Greene remembered how his mother had cried for three days afterwards. He was an only child and the departure of his father brought him and his mother even closer together. He had joined the force partly as an attempt at independence but had finally discovered that he preferred the doting of his mother.

Now he wondered what she was doing, fearing for her life even more than his own.

Sergeant Vic Hayes closed his eyes and massaged the bridge of his nose between his thumb and forefinger. He felt tired, depressed rather than frightened at the thought of what might confront them that night. He had been sergeant in this peaceful little town for more than fifteen years and now, in the space of a couple of months, all those happy memories had been superseded by the horrors which were occurring daily. He still found it hard to believe.

Tony Walford guided the car slowly through the streets of Medworth's largest housing estate, his eyes alert for the slightest sign of movement. He prayed that they wouldn't come across any of the things that night. Not because of the danger involved but because he didn't think that he could force himself to use his gun on any of them. The very idea of shooting another human being made him shudder. Human being. The words stuck in his mind. Lambert had said that they weren't human. Another thought struck him, one which made the forthcoming task even more difficult. He realized with horror, that he might even recognize some of them. Walford drove on, all the time mouthing silent prayers that they would not see any of the creatures.

'Puma One checking in,' said Chris Davies, holding the transmitter at arms' length to lessen the high-pitched whine of static which had invaded the wavelength. He waited for Grogan's reply, then flicked the switch to 'Off.' He replaced the hand set and returned to gazing out of the window. He and the other two men in the Panda had been given the task of patrolling the centre of Medworth itself. The shopping areas and parks which dotted the town like pieces in a grass and concrete jigsaw. Davies was pleased that they had been assigned this particular sector, as there was more likelihood of spotting something. He worked the pump action of the shotgun, chambering a shell; and smiled. God help you bastards, he thought.

In the back, Stuart Ferman was beginning to wish he had never joined the bloody police force. He felt giddy, the smell of plastic, sweat, and gun oil thick in his nostrils. He wished he were at home. He lived alone on the ground floor of a block of flats. Although, strictly speaking, he didn't occupy the dwelling totally without company. He shared it with two enormous Alsatians which he'd had since they were puppies. They'd been handed in to the station by some kid who didn't want them and Ferman had taken them home with him. He had cared for them with a love he didn't think he possessed, watching them grow into the magnificent creatures they were now. He wished he had them both in the car with him at this moment.

Ron Bell, driving, slowed the car as he saw something move ahead of him. He nudged Davies, who had been peering out of the side window and pointed to the area where he had seen the movement. All three men felt the tension rising as Bell edged the Panda closer. Its bright headlamps suddenly swung on the source of the disturbance.

It was a cat.

Caught in the sudden glare it hissed and fled from the blinding light. The trio of men in Puma One felt the tension drain from them and Bell breathed a sigh of audible relief.

They drove on.

Debbie Lambert had found what she searched for.

She had discovered the information about fifteen minutes ago and now she reread it, translating quickly, scribbling the words down like a journalist with a scoop. There were two entire pages about Mathias. She looked back through her notes, found that she was running short of paper and realized that she had more upstairs.

It was as she dashed into the hall that she heard the scratching at the front door.

'Puma Three to all cars. Anything to report?'

Lambert's voice rasped in the closed confines of the other two Pandas. Hayes and Davies responded that, as yet, they had seen nothing.

'Keep in touch,' ordered Lambert, 'over and out.' He replaced the hand set and wound the window down a little further, gulping in the crisp night air. They had now reached the edge of the industrial area and its countless tall chimneys towered above them as Briggs guided the car slowly along the wide roads, keeping it dead centre.

'If you see anything,' said Lambert, 'let me know.'

It was darker than he had imagined, especially in this part of the town, for there were no street lights, just the occasional naked bulb which shone outside a factory entrance. The Inspector made a mental note to have this area checked out in the morning. The things had to be hiding somewhere and out here offered countless possibilities. A thought crossed his mind. There was no evidence to support his own theory that they were, indeed, all holed up in the same place during the day and the thought that they could well be spread out all over town made his heart sink. It would mean searching every empty house, every cellar, every disused shop. He shook his head and sighed deeply.

When Debbie first heard the scratching she paused, heart pounding against her ribs, listening. It stopped abruptly but still she stood in the darkness of the hall until, at last, she sprinted upstairs to their bedroom and found some paper. When she reached the hall again, she switched on the light and stood there for a second. The lock and bolt were secure but she tested them just to set her mind at ease. Satisfied, but nonetheless uneasy, she returned to the living room which was comfortingly aglow with the light of three lamps. She sat down at her desk and reread the passage on Mathias, this time transcribing onto a fresh piece of paper. Her eyes stung from the hours of continual reading but she persevered, realizing that she had reached her goal.

The medallion glinted dully beside her and she looked at it for a second.

There was a rattling from the back of the house. Debbie heard it but ignored it, or tried to. She continued writing.

It grew louder.

A noise now at the front again. That scratching, only more insistent this time.

It stopped.

She looked up, glanced across at the telephone and wondered whether or not to call the station. But, when the sounds didn't persist, she shook her head, told herself that it was her imagination and returned to her work. The transcription was beginning to take shape, almost finished in fact. She read it through twice, struggling with its ancient construction. The meaning was in there somewhere, it was just a matter of finding it. The words on the paper stood out starkly, written in her own neat script. She read them to herself:

This year of the Almighty, 1596, in ground not Blessed of the Church is buried the one known as Mathias. This man did dare to oppose God: buried without tongue or eyes, removed in the sight of those present by hot pincers: Blasphemer, Servant of the Fallen Angel. Buried with him be the symbol of his evil. The instrument with which he hoped to reverse the very rightful process of death; to defy the Almighty; to bring life to the Dead.

Debbie shuddered. My God, that was the tie up. She looked at the medallion.

A MORTUIS EXCITARE - TO AWAKE THE DEAD.

She had more below that first transcription:

May he lie, buried yet whilst alive, forever in the place chosen. Without the Kingdom of the Almighty for the rest of Eternity.

So engrossed was she in her find, she didn't even hear the rattling begin once more at the back of the house. Debbie read on;

And now, though he wear that symbol of his Blasphemy let it not be removed; but, if so done, be it not returned to its owner for there is a power beyond that of man in its presence. Reunited with the symbol of his evil the one known as Mathias may yet attain The Power.

Debbie put down the transcript and looked at the medallion. She felt compelled to reach out and touch it but something told her not to. The gleaming metal winked up at her and she shuddered. 'The Power.' She glanced at her notes once more. At last, they knew the secret of the medallion.

It was then that she heard the rattling.

Breathing heavily, she got to her feet and crossed to the door which led out into the kitchen, suddenly aware of how cold it had become. She pushed the door and peered into the room, taking a step in, the linoleum cold against her bare feet. The rattling grew louder and she looked towards the locked back door.

The handle was being turned frenziedly back and forth.

'Oh God,' murmured Debbie under her breath. She flicked on the kitchen lights, watching as the bank of fluorescents burst into life. The door handle was slammed back and forth with renewed strength and now, a series of dull thuds began to break against it, gradually building to a crescendo which she realized were powerful blows.

She turned, slammed the door behind her and dashed for the phone in the living room. Her shaking fingers found the required digits and she dialled, the pounding growing in intensity. Her breath came in gasps as she waited for the receiver to be picked up at the other end. She heard three words;

'Medworth Police Station...'

The line went dead.

'Hello,' gasped Debbie, flicking desperately at the cradle. Her voice grew in volume. 'Hello!' Almost in tears, she flung the useless receiver down. She murmured Lambert's name, ran to the window and dragged back the curtains.

With a mournful puff, the street lamps blew out.

Debbie bit her fist and spun around, the smashing of glass telling her that the window had been shattered. Then, as she spun round to draw the curtains once more, she found herself staring into the grinning face of Ray Mackenzie, those twin blood red blazing orbs fixing her in an unholy stare and she finally summoned her voice for a scream.

Puma Three cruised around the industrial estate five or six times. Every so often Lambert and Jenkins would get out to check an open gate or some movement in the shadows, but each time, to their relief, they found nothing. On such occasions, one man would investigate while the other stood nearby, gun at the ready; never were they far from the car. Lambert told Briggs to keep his engine running whenever they stopped and its idling hum was something of a comfort in the stifling silence of the night.

Finally, satisfied that the area was clear, Lambert told Briggs to head for the outskirts of town with the intention of sweeping the country roads and outlying houses for any sign of activity. After that, they would head back into the built up areas.

As they drove, Lambert fumbled inside his jacket and pulled the Browning from its holster. He pressed the magazine release button and the slim metal box slid from the butt.

'Shit,' muttered the Inspector, noting that it was empty. He fumbled in his pockets, already remembering that he'd left the extra clips at home.

'Turn the bloody thing round,' he said to Briggs, 'we've got to go back to my house. I left the ammo for the pistol there.' He slid the empty weapon back into its holster, cursing himself. Briggs spun the wheel and the Panda completed a perfect 'U' turn. Within seconds they were heading back into town.

Debbie managed to step back from the window just as Mackenzie thrust a hand at her. It crashed through the glass, showering her with shards of crystal, one of which slashed her cheek drawing a tiny tear of blood. She saw others out there with him. A woman no older than herself, another man. She saw that Mackenzie wasn't looking at her but at the medallion. It glinted invitingly on the desk and the living dead thing grunted, stepping back. Debbie saw him launch himself at the bay window, almost rooted to the spot in awe and terror as his large frame smashed through wood and glass and landed on the carpet a foot or so from her. She screamed once more and grabbed the medallion, vaulting over the stunned man and grabbing at the handle of the hall door. Still lying on the floor, Mackenzie grabbed at her ankle and she felt his clammy hand touch her bare foot as she slipped by.

She didn't even see the kitchen door burst open and two more of the things rush into the living room.

Mackenzie, on his feet now, was racing up the stairs behind her, and Debbie was whimpering as she reached the landing. She could sense his closeness, and smell the fetid stench which came from his body.

A hand closed on her shoulder. Screaming, she fell against Mackenzie; the medallion falling from her grasp. She grabbed the wooden bannister rail to prevent herself from sliding down the stairs.

Mackenzie was not so lucky. The force of Debbie striking him was enough to make him lose balance and with a startled grunt, he fell back, rolling head over heels down the stairs.

Debbie scrambled to her feet, peering over her shoulder.

Mackenzie was on his feet again, coming up at her once more but now there were others behind him. She didn't stop to count, guessing that there were perhaps six. All ages, all sizes. All with one intent.

She grabbed the medallion, bolted for the bathroom and hurled herself inside, slamming the door shut. She slid the flimsy bolt. There were footsteps on the landing and she heard the sound of doors being flung open, then an almighty crash as one of them threw his weight against the bathroom door. She looked around frantically for a weapon. Anything to fight back with but, all she could see was Lambert's safety razor. She grabbed it, screaming as a fist punched through the thin wooden door. Debbie lashed out, slicing open the back of the hand, ripping away a large chunk of skin which stuck to the hooded razor blade. Blood jetted onto her and the hand was hastily withdrawn but the blows kept raining on the door and she knew that they would be in at any second. Big salt tears welled in her eyes and she said Lambert's name over and over again, watching as more of the door was torn away. She could see them all on the landing peering in at her. One of them, a man in his fifties, stuck his face into the gap and, screaming madly, she raked the razor across his lips. Blood burst forth but there was no expression of pain registered in his eyes because he had no eyes. Just those empty, red-rimmed holes. And yet they saw her. Saw the medallion. And they were grinning.

Lambert saw two of the things on his front lawn as Briggs swung the car into the street.

'Oh God,' he shrieked, with pained horror. Already he was grabbing for the shotgun.

Briggs stepped on the accelerator and the car sped forward. It mounted the pavement about thirty yards from the house, smashed through the hedge of the house next door and skidded to a halt on the grass in front of Lambert's house. Oblivious to the danger, with only thoughts of Debbie in his mind, Lambert leapt from the car, swinging the shotgun up as the two things cowered away from the blazing light of the car headlamps. The Inspector fired three times. The first blast hit the leading creature squarely in the chest, blew half its torso away and flung it a good twelve feet across the lawn.

'You fuckers,' screamed Lambert, now joined by Jenkins who also fired.

The second thing was caught in the crossfire and both men were almost joyful as they watched its head disintegrate, a dark shower of blood, brain and shattered bone spraying out into the night.

Lambert saw the broken front window, the front door hanging uselessly from one torn hinge. He dashed into the hall followed by Jenkins. Briggs, shaking with sheer terror, reversed and brought the headlamps of the car to bear on the front of the house, their powerful beams piercing the blackness and pinpointing two more of the creatures in the living room. He reached for his own gun and scrambled out of the car, aiming at the first of them, a man in his twenties.

There was a roar as he fired, the shot missing and blasting a hole in the wall beneath the window. Gasping, Briggs worked the pump action and fired again, screaming in terror as he saw the things scrambling over the window sill. Coming for him. He fired again and the discharge was on target. It hit the man in the lower abdomen, blasting away his genitals, almost severing his right leg. The second creature, a woman not yet in her forties, flung herself at him and the young constable went down under her weight. He felt sharp nails tearing at his face and his screams filled the night.

From his position on the stairs, Lambert could see from the concentration of the creatures clustered around the shattered bathroom door that Debbie was trapped inside.

One of them came at him and he fired from point blank range, ignoring the blood which splashed onto him. He dashed up the stairs, stepping on the body as he did so. Jenkins followed and the two men reached the landing together.

For a second, everything froze. A still frame in a broken down film. Suddenly, the film was running again. Jenkins raised his shotgun and fired twice, bringing down one of the living dead.

Lambert heard Debbie scream. A scream which was immediately replaced by the sound of snapping wood.

Mackenzie was no more than a foot from Debbie, his fetid breath filling her nostrils. Yellow, bubbling mucous trickling down his chin. He grabbed for the medallion and tore it from her grasp; she expected the grip of his bloodied hands on her throat at any second. But he turned and blundered out, clutching the gold circlet to his chest.

Lambert saw him and lifted the shotgun, jerking wildly on the trigger. The recoil slammed the stock back against his shoulder and the blast blew a huge hole in the wall beside the grinning Mackenzie who bolted for the tiny window at the far end of the landing. Lambert worked the pump action and fired again but he was too late.

Mackenzie launched himself at the window and hurtled through it. The Inspector's shot exploded beside him as he met the cool night air. The living corpse of Mackenzie hit the roof of the garage and rolled once. Lambert dashed to the window and looked out just in time to see him leap from the flat roof and lope off into the darkness.

He turned, cursing, and dashed into the bathroom, throwing the shotgun to one side and grabbing Debbie in both arms. She was sobbing uncontrollably. He closed his eyes and pressed her close to him, his own body shaking. She breathed his name over and over again, sobbing. He eased the blood-spattered razor from her hand and dropped it into the bath.

Jenkins appeared in the doorway.

'Check outside,' said Lambert softly and the constable nodded, stepping over two bodies as he made his way down the stairs. The house stank of blood and cordite and, Jenkins noted, something else. A carrion odour of corruption. He worked the pump action of his shotgun, ejecting the spent cartridge and walked out into the night. It was then that he saw the woman coming towards him.

She had him fixed in those gaping, empty sockets, and, in the glaring brilliance of the Panda's headlamps, Jenkins could see that her hands were soaked in blood. She raised them towards him and ran arms outstretched like some kind of obscene sleepwalker.

He took a step back, swinging the shotgun up just in time to get off one shot.

The blast tore through her shoulder, ripping away most of the left breast and splintering both scapula and clavicle. She staggered, the wound gaping wide, one arm dangling by thin tendrils of flesh and sinew. Then, to his horror, she started forward once more. He already knew that his gun was empty, realized that he would have no time to reload.

With all the power he could muster, he swung the shotgun like a cricket bat. The butt smacked savagely into her face. Her jaw bones crumbled beneath the impact. She fell to one side, empty sockets stared up at him. Revolted, Jenkins brought the wooden stock down repeatedly upon her head until it split open like a bag full of cherry syrup. Then he dropped the gun and retched until there was nothing left in his stomach.

He staggered away from the body, avoided the two other bodies laying on the lawn, and gulped down huge lungfuls of air. He leant against the side of the Panda for a moment, his breath coming in gasps, and the bitter taste of his own vomit strong in his mouth. His head was spinning.

'Oh God,' he groaned, rubbing his stomach with a bruised hand. For a second he thought he was going to throw up again but the feeling passed and he shook himself. He pulled open the passenger side door and climbed in.

The car was empty. No sign of Briggs.

Jenkins sat still for a second and peered out into the gloom, trying to catch a glimpse of his younger companion. Briggs' shotgun was missing from its position beside his seat and Jenkins assumed that the youngster must have got out of the car to help when they had arrived. He pushed open the door and stepped out, walking around to the other side of the car.

'Gary,' he called.

There was no answer. Jenkins stood in the reflected light of the car's headlamps, his face darkened into grotesque shadow. He looked down.

Lying just beside the driver's side door was Briggs' peaked cap. The other constable knelt and picked it up, noting with concern that it was splattered with blood. In fact, there was blood all over the ground near the door, great blotches of it staining the white paintwork of the car.

Jenkins picked up the discarded shotgun, suddenly afraid, and backed off towards the house, the barrel levelled. He stumbled over the body of the woman and nearly fell but he retained his balance and retreated into the welcoming light of the hall.

Footsteps behind him. He turned.

Lambert and Debbie were descending the stairs, the Inspector with his arm wrapped tightly around his wife's shoulders. Her head was bowed and Jenkins could see that she was sobbing quietly - tiny, almost imperceptible' movements of her shoulders signalling the tortured spasms. The constable suddenly thought of his own wife, of his child. Had she given birth yet? He drove the thought away.

'You all right?' asked Lambert, the shotgun propped up over his shoulder as if he were off on a hunting trip.

Jenkins, his face the colour of cream cheese, nodded.

'I can't find Briggs,' he said.

Lambert looked puzzled but his expression changed to one of worry when the constable held up the bloodstained cap. The three of them stood in the burning light from the car headlamps, the two policemen looking at one another, Debbie weeping softly. There was a harsh crackling, then voice from outside.

'The radio,' said Lambert, helping Debbie out, guiding her past the gun-blasted bodies of the living dead.

Jenkins nodded and crossed to the car. He picked up the handset and heard Grogan's agitated voice at the other end:

'Puma Three, come in.'

'Puma Three,' said Jenkins wearily.

'Thank Christ for that,' said Grogan, 'you hadn't called in, I thought something had happened.'

Lambert helped Debbie into the back seat of the car where she lay down, curling up in a fetal position, then he took the handset from Jenkins.

'Puma Three here, this is Lambert. Contact the other two cars, tell them we have encountered a number of the bloody things. Tell them the guns do work.'

Grogan muttered an affirmation.

Lambert continued, 'Anything to report, Grogan?'

'No sir, we've had a number of calls from people, sightings and what have you, but nothing from the other two cars. They both reported in a while back to say that they'd seen nothing.'

Lambert nodded as he listened, glancing over to where Debbie lay. Her eyes were closed, her cheeks tear-stained.

'Puma Three, out,' he said and switched off the set.

'What now, sir?' said Jenkins, sliding behind the wheel and locking the door.

'I want to get my wife to Doctor Kirby. Let's go.'

Jenkins nodded and started the car. The wheels spun on the grass but, as they reached the concrete of the road, they caught and the Panda sped off.

Lambert sat back in the seat and closed his eyes. Christ, the vile things had nearly killed Debbie. He prayed that she would be all right. Mackenzie had got the medallion, it seemed to have been the object of the attack. He gritted his teeth. It had to be the answer. No wonder Trefoile was frightened of the bloody thing. The Inspector realized that he would have to find out if Debbie had managed to discover the truth about it. He looked around at her. She was still curled up. Asleep.

At least the encounter had proved that the guns were of use. That much he was thankful for. He didn't dare think what would have happened if they had not been...

One thing did trouble him though.

Where had Briggs got to?

Run off in fright perhaps? Lambert wouldn't have blamed him if he had. He'd probably stagger in the next morning, ashamed of his own cowardice. Lambert half-smiled; he could quite easily have run off with him.

Even if anyone had noticed, no one would have wondered why there were blood spots on the trunk of the Panda. The whole car was splashed with the crimson fluid after all. What might have interested them was the contents of the trunk.

Gary Briggs had died painfully, his eyes torn from living sockets but now he lay in the boot of the car, fresh blood from the riven sockets still spilling down his cheeks.

He had had no chance against the woman who had attacked him. She had been too strong.

He had crawled into the trunk to escape the blinding lights of the Panda's headlamps. It was dark in there. It stank of petrol and rubber. But he didn't care.

He lay silently.

Waiting.

Thirty

Lambert breathed a sigh of relief as dawn clawed its way across the sky.

Now, as he stood by the window of John Kirby's spare bedroom, he had never been so pleased to see the light of day. He looked down at the cup of coffee in his hand and drained it, replacing the empty vessel on a small sideboard. He watched the sun appear, preceded by golden shafts of light and finally, a tiny portion of it peering over the horizon and filling the heavens with the first glow of morning.

He turned and looked at Debbie who was lying on a bed in one corner of the room. She was sleeping and the slow rhythmic heaving of her chest reassured him. He crossed to the bedside and knelt beside her, reaching beneath the sheets to grasp one of her hands. He stayed there for several moments, gripping her soft hand and gazing at her face. Eventually he got to his feet, kissed her lightly on the forehead and whispered, 'I love you.' Then he carefully replaced her hand under the sheets and left the room. He closed the door behind him and leant against it for a moment, exhaling deeply. The memory of the previous night was still vivid in his mind, burned deep into his consciousness like a red hot brand.

They had arrived at Kirby's at around three that morning. Bleary-eyed, the doctor had let them in and led Lambert, with Debbie's inert form in his arms, upstairs to this bedroom. He had sedated her with Thorazine. Then he and Kirby had gone downstairs to where Jenkins waited. Lambert had told the doctor what had happened and Kirby had listened, his apprehension growing by the second. Finally the doctor had treated their minor cuts and bruises and the three of them had then sat down over a cup of coffee to wait for morning. Jenkins had managed to catch a few hours sleep on the couch in Kirby's surgery. When Lambert walked into the kitchen he found the doctor sitting alone at the table.

'Is she all right?' asked Kirby.

Lambert nodded. 'Still sleeping.'

'She will be for quite a while; it's the best thing for her after what she's been through.'

The Inspector poured himself another cup of coffee and sat down opposite Kirby.

'Where's Jenkins?' he asked.

Kirby hooked a thumb in the direction of the surgery, 'He's still asleep too.' The doctor studied the young policeman's face, the beginnings of stubble on his chin, the dark rings beneath his eyes. 'You look like you could do with some rest yourself.'

Lambert smiled humourlessly and ran his index finger around the lip of his cup. Finally he looked up.

'They could have killed her, John,' he said, his voice softening.

'But they didn't,' said Kirby, trying to inject a note of reassurance into his voice.

'They were like animals. They would have killed her.' His voice broke and he lowered his head, his tone flat, dropping almost to a whisper, 'If I hadn't have gone back to the house; if...'

Kirby saw a single tear plop onto the table and, when Lambert looked up, his eyes were red-rimmed, big salt tears pouring down his cheeks. The Inspector clasped his fingers, propped his elbows on the table and rested his chin on his hands.

'I'm sorry,' he said, softly, wiping his face.

'Drink your coffee,' said Kirby, smiling.

Lambert managed to smile back. He coughed, shook himself, blew out a harsh lungful of air. He raised a hand to signal that he was O.K., nodding to himself as if to reinforce the idea.

'What's your next move?' asked Kirby.

'Find them. Find out where they hole up during the day. Find them and kill them.' He finished his coffee. He got to his feet, a new purpose about him, the old strength returning.

'If my theory is right,' he said, 'then they're all in the same place. They seem to function in groups, so it's only logical to assume they sleep in groups too. It's just a matter of finding the right place.'

He went through into the surgery and woke Jenkins. In minutes he was on his feet and the two of them were ready to leave. They paused in the doorway.

'How long before she wakes up?' asked Lambert.

Kirby shrugged, 'It's hard to say, four, five hours perhaps longer.'

'Let me know as soon as she does; it's important.'

Jenkins walked out to the waiting Panda, the blood on it now dried to a dull rust colour, and slid behind the wheel. Lambert paused and extended a hand which Kirby shook warmly.

'Thanks, John,' said the Inspector and he was gone, walking across to the car. Jenkins started the engine and Kirby watched as they disappeared from view down a sharp dip in the road. He went back indoors and poured himself another cup of coffee.

P.C. Bell was distributing cups of tea when Lambert and Jenkins entered the duty room. Mumbled greetings were exchanged and Lambert slumped down into a chair, dropping the shotgun down beside him. The other men looked pale but none looked as downright shagged out as he did. He later learned that they had taken it in turns to sleep as they cruised around. Two men in the front keeping watch while the third snatched a few hours in the back seat.

'We lost Briggs,' said Lambert flatly, taking the cup of steaming tea which Bell offered him.

'How?' Hayes wanted to know.

Lambert shrugged, 'I don't know.' He paused. 'My house was attacked last night; they nearly killed my wife.'

'Jesus,' murmured Walford.

'There were about a half a dozen of them. Ray Mackenzie was one.'

A chorus of sighs ran around the room.

Lambert continued. 'That medallion that we found at his place in the very beginning, my wife was trying to make out the inscription on it. I think she succeeded. Mackenzie stole it, he got away before we realized what was happening.' He finished his tea and stood up, crossing to the end of the room. The men's eyes followed his progress. When he finally spoke, his tone was flat, no inflection at all.

'We've got to find them,' he began, 'and we've got to do it before nightfall. Now that means searching every empty house, every cellar, every shop, every attic; anywhere where they could hide. Now, if you do find one of them I don't want any heroics. Get help, as much as you need and let's wipe the bastards out.' His face was set in deep lines as he spoke. 'Let's just pray that I'm right and that they're all in one place because that'll make our job much easier. Now, to date, there's upwards of ninety people missing. I want them all.' There were a vehemence in his last words which made one or two of the men sit up. 'Every last one of the fucking things has got to be found and destroyed. Understand?'

Nods and murmurs.

'Any questions?'

There were none.

'Right. Work in twos. I'll take my own car, and like before, keep in contact at all times.' Lambert made a mental note to pick up a walkie-talkie on the way out. He looked at his watch.

'It's five-twenty now. That gives us eleven hours of daylight.'

He mentioned something briefly about checking their weapons to make sure they had enough ammo. Hayes told him that it had already been taken care of. Lambert nodded. He picked up the shotgun and worked the pump action then, checking that this time the magazine was full, he slid the Browning from its holster and pulled the slide back and cocked it. The metallic click was amplified by the silence in the room. He stood before the men, grim determination etched on his face.

'Let's go.'

In the boot of Puma Three the thing that had once been Gary Briggs lay in torpor, hidden from the painful rays of the sun. It lay still.

Waiting for the night.

Thirty-One

Jenkins brought the Panda to a halt on the din track which ran alongside the hedge flanking the garden. The house, invisible behind the tall hedge, belonged to Nigel Moore, Medworth's most prosperous farmer. As Hayes stepped from the car he could see the gleaming metal towers of the pasteurization plant further back.

The farm was large. The house itself formed the apex of a triangle which was made up by a configuration of sheds and outbuildings at one corner and the actual pasteurization plant at the other. The area between the three buildings was part concrete (near to the house) and mud which was thick and clung defiantly to the sergeant's boots as he walked.

He could see cattle and the occasional horse moving lethargically about in the fields beyond. Hayes took a deep breath, enjoying the purity of the early morning air even though it was tinged with the pungent smell of manure. He didn't seem to care.

Jenkins flicked off the engine of Puma One and climbed out, carrying his shotgun at his side.

'You wait here,' said Hayes when they reached the rusty iron gate which opened into the farm yard. 'That way, you'll be able to cover me and hear the radio if anyone calls.'

Jenkins nodded, watching as the sergeant strode towards the house, avoiding the worst patches of mud. The constable glanced around him. There were plenty of places out here for the things to hide. He shuddered and looked up at the sun, finding reassurance in its growing heat. The sky was cloudless, a deep blue which promised a beautiful day.

Hayes reached the concrete path which ran up to the front door of the farmhouse and he scraped his boots clean of mud before proceeding. The house itself was traditional in appearance, white-washed, low roofed and covered with climbing ivy. There was a low wooden porch over the doorstep and the sergeant had to duck to avoid banging his head on it. He rapped three times and waited.

There was no answer.

He turned and shrugged at Jenkins who felt his own heart quicken. He gripped his shotgun tighter, his eyes scanning the empty yard furtively.

Hayes sighed wearily and knocked again. Receiving no answer this time, he took the narrow path to the back of the house. The sergeant took time to admire Moore's sizeable vegetable patch before knocking on the back door. After a few seconds he heard bolts being slid back and then the door swung open.

He found himself looking down the twin barrels of a shotgun.

'Morning, Nigel,' said Hayes, grinning and pushing the gun to one side.

Moore shrugged. 'Hello Vic.' He looked down at the shotgun. 'Well, you can't be too careful these days, can you?'

Hayes didn't answer, just looked around the kitchen and asked, 'Have you seen anything suspicious around here lately?'

'Any of those things you mean?' said Moore, his round red face lighting up excitedly.

'Anything?' Hayes repeated, refusing to be drawn.

'I checked all the barns and sheds myself,' he nodded vigorously, 'and the cellar and attic.' He smiled broadly. 'If any of the bloody things come round here they'll get a dose of this.' He lifted the shotgun proudly.

Hayes smiled, aware that the farmer was looking down at his own weapon.

'That bad, is it?' asked the man.

Hayes nodded, 'It's bad.'

Moore shook his head and sighed. 'You wouldn't believe it could happen in a place like this, would you?' There was a tinge of sadness in his voice.

Hayes turned to leave. 'You wouldn't think it could happen anywhere.'

Moore waved him away and closed the door behind him. Hayes took one last look at the expansive vegetable patch and made his way back to the waiting Jenkins.

'Nothing,' he said, 'old Nigel's fine; he says he's checked the place out himself.'

Jenkins nodded, relieved, and they trudged back to the car.

'If one of those things came up against old Nigel, I'd lay my money on him winning,' said Hayes, sliding into the car. They both laughed.

Davies checked his shotgun, running a hand down the sleek barrel, then he sat back in his seat and gazed out of the windscreen. The houses on either side were empty. The entire street was devoid of people. Those who had not been killed had simply packed up and gone. Redhoods Avenue was as dead as a doornail and there were many more streets in Medworth like it.

'Stop the car here,' said Davies as Greene turned into the road.

Davies sighed. There was no other alternative.

Each and every house would have to be checked individually.

'How do you want to do this?' asked Greene, a bead of perspiration popping onto his forehcad. 'You take that side, I'll take this one,' said the older PC.

Green swallowed hard, 'That's what I was afraid you were going to say.'

Both men swung themselves out of the car, checking their weapons once more, stuffing handfuls of extra shells in their pockets. Greene prayed that they wouldn't have the need for them. He watched as Davies reached for the radio.

'Puma Two to base.'

Grogan acknowledged.

'This is Davies. We're leaving the car to check every house in Redhoods Avenue, right? Over.'

Grogan said something about reporting in if they found anything.

'Will do. Puma Two out.'

The two policemen looked at each other for a moment, both sensing the other's fear.

'How do we get into the houses?' Greene wanted to know.

'Break in,' offered Davies and he walked away, the shotgun slung over his shoulder. Greene watched him walk up the path of the first house in the road, check the front door and then disappear around the back. The younger constable heard the crashing of glass as Davies broke a window and he realized that his companion must be inside by now. He stood still beside the stationary car for long seconds, just looking down the street. A street just like any other on any normal housing estate in any town in the country. A narrow road flanked on both sides by grass verge and carefully planted trees, their branches still, bare. Just an ordinary street.

He was sweating profusely as he set off for the first house. It lay directly opposite the one which Davies had entered, and, like his companion, Greene found that he had to break a window to get in. Using his elbow, he smashed a hole in the frosted pane set in the back door and reached through, fumbling for the key, wondering whether anything were going to grab his exposed hand. He breathed an audible sigh of relief as the lock gave and the door swung open. Clutching the shotgun, he stepped inside.

The kitchen was small, identical to all the others in the street. There was a yellowing calendar on the far wall and Greene noticed that it had not been turned to the appropriate month. It was two behind. He wished that time could, indeed, be reversed, so that all this had never happened. He drove the thought from his mind and continued through into the living room, pleased to find that the curtains were drawn and sunlight was flooding the small room. Tiny particles of dust fluttered in the golden rays. Nothing here. Shaking a little more, Greene made his way upstairs towards the narrow landing.

Three doors faced him. Two open, one closed. All the houses on the road had either two or three bedrooms as well as an inside toilet. Greene could see through the two open doors that the rooms were both bedrooms. Not much chance of anyone hiding out in a bathroom, he told himself, trying to find reassurance in the assumption. He placed a hand on the knob of the closed door and, praying, shoved it open.

Nothing.

The house was empty. Thankfully, he hurried back downstairs out of the back door and made his way to the next house.

Meantime, across on the other side of Redhoods Avenue, Davies too had found the house he was searching to be empty. Almost disappointed, he left the building vaulting the low fence which divided the adjacent garden.

There was a loud crash, a shattering of glass and Davies looked down to see that he'd landed in a cold frame. He groaned and stepped clear of the wreckage, cursing himself for not being more careful. The grass of the lawn hadn't been cut for a while and it grew knee high, competing for supremacy with large growths of chickweed and dandelions. There was a rusted lawn roller propped up against the fence beside the remains of the cold frame. The constable walked up the path towards the back door which he found was already open. The lime green paint had peeled away in places, leprous slices of the stuff chipped away to reveal the thin wood beneath.

Davies lowered the shotgun, the barrel pointing ahead, and took a step inside. The kitchen smelt damp; the cloying stench mingling with something else. A more pungent odour which caused the constable to cough. He looked around, searching for the source of the odour. There was a white door to his right which he took to be a larder and, as he took a step towards it, he realized that his suspicions were right. The stench grew stronger.

Davies lowered the shotgun and pulled open the door.

'Christ,' he grunted, discovering the source of the smell. On the lowest stone shelf of the larder was a rotting joint of beef. It lay on the place in a solidified pool of blood which spread into a rusty circle around it. Davies heard the somnolent buzzing of flies; some were crawling on the meat. He also noted with disgust the loathsome writhings of maggots on the joint.

He pushed the larder door shut and walked into the living room. The curtains were drawn here, the room in semi-darkness but for the thin beams of sunlight lancing through gaps in the dusty drape. Wary of the darkness, Davies advanced further into the room and tore the curtains down, flooding the room with bright sunlight and throwing up a choking cloud of thick dust. The policeman stepped back, eyes darting round the room. Come on you bastards, he thought, where are you? Satisfied that downstairs was clear, he pushed open the hall door and made his way up the narrow staircase finally emerging on the landing.

Four doors. Two bedrooms, an airing cupboard and a toilet. All empty.

Shaking his head he descended the stairs and made his way across the front lawn to the next house, wondering how Greene was doing across the road.

As it turned out, his younger companion was having as little luck as he in finding anything. There were not even any signs of the creatures and Greene was beginning to think that the search of the street would end up being fruitless. At least that was what he hoped. The perspiration which soaked his back was beginning to stain his uniform as he began searching the fifth house. He didn't even attempt to tell himself that the sweat was heat induced. It was the product of fear. Pure, naked fear. He wiped his brow and pushed the door which he knew led into the living room of the house. The curtains once more were open and he passed through without checking, anxious to scan upstairs and get out of the bloody place. There was a sofa and two chairs in the room, and no carpet on the floor. The sofa was stretched across one corner of the room, a sizeable gap behind it.

It was as the young constable made his way up the fifth staircase that morning, that the sofa was pushed forward and the creature sheltering behind it crept slowly forward.

From his position in one of the bedrooms, Greene didn't hear the slight squeaking of castors as the sofa moved. Having thoroughly searched the upper story, he hurried downstairs once more, his heart slowing a little.

He walked into the living room.

All he heard was a high-pitched rasping sound as the thing launched itself at him.

Greene screamed and swung the shotgun round, his actions accelerated by sheer terror. Luckily, the monstrous discharge hit its target and the young constable slumped back against the wall gasping.

At his feet lay what remained of a cat. It was now little more than a twisted heap of fur and blood, large lumps of it splattered around the room by the horrendous force of the blast. Had it not been for the fact that the partly obliterated head stared up at him, Greene wouldn't have known what he'd killed, so great was the destruction wrought by the gun.

He bolted from the house. Fortunately, he managed to reach the back door before vomiting. Sweating profusely, he leant against the wall, gulping in the grass-scented air and shaking madly. It was some time before he found the courage to move on to the next house.

Across the road, Davies has heard the shot and he smiled. That's one of the bastards gone, he thought. He was surprised that Greene had had the guts to use the shotgun, he seemed such a spineless little sod. Davies himself was more than half way down the street by now, having discovered nothing so far and he, like Greene, was beginning to suspect that all the houses were, indeed, empty. The house he was in this time was built somewhat differently from those further up. He stood in the kitchen, his eyes alert. No pantry here, just a door in front of him, which, he found, led out into a hall. Peeling wallpaper once more, flaking away like dried skin. There was a door to his immediate right and another to the left. Between them lay the staircase. He chose the right hand door first and found that it was a bathroom with toilet. Piss stains up the wall, more flaking paper and a yellowed plastic shower curtain. The place smelt like a urinal.

Davies closed the door behind him and nudged open the other across the tiny hall with the barrel of his shotgun. The living room. He checked it quickly, anxious to inspect the upper floor but even more anxious to get out into the sunlight again. He left the living room and started slowly up the uncarpeted stairs. His heavy boots sounded conspicuously loud in the deathly silence and the policeman swallowed hard, aware that anything up there would most certainly have been alerted to his presence by now. There was a small guard rail running along the side of the landing and, through its wooden slats; he could see the half-open door of a bedroom. It was in darkness, the dirty blue curtains drawn tight against the invading sunlight. He gripped the shotgun tighter and finally stood still on the cramped landing.

Two more doors in addition to the one he had already glimpsed. He kicked open the nearest and walked in. Nothing in there, just bunk beds and an old dressing table. At the far end of the room, a cupboard door had fallen open, spilling toys across the wooden floor. Davies closed the door behind him and crossed to the second bedroom, pulling at the curtains as he did so.

It too was empty.

The last of the three doors was locked tight and the handle twisted impotently in his grasp. He took a step back then threw his weight against it. There was a shriek of buckling metal as the lock broke and Davies tumbled into the room. He sprawled heavily. The shotgun fell from his grasp and skidded across the floor. Suddenly seized by a spasm of terror, he grabbed for the weapon and looked up.

The room was empty. He cursed himself, realizing that the atmosphere was getting to him. Another empty room he thought and shook his head. Where the hell were the bloody things hiding?

It was as he emerged onto the landing that he heard the scraping from above. His heart leapt, thudding against his chest, the breath catching in his throat. He looked up.

'Oh God,' he gasped.

The trapdoor of the attic was out of place, half of it drawn back, revealing the impenetrable blackness within. The sound came again, louder this time. Davies leant back against the wall, his eyes fixed on the half open hole. My God, he thought, it was so obvious. The attic. What better place for them to hide? It was dark, out of sight, not easily accessible. His heart began racing and he took three deep breaths, forcing himself to calm down. Perhaps his imagination was getting the better of him, maybe it was just birds up there. They very often nested in lofts. Nevertheless, he would have to know for sure. But how to get up there? He looked around for something to stand on and remembered a chair in the second bedroom. Hastily retrieving it, he positioned it carefully beneath the black hole, his eyes constantly alert for any sign of movement. Cautiously he climbed onto the chair and found that he could reach the wooden surround of the attic entrance. He shook his head. That would mean him hauling himself up gradually, getting a firm handhold and dragging his bulky frame into the enveloping darkness. It was too risky, besides the fact that he would be momentarily unable to use his gun if there were any of the things up there. He shuddered at the thought, leaning against the guard rail which ran along one side of the landing.

That was the answer.

If he could use the guardrail as a further step up from the chair then he could ease himself up into the attic and still retain a firm grip on his gun. Davies set the plan in motion, finding that it was not as easy as he had anticipated. The guard rail creaked protestingly under his weight but he grabbed the wooden lip of the attic entrance, laid the shotgun inside and hauled himself up.

Christ, it was dark in there. He reached for his flashlight, fumbling around inside his jacket. He grabbed it and swung its powerful beam around the inside of the attic.

There were four of them in there and, even though he had half expected it, Davies was still shocked by their appearance. In fact, one, a man in his fifties, was already on his feet and advancing towards the policeman. Davies shone the light in his direction and the man covered his face against the bright light. The eyeless sockets remained open, glaring at Davies through meshed fingers. With a grunt of disgust, the policeman fired.

The blast hit the man in the chest and blew him across the small attic, but now the others were stirring and Davies realized that he couldn't hold the light up and fire at the same time. Praying, he fired off the remaining four cartridges, using each subsequent muzzle flash as a guide. When he'd finished, the room stunk of cordite and his ears were ringing from the swift deafening explosions. Hurriedly, he reached for the light and shone it in the direction of the living dead things. Joyful at first, he counted three bodies but then suddenly the awful realization hit him. He had seen four when he first entered the attic. Where was the fourth creature?

He swung around in time to catch it in the beam. What had once been a girl in her twenties, her eyeless sockets still caked with dark dry blood, ran at him, dark liquid gushing from a savage wound in her side which had exposed the intestines. Her mouth was open in a soundless scream of rage and, arms outstretched, she lunged at Davies. He rolled to one side and the girl tripped, falling head first through the open trapdoor. There was a sickening thud as she hit the landing below. Davies leapt down after her, his full weight landing on her torn body. His gun now empty, he snatched up the chair and brought it crashing down on her head. The one blow was all that was needed. Her skull collapsed like an egg shell, greyish slops of brain plopping onto the carpet. Seized with an almost insane hatred, the policeman reloaded his shotgun and fired two more shots into the inert form as if not quite satisfied that the creature was finally dead. The second blast tore off her head. What remained of it.

He stared down at the body, shaking with rage and fear.

'Bastard,' he said. 'Bastard. Fucking bastard.'

It was a moment or two before he recovered his composure and left the house, wondering what he would find in the next.

Walford brought Puma Three to a halt in the car park at the back of the block of flats where constable Ferman lived. The two of them had been ordered to check out the block with its twelve storeys and ninety flats. The two men sat in the car for a moment, gazing upwards to the top storey.

'Shit,' muttered Walford, 'we'll be here all day checking this lot.'

Ferman grinned and climbed out of the car. Walford followed a second later, wondering what his companion found so amusing.

'Don't worry about it,' said Ferman, 'we'll have this done in less than half an hour.'

They were already inside the main entrance hall, the lifts in front of them, two corridors on either side stretching away for hundreds of yards.

'Half an hour my backside,' said Walford, indignantly.

'Just shut up and come with me,' Ferman told him, heading for the flat nearest them. He fumbled in the pocket of his trousers and produced a key. 'My flat,' he announced. He opened the door and Walford shrank back. Curled up in front of the dormant gas fire were two of the biggest Alsatians he'd ever seen. The first animal looked up, saw Ferman and bounded across to him. He smiled and grabbed the dog, patting it and running his hand along its sleek body. 'This is King,' he announced, stroking the animal which looked at Walford lazily, regarding him as if it were looking at its next meal.

'They're big bastards, Stuart,' said Walford, trying to hide his apprehension. He wasn't too keen on dogs at the best of times and these bloody things looked like ponies, he'd never seen any as big.

'I look after them,' said Ferman proudly, stroking the second dog which licked at his hand. 'This one is Baron. If they can't sniff out those bloody things then no one can.'

'You know, you're not as daft as you look,' said Walford, smiling.

Both men checked their weapons. Ferman led the dogs out into the corridor and hastily locked his flat door behind them.

'What makes you so sure they'll be able to find anything?' Walford asked as they set off up the first corridor, the dogs leading.

'Dogs can usually sense when something's wrong,' Ferman said. 'It'll save us a lot of time if they can.'

They checked the place, floor by floor, all the time their ears and eyes alert. Ferman watching the two dogs, observing their reactions as they paused now and again at a door, one of them sniffing around, the other pacing back and forth.

On the fifth floor a door opened and a woman stuck her head out, suddenly alarmed by the sight of gun-carrying policemen and dogs.

'What's going on?' she asked, worriedly.

'Nothing to worry about,' lied Walford, 'just a check. We got a call from someone in the flats who'd reported someone suspicious hanging round.'

The woman looked at the two men and then at the dogs. She hesitated a moment then closed her door and both policemen heard a bolt being slid into place on the other side. They walked on.

'Mrs Cole,' Ferman announced, 'we probably interrupted her and one of her customers.' He laughed to himself. Walford looked puzzled. 'She's a bit of a goer if you get my drift.'

Walford did.

'Her husband's in the nick, some big black bloke. Right fucking headcase, alcoholic too. He used to knock the shit out of her. I dragged him in twice for assaulting her but she stayed with him. I suppose she's making up for lost time now. There's a different bloke in there every night.'

Walford started to sound interested. 'How old is she?'

'Thirty, maybe younger. Who knows?'

They reached the flight of steps which led up to the sixth floor and the dogs raced ahead. Ferman watched them go, wondering if they'd found something at last. When he and Walford finally caught up with the animals he saw that it was a false alarm. They continued their endless trekking along the maze of corridors. Doors were tried; those that were open they investigated, the ones that were locked they bypassed.

'I hope you're right about these bloody dogs,' said Walford. 'I mean, what if they've missed something?'

Ferman shook his head. 'No chance. If there's anything here, they'll find it.'

Someone else popped their head out of the doorway on the tenth floor. Mr Wilkins. A retired solicitor, Walford was told afterwards.

'Pompous old sod,' said Ferman as they walked on. 'He's a nosey old cunt, too. There's not a thing goes on in this bloody block that he doesn't know about.'

'Do you know everyone who lives here?' asked Walford, irritably.

Ferman smiled.

Eleventh floor and still nothing. The sun was beaming in through the huge picture windows at either end of the corridor and Walford leant back against the wall to rub his aching thighs.

'Only one more floor,' Ferman told him.

'Thank Christ for that. My bloody legs are killing me, all these stairs.'

It was King who started barking first. Walford looked around to see the animal standing at the far end of the corridor, hackles raised, barking madly at something which he couldn't see. A second later, Baron joined in and the entire corridor was filled with a cacophony of harsh yapping and growling. King began scratching at the door, growling, backing off then barking once more. The two policemen ran to where the dogs stood and Ferman grabbed their collars, pulling them back, finding that he needed all his strength to do so.

'Try the door,' he said, watching as Walford gently turned the handle. The dogs' frenzied barking had now subsided to a low guttural growling; both had their sharp eyes fixed on the door as the policeman turned the handle and pushed it open a few inches.

'What do we do?' asked Walford. 'Let them go in?' He nodded towards the waiting animals.

Ferman bit his lip contemplatively. 'There is the chance they could be wrong.'

'You said...'

'All right. But I'll go in with them.' Ferman swallowed hard. He told his companion to hold the two Alsatians while he himself worked the pump action of his shotgun, chambering a shell.

Walford held the dogs as best he could, stunned by their power.

'Let them go,' snapped Ferman, simultaneously kicking open the door.

The two animals hurtled in, Ferman following. There was a flurry of barking and howling from the room beyond him as he ran to catch up with the dogs. They had barged through a half open door inside which the policeman knew led into one of the bedrooms. All the flats were built the same; this one was no different to his own. He kicked open the second door and froze.

What had once been a man in his forties was struggling with the two animals, yellow spittle dribbling over his chin. He snarled and bit like they did, uttering the same harsh animal sounds so that it was difficult to determine who was making the noises. He had one hand clamped round Baron's throat, while the bulk of King clung to his other arm, teeth firmly embedded in the flesh. The living dead thing grunted and hurled Baron away, the animal smashing into the far wall, staggering for a second then racing back at the creature. He tried to bludgeon King away and, by turning, left his face exposed. Baron launched himself at the man's unprotected side and tore away a large chunk of skin. Blood spurted into the air and the dog fell away. The living dead thing spun round, bringing one hand down hard on King's head. The animal dropped like a stone and Ferman raised his shotgun, anger boiling within him.

'You bastard,' he muttered, and fired twice. Both shots hit their target and the man was slammed back against the wall. He stood there for a second before slumping forward, a huge crimson smear trailing out behind him, his entrails spilling in an untidy pattern on the floor before him.

Ferman dropped his gun and ran to King. He knew before he reached it that the animal was dead, its skull crushed to pulp by the powerful blow it had received. Baron, whimpering softly, licked at the policeman's hand and he had to fight hard to keep back a tear.

Walford appeared in the doorway. He looked in, saw the dead dog and the corpse and left, staggering into the corridor outside. Ferman finally emerged, carrying the body of the dog, Baron close behind him. The policeman's face was set, his jaw firm, the knot of muscles at its side pulsing angrily.

'I loved that dog,' he said, softly. And Walford reached out to touch his shoulder.

'Come on,' he said, still shaking from what he'd just seen, 'we'd better report in.'

Lambert was surprised at how many people there were in the centre of Medworth that morning. Perhaps they just chose not to hide or realized that they were not in so much danger during the daylight hours. The sun shining brightly overhead seemed to add much needed reassurance.

He had just received the reports from the three other cars, well over half the town had been covered now and, as yet, only eight or nine of the things had been found. The evidence seemed to support Lambert's own theory that the bulk of them hid together during the day. But where?...

He glanced up at the clock on the council offices as he guided the Capri along the main street. It was 1:30 p.m. They had less than five hours of daylight left. Bell and he had covered an extensive area themselves that morning but had found nothing. A search of two pub cellars had revealed nothing, neither had a house to house probe which had taken in most of Medworth's largest estate.

Lambert swung the Capri round the roundabout at the top of the main street and guided it into the narrow delivery road which led up to the back of the suupermarket which was the next sight of their quest. It had, up until three days ago, been a large branch of Sainsbury's but, as events in the town had become progressively worse, the management had pulled out, closing the store down. The Inspector brought the car to a halt in one of the loading bays and shut off the engine. Better to go in the back way, he thought. The people in the town were jumpy enough without seeing two coppers walking around with shotguns. He radioed in to the station, telling Grogan that they were going in. The Inspector hesitated a second, considering the handset which he held, then, almost as an afterthought, he said, 'Any word from Doctor Kirby yet?'

Grogan said that there wasn't and Lambert switched off the set. He sat for a second then reached for his shotgun and swung himself out of the car. Bell followed. As they reached towards the twin doors which marked the back of the supermarket, the Inspector's thoughts returned to his wife. Kirby had promised to contact the station as soon as Debbie woke up. He must have given her a pretty strong dose of sedative if she was still out. Lambert hoped that she would wake up in time. She was, after all, the only one who knew the horrendous truth behind all that had transpired these last two months. He hoped that her knowledge would be enough.

The two men reached the large doors and Lambert pressed down hard on the locking bar. It wouldn't budge an inch either way.

'Stand back,' he said, working the pump action of the shotgun.

Bell took several steps back and watched as his superior fired a blast, point blank, into the end of the bar. Lumps of metal and pieces of shot ricocheted into the air. Lambert kicked at the bar and it gave. The door swung back.

Both men looked at one another and, with the Inspector leading, walked in.

From the piles of boxes and cans, both men realized that they were in the supermarket's vast storeroom. On all sides, every kind of tinned and packaged food rose in huge towers and Lambert almost smiled to himself. Christ, the owners must have been anxious to get out to leave this amount of stuff behind. There was a fruity smell in the room, a more pleasant odour than the perpetual mustiness they had encountered nearly everywhere earlier in the day. They separated, ensuring that every inch of the storeroom was searched.

Away to his left, Lambert heard a crash and spun round, the shotgun at the ready.

'Bell,' he called.

'I'm all right, sir,' came the reply. 'Just tripped over a box of bloody baked beans.'

Lambert smiled and made his way cautiously towards the next set of doors which confronted them. Bell joined him and the men found themselves faced by row upon row of shopping trolleys, all arranged in front of the doors. They heaved them to one side, making a path. Lambert pushed the doors, relieved to find that they opened easily. The two policemen found themselves in the supermarket proper. He remembered it when it had been full of people, bustling up and down the aisles like ants moving around the nest, snatching things from the shelves to put in their baskets and trolleys. Now the place was deserted, as quiet as a grave, its once powerful banks of fluorescents now dead, leaving the entire huge amphitheatre in a kind of semi-darkness. Lambert thought about turning on his flashlight but realized that he could see perfectly well without it. Away to their right was another doorway, this one open; it led into the meat storage area. There would be time later to check that.

'You take the end aisles,' said the Inspector, softly, almost reluctant to disturb the peace and solitude within the vast empty building. 'Work your way to the middle. I'll do the same from that side.' He hooked a thumb over his shoulder. Bell nodded and walked off, his boots echoing conspicuously on the tiled floor.

As he made his way slowly down the furthermost aisle, Lambert had already made the assumption that this was not the resting place of the creatures. It was too open, even the fridges didn't have tops. He reached the bottom of the aisle and peered across through the gloom to see Bell emerge at the far end of the supermarket. The constable raised a hand and Lambert nodded. They both started up the next aisle, giving mutual signals when they reached the end.

This procedure continued until they met in the central aisle.

'What now?' said Bell, relieved that nothing had turned up.

'The freezers,' said Lambert, motioning with the barrel of his gun, 'where they keep the meat.'

The two men headed for the storage room, Lambert noting that a pile of cans was strewn across the floor near the entrance. Probably someone had knocked them over in their hurry to leave. Or perhaps....

The door to the cold storage room was open and the Inspector walked in. The place was larger than he'd expected. All down the left hand wall was a stainless steel topped work bench, the butchers' implements still spread out upon it. Carving knives, cleavers, saws and the Inspector could see that some of it was still dark with dried blood. Running the full length of the room were six metal rods, each about four inches thick and placed more than six feet from the ground. A number of meat hooks hung from them, suspended from one of which was a Whole pig. Lambert wondered why just one carcass should have been left behind. Probably no reason at all; maybe his imagination was getting the better of him again. The far end of the room was made up entirely of fridges, huge coffin-like things which must have been more than four feet deep. The white tiled floor was spotted red in places and, with the coolant turned off, both men began to notice the pungent odour of putrifying meat. It was dark in there, very dark and now both of them switched on their torches. Lambert smelt another odour, the sharp smell of sweat which he realized was his own. He swallowed hard and walked slowly towards the waiting fridges at the far end of the room, gun in one hand, torch in the other. Bell followed his example. They reached the first of the freezers and Lambert laid his flashlight on top of the adjacent fridge.

'Shine the light here,' he told Bell, both men's faces looking white in the powerful beam. The constable obeyed, watching as Lambert hooked one powerful hand under the lid and flipped it back.

Empty.

Both men breathed heavily and Lambert's voice was low when he spoke:

'I'll start at the other end. We'll check each one. Then we'll get the hell out of here.' He was nervous and he didn't mind admitting it. He retrieved his flashlight and hurried to the end of the line of fridges. There were eight in all. He laid his light on top of the metal lid of the next freezer along and, propping the shotgun up against the wall, raised the first lid.

Empty.

Further along, Bell was repeating the procedure. He too, found nothing. Both men moved along, hearts thumping and, twice; Lambert was forced to wipe beads of perspiration from his forehead.

He opened his third fridge and found it empty. Bell actually had his hand on the lid when it shot up, knocking the shotgun and the torch from his grasp. He shrieked and Lambert spun round, the torch beam highlighting the horror before him.

The creature, a woman (Lambert wasn't sure because of the long hair and bad light), had one powerful hand clamped around Bell's neck and was dragging him into the fridge. He clung to the sides, fighting against the strength which held him, his eyes bulging wide in pain and terror. Lambert reached for the Browning but, as he pulled it free of the holster, he realized that he dare not shoot for fear of hitting his companion. He shone his flashlight full in the face of the thing which he now saw was a youth in his early twenties. The creature opened its mouth in silent protest, trying to shield its eyeless face with one hand while throttling Bell with the other. Lambert ran forward and struck the thing full in the face with the flashlight. The room was plunged into darkness and Bell fell to the ground. Lambert flung himself down, his desperate fingers searching the floor for the dropped light.

Grinning, the thing was dragging itself out of the fridge.

Lambert saw the light, lying not more than ten feet from him. He threw himself towards it, hearing Bell shriek again as the thing grabbed for him. The constable rolled clear and the living dead creature was caught in two minds for a second, not sure which of the two men to pursue. It saw Lambert reach the light and came after him, anxious to extinguish it. The light which brought so much pain.

The Inspector felt the crushing weight of the creature on him and powerful hands snaked around his neck, choking him. He gripped the hands and tried to pull them free. Bell stood motionless, watching the tableau, too frightened to move.

'For fuck's sake get it off,' screamed Lambert, his shout finally galvanizing the stunned constable into action. He looked around for a weapon, squinting through the gloom to the table of butcher's implements. His eyes sought, and found, the cleaver. Whimpering, he grabbed it and brought it crashing down on the living dead corpse, aiming for its head. But the blow missed by inches, sliced off one of its ears and powered into the shoulder at the point of clavicle and jugular vein. There was an enormous fountain of blood which sprayed out like a crimson jet.

Lambert felt the pressure on his throat eased and he struck out, knocking the creature off. It fell back, the blood still spouting from its neck but, in the darkness, both men saw it wrench the cleaver free and, despite the frenzied spurtings of dark fluid from its wound, come at them once more. Scarcely believing what he saw, Lambert backed off. The thing made a last desperate charge and brought the cleaver hurtling down with the force of a steamhammer. Bell, retreating also, slipped in a pool of blood and raised his hand to shield himself from the attack.

The bloodied blade sliced through his arm just above the wrist, the severed limb flying into the air. He began screaming, holding up the shattered stump as if it were a prize, blood pouring from the remains of his arm.

Lambert at last had a clear shot and, with Bell's screams ringing in his ears, he squeezed off two, three, four shots.

Moving at a speed of over 1,100 feet a second, the heavy grain bullets tore into the living corpse, blasting exit holes the size of fists. The impact hurled it across the darkened room where it slammed into the fridges, blood spattering up the smooth white sides. Lambert fired again, again, again. Blasting the body into an unrecognizable bloody rag. Finally he lowered the gun, the muzzle flashes still burned onto his retina, the roar of fire in his ears but, above all that, the delirious screams of Bell as he staggered a couple of feet before dropping to his knee still holding up the stump of his wrist.

Screams. Screams.

Lambert vomited. Only by a supreme effort of will did he manage to stop himself fainting. Leaving Bell alone in the store room, he staggered out.

He managed to reach the Capri and radio for help, but then, as he dropped the handset, he lost his fight and finally did pass out.

Thirty-Two

Lambert sat up, felt hands on his shoulder. He grunted and reached for his gun, suddenly frightened. But slowly; his wits returned to him, he saw the face of Hayes looking in at him.

'You all right, guv?' he asked, his big hand still on the young Inspector's shoulder.

Lambert was still dazed. He saw the two dark uniformed men carrying someone to the back of a waiting ambulance. Its blue light was spinning and the engine was humming but there were no other sounds. He caught a brief glimpse of Bell's face, milk-white as they manoeuvred him inside the vehicle. The Inspector exhaled, running a hand through his hair.

'Where the hell did you come from?' he asked, groggily.

'Grogan picked up your message. We were the nearest car, so here we are.' The sergeant smiled.

'I blacked out,' said Lambert, not that the explanation was really necessary.

One of thee ambulancemen, a tall man with sad eyes, walked across to the car and looked in at Lambert.

'Will you be O.K. ?' he said.

The Inspector nodded. 'Thanks.' He paused. 'What about Bell?'

'He'll live, but he's lost a lot of blood.'

Lambert nodded again and rubbed his face in the imitation of washing. The ambulanceman took one more careful look at him then walked away and got into his vehicle. In seconds, it was pulling out, the scream of its siren now filling the air. Lambert shook himself, then felt something being pressed into his hand. He looked down to see that it was a silver hip flask. Hayes nodded towards it and the Inspector drank, allowing the liquor to burn its way to his stomach.

'Purely medicinal of course,' said Hayes, smiling.

Lambert too found the strength to grin, handing the flask back to the sergeant. A thought suddenly struck him.

'Any news of my wife?' he asked, hopefully.

'Grogan called about ten minutes ago. You must have been in there,' he pointed to the supermarket, 'at the time. Doctor Kirby says that she's conscious.'

Already Lambert was starting the engine but the sergeant reached out a hand and switched it off.

'What the hell are you doing?' snarled Lambert angrily.

'Let me drive, guv,' said the sergeant softly.

The Inspector nodded. 'I'm sorry.' He slid across, allowing Hayes to settle his considerable bulk behind the wheel. He called to Jenkins to follow them and the constable nodded, gunning Puma One into life.

The two cars swung out of the loading bay and, within minutes, were on the road leading to Kirby's house.

Kirby had hardly got the door open when Lambert barged in.

'Is she all right?' he demanded.

Already he was bounding up the stairs to the bedroom where he knew Debbie to be. He flung open the door and she turned her head and smiled at him. Lambert rushed across to her and took her in both arms. They hugged each other for long minutes. Finally, he let her go and he saw the tears in her eyes. She gripped his hand and he reached out to brush her cheek with his finger tips.

'Are you O.K.?' he asked, his voice little more than a whisper.

She nodded, squeezing his hand harder. 'Tom, those things.' He saw more tears welling up and ran his hand over her forehead.

'Don't worry, we found some of them this morning.'

'And?'

'We killed them.'

She seemed reassured and her tone brightened a little, but her voice was still croaky. He saw a jug and glass on the small bedside table and poured her some water. She drank and handed the glass back to him.

'Tom,' she said, 'I found out about Mathias, about the medallion. What Trefoile told us about him was true. He was a Black Magician, and that medallion belonged to him. He'd found the secret of reversing death, bringing the dead back to life. That's what the inscription on the medallion means; "To Awake the Dead." ' She gripped his hand and he edged closer, putting one arm around her shoulder as she continued.

'Mathias was buried alive for his crimes, his blasphemies they called them, but before that, his tongue was torn out and he was blinded. They gouged out his eyes. It was some old superstition, so that he couldn't see or speak of the evil he'd committed. It's all in my notes at home.' As she mentioned the word he felt her body stiffen.

'Oh God, I don't think I can ever go back there, Tom, not after what happened last night.' She hugged him, fighting back the tears. He ran his hand through her hair, kissing the top of her head.

Kirby appeared in the doorway.

'Come on, Tom,' he said, quietly, 'don't tire her too much.'

Reluctantly, Lambert broke away but Debbie held onto his hand. 'What are you going to do?'

'I'll drive back to the house,' he told her. 'See if there's any clue in your notes as to where Mathias's grave might be.'

'It said he was buried in ground not blessed by the church. Unconsecrated ground.'

Lambert nodded.

'Tom.'

He looked at her.

'You know why they took the medallion?'

He looked vague.

'If it is ever returned to Mathias, it'll enable him to rise again. They must know where he's buried.'

Lambert looked across at the clock on the dressing table. It said 4:30 p.m.

They had ninety minutes of daylight left. Lambert's mind was spinning. He had to drive back to the house, pick up Debbie's notes, praying that there might be some clue as to where the grave of Mathias was, but, above all, he had to find the remaining living dead before nightfall. He shuddered. Debbie pulled him close one last time and this time the tears flowed in an unceasing river. They held each other for a long time, Debbie sobbing softly, her head buried within his arms. Finally he pulled away, supporting her head in his hands. He kissed her.

'I love you,' he said, softly.

'Tom, for God's sake be careful,' she sobbed.

He kissed her on the forehead and then he was gone, his heart seized with the icy conviction that he might never see her again. But overriding that feeling was one of grim determination. As he left Kirby's house, the doctor heard him muttering one phrase over and over to himself, like some kind of litany-

'I'll get you, you bastards. All of you.'

He bypassed Hayes and Jenkins and climbed into the Capri, shouting at the two other policemen to keep up their search. Then he drove off, not even thinking to look up at the bedroom window where Debbie stood, watching as the car disappeared out of sight.

Already, the first warning clouds of dusk were beginning to gather on the horizon.

Thirty-Three

Lambert sat in the Capri for precious minutes before he could actually pluck up the courage to walk up to his house. The memory of the previous night was burned indelibly into his mind and he wondered if the image would ever fade. But, at the moment, time was the important factor so he swung himself out of the car and headed up the path towards the front door. There were tyre tracks on the front lawn, patches of dark blood spattered over the front of the house. He walked in, through the still open front door, hanging by its single remaining hinge. He cast a furtive glance up the stairs as if expecting to see the things waiting for him once more. There was more blood on the stair carpet and up the white walls. He entered the living room, a cold breeze blowing through the smashed bay window. It stirred the papers scattered across the floor.

More blood and the pervading stench of death. Lambert hunted quickly through the papers strewn across the carpet and desk. Even some of these bore tiny specks of dried crimson. It took him about ten minutes to find what he sought. He gathered up the necessary information and hurried from the house back to the warmth and safety of the car. There, he read through Debbie's notes, found it all just as she had told him earlier. He reread, his eyes straying back to that one phrase:

... in ground not Blessed of the Church is buried the one known as Mathias.

Unconsecrated ground. Christ, that could mean anywhere. He laid the notes on the passenger seat and started the engine, swinging the Capri round and driving back into Medworth.

As he drove, reports came in periodically from the other cars. All of them the same. Nothing to report. Not one of the things had been sighted since the morning. Lambert glanced at his watch. Nearly five o'clock. Less than an hour until nightfall.

He took the route through the already quiet town centre. There were only a few people about, all of them anxious to be home before darkness. The Inspector drove past the huge silent edifice of the deserted cinema, glancing at it as he did so. The letters above the entrance had fallen in places, blown down by the wind. He smiled as he read the sign:

TH EM IR C NEM.

It towered over him as he drove past, a monument to obsolescence.

Lambert slammed on the brakes, the Capri skidding to a halt.

One of the cinema's side doors was slightly ajar.

He sat still, his breath coming in gasps. The place had been closed for over two years now. And yet, the wooden door was propped open, wide enough for a man to squeeze through. Lambert snatched up the shotgun from beside him, made sure the Browning was loaded and got out of the car. There were two sets of doors facing him. He had been in the cinema a number of times before it closed down and he knew that both sets of doors were exits. One from the stalls, one from the balcony. But right now he couldn't remember which was which. He pushed the open door and it moved slightly, the hinges shrieking in protest. Lambert squeezed through, surprised at how light it was inside. He knew immediately, from the wide flight of stone steps which faced him, that this exit led down from the balcony.

Moving slowly, his ears alert for the slightest sound, he began to climb.

Half way up, the staircase turned in a right angle, flattening out into a small landing before rising, in another flight of steps, towards the doors which led into the balcony itself. There was a large frosted glass window set in the wall and that was where the light was coming from. The window itself had been broken in two places and a cold draught blew through, creating an unnerving high pitched moan.

A few feet away from him, its door cracked and peeling, was the toilet. A rusty sign on it proudly proclaimed - Gentlemen.

The door was closed. Lambert crossed to the door and, swallowing hard, pulled it open. He stepped in. The place stank of damp and blocked drains. The single window had been bricked up and the Inspector found it hard to see in the gloom. There was a tiled urinal area and a single cubicle. He pushed the door open and found, to his relief, that it was empty. The persistent drip, drip of water from the old cistern added background to the Inspector's laboured breathing. He left the toilet and began climbing the second flight of stone steps which would take him into the balcony itself. The twin doors which led into it were firmly closed. Heart thudding against his ribs, he pulled open one of the doors and stepped inside.

The darkness was total. Almost palpable, like some thick black fog, totally impenetrable and clinging around him like a living thing. Lambert, literally, couldn't see his hand in front of him. He fumbled in his jacket for his flashlight and realized, angrily, that he'd lost it earlier that afternoon in the supermarket. He fumbled for his lighter and found it, the yellow light giving him a few precious feet of visibility.

Using its light as a guide, he climbed the steps which eventually levelled out onto a kind of walk way, separating front from rear balcony. He knew, from memory, that the main entrance was about twenty yards to his right, but in the all enveloping darkness he could see no farther than the glow his lighter allowed him. He walked on, heading for the entrance, becoming more aware of the stench which filled the place with each passing second. Not just the odour of dampness which he expected, but something more powerful. The carrion odour of rotting flesh. Excrement. Death.

There was a movement behind him and Lambert spun round, the dim light from the lighter totally inadequate for the task. He saw nothing but remained in that position, gun at the ready. Waiting and listening. Then finally, slowly, he turned again.

The dull glow of the lighter shone straight into the grinning face of Ray Mackenzie.

Lambert shouted in sudden terror, dropped the lighter and was plunged into total darkness once more. He rolled away, knowing that Mackenzie was coming for him. The Inspector fired one blast into the air.

In the thunderflash explosion of the discharge, the entire vast amphitheatre was momentarily illuminated and Lambert saw an image which he had always suspected. Always feared.

In the swift blinding light he saw them. Fifty. Sixty. Probably more. Living corpses all around him. He cursed himself for not having had the place searched before. It was so simple.

But now, in that brief moment of light, he knew he had found them.

Thirty-Four

For untold seconds nothing happened, then Lambert fired again, using the gun as a source of light. He fired off the five cartridges in rapid succession, moving towards the area where he knew the stairs to be. He didn't even know whether he hit any of the creatures with his blasts, but as his finger jerked a last time on the trigger, something warm and wet splashed across his face. His hand found the banister which led down the short flight of steps to the balcony entrance, He tried to jump the distance, tripped and tumbled to the bottom of the stairs, losing the shotgun in the process. He pushed open the door and a kind of dull half light flooded the bottom of the staircase. Lying at the bottom, Lambert looked up and saw the things crowding above him, Mackenzie at their head. The light stunned them for a second, long enough to enable Lambert to clamber to his feet and burst out of the balcony doors. He heard them thundering after him.

A few feet of carpeted landing and he was at the stairs which led down into the foyer.

Mackenzie burst from the doors in pursuit, others behind him and Lambert could smell their stench as he ran, taking the stairs two and three at a time. He reached the bottom and flung himself the last few feet, skidding across the tiled foyer floor.

The living dead pounded down behind him, one or two of them reaching the ground floor a mere second after him.

Lambert spun round, pulling the Browning from its holster. He fired with one hand, the recoil almost breaking his wrist, but by some miracle the shots hit their target and two of the creatures were felled. But now more were flooding the foyer and Lambert dashed for the twin sets of double doors, smashing the glass in one as he slammed into it, desperate to reach the main doors of the cinema. The things clattered after him, pausing a moment when he shot down two more. But now it was Lambert's turn to pause.

He turned to the great, steel braced glass doors and almost shrieked when he saw the chains and padlocks which held them firmly shut.

The first of the creatures came at him through the double doors and he blew half its head off, then another, recoiling from the light, shielding its eyeless sockets in pain. Lambert realized that the light was his only hope. He tore down the curtains which masked the twin sets of double doors, flooding ten feet from him. The Inspector felt sick, overpowered by the collective stench which emanated from them. He gave himself a moment's respite and fired at one of the padlocks. The heavy grain bullet shattered it and Lambert tore the chain free, kicking at the heavy door, shouting when it stuck. He threw all his weight against it, aware that the bolder of the creatures were drawing closer to him. He fired. The first of them went down, blood jetting from the wound in its throat.

Mackenzie ran at Lambert, his lips drawn back in that familiar hideous feral grin.

It was the force of his charge which finally catapulted Lambert through the half-open door and onto the pavement outside.

The other creatures cowered back from the light which flooded in through the glass and Mackenzie was left outside. Lambert felt his weight on him and struggled to free himself, aware that his attacker was becoming weaker in the light. Lambert remembered that he still held the length of chain and he lashed out savagely with it, catching Mackenzie across the cheek and laying it open to the bone. Those burning red orbs glowed intensely, defiant to the end. Lambert brought the chain whipping down across the man's skull. The heavy links split the flesh of his scalp, tearing away hunks of hair. Mackenzie dropped to his knees, his blazing red eyes still fixed on Lambert who had retrieved the Browning.

From point blank range, the policeman fired, almost shouting his delight as the bullet slammed into Mackenzie's jaw just below the ear, tearing it off before erupting from the back of his neck. Mackenzie sagged forward in a spreading pool of blood and

Lambert put three more into him, finding something akin to pleasure in the damage the bullets wrought. He stared down at the body, frightened it would get up. At last he bolted for his car and snatched up the handset.

'Grogan,' he barked, continuing before the man had even had time to acknowledge, 'get all the cars to the Empire in town. The cinema. They're here. All of them. They're here.' He was shouting now. 'And I want petrol, lots of petrol and tell them to hurry, for fuck's sake tell them to hurry.' He threw the handset back inside the Capri and dashed back to the front of the building, peering in at the remaining living corpses. Jesus, there must be upwards of eighty, he thought. He looked at his watch.

5:30.

Night was drawing in fast. Lambert prayed they would make it in time.

The three police cars arrived within minutes of one another. Lambert told all of them to switch on their headlights and keep them trained on the front of the cinema.

'What about the petrol?' asked the Inspector, looking at Hayes.

As if in answer to his question, a Shell delivery tanker rumbled up the street and Lambert caught sight of Grogan behind the wheel. The policeman drove up onto the pavement in front of the cinema and leapt down from the cab. Together, he and Lambert pulled the hose free and Lambert placed the nozzle just inside the main door of the building.

'Turn it on,' he shouted.

Clambering back into the cab, Grogan flicked a switch and gallon after gallon of petrol pumped into the foyer of the cinema. The policemen in the cars could see the living dead cowering back from the blazing headlamps, stepping in the flooding petrol, falling over one another in their attempts to reach the darkness. Many stumbled into the stalls for shelter but Lambert had men posted at each exit with orders to shoot anything that came out. Nothing would come out of that place tonight.

A red light winked on the dashboard of the tanker and Grogan yelled that the tank was empty.

Lambert ran to the safety of the nearest car then, taking a shotgun from Walford, fired four times into the petrol flooded cinema foyer.

There was an ear splitting roar and a blinding flash as the flammable liquid went up with a high-pitched shriek.

The creatures not immediately incinerated in the conflagration were either burned as the fire took hold throughout the entire building or shot down as they bolted from the exits.

Almost in awe, the men of the Medworth force watched as huge tongues of flame licked up the outsides of the building, the entire place transformed into a huge oven. For four hours it burned, the smoke rising thickly into the night sky until at last, gutted and destroyed, the roof collapsed, sending out a blistering shower of sparks.

By first light the next morning all that remained was a gigantic blackened ruin, like some huge pile of charcoal, choking black smoke still drifting from the remains.

The men had stood silently for a while, not daring to believe that it was all over but then Lambert had given the order for them to leave and, led by him, they had driven off.

Lambert felt no elation, merely a crushing weight of weariness, of total emotional and physical exhaustion. His desire to rest overwhelmed all but one feeling.

He thought of Debbie.

No one had seen the thing which had once been Gary Briggs crawl from the boot of Puma Three that night. All had been too intent on watching the incineration of the living dead.

When they left, the Briggs thing crept into the ruins of the cinema, searching. It knew that it would have to be quick for the sun would be at its zenith soon and the pain would be too great. But it found what it sought and it left the blackened hell where the other living dead had sought refuge.

Now it hid in the church up at Two Meadows, sheltering from the light. At home in the bell tower where no sun could reach it.

It knew what it had to do and knew how to do it. It rested, clutching the medallion to its chest.

It waited for the coming of night.

Thirty-Five

'You'll do,' said Kirby, tucking away his stethoscope. Lambert pulled his shirt back on and began fastening it.

'What about the rest?' asked the Inspector, tucking the shirt into his trousers.

'They were fine too,' Kirby told him. The two men looked at each other for a moment then the doctor said, 'Back to normal eh, Tom?'

Lambert shrugged, 'I don't think anything will ever be bloody normal after what's happened here these past couple of months.' He ran a hand through his hair, 'I'm just pleased it's over.'

'Amen to that,' said Debbie, who was sitting in a chair across the room from the couch on which Lambert perched. They were in Kirby's surgery.

'I hear Jenkins' wife had a little girl,' said the doctor, smiling.

Lambert nodded, 'I sent him on leave to be with her. Walford and Hayes are off too. They deserve the rest after what they've been through. The others will get their chance in a couple of weeks.'

'And what about you?' asked Kirby.

'What about me?'

'When do you take your leave?'

Lambert slid down from the couch, 'I don't. There's still work to be done, John. I'm in charge of the force here; it's my job to see that it gets done.'

'Tom, be sensible. After what you've been through, you more than anyone need a couple of days off.'

'We all went through the same. What about Bell, what about Briggs? At least I'm still alive.'

Kirby turned to Debbie. 'Can't you talk some sense into this hard-headed bastard?'

Debbie smiled humourlessly and shook her head, 'I gave up trying to do that a long time ago.'

Lambert extended a hand which Kirby shook warmly. 'Thanks for everything, John,' said the Inspector.

'You can stop here as long as you like, you know,' Kirby told him.

Lambert shook his head.

'You're not going back home, then?'

'Not after what happened there,' Lambert told him. 'I don't think either of us could face it again. There's a little place in Bramton, about twenty miles from here. I don't mind the journey every day. We couldn't stay here after what's happened.'

Kirby nodded. Debbie got to her feet and joined her husband and they walked out to the car with Kirby at their side. He kissed Debbie lightly on the cheek and watched as both of them climbed into the Capri. Lambert rolled the window down and looked up at the doctor.

'I'll be in touch,' he said, and started the engine. The Capri moved off and Kirby watched it disappear out of sight over the hill. He stood for long moments alone on the hillside, until at last the cool breeze drove him back inside. Into the warmth.

'Are you really going back straight away?' said Debbie, studying Lambert's profile as he drove.

'What choice do I have?' he asked.

'Can't you put someone else in charge for a couple of days? Christ, Tom, two days won't hurt will it?' There was a note of exasperation in her voice. He reached across and placed his hand on her thigh.

'We'll see,' he said, smiling.

They drove for a long way in silence, the policeman taking back roads, dirt tracks, anything he could to avoid the hustle and bustle of main roads. When they had reached a particularly secluded spot he stopped the car and got out. Debbie followed him. He walked away from the vehicle, catching her hand and pulling her close to him. They stood on the hilltop, the whole of Medworth and its surrounding countryside spread out before them. The air was fresh, filled with the scent of damp grass and wild flowers which added an occasional clutch of colour in the all encompassing greenery of the fields. Lambert bent and picked a single bloom, sniffing it before he handed it to Debbie. She kissed him, pulling him down on top of her in that damp field. Their hands sought each other's bodies, their tongues eager for the taste of the other's mouth.

There, in that open field, high on the hill side, they made love with a passion they had never before experienced.

High above the sun shone down, its warming rays covering them.

Lambert woke with a start and looked at his watch. He sat up, startled, shivering. Beside him, Debbie stirred and nestled closer to him for warmth. Lambert began to laugh. He laughed until the tears ran down his face. Debbie looked up at him, his own merriment contagious. She too began to laugh.

She realized what he was laughing at. They were naked. Both of them, there on the hillside. They'd fallen asleep after their lovemaking, beneath the comforting warmth of the sun. She checked her own watch.

Four-fifty.

Still giggling, they dressed quickly and retreated to the safety of the car just as spots of rain began to fall from the rapidly darkening sky. They sat there for a moment, both now free of the tension which they had felt for so long.

'Maybe just two days,' said Lambert, smiling.

Debbie leaned across and kissed him.

He started the car and drove off. It wasn't until they reached the centre of Medworth itself that she realized what he was doing. Even after all he had gone through, the memory was still with him. She realized he was heading for the cemetery. To take one last look at his brother's grave. Lambert still bore the sting of guilt, but now, somehow, he had managed to come to terms with it. He had to see Mike's grave once more.

By the time they reached the cemetery, the sun had retreated from the sky, driven away by a combination of gathering storm clouds and the onset of night. Twilight hovered like a hawk in the darkening heavens.

Lambert shut off the engine and looked across at Debbie.

'Stay here.' He smiled, warmly.

But she was already out of the car, reaching for his hand, their feet crunching on the gravel of the driveway. An icy wind had sprung up and the first large spots of rain were beginning to fall as they left the driveway and walked the pathway which led to Mike's grave.

A silent fork of lightning split the clouds and Debbie jumped. Lambert smiled and hugged her tighter as they walked. They finally reached the grave and stood beneath the big oak tree which hung over it, listening to the rain pelting down. Lambert read his brother's name and felt no pain, just a deep sense of loss. The wound was healing and he knew it. He had at last found the strength to come to terms with his brother's death. It was as if the destruction of the past two months had somehow put it into perspective. What was the phrase... ?

Just a drop in the ocean...

They stood for long moments, close to one another, ignoring the rain which dripped onto them. Then finally, Lambert said,

'Come on.'

It was as they turned that they saw the figure emerge from the church.

At first neither moved and it was obvious that the person hurrying across the cemetery had not seen them. The oak hid them from its view. Lambert squinted through the pouring rain to get a glimpse of the figure, which seemed to be dressed in a uniform of some sort. And it was carrying something....

There was a blinding explosion of lightning and Lambert saw who the person was.

'Oh my God,' he breathed, 'it's Briggs.'

Debbie didn't understand but she felt a sudden, ungovernable terror rise in her.

'He's got the medallion,' gasped Lambert, watching, riveted, as the living dead thing shambled quickly towards the patch of waste ground a hundred yards away. Waste ground. Outside the boundaries of church land.

The realization hit them both like a steam hammer, but it was Debbie who spoke first. 'Tom, the Unconsecrated Ground. Mathias's grave must be there.' She was pointing to the line of trees which marked the outskirts of the scrubland. Lambert was running, screaming at her over his shoulder to get back to the car, bellowing to make himself heard above the driving rain and persistent roaring of thunder. Debbie watched him for a second then she too ran, the breath rasping in her lungs, heading for the cemetery gates and the safety of the car.

Lambert reached the crest of the ridge in time to see Briggs tearing clods of earth up with his hands, furiously digging deeper.

The Inspector paused and pulled the Browning from his holster. He steadied himself, aimed and squeezed off a shot. It threw up a small geyser of earth a foot from the rapidly digging Briggs who paid it no attention. Lambert fired again.

This time the shot sped past its target and disappeared into the distance.

The rain seemed to have intensified and even the loud retort of the Browning was drowned by the persistent rumbling and crashing of thunder.

The Briggs-thing felt its fingers connect with wood and it redoubled its efforts, tearing the coffin lid free and exposing the mouldy skeleton of Mathias. Grinning madly, the living dead corpse picked up the medallion, holding it aloft for a second, then placed it carefully on the chest of the skeleton.

Lambert fired a last time and ran towards the thing crouching in the centre of the waste ground.

His final shot was on target. It powered into Briggs' side just below the right armpit, tearing through the rib cage and exploding from the other side to send a confetti of shattered bone and gobbets of lung tissue flying into the air. The impact toppled the creature but didn't kill it. Blood pumping from its wound, it staggered to its feet to meet Lambert's onslaught. The Inspector used the butt end of the pistol like a club, smashing it down on Briggs' head with a force that buckled the metal. The head split open and the creature keeled over.

Lambert, gasping for breath and almost blinded by the rain turned and looked down into the coffin where Mathias lay. He saw a bony hand grab for his ankle, but as he backed off he realized that he was too late.

Debbie had never worked a handset before and now, in the moment when she most needed it, she couldn't find the knowledge what to do next. She suddenly had an idea. The Capri roared into life as she twisted the ignition key. She stepped hard on the accelerator and it shot forward, spraying gravel out behind it.

Mathias stood erect in the centre of the waste ground, the medallion gleaming around his neck.

Lambert was shaking, his eyes riveted to the spectre of pure evil which confronted him.

It must have towered a good six inches above him, and he guessed its height to be somewhere around six feet six. The tattered shroud which was the only thing that covered its body hung in gossamer wisps, scarcely hiding the yellowed flesh which was stretched over thick bones like parchment. And yet there was a power there which Lambert could almost feel, not least in those gaping black eyeless sockets which fixed him in their stare, tiny pinpricks of red light at their centres gradually expanding until they filled the whole gaping maw. Two blazing red orbs which glowed like the fires of hell and made the Inspector stagger. He was gripped by a cold so intense it penetrated every fibre of his body until even the slightest movement seemed a monumental effort:

He realized he still had the Browning and he fumbled in his pocket for a fresh clip, slammed it in and raised the weapon. The trigger wouldn't move. The impact on Briggs' skull must have damaged the firing pin in some way.

With a shriek of terror, he flung the pistol at Mathias and finally found the strength to run.

He knew without looking round that the thing was after him. Gasping for breath, Lambert climbed the short incline and went sprawling on the gravel drive, cutting his palms. Then, all at once, he saw the twin beams of the car headlights speeding towards him.

'Oh God,' he gasped.

Debbie saw him and slammed on the brakes. Then she saw Mathias behind him, no more than a yard behind him, and she screamed. The Capri skidded on the gravel, spinning round once. Lambert grabbed for the handle of the passenger door and flung himself in. Debbie immediately drove her foot down on the accelerator and the car burned rubber for precious seconds.

There was a fearful explosion of glass which showered them both as Mathias broke the back window with a single blow of his fist.

The car jerked forward and the Black Magician pulled his hand free just in time to prevent it being torn off at the wrist. Lambert looked over his shoulder and saw the vision of the creature receding, but just as it was leaving his field of view he saw it raise both arms skyward.

He heard Debbie scream and turned round in time to see that the cemetery gates had slammed shut. She twisted the wheel, stabbing at the brake simultaneously. The car slowed down a little but not enough. It left the driveway, the wheels skidding on the wet grass, sped a few yards and slammed into the high wall surrounding the cemetery. Lambert felt his head snap forward, crashing hard against the dashboard and blood ran down his face. Debbie slumped back in her seat and he had to shake her out of unconsciousness, gratefully realizing that she had only fainted. She shook herself and looked at him, the blood pouring down his face.

'We've got to get out,' he panted, throwing open the door and taking her hand.

As she clambered after him she saw the image of Mathias filling the rear view mirror and she could swear that he was grinning.

'The church,' shouted Lambert as another bolt of lightning tore open the clouds.

They ran with a speed born of terror and reached the hallowed building, praying that the door wasn't locked.

Lambert pulled on the metal handle and the door gave. They tumbled in, immediately enveloped by a stench of dampness. The sound of their footsteps reverberated throughout the ancient building as they ran towards the altar. Within seconds,

Mathias was driving the first of a series of powerful blows against the massive oak door of the church.

Lambert looked around, searching desperately for something with which to defend them. He glanced at the door.

'That won't hold him for long,' he said.

Debbie was close to tears and Lambert found his own breath coming in gasps. He scanned the building frantically. There was another powerful blow on the church door and the wood bent inward a fraction.

'The medallion is giving him his power,' said the policeman. 'I've got to get it away from him somehow.'

Debbie grabbed his arm, 'Tom, he'll kill you.'

The tears were streaming down her face. 'That's no man out there.'

Another thunderous bang and a large portion of the church door showed a split from top to bottom. A minute more and Mathias would be in. Lambert's head was throbbing, both from the pain of the gash and also from the effort of trying to find some way of saving them from the horror awaiting them. He held Debbie tight and looked into her face.

'You must get out, understand? When I distract him, you run for the door. Get help, just get out of here.'

She shook her head despairingly, the tears coming with renewed ferocity.

'Do it,' he said, his voice low but full of power.

He pushed her behind him as the first panel of the door splintered inwards.

'Behind the altar,' he told her, his gaze now fixed to the sight before him.

With four powerful blows, Mathias demolished the door, huge lumps of metal and oak flying into the church under the impact of his onslaught. He passed through what remained of the door and stood in the entrance, peering into the church. In the cold light cast by the frequent flashes of lightning, the golden medallion winked evilly at Lambert who reached behind him and grasped a metal candelabra for protection. He also found a heavy golden cross which he picked up.

Mathias advanced slowly down the central aisle, heading straight for the waiting Inspector.

Lambert gripped the puny weapons until his knuckles went white, then, with a scream of angry fear, he ran at the Black Magician and swung the candlestick. The creature raised one hand to shield its face and the metal cracked savagely against its forearm. There was a snapping sound as the bone broke and Lambert pressed his advantage, using his own body as a battering ram, actually managing to knock Mathias to the ground. The two of them crashed into a row of pews and Lambert felt a powerful hand hurl him effortlessly to one side. He rolled once then was on his feet, brandishing the cross and candlestick before him. Mathias lunged and managed to grab the candlestick and Lambert felt the power in that ancient hand as it forced him back. And all the time, those blazing red orbs fixed him in an unholy stare. The thin, almost transparent lips drawn back to reveal rotted teeth, the mouth opening occasionally to reveal the gaping maw within. The stench was unbelievable.

The Inspector felt himself being forced to the ground and struck out with the golden cross, driving the end towards the empty socket which had once housed an eye. The top of the cross disappeared into the hole, swallowed up in the red light which filled the eyeless pit. Mathias only grinned and struck the weapon away, seizing Lambert in a vice like grip, and lifting him by his throat in one huge powerful hand.

'Run,' shrieked the Inspector, and he caught sight of Debbie dashing past them towards the remains of the door. Wind and rain blew in and she could feel them on her face.

Mathias turned, still holding Lambert and pointed his other hand towards the escaping Debbie. The Inspector felt a force like an electric shock run through his entire body as, through pain-clouded eyes, he saw one of the huge wooden pews at the back of the church lift a good six feet into the air and hurtle across the entrance of the church.

Debbie screamed and fell back. Mathias now seemed to have tired of the Inspector and, with a contemptuous heave, flung him to one side. Lambert struck the cold stone floor of the church and looked up, stunned, to see the figure of Mathias raise both arms skyward.

There was an ear-splitting roar and a large rent appeared in the church roof. Masonry tumbled down. A particularly large lump hit a pew and splintered it to matchwood. Rain poured in through the hole but the Black Magician was oblivious to it and remained where he stood.

Lambert looked on in horror as a large crack appeared in one of the thick stone columns supporting the roof. Dust and ancient stone fell to the floor, mingling with the rain that was now pouring in through the roof.

And the cold. Lambert felt it once more, seeping into his bones, a cold the like of which he had never known, and with it, came the overpowering stench of rotted flesh.

Mathias was grinning, those blazing pools of blood glowing with even more vehemence.

There was an explosion as the stained glass windows shattered inward as if pushed by some giant hand from the outside. Huge jagged shards of coloured glass rained into the church, some remaining intact, others splintering again as they hit the ground. The wind rushed in through the holes, drowning out all other sounds. Lambert tried to stand and found the effort impossible. Debbie too, found herself pinned to the ground by the enveloping force which was invading the church with each second. She could only gasp as she saw her husband dragging himself across the church towards one of the broken windows.

Lambert felt as if he had lead weights secured to every limb and the act of crawling seemed an impossibility. His teeth were chattering, the combination of the driving rain and unbearable cold making his task all the more difficult. Glass cut his hands and knees as he crawled but he ignored the pain and reached out to grasp a long shard of glass which bore the face of Christ. The policeman gripped it, disregarding the blood which ran from his cut palms. He wanted to scream. He felt the cold growing more intense. The sound of the rain and the intensifying storm outside deafened him but he crawled on. Finally, by a monumental effort of will he dragged himself to his feet.

'Our Father, who art in Heaven,' he began, under his breath. Each agonized step brought him closer to Mathias who still stood with his arms outstretched. His back to the advancing policeman.

'Hallowed be thy name.'

The cold wrapped itself around Lambert like a blanket, slowing his already faltering steps.

'Thy Kingdom come, thy will be done.'

He drove himself on, tears of fear and frustration now coursing down his cheeks. The blood from his head wound still dribbling down his face. His hands, slashed open to the bone, gripped the dagger-like shard of glass. The face of Christ suddenly ran red with Lambert's blood as it cascaded over the coloured crystal.

'Give us this day our daily bread and forgive us our trespasses, as we forgive those...'

Mathias was no more than a yard away, his back still to the Inspector.

There was another resounding explosion as a further crack appeared in the central roof support pillar. More masonry sped down, shattering on the stone floor and spraying out like shrapnel.

'... Who trespass against us. And lead us not into temptation, but deliver us from evil.'

Deliver us from evil.

Mathias turned, bringing the full fury of those burning red pools to bear on Lambert.

The Inspector gave a last despairing scream and lunged forward.

Mathias couldn't avoid the thrust and, as Lambert drove forward, the Black Magician opened his mouth in silent agony as the razor sharp shard of glass pierced his heart. Lambert twisted it, indifferent to his own pain. Blood from Mathias' torn heart sprayed him, a thick, almost black ooze which stank of corruption. Lambert staggered back, watching the pus-like fluid spouting from the creature's chest.

Mathias made a desperate attempt to tear the glass free but his hands could gain no firm grip on the slippery weapon and he staggered drunkenly for a second before toppling back.

The blazing red of his eyes dulled momentarily before glowing even stronger and then, as Lambert watched, twin fountains of blood, brighter than that gushing from the creature's heart, spurted from the empty eye sockets. Mathias opened and closed his mouth, speaking silent curses, then, that too filled with dark blood.

Lambert swayed, thought he was going to faint, but Debbie's screams brought him back to his senses and he looked up in time to see that the central roof column was crumbling.

Finding new strength, he ran, vaulting the transfixed body of Mathias and reaching the door of the church just as the roof folded inward.

Debbie and he ran outside, the rain and wind buffeting them about like leaves in a gale, but they fought against it, not even turning to watch as the last remnants of the church roof crumbled inwards. Tons of old stone and rubble crashed down, shattering pews, altar, everything. Burying the body of Mathias for the last time.

Lambert collapsed on the wet grass, finally aware of pain in his hands and head. Every muscle in his body ached and, even with Debbie supporting him, he could hardly make it to the car. She helped him in and then went and hauled back one of the heavy gates at the cemetery entrance.

The engine spluttered as she started the car, and for a second, she wondered if it would move. Its wheels spun only for a second before catching and she guided it out of the cemetery.

Beside her, Lambert was barely conscious. He was covered in blood, his own and that of Mathias. The stench in the car was unbearable and Debbie wound the window down, ignoring the rain which spattered her. She looked across at him every few seconds, the tears filling her eyes.

He smiled weakly and reached for her knee with a bloodstained hand.

'Now it is over,' he croaked, the smile still on his lips.

When she looked back again, he'd passed out.

Thirty-Six

Time passed slowly in Medworth and it was nearly two years before the town finally returned to something like normality. It grew in size, its small industries expanding and attracting new inhabitants, becoming a part of the progress which it had always resisted.

Those who moved there never knew anything about what had happened. Nothing had been printed in any papers about it. The deaths were never explained. Indeed, how could they be?

Lambert was promoted. He and Debbie moved further North where he took over command of a force three times the size of the one in Medworth. Once a month they returned to the town to visit the cemetery, to plant fresh flowers on Mike's grave. Lambert had finally found the peace within himself which he had always sought.

The church was never rebuilt. It remained a roofless shell, home only to those animals who would enter it. Moss and lichens invaded it, and, some said that there were rats as big as cats in there. Visitors to the cemetery gave it cursory glances as they passed by.

As time passed, it was forgotten.

EPILOGUE

The boy was frightened. Not only of the church but of what his mother would say when he got home. He looked at his watch and saw that it was approaching eleven p.m. God, she'd skin him alive when he got in. She'd warned him before about hanging around with those Kelly boys. They were always in trouble with the law, she'd told him. The boy knew she was right but he also knew that if he ducked out of this prank, he'd be a laughing stock at school next day. That fear overshadowed anything his mother would say. So now, he stood in the ruined church staring around him, his body coated in a light film of perspiration. But this was part of the initiation ceremony. The Kelly brothers had told him so. Enter the church and bring something out to prove that you've been in there. All the other gang members had done it at one time or another.

The boy was sixteen, his imagination vivid. He had heard the stories of the giant rats nesting in the ruins and that thought was strong in his mind as he rooted amongst the rubble, shining his torch before him as he tried to find a likely prize.

The beam alighted on something golden lying at his feet. He bent to pick it up.

It looked like a medallion of some sort and there were funny signs on it. This would do perfectly. The boy snatched it up, anxious to be out of the church. It was only as he lifted it that he felt the heat.

It intensified until he dropped the gold circlet. He rubbed his palm against the seat of his dirty jeans and picked it up again, more cautiously this time. No trouble. No heat. He dropped it into his pocket and ran out.

The Kelly brothers accepted him as a member of the gang and that pleased the boy. He kept the medallion in his pocket, careful to hide it from his mother when he finally did get home. She shouted at him just as he'd expected and so did his father. The boy ignored them and went to bed.

He sat up for a long time looking at the medallion, but finally he switched off his bedside lamp, surprised at how much the light hurt his eyes.

Besides, he had a terrible headache.

Also by Shaun Hutson

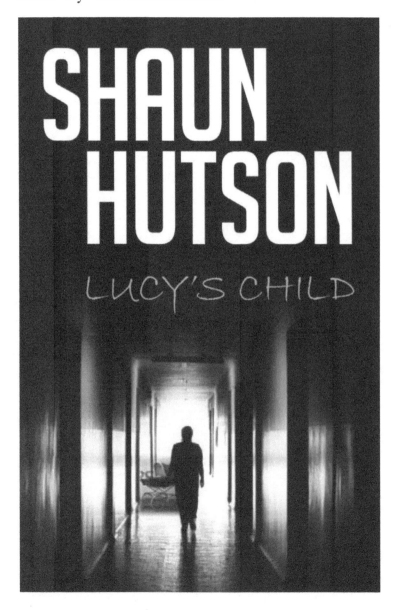

SHAUN HUTSON

LUCY'S CHILD

SHAUN
HUTSON

NEMESIS

SHAUN HUTSON

SLUGS